A Chasm of Night

Peter Eliott

A Chasm of Night by Peter Eliott
Published by Further Press, LLC
PO Box 314 Amagansett, NY 11930.

www.petereliott.com
Copyright ©2024 Peter Eliott

All rights reserved. No portion of this book may be reproduced in any form without permission from the publisher, except as permitted by U.S. copyright law. For permissions contact: publisher@furtherpress.com

This is a work of fiction. Names, characters, business, events and incidents are the products of the author's imagination. Any resemblance to actual persons, living or dead, or actual events is purely coincidental.

Cover by: Jeff Brown
Editing by: Sara Kelly
Page Design and Typesetting by: Iram Allam
Author photo by: James Asnes

Libary of Congress Control Number: 2024919449

ISBN Print: 979-8-9867065-6-6
Ebook: 979-8-9867065-7-3

Printed in USA
First Edition

To John and Isabel,
the two most supportive siblings, and enthusiastic readers,
a guy could ever ask for

"The road to great change is paved with the stones of seduction. Tempt the people into the dream that is you, and in time, they will be tempted into the dream you carry for the world."

~ The Empress Asadeissia Besidian

"Upon this city, upon its culture, upon the flesh of the people, I will leave my mark."

*~ High Lord Ulan Gueritus,
the Raving Blade of Hell's Labyrinth*

PART
I

1

ARCADIUM

They could see the sails from the main door, a thousand brushed white bulges, pregnant beneath a cobalt sky. The armada rested exactly 412 feet away, past 48 columns, under 24 ribbed vaults, between the breathing mirrors of 8 narrow pools. At that distance, the finer details could not be appreciated; however, as the architect had calculated, the broader sweep of the piece could be thoroughly absorbed, for this was *Ventrilus's Taking of the West*, the single grandest painting ever created.

Most of the arriving guests had seen the image already, but still they paused to give it reverence. Through the domed hollow of the entryway they ambled, first into a vestibule where wet cloaks and coats were received, then through the second set of wide glass doors—propped open now, for it was pleasantly warm inside, heated by twelve enormous fireplaces spaced along the length of the main hall, and additional stoves unobtrusively hidden behind heat-emitting grills. As they stepped onto the polished marble of the grand arcade, the dull clocking of their heels and the chirping of their banalities were lost in the murmur of dozens who had come just before.

The sounds of a small orchestra soon arose. Resonant and spirited, the musical selections that night had been meticulously considered, and this cloud of sound lulled away whatever discomfort lingered from the inclement journey. Drinks were in hand within minutes, followed by appetizers, all of this shuttled on burnished platters by impeccably dressed staff. Then the gentle admonitions began, to move deeper into the hall where the night's exhibition was housed, though the staff soon learned that it was difficult to influence the movement of these people who were, themselves, the epitome of influence. Titles abounded. Names were drawn from all the top houses in the region, including the ruling family, and while there were a few distinguished visitors from the Midlands, autumn was never a great season for travel, making tonight's event primarily a Sullward affair.

This building, ironically, did not seem like a thing of Sullward at all, but rather a preposterously elongated hall from the Imperial Square in Tergon. Stretched out to the length of three enormous war galleons, Horatio Ussard's signature Arcadium was a masterpiece of classical architecture. This too was ironic, for the storied master builder was anything but a classicist, but in designing a space so thoroughly mismatched to the intimate viewing of art, it became its own form of Ussardian idiosyncrasy.

The main premise had been fulfilled, however: build an appropriate home for the greatest artistic treasure ever bequeathed by one nation to another. *Taking of the West* had been commissioned by the fabled Empress Asadeissia, then gifted to the city of Sullward for its unequivocal embrace of the Dawn of Reason, and the blood that had been shed to rid the North of zealotry. The gift was also, unmistakably, a warning that those same terrifying sails might appear upon Sullward's horizon one day if the Empire's new irreligious decree was not strictly enforced. Asadeissia had not chosen to have Ventrilus depict a scene near and dear to the heart of the recipients. Instead, she picked one of the proudest moments of Tergonian expansion, when the Imperial Armada crossed the Derjian Sea and conquered the region known as Kaszia, reversing the Eastern emigration that had occurred many centuries earlier. Such was the way with this brilliant leader, a benefactor who offered gifts that were warnings and warnings that were, in the end, gifts, for in heeding them, the foundation was laid for a better world.

But the guests tonight cared little for that history. They saw no snub in the theme, since Asadeissia and Ventrilus and Horatio Ussard were over two hundred years dead and buried by then, and the Dawn of Reason had taken such firm hold throughout the lands of Derjia, one could hardly imagine that religion had existed at all. What had been viewed, two centuries earlier, as an act of staggering political risk by a Tergonian Empress was now universally accepted as the norm.

So, wine and cheese ruled, along with equally delectable helpings of gossip. The unfriendliest of the night's prattle focused on the artist of the hour. Jaiden Denevaego, youngest son of the current monarch and scion of the ruling dynasty, had decided to try his hand at painting, and while he was not entirely without skill, nothing he had thus far rendered warranted wall space in the Arcadium. Most of his works would be hard-pressed to make it into the galleries lining the six twisting streets of the Virtuoso. He bore the name Denevaego, however, so here they were—his pleasant, neatly brushed but ultimately spineless collection, taking up valuable room in the grandest art museum of the North. What's worse (and the source of the night's nastiest mirth), most of these uninspired pieces would find their way, at enormous cost, to the households of these very guests. What better way, after all, to curry favor with a king than to suffer the artistic mediocrity of his delusional son.

Thus, the hours passed, the music growing in tempo, the crowd growing in size, enough figures now to fill the entire middle section where Jaiden's collection hung. Laughter, at times uproarious, spiraled its way to the arched ceiling, while ripostes became overt, often inappropriate, as the heat of so many bodies caused ermine collars to come unbuttoned.

"You must have stolen that blouse on your last trip to Tergon… may I steal a peek inside?"

"I think, dear fellow, they retired that cut last year."

"You certainly are brave to bring your little harlot here."

At a certain point, some fashionably late arrivals found their way into the throng, flushed and dripping, recounting their misadventures to reach the Arcadium amidst some of the worst weather they had seen in years. The drunken responses were mindless and predictable.

"Had I known, I would have brought my caravel!"

"I'll just take the wheels off my carriage and float home."

"Hahahahaha…"

Up to the vaulting spun the laughter, down the gullet went the wine, and now making the rounds, several trays of decadent pastries.

Eventually the entry guards closed the two glass vestibule doors, for the wind was starting to come off the river with such force it began to gutter the lanterns and chandeliers. The main entry remained open, however, for these fortress-style doors were only shut when the museum closed, and there was a sizable awning to prevent the incursion of wind-driven rain.

When the first of the fireplaces went out with a drenching hiss, there were merely groans, macabre jokes, and more idiotic laughter. When it was followed fifteen minutes later by a second, with enough sooty rainwater pouring through the flue that it sheeted onto the marble floor, the tenor of the talk grew a bit uneasy but ultimately droll, for with alcohol lubricating imprudence and the storm fueling a comic sense of fatality, jokes returned to their source.

"Methinks the Dark Gods are making a statement about poor Jaiden Denevaego's artistic prospects."

"Apart from getting us all soaked and sloshed one evening, the dear boy won't be remembered at all."

How right they were.

Fireplaces three and four had just sputtered down to steaming piles, and smoke had begun to backdraft heavily into the hall when they felt the tremor starting to rise from the floor. It was a faint, quailing rumble, something easily confusable with the orchestra's base, except that the musicians had taken a brief pause for refreshment. If the crowd had been dancing—and it wasn't—the impact of all those cavorting feet still would not have created a vibration of this steadiness, a shudder so weirdly subterranean one might imagine that a team of drummers was playing in the Arcadium basement. The guests stood and listened. When a few ventured nervous witticisms, they were quickly shushed, and Jaiden's elder brother, Godvin, raised a hand as he called for silence from all corners of the hall. It was into this eerie, awkward stasis that the full force of the cataclysm came.

The shattering of the two glass vestibule doors produced a booming crash that was so shocking, so breath-stopping, that it could only be likened to the striking of a wildly oversized gong in a wildly undersized space. Straight down the walls of the Arcadium it reverberated, drilling through eardrums and hearts, dropping drinks and pastries, bottles and trays. An instant later, when breath returned, they screamed, one and all, lifting their terrified cries into a secondary clamor; for, frothing towards them, through that lacerating waterfall of glass, came the nightmare.

For those deepest into the building, the scale of the thing seemed impossible—a looming gray wave, surging up higher than the doorframe, turning the guests nearest the entryway into a terrified, twitching carpet. A large carriage, along its entire team of horses, was swept straight through on its crest, rolling over and over again, a shiny toy box with hypnotically spinning wheels. One of the horses broke the surface briefly, releasing a dreadful neighing scream, while the haunches of another emerged just after, its palsied beetle legs kicking madly in the foam.

And in this way, the dirty waters swallowed them. Those in the first half of the hall were quickly enveloped, along with candelabras, statuary, pedestalled vases, and every last painting on the walls. The other guests, farther along, had more time to flee, turning in their fancy slippers and high-heeled boots and then tripping over serving staff, fallen instruments, and their own extravagant gowns. Those who fell were trampled. Those who tried to help others were laid low by the thundering wall—swept up in its frigid mouth, spun and tumbled, dashed and drowned. A woman, belly up and screaming, snatched at her own strangling emerald necklace, opening her mouth wide to breathe; but into that orifice poured the Derjian Ocean, filling her throat and sternum, then her stomach and lungs.

Some got away. There were hidden staircases accessible from the main gallery, but these were at the end of narrow hallways, and they led to staff offices and storage chambers, not readily known to the well-heeled clientele. Those who ventured into ancillary galleries found themselves caught in deathtrap grottos, while the main hall became a vast, surging tank. Eventually, the upper windows shattered. This began to release the water, maintaining a large pocket of air at the vaulted ceiling; however, only the hardiest swimmers lasted that long or had the upper body strength to pull themselves up onto the chains of the chandeliers. The others fell prey to the frigid temperatures, the churning currents, the panicked grasping of the other guests; or, if they managed to survive all of that, many were spat straight out the broken windows and dropped helplessly into the full force of the storm.

Taking of the West was, itself, eventually taken. When the waters rose high enough, they hoisted the work off of its mounting hardware, causing the full, forty-foot height of the enormous piece to crash forward onto the swimmers like a chainless drawbridge. Down swatted the huge, crushing canvass; down drove those thousand menacing sails. One last grisly assault for the armada, before everything, including the painting itself, was unceremoniously swept away by the storm.

"Vazeer."

I was painfully startled by the sound of his voice. It wasn't loud or grating, but it entered my reverie like the slam of a door.

"What?"

"It's time to go in."

My face felt sullen and unpleasant as I tried to fend him off.

"Not yet."

For several long moments, he considered this, his neatly groomed head adopting an inquisitive tilt.

"What are you waiting for?"

"I'm waiting till I feel ready to die."

I turned back to the looming darkness of the ruin. The Arcadium, when all was said and done, wasn't truly narrow; however, the extraordinary length made it appear so, and as my eyes followed the long, crumbling spine—ridged and damp and greasy with muted moonlight—I found something almost crocodilian about it. The gaping mouth of the beast pointed obliquely towards the river, with the remnants of a neglected stone dock still visible, which was, as the storied builder explained it, a wonderful way to invite waterborne travelers straight to its doors.

"A nice touch, Ussard," I muttered, "a nice, incredibly ill-considered touch."

"Vazeer?"

"Nothing," I said, and I now pivoted back to him. "Just talking to myself. This building gives me the creeps."

"It was a museum once?"

"Yes."

"But nothing else since?"

"A graveyard, more or less. I'd rather not join the interred."

We were at the cusp of the northernmost residential ruins, close enough to the nighttime river to see its black, slippery skin, and about a hundred yards from the titanic carcass of the museum. The air was frigid and blurred by mist, yet in the dankness of our sheltering alley, I detected some warmth. It was on his face, for his lips hiked wryly at the corners, suggesting a rather welcome return to humorous form.

"It's risky for you to go in there alone," he said.

"It's even riskier for you to come with me. I may be forever linked to the Narrow Bid, but you're the bastard who actually wielded the blade."

Radrin Blackstar did not so much as flinch at those words. He seemed (and there was something improperly comforting about this) entirely without remorse or regret. Standing there beside me in the shadow of Lower City buildings, his spotless face partially obstructed by haze and gloom, he was, as always, a creature of calm conviction. His cloak, with its raised collar, was a slightly different shade of black tonight, or perhaps the weave was finer, but either way, I was glad to see that the man was capable of changing his clothing.

"Eleventh Bell rang almost twenty minutes ago," he said. "It isn't wise to keep these men waiting."

Yes, he had a point there. This wasn't a good meeting to be late to or, for that matter, early. If one really wanted to be a stickler about it, this wasn't a good meeting at all, but we had already moved past such considerations.

"A few minutes more won't make a difference."

I returned to my surveillance. Up on the museum's roof, I saw many dark spots where the dull lunar haze found nowhere to land. Those were the copious holes, places where shingles, grout, cement had broken away, or the roof had collapsed entirely, which, given the intermittent rain of the last few days, couldn't have made for a very pleasant encampment. But it was defensible. The huge structure was located farther north than the other major landmarks, and it did have that battered but serviceable dock for those who might need to escape the area on short notice. I was, arguably, one of those people.

By setting foot inside that building, by surrendering weapons and freedom, not to mention the popular notion that I was already dead, I would be effectively walking into an ambush. Somewhere inside this vast derelict hall was Count Halsin Tygean, formerly the number three man in Hell's Labyrinth, and now the main opposition to Count Ulan Gueritus—otherwise known as the

Raving Blade. Given how poorly my last two Underlord meetings had gone, there was little cause for optimism here. But it was necessary, or so Radrin and I had concluded after exhaustive planning. Not only did Tygean have the manpower to hold off Gueritus's army, at least temporarily, but he was also the ultimate piece of bait to draw our target out into the open. That was, if Count Tygean could get over the small fact that I had caused the death of his High Lord and thereby brought about the worst of his current troubles.

Making contact with this Underlord had not been easy. It had required first finding another man, a former associate who might have been dead, or possibly worse than dead (which, in my city, you could actually be). That man was Sebastien, a Sullward watchman who had run afoul of the Raving Blade while performing a difficult favor for me. Sebastien had lost his tongue in that encounter, and I was determined to find out what happened to the rest of him.

When I located Sebastien, he was neither a corpse nor a subhuman thing, twitching and squatting with other unfortunates in an old ruin. He was sitting alone in his Dockside apartment, brooding. Fate had it that he had only lost his tongue, though he had been gifted with the branded image of two swords, coiling like serpents in the burned flesh of his forehead. This was the mark of Ulan Gueritus, and there it would remain forever, a warning to all who might utter forbidden secrets from the realm of the Underlords.

Sebastien was angry. He was angrier than I had ever seen him, and while some of this was directed at me, much more was focused on the people who had maimed him. Being a literate man, he was quite capable of scribbling out furious messages on parchment, and Sebastien quickly made it known that he was ready, willing, and able to do whatever was necessary to bring down Count Ulan Gueritus, along with the man's chief torturer, Viscount Dubin Haiyes, aka "Dubin the Dicer."

Privately, I was somewhat taken aback. Never a paragon of courage or conviction, Sebastien was displaying both qualities, along with a complete disinterest in narcotics, prostitutes, gluttonous eating habits, and assorted dissolute behaviors that had made him an easy target for bribery.

And so, this transformed man, prominently bearing the mark of his punishment, wandered the domain of the Underlords in search of Count Tygean. Sebastien became the perfect, dismissible nobody to hunt the ruins of the Lower City, and then, upon locating the rebellious count, to convey transcribed missives that would appear trustworthy. After all, Tygean and his people would be hard-pressed to imagine that one of "the Raved" was devising a trap on behalf of the Raving Blade, and in this way, Sebastien had been extraordinarily successful in setting up our meeting. Of course, none of this guaranteed that a trap was not being devised for me, who had brought so much trouble into this clandestine world.

"Vazeer…"

Startled again.

"Just remember," I muttered, "if I don't come out of there, you'll have to go gather the others on your own."

"Just see to it that you come out."

I gave a noncommittal wave and started forward towards the meeting site.

There it sat, doorless and haunted before me, the yawning face still looking like a thing gasping for breath. It was here that I intended to sow the seeds of a better future, one that might offset the tragedies of the past. With this unreasonable hope drawing me forward, I entered the cavernous ghost of the Arcadium, where one terrible autumn night two centuries before, the dream of the artistic city-state met its watery end.

2

THE REBEL

I hadn't ventured more than ten feet inside before they had me entirely surrounded. This I expected. They took my weapons immediately, at least the ones they could find, which I also expected. Then they shoved me along, one soldier palming me in the back of the neck so hard that I stumbled over a pile of rubble, and this part I didn't quite expect or appreciate. However, such is the deserved comeuppance for idiots like me, who go handing themselves to the enemy.

The air inside that colossal, festering hall was moist to the point of swampiness. There was a cold, muddy smell that lacked the freshness of nature, and I found each inhalation skewing towards impurity, my mind failing to separate the physical realities from the knowledge of what had happened here. As I navigated a series of roughly laid planks, bouncing grimy wrinkles across the lake floor, I took in the sights as if being led through a crime scene.

The eight soldiers moved in single file, with me in the middle, and since the men in front and back carried torches, I was able to use their trembling flames to observe the arched ceiling. Gap-riddled and slick, the plaster surface picked up the torch shine as if it was a traveling spirit, and I watched that unsteady bead as it jerked across cracks and craters, wormed its way over ribbed stone vaults and the dangling chains that had once held chandeliers. I could also see the walls, and here and there I noticed the rusted scars of mounting hardware. Around us on the puddled floor lay an archipelago of fallen sections from the roof, broken pillars and assorted vagrant trash. Plus (and I really couldn't know this without moving closer) I saw what appeared to be older relics: rusted picture frame angles, the heavily corroded legs of a musician's stool. At the mouth of one of the side galleries, I believe I spotted the iron rim of a carriage wheel. I slowed a moment, looking for an accompanying hub, but the man behind me gave me a hard elbow, indicating that archeology wasn't part of today's tour.

These soldiers were of the distinctly battle-hardened variety, and while they didn't have quite the look of callous depravity that had marked Gueritus's army, they weren't a likeable bunch either. I observed what seemed like fresh injuries on two of the men—a large scab on one soldier's neck, a bandage on another's thigh. This told me that the so-called "simmering" war with Gueritus had now moved into a hotter phase.

We reached the midpoint in the hall, and, gazing up at the looming walls, shattered with fractures, I again thought of budding painter Jaiden Denevaego. He had stood in this very spot on that fateful night, his artistic hopes buoyed. And it was in this very place that the waters killed him, along with his entire forgettable collection. A little farther along, we passed the side gallery where Jaiden's older brother, Godvin, had expired. Embracing his natural role as a leader, Godvin lingered too long ushering others towards a staircase, and was sucked into an airless cavity from which he never returned.

At last, we turned from our path and entered one of the side corridors, passing two sentries, then another just before we climbed a staircase. While many years before, I had poked my head into the main hall of the Arcadium, I had never made it upstairs. However, possessing two of Horatio Ussard's private journals, I was well acquainted with the layout, and I knew that above the two wings of the central gallery there was a whole realm of interconnected staff offices, along with secure storage chambers used to house artwork currently out of rotation.

We soon arrived at the museum director's office. The air up in this section of the Arcadium was dryer, suggesting that the living accommodations for the Count and his staff were significantly better than what I had experienced on the ground floor. After a light knock, the lead soldier pushed the door open, then shoved me inside.

There were three men in the room when I entered, and the soldier who had commanded my entourage followed me inside and shut the door. I managed only a quick glance about, taking in the general dimensions of the space—big, which is what one would expect for the Arcadium director—before the interrogation began.

"Did you kill him?"

This came from a man sitting at the far end of the room behind a large desk. There were a couple of oil lanterns burning on wall hooks, and once I was nudged closer, I saw him quite well. At the latter end of middle age, he had mid-length, sandy blond hair, touched only in passing by needles of gray. His eyes, well-illumined by the lamps, were of a deep, cerulean blue, that moody shade unique to northerners, and quite distinct from the brighter tones from the South.

The trailing soldier bumped up so close I could feel the buckles and plated sections of his chest armor. Down at belt level, I heard the light, frictional rasp of a blade coming out of its scabbard, telling me that I had better answer this question correctly.

"No."

Next to the man at the desk sat a tall, slender figure whose expression was so intense it flirted right on the border of enraged. He had extremely short, reddish-brown hair, and his eyes, in marked contrast to the pleasant, neighboring blue, were of a drilling darkness, boring into me so deliberately that when recognition came (and it unpleasantly did), the experience manifested more as a physical reaction than a cognitive process. This was the intimidating Chief Legate who had laid down the law for me at the end of the Gaff saga. In addition to providing me with the nonnegotiable terms of that deal, the man had also bestowed my street alias, which he used now.

"Vazeer the Lash," he said, in a brusque voice I remembered well. "My lord is going to ask you a series of questions. If we catch you deviating from the truth in any small way, Mogen there will skewer you like a spit roast, then toss your body into the river. Do you understand?"

"Yes."

The final figure in the room, an armed young man, standing in the corner behind the desk, shifted his stance. Every bit as hostile as the Chief Legate, his posture suggested that he would welcome the opportunity to rush forward and assist with the skewering. Because of the man's close proximity to one of the oil lanterns, I easily noted his rich blue eyes, which were rather like those of the first man who spoke.

Let me spare you the mystery here: I already knew that first man to be Count Tygean. I had seen him a few times over the years—twice in The Crossbiter, once in Dockside, another time dining in the finest tavern in White Hill—but since it was never wise to stare too long at such figures, especially with his soldiers staring back, I'd always failed get a good look at him. Now, I noted that he was quite handsome, with a full face, a narrow, straight nose, and long eyebrows that were curved in a pleasant script. While he didn't exude the dashing regality of the former High Lord, Beranardos Sherdane, Tygean's appearance was certainly an improvement over that of the ghoulish Ulan Gueritus.

"Let's get on with this," said Count Tygean from behind the desk. "Did Lave Kaszivar hire you to ferry her to Sherdane's compound?"

"No."

"Were you hired by a Sketcher for a Narrow Bid?"

"Yes."

"Did you understand the full implications of that contract?"

Here I hesitated.

"Not exactly."

My host shifted forward, sliding his arms onto the wooden surface and extending himself just a little closer. Count Tygean was not wearing sartorial finery and was only slightly better attired than a standard Underlord soldier, with a gray house cloak over a simple blue tunic. I noticed some bulky spots under the shirt that suggested he wore armor.

"Why don't you explain it to me then," he said.

And I did, or at least the broader details from the boathouse meeting. I described how the Sketcher, in an artful, surreptitious manner, implied that Count Ulan Gueritus was the target of the Narrow Bid, not the High Lord. I also noted how one of our group members used the name "Gueritus" as the presumed target, then called him "the Raving Blade" for good measure. The Sketcher did not deny this, though he was clearly unmoored by the lapse in protocol.

I watched Tygean exchange glances with the others, then he turned to confer quietly with his Chief Legate.

"Vazeer the Lash," said Tygean. "I understand that you live by certain codes and that it violates those codes for you to mention the names of the other operatives who joined you on the bid. But codes mean very little to me right now, so I'm going to ask you to provide a full description of what happened that night, including the identity of the other Bidders. As Viscount Grieves here already warned you, we will show no mercy if you lie to us."

What was I to do? There really was nothing for it but to lay it all out for him, which I found abhorrent. In addition to being a gross violation of protocol, I just plain hated telling the story itself, which I'd been forced to do now on three occasions: the second half of it to Nascinthé of Levell, the whole thing to Holod Deadskiff, and now this third rendering for Count Tygean—a Shadow Bidder, a Contract Broker and an Underlord—who represented, I supposed, a rather decent cross section of my criminal world.

I imparted the tale accurately. I described our admission into the compound, Nascinthé's extraordinary performance in the entry vestibule, and then (and I debated this part with myself fleetingly) I went ahead and revealed High Lord Sherdane's love affair with the Countess Shaeyin Odel. This bit, for some reason, I wanted to omit. Possibly it was to safeguard the memory of Beranardos Sherdane, or maybe it was to protect the reputation of Countess Odel, a woman my friend Merejin believed would be the next Empress of the Tergonian Empire. Nonetheless, I told them everything that had been revealed on this, since it was simply too dangerous to waste my integrity here.

As I relayed these details, I carefully watched my audience. The Chief Legate, whom I now knew as Viscount Grieves, visibly winced, and he glanced down at the floor, either with embarrassment or disgust. The young, blue-eyed soldier squinted owlishly, then blinked anxiously, and this certainly looked like mortification. Count Tygean alone seemed unsurprised.

"I knew it," he muttered. "It's the only thing that made sense."

Nobody seemed interested in lingering on this part, so I moved things through the harsher portions of the tale—the killing of Jevar the Legate, the soldiers storming the Ripening Hall, our mad efforts at escape. Precise details, like Fe Gesbon's stupid antics in the Hall and Nascinthé's mute compliance, were of no relevance to these men, so I dispensed with them. I did mention my Brood sister, Flerra Tellian's, torture and death, passingly (which was all I could handle), and when I reached the water door, I presented Nascinthé's exit as a logical course of events. The Masque was of no further use on the mission, I said, so I encouraged her to hide in the marsh until the storm passed and then flee the city after that. She had not been seen since and had likely drowned in the flood.

Curiously, at this point in the story, I noticed a little droop in Count Tygean's countenance, a crestfallen reaction by any measure. His fingers kneaded with a sort of methodical heaviness against his jaw and lips, where there was the light dash of a blond mustache. He did this several times, and I had the distinct sense that we had just hit a particularly objectionable part of the story.

When, at last, I brought us to the death of the High Lord, I undertook my most dangerous dance with falsehood by altering a small but critical detail. I implied that the tunnel where Sherdane died was much darker than it actually was, with only a single torch burning some distance away, and that we were given no hint of the High Lord's identity in advance. This was a necessary lie, which I had explained to Radrin repeatedly. And repeatedly, Radrin had countered with treatises about the code of Finishers and the need to follow through with contracts at all costs. Hearing him mouth this garbage a few times was enough to ensure he wasn't coming to this meeting.

"Your Finisher, this *Blackstar*, you are still in communication with him?" Tygean asked.

"He's part of my proposed plan."

"Yet you didn't bring him here tonight. Why?"

I hesitated, but only briefly, for there was ultimately no use in lying about this part.

"I thought you might kill him."

A rather dour smile appeared on Tygean's lips.

"Very astute of you, Vazeer the Lash. Have you ever hired a Finisher?"

I shook my head.

"I have, many times. If there's one thing I know to be true of them, they go to great lengths to confirm the identity of a target. While I understand that there was deception in this bid, I have trouble imagining that your man pulled that knife across Beran's neck still thinking it was Ulan."

"Yes, I have trouble believing it too."

Count Tygean shifted back in his chair, and his shoulders widened out, as if prepping himself for whatever legerdemain was about to follow. To be sure, I did have some legerdemain, and it came complete with ample helpings of ethical complexity; however, it also happened to be the truth, more or less.

"Count Tygean," I said, "there aren't enough words in the Derjian tongue to express how appalled I am by what happened that night. It was, for me, a tragedy on every level. Losing fellow Bidders on a job is always bad, but that night I lost a woman who was, for all intents and purposes, my sister. I didn't just lose her; I had to witness and listen to her being tortured to death. After that I faced an even greater misery, when I inadvertently assisted with the murder of Beranardos Sherdane, the man who, perhaps more than anybody else, was responsible for my prosperity in this life. In the aftermath of that terrible act, I was on the verge of attacking Radrin Blackstar myself, but then the Swell Driver arrived, and all of my efforts were focused on escape.

"So yes, I question whether the Finisher was truly ignorant in that moment when his blade did its work. However, what's done is done, and I have to keep my priorities straight. You've hired Finishers, but I've actually collaborated with this one, for some time now, and I've learned at least this about him: if, somehow, Blackstar felt the need to complete that contract because it upheld his code in some manner, then his desire to complete this current contract is even stronger. The Finisher is more committed to the death of the Raving Blade than any of us. The only other person who comes close is me, and we are both prepared to do whatever it takes, go to any lengths, to avenge the treachery that was committed that night."

My little speech rested in excruciating silence. Tygean and Grieves again exchanged glances, communicative glances, and when the Count finally turned back to me, he looked like he had just been given council.

"Mogen," he said, addressing the soldier directly behind me. "Please go get an extra chair, along with a bottle of wine. It would seem that Vazeer and I have some planning to do."

3

GRAND DREAMS

The chair and wine soon arrived, and as I took my seat, Mogen filled three glasses. Thereafter, an interesting drama unfolded.

When Count Tygean tried to send away the young, blue-eyed soldier who had been standing at the ready, there was some aggressive pushback.

"I won't leave you alone with this contract scum," the young man snapped. "He's already killed Sherdane, what's to say he won't try and kill you too? Besides, I should be a part of this."

"What you *should* be, Devlan, is obedient to my orders," Tygean replied, twisting angrily. "That would be the most useful thing. Grieves and I can handle a single, unarmed man. Now go on, and make sure that the patrols are being properly manned."

"That's Mogen's job, Father," Devlan shot back, exposing his identity and his petulance in one breath. "When are you going to learn that I can do—"

"Enough!"

Devlan shut his mouth, reluctantly. He lingered for a few moments in this sulky state, and when he eventually headed for the door, he leaned towards me aggressively.

"Just because you're sitting here with noblemen doesn't make you noble, bid man," he spat. "And if you so much as touch a hair on my father's—"

"Devlan!"

Count Tygean appeared genuinely furious. He was also, I think, embarrassed, and he glanced over at me with an exasperated lift of his eyebrows that possibly sought commiseration, which I couldn't give. I knew nothing of fatherhood, and while I suppose Cad had caused me enough trouble over the years to qualify me for something, he had never sunk to the level of this belligerent brat. Devlan the man-boy possessed all the conceit of a Tergonian aristocrat without any of the dignity, reinforcing the idea that pretenders to something are always far more arrogant about it than their genuine counterparts.

Once Devlan and Mogen were out of the room, Count Tygean formally introduced me to Viscount Grieves, then I was told to explain my plan of attack.

The strategy I presented was complicated. Radrin and I had spent days on this, hunched at my apartment dining table, running our fingers over every inch of my most up-to-date map of the Lower City. All of that hunching and pointing, debating and planning had led to one indisputable conclusion: there was no way to accurately predict where and when the Raving Blade would be moving around our city and with whom. Enrolling Count Tygean into the plan could possibly take care of the "when" but not the "where." Still, we felt we had the bones of something we could work with. It went like this:

Upon solidifying our alliance tonight, I would leave this meeting armed with the Count's backing and begin recruiting the Shadow Bidders I felt would be most useful and loyal to our cause. Telling these Bidders that they could rely on Tygean's support, and also some of his funds, would make everything go a lot smoother. Once this team was in place, Count Tygean would then send an emissary to the Raving Blade and request a meeting at a neutral site. The purpose of the meeting, ostensibly, would be to discuss a truce, predicated on the notion that this slow, debilitating war of attrition was harmful to all. The longer it lasted, the less able the Lower City would be to salvage all of the flooded inventory and get on with the business of fencing stolen merchandise.

Gueritus would agree to this. As I had learned at The Crossbiter Tavern, he was quite eager to bring Tygean in as his chief vassal, which would, as he saw it, return stability to the Labyrinth and allow his own coronation to proceed without contest. The Raving Blade would pick the meeting location; we already knew this. He would also arrive heavily defended, and we anticipated advance reconnaissance of the site, as well as the route to get there. This made an ambush a tricky endeavor. When asked how I planned to overcome these obstacles, I gave an answer that I knew would not be much appreciated.

"You need to swear fealty to Gueritus, Lord Count. You must officially make him High Lord."

The outrage commenced immediately.

"Have you lost your bloody mind, Grell Runner!" Grieves barked.

Tygean simply shook his head.

"That's out of the question. In every way, it's counter to what I believe. It's counter to who I am."

"Which is precisely why it will work. That symbolic victory might, just might, cause Gueritus to relax for a few minutes, which will give my team an opening to create a violent distraction, thereby allowing the Finisher to do his job."

Tygean's obduracy set itself into the lines around his mouth.

"It's time I explained something to you, Shadow Bidder," he said, dispensing with my name, which I did not see as a good sign. "If somehow, we can rid ourselves of Gueritus, there's going to be a major power vacuum in this city, which I will need to fill. Donblas has not been heard from since the storm, which means he's probably dead—either by one of Ulan's agents or the flood."

Count Donblas was the third of Sherdane's three direct vassals. The former High Lord, in keeping with tradition, wanted three Counts below him, so he elevated one of his own staff members to the role. Donblas had never been viewed as a figure on par with Gueritus and Tygean. The limited size of his army and inventories made him only slightly more formable than the Raving Blade's two Viscounts; however, as a former staff member to the High Lord, his loyalty had bordered on fanaticism. Which was probably why he had conveniently disappeared.

"If…and it is a big if," Tygean continued, "I manage to assume the role of High Lord, something that I have never sought and still don't, then I will need credibility with the Underlords who remain, as well as their soldiers. An act of betrayal on the scale that you describe—first swearing fealty, then turning around and orchestrating the murder of the new High Lord—will make me a traitor on par with Gueritus."

I slid a little closer on my elbows, then put my palms down flat on the table.

"*Treachery*, Lord Count, is literally the only way we will beat this man. You know it, I know it, so can we all stop pretending here?"

It was a long, painful wait for a reply. As a fretful distraction, I studied the space behind them, noting that the blank plaster wall bore a sizable crack where painting hardware had once been nailed and also a green, speckled bleed in the surface where moisture had created its own abstract piece. Meanwhile, I tried to stuff down my apprehension. Only one of these men was capable of responding, for it was *his* reputation on the line, not to mention his life.

"You know," Tygean finally said, scratching at his mustache, "all of this, all of these plans, probably just guarantee our demise. I ought to tell you that some of the rumors that have developed since 28 Dekharven are now coming to pass. Lave Kaszivar, who has supplied as much as a third of all our merchandise over the years, has finally turned against us. I have it on good authority that the entirety of her armada is, at this very moment, pulling into her Kaszian port and making ready for a land assault. It can't be more than a month before she arrives here in force and takes whatever remains of our inventories, not to mention our coin. With a haul of that magnitude, she'll be able to pay her soldiers the tolgens, then create her own Ripening Halls for the merchandise, putting us permanently out of business."

I had actually given a warning along these lines to Count Ulan Gueritus at The Crossbiter Tavern, for it seemed impossible that the infamous pirate financier Lave Kaszivar—otherwise known as the "Red Siren"—would pass up an opportunity like this. The question was, could this information work to my advantage a second time?

"This only makes your peace offering more appealing, Lord Count."

"It also makes my treachery all the more heinous," Tygean replied. "I probably should be looking to swear fealty for real. And, as a nice coronation gift to my new High Lord, I can provide to him the identities of the women who are compounding the Kaszivar threat here at home—a certain group of Shadow Bidders who are scrawling insurrection and blasphemies all over

Dockside. Their words appear to be raising the Red Siren to almost mythical stature, which likely won't tamp down her ambitions. I have plenty of spies, Vazeer the Lash, and one of them happens to live on a certain charming street that you yourself frequent. He has witnessed some interesting comings and goings of late."

Like a mainsail boom that jerks back in a sudden, squally reversal, this piece of information slammed straight into my gut. Things really had been going a little too smoothly for comfort. This reference to my ex-lover, Terza Falconbrow, my never-quite-lover, Adelyn, and my Brood sister, Heshna the Seer, along with whichever other reckless Shadow Bidder women had been recruited to their matriarchal cause, was a clear reminder that barriers still divided our criminal world. As odious as the Raving Blade was in Tygean's eyes, he was still an Underlord, while the rest of us were not.

"Of course," Tygean continued, "these writings are not entirely harmful to me so far, since they are more of a nuisance for a man slated to be High Lord than one who acts the part of a rebel. But they will become harmful, should I ascend to the top position."

"They will stop well before that, Lord Count," I said.

"You can assure me of this?"

"Yes."

"That's good, then," he replied. "After all, I assume one can't wield a paintbrush and a blade at the same time. I'm going to hazard a guess that at least some of these women are the ones you plan to recruit for our plan."

Here, again, the swinging boom caught me off guard, and this time I really must have shown it.

"Don't look so surprised, Vazeer the Lash," said Viscount Grieves, his colorless lips doing something satisfied and unpleasant. "You think we don't know everything about you? We have a fairly good idea of where you will turn for help. And, let me be plain, they better be helpful. As far as I know, only one of those Bidders is a true fighter, and her dedication has been lacking at times. When you last shared a boat with her, she turned over the goddamned cargo."

I was starting to find this novel breakdown in Labyrinth barriers less than gratifying. Even the Raving Blade didn't seem to know this much about me.

"Let's not give our guest such a hard time, Owen," said Count Tygean, and he patted his Viscount's forearm. "He's offering a lot. And he won't be doing this with any advance funds from us, in case he was hoping for that."

Yes, I was definitely hoping for that.

"Sorry," continued the Count. "I have already been cutting my soldier's pay as it is, since I can't access my vaults. Several men have defected from me in the last week, so losing more isn't an option. You'll have to front any money required to hire your people with the understanding that I will reward you all handsomely on the back end."

When I failed to reply—failed, quite frankly, to maintain even the pretense that I was happy with any of this—Tygean made a conciliatory proposition of sorts.

"I can see that this isn't turning out like you hoped," he said. "And I do acknowledge that a lot will be asked of you in this plan, so the least I can do is to make a sacrifice of my own. If you can gather a team that is capable of staging a proper ambush, and your Finisher remains committed to the job, then I will set up a meeting with Gueritus, as requested. And in this meeting, I will promise fealty. It won't be the official ceremony, which still gives me an out later; however, for all intents and purposes, it will achieve our aim. Ulan will not expect me to go back on my word. That's not something I do, or haven't."

I consented, but I didn't like it. The warning bell was starting to ring in the back of my brain, one that told me I was relying too much on the word of this man.

"I've been meaning to ask you something, Vazeer," Tygean said, craning forward to peek inside my cup. Seeing that it was half-empty, he grabbed the bottle and poured me a little more, then provided a topper for himself and Viscount Grieves. I took a small sip, mostly to be polite, before I set the cup down, awaiting the next development I wouldn't like. Tygean drank heavily, then held the cup at mid-height, swirling the liquid unconsciously.

"That Masque from your Narrow Bid," he said, "*Nascinthé of Levell*. Did you really send her alone into the marsh on the night of a storm? According to your rendition, her brilliant performance saved you all—her ability to play two roles at once. Would you really put her at such risk after that? This seems a strange miscalculation for a man who knows the environment so well."

The creeping unease now grew into something worse. I raised my cup to my mouth, mostly to give my twitchy hands a menial diversion, and also to cover my face. Viscount Grieves's stare was nothing less than a carpenter's bore, and I was present, again, to the ways in which the threat from the various Underlords differed—Sherdane assuming the role of an all-powerful monarch in his subterranean palace, Ulan Gueritus that of a devilish father, lording over a family from Hell. And now this new form of Underlord peril: the mild-mannered, insidious spymaster, whose knowledge of my life, my past, and, quite possibly, recent personal events, made him just as dangerous as the others.

"I have been in the marsh during storms before, Lord Count,"

I said from behind my cup. "The water at most rises an extra foot. We have never seen anything like what happened that night."

"Yes, I suppose not," he said, and he leaned back in his chair, massaging his left hand over his cheeks. I had earlier noted a couple rings on his fingers, though only now could I see them clearly: one set with sapphires, the other a simple gold band, worn on the traditional matrimonial finger.

"I told my wife that we likely had a very special visitor to the Lower City," he continued. "I don't think I'll tell her the unfortunate upshot."

Now, my anxiety shifted towards perplexity, which the Count misinterpreted.

"It's alright, I know; or rather, I know the presumption. We have, in our custody, the Sketcher who presented the Narrow Bid to you in the boathouse. He's on the outs with Ulan, for his mistakes during the sketch, and also his miscalculations overall, and he actually came running to us to avoid a Raving. He's the one who insists it was her. That's why he recruited her, because of her past and the belief that it would allow her to pull the whole thing off. So, let me ask you, you who worked with the woman in close quarters, do you think the Sketcher's right?"

"I'm sorry, Count Tygean. I really don't know what you're asking."

"I'm talking about the *Spellbinder*," he said, dropping his hand. "Do you think your Masque was really her?"

Now, in some recess of accumulated knowledge, a memory stirred. I had heard this name "Spellbinder." My cultural appetites had focused on those mediums with which I could readily interact—architecture, literature, paintings, sculpture. Theater productions, which I would no doubt enjoy, were nonexistent in

Sullward and had been for over two hundred years. There were occasional ribald street shows in Dockside; however, this was decidedly lowbrow fare and held nothing in common with the grand performances that used to be held in the Lower City's vaunted Drover Theater.

In the Tergonian Midlands, however, the theater was alive and well, and while I was only marginally familiar with the oldest and most esteemed works and even less acquainted with revered thespians throughout history, I did recall that in recent times there had been a famous Tergonian player with the stage name "Spellbinder." I hadn't heard this person mentioned in years, and, quite honestly, I wasn't even sure if it was a man or a woman.

"My wife, daughters, and I sometimes venture down the coast to Gealtwhal to catch a show," Tygean continued, "and though we tell ourselves afterwards that we have witnessed something of consequence, we know we haven't. The Midland troops never make it that far north, so even if that theater puts on a play of some merit, the acting is so poor you have to squint and half cover your ears to make the whole thing passable. I don't discuss many details of my work with my wife, but I assured her that if, indeed, the Spellbinder was here in our city, contracting bids, I would pluck her from this system and see to it that her talents were put to better use. I have even joked—half joked—that one day when I am High Lord, I will restore Drover Theater."

This was a lot to take in. I glanced over at Viscount Grieves, and while that penetrating glower continued, I now saw it in a different light. Whether or not these issues interested him personally, they were important to his lord. As such, he would see to it that I provided any and all useful information on the subject.

"Answer him."

"I really can't say, Lord Count," I replied. "I have little knowledge of cultural figures from Tergon, and I did not get to know the Masque very well—"

"Knock it off, Shadow Bidder!" Grieves snapped. "Assume that we know everything, because we do. The Sketcher told us how you gawped at the woman in the boathouse."

"Yes…how could I not? This doesn't mean—"

"And Sherdane's surviving soldiers told us that you fought like a thing from Hell to protect her. That you became a creature possessed in your efforts to get her to safety. Some of those very men were in your greeting party downstairs."

Another mystery solved. That group did seem a particularly inhospitable bunch, and my efforts at deception in this meeting were falling decidedly flat. I was now being forced towards a choice, a dangerous choice, and with Viscount Grieves drilling me with his inquisitional stare and Count Tygean acquiring, again, that vaguely gloomy expression, I took what I felt was the wisest route under the circumstances. The Raving Blade would soon have no reason to terminate Nascinthé, since his stratagem was about to be exposed, and of those who would seek revenge against her, none should have greater cause than this man sitting across from me. Revenge, it seemed, was not on his agenda.

"She survived, Lord Count," I said. "She's alive, and she has fled south. I will say no more about it than that, no matter what you threaten to do to me. As to whether she is this *Spellbinder*, I honestly can't say. She never mentioned that name, and I didn't know enough to ask. But…why not tell your wife that it was her, because it very well may have been. I have worked with many Masques in my day, seen some extraordinary things, but never, and I truly mean never, have I witnessed a performance on par with what occurred that night. It was, for all intents and purposes, a *spell* cast over us all."

Tygean's hands worked against each other in an operose, meditative grind.

"You're not just telling me this because you know it's what I want to hear?"

"Just the opposite. It's really the last thing I wanted to reveal. I'm only telling you the truth because you backed me into a corner. Plus, I'm fairly sure she's safe at this point, which is another thing you can tell your wife. I don't know if Nascinthé of Levell will ever come back here, nor do I know if she will ever return to the stage, but if she does, it will only be because of the money she earned in Sherdane's contract system. Our city, and that horrible, duplicitous bid, actually gave her a second chance at life."

On occasion—quite rarely—I say something that causes a person's poor mood to entirely reverse. I had achieved this with Flerra sometimes. It was difficult to convert that scowly little mouth into beaming brightness, to induce a string of shrill giggles in a place where irritable snips ruled, but it was worth the effort, for whenever I succeeded, I could feel the foundation of our relationship deepen.

Something along those lines occurred with Count Halsin Tygean. I don't know if it deepened our relationship or, more accurately, created one, but the man's melancholy, contracted mien now broadened into a much warmer version of itself. He looked heartened. Given that he had a limitless storehouse of worries with which to concern himself, most of them pertaining directly to his own survival, it was hard to fathom why the safety of this one Masque would lift his spirits. Perhaps it was because he did not have to contend with the fact that his city—corrupt, decrepit, tumbled from its former glory—had actually gone and murdered a shining talent who would, in Sullward's heyday, have proudly called it home. Whatever the reason, this seemed to mark a clear turning point in our proceedings.

"You hear that, Owen?" he said, smiling towards the somewhat less enthused Viscount Grieves. "A second chance, the very thing I dream of sometimes."

"Don't we all, my lord," said Grieves.

"Do you?" I blurted.

They turned, of a piece, amused. Count Tygean seemed like he actually might laugh, and Grieves now sported a droll smirk. Taken together, they had the look of two men speaking with a child—a little boy who hears some common idiom ("It's raining cats and dogs" or "I turned a blind eye to it all") and interprets it literally.

"You ask that question with such seriousness, Vazeer," said Count Tygean. "I think I was just making a general observation."

"Were you? Because it seems to me, seems from my vantage, that something about this topic has roused you."

Viscount Grieves unwound his smirk, and his expression became severe again. He was probably about to tell me to mind my own business, but Count Tygean spoke before that could happen.

"I suppose we all, all of us living in this place," the Count said carefully, "imagine, at one time or another, what it might be like to live a normal life."

"That's all I imagine."

"But you didn't flee. With the money you were paid for the Narrow Bid, surely you could have relocated elsewhere."

"I didn't say I wanted a normal life somewhere else, Lord Count. I want it right here, in this city. And you…"

My mind tossed through a swirling amalgam of ill-advised thoughts, which were on the brink of becoming ill-advised statements. It wasn't my intention to raise this topic tonight, a subject that I no longer even mentioned to Shadow Bidders, let alone Underlords, except that I was sitting in the forlorn shell of the Arcadium, a place where lost dreams hung in upended suspension like bats.

"You," I said again, "have the power to change life for all of us."

He appeared to consider this for a moment, then nodded quickly, which clearly meant he had no idea what I was talking about.

"If you are referring to the continuance of the contract system," said Count Tygean, "you can rest assured. The Shadow Bidders will be restored to their former role."

"No. I mean something different."

There were several ways to approach this topic, each of them foolish in their own way. Because I am inherently a fool, I used the one that carried the most risk, for it was personal to Count Tygean.

"I have heard it said, Lord Count, that you originally hail from the North Derjian gentry. Is this true?"

I didn't need to look at Viscount Grieves to see how poorly he reacted to this. In my peripheral vision, I could see him jerking forward in his chair, though Tygean raised a hand to still him.

"It's true," the Count replied. "I was the only one among our ranks, as far as I know. Why do you ask?"

"My tailor, Osvert Gromwell, lives on the Virtuoso, and I wondered if he was a relation of yours; also, maybe, your spy."

I received the foreseeable fall-off in goodwill, and now I saw a rather icy look intrude into Tygean's dark blue eyes.

"It's not him, and I won't say what house I'm from. You'd better have a very good reason for asking me these questions."

"I think I do. Or at least I hope I do."

Here I mustered the sum of my articulacy and stupidity, then promptly spat it all out.

"Lord Count, why must your talk of restoring Drover Theater be but a private joke between you and your wife? Why not do it for real? If you want to bring the Spellbinder back to Sullward, this is the way to achieve it. And while you're at it, why not restore this very building in which we sit? That would certainly put an end to the meaningless graffiti in Dockside. The female Shadow Bidder who wields that brush, whose dedication Viscount Grieves questions, has just created a painting of such staggering power and artistry that it would be a crime for it not to be hung in a museum. Which, as you may have noticed, we don't have. Nor do we have a hall for musical performances, nor a school for architecture. Except...of course, we do. We have all of these, but they have been allowed to rot right beneath us."

"Enough of this!" Viscount Grieves snarled from where he sat. "We're Underlords, not Midland art dandies."

"The people who founded the Lower City weren't dandies," I shot back. "They were as tough as they come, but they were also visionaries, noble dreamers, who carved a cultural nexus right out of the whirling mists and bedrock."

"You're way off base, Shadow Bidder," said Grieves.

"Am I?"

I swiveled to Count Tygean.

"I think you, Count Tygean, could be a different sort of leader. I don't know what led you to this life, but it's obvious that some part of you retains your former education. Why not return to that side of yourself, allow it to drive you, as you create a new system?"

"What system?"

"A hybrid."

"A what?"

"A hybrid approach that keeps the fencing operation running, but which also diverts a portion of the funds towards restoration. The entire Lower City will take a generation to revitalize; however, key portions of the inner core could be repaired quickly, and that would begin to attract a new source of revenue."

He simply stared at me blankly, his two hands rising in an inquisitive flail.

"Cultural visitors," I clarified. "The aristocracy of the Midlands, also the gentry and merchantry masters, who have more money than the other two classes combined. Let's make this city beautiful and safe again, draw them back, allowing them to spend their money here. Great hordes of money, to create tax revenues, to begin to stamp legitimacy on this place again, so that you don't have to waste so much of your money on bribes."

"Stop this already!" Viscount Grieves shouted, and he slammed his fist down on the table. "We agreed to meet with you, Shadow Bidder, because we want you to kill our enemies, not spin fairy tales. You seem to forget what this meeting is and who we are."

I glared right back at him, emboldened, maddened even, by the wildness of my own ideas.

"You are whoever you say you are. *Viscount*."

"You forget something else, Vazeer the Lash," said Count Tygean, who appeared less irritated than his vassal. "There is the small matter of a certain meteorological event that comes at random to our shores and seems to target this neighborhood in particular."

"Of course," I said, pressing eagerly forward. "And there are plans to deal with it, real plans, not another worthless jetty. In fact, I have a copy of those plans—specifications for a massive northwestern sea wall, designed to deflect the surge waters so that they swing wide and roll off of the cliffs to the southeast. Engineers drew these up just after the first Great Storm, but King Denevaego was so delirious with grief over the loss of his two sons, he was incapable—"

"Lord Count, you have to stop listening to this!" Viscount Grieves roared, and he half stood in his chair, ready, it seemed, to throttle me.

"Yes," Tygean muttered. "Owen's right. This is off purpose, and not why we brought you here. Let's get on with it…this plan to kill him, which is what we must do."

He then went back to his habit of expressive face-rubbing, which, if he was a card player, would probably reveal everything to the other players. I had little experience with gambling, but I certainly knew the man was agitated.

"How long will it take you to gather your team?" Grieves asked.

"I'm not sure. Probably a week."

"Make it quicker than that. We're running out of time. And when you're ready to give us the signal, send your messenger, don't come yourself. As it is, you'd better be sure not to be spotted leaving here. That would put a quick end to all of these plans."

I nodded.

"You thought this thing through?" Count Tygean asked me.

"The ambush?"

"No, the restoration plan."

"Yes, it's pretty much all I think about. I have one of Aurellis Kaennamin's original maps of the city, and I stare at it every night before bed, planning the exact order of repairs."

"Lord!" Grieves snapped. "No more of this foolishness."

"You're right, you're right." Count Tygean sighed, and he leaned back in his chair and stared up at the ceiling. He rolled his neck in a few kink-expelling rotations, while his hand travelled unconsciously to his wine cup. His fingers hooked over the lip of the vessel, and he bobbled it about for a few seconds, his wedding ring catching the lamplight and creating a crisp amber spark. Finally, he dropped his chin and stared at me directly, the mildest density of a squint marring his brow.

"Just out of curiosity," he said. "How would the restoration begin?"

4

INSTINCTS

I left the enormous decaying gullet of the Arcadium somewhere after morning's Second Bell, and while I tried to be stealthy, as Viscount Grieves demanded, Radrin showed me that I had failed. He came up behind me as soon as I reached the first phalanx of surrounding buildings.

"I thought they had taken their revenge," he said.

We were one block from the river now, in a dense knot of stone residences that comprised this northern section of the Lower City. Some of the wealthiest families had once lived here, for these buildings were considered especially prestigious, providing easy access to both the museum and the river. However, the first Great Storm had done such damage that few Underlord retainers had since chosen to make use of them.

Radrin ushered me into a narrow side street, and he pulled me back towards a wall.

"Did he agree to our proposal?" he asked.

"He did."

"The fealty too?"

"More or less."

"Less? Which part was less?"

I waved dismissively, as if I felt dismissive, but what I really felt was nervous. I knew this was going to be a sore point.

"He won't actually go through with the ceremony. It's apparently a drawn-out affair, involving kneeling to a sword, ring kissing, specified witnesses, etc." (Honestly, I didn't know what the ceremony entailed, so I simply rattled off some twaddle I had read over the years about Tergonian nobility.) "But he'll tell Gueritus that the fealty is coming soon."

"That's insufficient."

Radrin's admonition was now making a sudden, unwelcome reappearance. The unsplintered hillocks of his cheekbones looked notably stark in the faint moonlight. There was a lantern burning just beyond a white window shade two buildings away, and with Radrin facing partially that direction, I could see the inquisition readying itself behind the smokey green of his eyes.

"Has he at least agreed to join the attack, once the ambush is sprung?"

Hand gestures were too cavalier for this question, so I provided a noncommittal nod.

"It was implied."

"Implied? How do you 'imply' such a thing? Either their blades will be joining ours in the attack or they won't."

"Look," I said, trying to sound too exhausted to argue these points, which, now that I checked in with myself, I was. "There was a lot to cover in this meeting. The logistics can be discussed once we have our team."

"What *did* you cover? You were in there for over two and a half hours."

Down the bend of the narrow street, I noticed three figures moving cautiously away from one of the buildings. They didn't quite look like soldiers, so I had to assume they were Underlord minions of a less martial variety. Still, it paid to be cautious.

"Let's get out of this neighborhood, Blackstar. I shouldn't be seen here, or anywhere for that matter. Dead men aren't supposed to hold meetings."

Indeed, "being dead" was one of my few protections right now, for ostensibly I had been killed by a Finisher named Shade of Night, hired by Count Ulan Gueritus. The woman's frustrated attempt on my life (and the likelihood that she would try again) were the main reasons that Radrin was acting as my bodyguard tonight.

So, we charted a route that wove us quickly towards the least inhabited section of the Outer Ring. Despite its distance from the sea, the northernmost regions of the Lower City had taken a great deal of damage from the two storms, as the Grells was narrowest there and had created a funnel effect for the surge. Radrin and I found ourselves leaping over deep puddles, inhaling moist air that had an almost viscous density to it.

In this fringe of the Lower City lay a sub-section of the neighborhood where artists of all sorts had once taken residence. Passing through this cluster of three- and four-story buildings, I stared up at what had once been creative imagery: bas reliefs of dancers, lyre players, thespians, figures scribbling with quills, and those working at kilns. The stonework had suffered with the passage of time, and the mildewed facades were a lattice of chipped limbs, missing instruments, and heads ground down to noseless blobs.

Even so, I found the sight inspiring. These homes had originally been a patronage project by the founding Kaennamin family, with the goal of allowing lesser-known artists to afford the rent. Northern aristocrats and merchants in good standing were expected to sponsor two or three artists, which did wonders to draw talent to these gorgeous buildings. Count Tygean and I had actually touched on this topic tonight. A patronage program, sponsored first by the Underlords, followed by the local gentry, then finally prominent families in Tergon, would be essential to seeing the restoration plan through.

"There, Gistward," Radrin said, pointing between two buildings towards the lamp-blushed profile of a bridge. Gistward was the second to last of the five bridges that spanned MidRiven, the blade-straight canal that separated the Lower City from the Middle City. As we crossed the stone surface, I paused at the apex. The canal was a full twenty feet across, and from my perch, my gaze was drawn along the sheening water by the pulse of streetlamps. I spotted the Mercantile Exchange, the Tergonian Embassy, and the Imperial Garrison along its southern lip. Then, farther south, near the heart of the Middle City, I could easily pick out the domed crown of Government Hall, a majestic, spired building that, in the days of the Old Calendar, had been the royal palace, but which now served as the home of the State Senate and the Governor's office.

Tygean and I had not quite reached this place in our discussion, but we came close. The next leader of Sullward—its true leader, not the bribed figurehead—could conceivably hold court there. At the very least, the curtain of deception that separated the two worlds could be lifted, so that matters of state could be openly decided by the man who actually ran things. The startling possibilities of what lay ahead were creating a light prickle in my throat.

Radrin and I stepped off into the Middle City and quickly made our way to the sheltering bulk of guild halls. I spotted a pair of Imperial soldiers making the rounds just past the tawny mass of the shipbuilder's guild. At the corner of Justice and Colvin, we found a safe area, where two stone halls and two timber-framed houses made a neat four-point junction. The windows of the closest buildings were all dark, and we had a good view down both streets.

"Tell me what happened," he said.

I quickly recounted things. I got us as far as Tygean's grudging compliance to the meeting with Gueritus before I was cut off.

"Did they advance you funds?"

"No. They can't access their vaults."

Radrin made a low, murmurous noise, which definitely didn't sound like approval. Two well-heeled pedestrians were moving some distance off, conversing as they ambled across Colvin, then down another street.

"You keep giving me bad answers," he said.

"You keep asking bad questions."

"Are there any good questions?"

"Yes, I think there are."

I could already feel I was about to blow this part, for I was tired and not likely to spin it correctly.

"This Underlord seems different than the others," I ventured.

This won me no response, just a curious ascent of the eyebrows.

"He's from the gentry, originally."

No verbal response here either, but those nicely groomed eyebrows dipped slightly in confusion. I tried to see if somewhere in that half-shadowed face, behind the scolding green of his eyes, I might spot recognition. I saw nothing.

"He's also married," I continued.

Now Radrin shifted in place so that he was looking at me

from a somewhat different angle, trying, perhaps, to see if my right eye looked a little saner than my left.

"Vazeer?" he said in a low voice that sounded troubled.

"I know what you're thinking," I went on. "You think that can't possibly have anything to do with anything, but actually it does. I'm sure it does, because I've met very few people who are married, and of those I know…especially this one friend of mine, or former friend, the person who rents me my skiffs. He's a real straight player, someone who honors his word. So, my sense—"

"Vazeer." This was said with a brisk finality, precluding further discourse on the virtues of marriage. "What, exactly, did you talk about for almost three hours inside that building?"

"What we talked about was a vision of this city that would eventually have no use for criminals like me."

I watched Radrin work on this for a moment.

"Didn't the Raving Blade also present that vision?" He finally asked.

"I couldn't begin to tell you what the Raving Blade was presenting. A fencing operation run in broad daylight? In open defiance of Tergon? It made no sense."

"And this thing that you and Count Tygean discussed somehow did?"

"It definitely did."

"A resurrection of the city of old?"

"Exactly." And now I felt a pyretic little quiver. The fact that Radrin even asked that question, phrased it in that manner, meant that he grasped at least the general concept.

"It wouldn't happen immediately," I went on excitedly. "The fencing would need to continue for a decade, hopefully a little less; however, Tygean isn't old, so he would have plenty of time to see the transition through. We discussed it—the order of restoration, and how revenues might be—"

"Enough."

Imperious Blackstar was now the only version of the man present.

"Do you not see what he's done?" Radrin asked. "He played you. Count Tygean is clearly an intelligence gatherer. He knows this fixation of yours, could have learned it any number of ways. I gleaned it in but a few hours, watching you pore over your Lower City map, digressing constantly to talk about old buildings. The Count dangled these absurd ideas to get what he wanted."

"I'm the one who brought it up."

"Or so you imagine, but any good confidence scheme works that way. A clever manipulator can steer you within striking distance of a topic, so that you believe you thought of it yourself."

Oh, that one struck a chord. Into my mind crept the memory of that first promising utterance from Count Tygean, the one that had instigated everything: *"A second chance, the very thing I dream of sometimes."* That did seem like an oddly wistful comment from an Underlord.

"But he would have nothing to gain from doing this. How does this help his cause?"

Now Radrin slowly swung his chin back and forth in a headshake that seemed part pity, part distaste.

"He got everything. He has advanced us no funds for recruitment. He has only to set up a harmless meeting with the Raving Blade, where he will promise nothing of substance. On the way home from that meeting, the Raving Blade will suffer an attack from a team of vengeful Shadow Bidders who may or may not succeed in killing him. Certainly, some of his men will die, weakening him at the very least. And does Count Tygean need to join in this attack? To the contrary. He can flee to safety, absolving himself of the incident. If the intended purpose is achieved, he can then hunt us down and destroy us, to gain the confidence of Gueritus's surviving soldiers. If, instead, the assassination fails, he can claim total ignorance of our intentions. The Raving Blade may or may not believe him, but Tygean will be no worse off than he was before, and probably a bit better. Our attack will do damage."

I abruptly teetered on the edge of horror. Somewhere in the early portion of my meeting with Count Tygean, thoughts along these lines had crossed my mind, but they had been largely overwhelmed by all that followed.

"I refuse to believe this about him."

"Why, because he's from the gentry?"

"It's not that simple."

Actually, it kind of was. I felt that the Count, unique among others of his world, inherently valued so many of the things I valued and was depleted, unmistakably, by the very things that depleted me. I couldn't help feeling that Halsin Tygean and I were kindred spirits. But this would not be well received by my co-conspirator, so I said no more.

Near the place where Justice Street ran into the Courthouse, I spotted two figures approaching. They were not the same pair that I had seen earlier, and though far off, years of Grell Running paranoia alerted me to the danger. The shape of one of the individuals—shawled, narrowly hatted, with the skinny legs of a man wearing hose—suggested a government official, which wasn't a threat. However, the other—broadened by armor, the jutting protrusion of a scabbard, no helmet, cloaked to a certain midlength—possessed a shape that would have been recognizable in near total darkness, which this wasn't.

"Constable," I murmured to Radrin with a flick of my chin. "I can't tell which of the nine it is, which means he doesn't recognize me yet either. Let's get out of here before that changes."

But we weren't quick enough. The law officer put up a restraining hand to his companion and then released a shrill, keening shriek, not unlike the cry of a hawk. That goddamned noise. The Imperial constable's whistle was a horrible thing, a three-inch-long brass contraption, so lightweight that it could remain in the lips for long stretches, keeping the hands free. Its piercing note was, arguably, the single worst sound a Shadow Bidder might hear in the course of their career.

Radrin and I sped across Justice and darted down Colvin in the direction of Dockside. While this neighborhood had the advantage of being free of Lower City men, Imperial agents roamed the area at all hours, often accompanying politicians back to their Middle City residences. Whoever that whistle was calling, and whatever they thought we were (Underlords, probably), interrogations were coming, followed by a detention of an indefinite length. We needed to get out of the Middle City quickly.

We raced along Colvin until we reached the end, and here we found ourselves at the edge of a large, open fairgrounds. In better times, this was where public events were held, including a weekly bazaar where Terza Falconbrow used to display her works in a pleasant little art stall. Crossing the Fairgrounds after dark definitely wasn't the best way to reach Dockside, for I had noted a large number of ratty tents, broken wagons, and assorted makeshift dwellings since the storm. Displaced people of all sorts were living here, and such enclaves were invariably crime-ridden and filled with desperate souls. However, that whistle left us no choice, so Radrin and I quickly fled the exposed world of streetlamps and made our way out onto the sheltered gloom of the muddy lot.

"Sometimes I need to trust my gut about someone," I said when we were a third of the way across the saturated field of footprint puddles and wheel ruts. While the area was dark overall, I kept seeing the blurred crescent of the moon appearing here and there on the slurpy ground.

"Trust it like you did with Shade of Night?" Radrin asked.

Damn. This topic of my seduction and defeat by the deadly Finisher, Shade of Night, was something that Radrin had generously avoided in the last few days, possibly in deference to my wounded pride. That moratorium was clearly over.

"I was in a particularly vulnerable place that night," I replied. "She wouldn't have such an easy time of it if she ever tried again."

"She will try again."

I stopped and squared with him, and when he followed suit, the two of us faced off in the center of the bumpy field. A powerful loamy smell filled our nostrils, and a few feet to my right, I saw a soiled twist of a stall banner curled in the mud like a sleeping animal. Tents and improvised housing appeared like woeful dunes a hundred feet or so behind Radrin's back, and closer to me, I saw what looked like an overturned wagon.

"What's your history with Shade?" I asked. "Similar to mine?"

"Certainly not."

"Then what?"

"We were double proffered on a bid once. This doesn't happen often, but when it does, the contract becomes a competition."

"A competition…? Who won?"

Now a lean, cynical twist appeared on his lips.

"She did. Shade of Night usually wins, which is something I'm afraid you're going to learn."

In the open space beyond Radrin, I saw movement. It was dozens of feet away, but with some straining, I picked out a pair of tousled shapes fast approaching. I flicked my chin as an alert, a gesture which Radrin quickly mimicked. At just that moment, I heard sodden steps behind my own back, and when I turned, I was met with the sight of two lurching figures, very close, who had likely emerged from the underside of the wagon. I understood immediately that this was a robbery. I also understood that it had been staged in the hopes that some rich, Middle City resident would be stupid enough to make this crossing at night.

The pair came at me from either side, which showed at least a measure of coordination, and they instantly grabbed pieces of my clothing, trying to stop me from drawing a blade. None of this was terrible planning; however, they sure blew it with their reconnaissance. Of everybody in this entire city, I was pretty much the worst person to grab.

The man on my left seized my upper arm, while the man on the right, who was appreciably larger, used a more bullying approach. He snatched the fabric on my upper chest and yanked me up to my toes. I could see that both of them had weapons in their other hands.

"Ya gonna give me all ya got," snarled the big one, "or else ya...ahhhhhoooowwwww...yeeeeee...gawwwds!"

Let me explain.

Here's the thing with grabbing somebody on their chest and then compounding the error by hoisting—you leave the pinky exposed. I don't care how big you are, your pinky is weak, and if your so-called "victim" can separate that one digit away from the grabbing hand, and then bend it backwards, terrible pain follows. It doesn't matter that it's only the pinky and it can be splinted later, because you don't think any of that. Instead, you make sounds like this fellow and go twisting yourself like a circus freak to relieve the pain.

My mentor, Holod Deadskiff, had taught me this (along with every other dirty trick in the book), and I must say I executed it to perfection that night. I needed to, because the big, clutchy shit had a rusty spade in the other hand, and only by means of his rearward contortions was I able to put the weapon out of reach. But my success was even more thorough, because as I used the right hand to take care of him, my other arm was freed up to handle the man on the left. Of the two, this one had made the dumber choice, since there's a very good counter to his grab, which you might want to learn. If somebody seizes your upper arm from the side, all you need to do is lift your arm up, swing it back and then quickly hook it forward again, and you'll pin him in a potentially shoulder-dislocating trap. Try it. You can improvise with a friend (lightly), and you'll see what I'm talking about.

Anyway, this is what I did (not lightly, because this unkempt horse's ass wasn't my friend), and I actually heard the dull pop of his bone coming out of its joint. To his credit, the man merely grunted, and he still had the wherewithal to make a go of it with his weapon. The issue for him, and I had noted this at the outset, was that he carried a long staff as his tool of the trade. This wasn't inherently a bad weapon, especially for an unskilled combatant, but it proved quite useless here. All the wretch could do was swat at me across his own body. He struck my far arm a few times, rather irrelevantly, and the only real success he achieved was getting me to torque away, thereby igniting some pain in my injured hip. This was from my duel with Coljin Helmgrinder at The Crossbiter, and while it was healing well, sudden movements of this sort aggravated it.

It only took about four or five seconds of administering these bone-cracking agonies before both men started to cry out plaintively. So, I released them and stepped back out of range. My hands were ready to draw blades, but I saw that this wouldn't be necessary, as both dropped their implements and clutched their injured joints. Shortly after that, they stumbled away into the darkness, mewling.

I turned back to Radrin and found him both physically (and by all appearances, emotionally) unmoved. While the dim lighting made it difficult to do much of a survey, I saw no sign of the figures who had been approaching him from behind, so I had to assume they sprinted away at the start. They were probably frightened off by the ease with which I handled their cohorts, something my own cohort might wish to note, for the services of a "bodyguard" were obviously superfluous.

Then I observed that Radrin was doing something interesting with his hands. He was engaged in a dexterous little motion, about stomach height, which seemed familiar to me. In fact, it was so familiar that I actually felt a bit queasy, for this fastidious ritual always signified something horrible. Radrin was cleaning that dagger of his with a black cloth.

I looked down at his feet and saw two new lumpy mounds in the mud on either side of him. They were bodies, splayed out in vulgar lifelessness.

"We should get moving back to your apartment," he said, nodding in that direction. He stuffed his cloth and dagger away, then started walking towards Dockside, forcing me to hobble to catch up.

"Was that really necessary?" I asked as we came in sight of the dense irregularity of the Dockside buildings. "These people—"

"Shade of Night has had ample time to recover," Radrin said, resuming our prior conversation. "She's likely to come for you soon."

This wasn't the easiest adjustment for me. The casualness with which this man dispensed murder made the act seem about as consequential as sneezing (something I had yet to see him do, by the way). Not until we had come under the first timber-framed shadows could I bring myself to mutter out a response.

"Shade won't come for me yet. You may know Finishers, Blackstar, but I know women, and I saw the look in her eye when she left that night. She's going to give me a little time to keep my vow."

We entered the street, which was slick with the recent rains and entirely empty.

"You're being overly optimistic again," said Radrin as we worked our way down the glossy, irregular path of cobbles. "You're not dealing with a normal woman, just as you didn't meet with a normal man earlier this evening. Assigning typical motives to either of them would be a mistake."

I led us into a nameless shut that would link up with Ghailbrath Road and bring us, eventually, to the alleys behind 44 Masthead. We worked our way, single file, through these narrow passages, and all the while my mind was churning. The issues surrounding Count Tygean needed more time to contemplate, including steps that I might take to avoid betrayal. When it came to Shade of Night, I had already applied the obvious safeguards.

The day following the Finisher's attack, I had lumbered down to Everine Agaedus's office and confronted my landlady about her involvement. It can be gratifying sometimes to induce terror. As Everine watched me limp towards her—slashed, battered, heavily armed, and angry—even the clownish coating of rouge could not mask her panic. I was, for all intents and purposes, the walking dead.

"It can't be," she whispered.

She slid back against the wall of her office, her hand groping across a shelf for support.

"But somehow it is," I replied.

Everine's eyes traced a path up, down, and around as she took in my injuries, particularly the cut across my ear. Existing as it did so close to the all-important jugular vein, my landlady was clearly wondering how her charming property manager had failed to finish the job.

"You really are unkillable," she wheezed. "You're the first I've ever seen survive."

And so, it all came out. Frightened and remorseful, Everine confessed how, early in her investment career, she had employed Shade to remove a hateful competitor who was threatening to ruin her. Not yet rich, Everine was incapable of paying Shade's exorbitant fee, so instead the two women struck up an arrangement. This included on-demand residency in the Agaedus buildings when Shade was visiting Sullward for a job and also the occasional use of "special access" apartments for more sinister purposes. Secret window latches, liftable door hinges, and hidden floor hatches had been installed in Everine's six buildings at Shade's insistence.

"Vazeer, I have been absolutely sick about this," Everine said, some of the color reemerging behind the facial putty. "Shade always targets such bad characters, which has made it bearable. But when she told me it was you, I was heartbroken."

"You didn't seem heartbroken when you asked me to strong-arm Breaker Tabard."

"I was, but I covered it."

"Whose idea was that…the bit about Tabard?"

"Hers. She always comes up with these plans, including the backstory about being a family friend. Sometimes I think she prefers to make things more complicated, just so that she has an entertaining game to play."

"I noticed that. If I was any less entertaining, I'd be dead."

Thereafter, I made my demands. I really wasn't interested in harming Everine, though I kept up threatening appearances. The first requirement was obvious: she needed to instantly send people to fix my window bars, and any other secret Shade of Night access points I might not know about. After that, I had her change both of the exterior door locks for building 44, which involved the not insignificant trouble of distributing new keys to all of the tenants. Finally, I worked out an arrangement similar to Shade's: I was given permanent residency, including as many candles, bundles of firewood, and blocks of ice as my heart desired. These, Everine would deliver herself. None of these measures would protect me while I was out in the Sullward streets, but at least I could feel a degree of security at home.

Radrin and I arrived at last at the rear entrance to 44 Masthead Lane. This was my clever little safe haven, which had been neither safe nor clever so far; however, it was a lot more discreet than my townhouse. Before reaching the door, I pulled up short, which was my signal that I didn't want Radrin to come up. In the last week, he had spent most evenings with me upstairs, going over all the details of our coming operation, and I was sick of it. If he repeated the performance, I wouldn't get to sleep until dawn, and he'd no doubt rebuke me continually for lapses during my meeting with Count Tygean. Still, a degree of decorum was necessary.

"Listen, Radrin," I said. "I owe my life to your penchant for caution. But some things lie beyond the reach of odds. I'm not a Masque, but I do have instincts about people, and I have a very good feeling about the Count, who I don't think wants to betray us. And I also have an instinct about Shade of Night. Her curiosity is too strong to simply kill me at this point. She'll watch a bit first, to see what crazy thing I do next."

"It's the crazy thing that *she* does next that worries me," said Radrin. "The woman is not stable."

"No, definitely not, but that's also why she won't obey all of your precious codes. She operates according to her own rules."

"All elements that make her so dangerous," he said. "There's a reason she's considered the best."

"Is she? Is she the best?"

He contemplated this for a moment.

"By the time our mission is through," he replied, "she and I will face off again. One of us will walk away from that encounter, the other will not. At that point the question will be settled."

This was a grim prophecy, one which I quickly tried to lighten with a little smile.

"Perhaps she's too unpredictable to show up for that meeting. In the meantime, trust me, Shade doesn't want to finish me yet. I've got another week, probably two, before she starts to get impatient. By then our operation will be underway, and at that point, she'll want to watch to see how it unfolds."

"I hope you're right."

"I know I am. She's a strange one, but I feel certain about this."

At last, we bid each other good night. Radrin lingered a moment to watch me enter the building. His own Locksmith had already switched out my apartment locks and also checked on Everine's repairs, so I was effectively safe now, and when I glanced back through the door's viewing glass, he was gone.

I had just taken the first few steps up the staircase, when Shade of Night emerged from the gloom of the building's interior and came to take her revenge.

5

PAYMENT

The first thing I felt was the fiery sting of a knife in my back. It went straight through the leather cuirass with a livid creak, just shy of full penetration. My cloak had been brushed aside in the process, and I felt her other hand clamp securely onto my belt.

"If you make any sound, I'm finishing you right here in the hallway. Interlace your fingers behind your head."

Her voice was low, hoarse, and without any hint of playful mockery. The guttural inflections of her indeterminate accent were a little less pronounced than they had been in the past.

I raised my arms and did as told.

"Now, we're going to slowly climb those stairs, and you're not going to make any sudden movements. Do you know where this stiletto is pointed? Nod your head if you do."

I nodded, because I did. The tip of her blade had penetrated as much as a quarter of an inch into the flesh of my left middle back, directly over one of my kidneys.

"Good, then you know with just the slightest pressure, I'll pierce your kidney, causing unbearable pain, then death. Not a quick death. I'll have plenty of time to carve all those bits I promised the proffer. I've done this many times, and I can assure you, you won't have the strength to fight back."

I was fairly sure she was right. I'd heard enough stories about kidney wounds over the years and delivered a few myself, so this did not seem like hyperbole.

"Now, up we go. Slowly."

And so it went. I was exhausted, and though my prior injuries were on the mend, I had just re-ignited the pain in my hip, so I definitely wasn't primed for some sort of brilliant reversal. Plus, this wasn't some cretinous wagon-dweller; this was the top Finisher in Hell's Labyrinth, possibly the Empire at large, and she knew exactly what she was doing. Each movement I made she mirrored in perfect tandem, stepping with my step, balancing with my balance, maintaining an acute, needling pressure the whole time with that blade. Her short stature worked to her advantage here, for even if I swung my elbows around and tried to catch her in the jaw, her head was down close to the level of the stiletto, and therefore almost impossible to hit from that angle.

Slowly, agonizingly, we climbed, and at each landing, dimly aglow with the throb of an oil lantern, I prayed that nobody would open their door. The clanking shock of it would almost certainly have Shade driving her knife straight through my kidney out of reflex, and then she would kill the tenant afterwards to tie up loose ends.

By the time we reached the third floor, I could feel the gummy ooze of my blood creating warmth on my lower back. My legs were on the verge of cramping from moving so slowly, and even the act of holding my arms up high with the elbows flared was remarkably enervating, like a mini crucifixion. The stairs beneath me groaned and creaked. Her footfalls, by contrast, were pillowed—no clomping or scuffing—which told me she was either wearing slippers or soft-soled shoes, all the better to ambush some moron in his own lobby.

My mind, in its stressed state, latched on to details of no relevance whatsoever—a brown smudge on the third-floor chair rail that looked vaguely like a turkey's head, the small paisley twirls in the stairwell wallpaper, which, taken as a whole, read almost like falling snow. I smelled the radishy odor of trash, likely emanating from one of the apartments and which, if I managed to live through this, would probably always be associated with this assault.

We eventually reached the fourth floor. I was amazed by the fact that at no point in that ascent did Shade's grip relax, indicating a loss of focus or an awkward step. We came around the L of the hallway and eventually arrived at my front door.

"Very slowly, with just your right hand, reach down and get your keys out of that pocket where you keep them. If you so much as twitch towards one of your blades, it's over. Do you understand?"

"Yes."

A fierce, terrifying burst of pain tore through the nerve endings in my back as Shade exerted a jiggling poke of the stiletto, driving me face-first into the door. My chin collided with the lacquered wood, making a dull, oaken thud, and my body squeezed against the paneled surface as I tried to escape the agony.

"I told you not to make a sound, you idiot!" she said. "My blade is so close to your kidney I can tickle it. Another mistake and you're gone. Grab those keys and open your locks."

This I did carefully, not moving in any erratic ways, and though it was difficult to keep from shaking, I got all three of the locks open in short order. After that, with my left hand still up behind my head, I used my right to turn the knob and push slowly inside.

The space within was dark and slightly stuffy. There was a dense, pleasant aroma of the stew I had cooked earlier, mixed with the apartment's inherent plaster and wood smell.

"Light the front hall lamp."

With the door still open and some radiance creeping in from the outside hallway, I pulled the flint lighter from the front console table and set to work on the lamp. Once lit, Shade had me close, lock, and bar the front door before we moved in this excruciating couplet to the middle of the living room carpet.

"Use your left hand to free your cloak."

I let it fall to the floor between us.

"Now, down to your knees, very slowly."

This was harder to accomplish than I would have thought, as my quad muscles were already quivering from the anxious climb, and with my hands still up behind my head, I thumped down awkwardly onto my kneecaps, then almost fell forward. Shade hauled me back by my belt.

"Clumsy oaf," she spat.

Pulled back as I was, her breath was suddenly hot against my ear, damp and astringent. For one merciful second, I felt the sting of the blade release itself from my back, but this was merely because she whipped the stiletto up to my throat, where it pressed so hard against my jugular I truly feared it would go through.

"Remember this posture?"

And before I knew it, I was right back in her favorite clinch, with her monkey legs finding their way around my waist from behind and my head cocking, and indeed cracking, as her other hand leveraged it to the right. She drew me backwards so that my feet were forced off to the sides and then eventually around to the front, at which point I found myself slumped back on her, with that terrible angle in my neck. It had taken me days to get the painful kink out last time, and now that it was happening again, I let out a little squeak of pain.

"No squealing, piggy," she rasped hotly against my ear.

Again, I was present to how utterly stripped this voice was of cooing or playful teasing.

"You have more blades this time, so let's take care of that. Reach down and unbuckle your weapon's belt, and push it across the floor. If you so much as touch one of your implements, you die."

Trying not to cut my neck in the process, I fumbled my hands down to my waist and got the belt off, and was able to writhe until it was out from under me. From there I swung it on the carpet, though the two spades caught on the plush tan fabric and didn't go very far. Shade simply turned us slightly so that the weapons were out of reach.

"We also have more clothing in the way. Unbutton your pants, then slide them down around your ankles."

If going gracefully to my knees was difficult, this was so much worse, and far more embarrassing. It required a thrust of my pelvis off the floor, followed by an extended, shimmying wriggle to get my trousers down to my boots. A brief, unpleasant conversation about undergarments made it clear that those needed to follow, and by the time my privates were fully exposed to the wide plank ceiling, my legs were effectively pinioned by a twisted mess of cloth.

But she wasn't done. The striptease continued, for now came my cuirass and tunic, and this part she accomplished with what I can only describe as cunning depravity. Forcing me to roll over onto my stomach, she slid down my back, and with terrifying quickness, she had reached between my legs and snatched my most vulnerable parts in a fierce crabbish clutch, driving the edge of her blade like a tiny guillotine against them. I literally shrieked. It wasn't a manly sound, or even a boyish sound, but something an adolescent girl might emit when pinched or jabbed, and this managed to draw the first humorous noise. She chuckled in that brisk, unmelodious rattle—the laugh that had, at one time, minimally charmed me for its unadorned quality.

"Does my piggy fear for his little package? Imagine what a racket he's going to make when I start carving him for real. Now, off with that tunic and armor."

And so, it progressed. Throughout my slow, shameful disrobing, I was intensely aware of how practiced Shade of Night was with this. Either she had guided many unfortunate victims through this sequence, or else she had obsessively thought through the logistics of our meeting and was executing her plan to perfection. At no time did I ever detect the slightest hesitancy or complacency. Which is not to say that I couldn't have made a move. There were key transition moments, as we shifted from one parasitic pairing to another, that my odds improved slightly, but only slightly, and part of the fiendish cleverness of the assault was the fact that I kept thinking I would get a better chance later on. "Later on," I now learned, was me on my stomach with my most helpless pieces in her grasp and a razor-sharp blade ready to sever them from my body. A kidney wound was starting to look more attractive by the second.

But everything else was looking less attractive, including my most hopeful ideas. For starters, my character judgement was just plain awful. If I could be so wrong about Shade of Night, then how right could I possibly be about Count Tygean? All the pesky warnings from my co-conspirator had to be viewed in a different light.

Sorry, Radrin, I thought as I lay there, a fraction of an inch from castration. *You really did pin your hopes on the wrong man.*

Shade again made one of her moves, springing up my torso (sliding, actually, for my blood had glazed my lower back like millwheel grease) and was at my head again, with one hand gripping my hair and the stiletto at my jugular. I knew right away that this was going to be my best chance. The throat is nothing to play around with; however, it sure beat the last body part, and I was finally feeling ready to take a risk. Shade, unfortunately, knew this.

"I can hear you thinking," she whispered into my ear. "Your mind is telling you that this is your moment. Many corpses thought the same thing. Remember, your Finisher creep isn't here to distract me this time, and your legs are bound by your pants. You would have to get control of my blade, and that will be almost impossible in this position. Not to mention, I have other weapons, ready to pull, and you have no armor, so I can stab your organs at will; and believe me, I know where they all are. This will turn into a gushing, bloody mess, with you leaking out all over Everine's carpet. Your best chance was in the lobby downstairs."

This was all true, and I was consumed, in that moment, with the depth of my stupidity. On the night that Shade seduced me, my conscience probably would not have allowed me to drive the knife home myself, but I certainly could have allowed Radrin to do it. How many times did I stop him from destroying the threat? Three. Once in the bedroom, then twice in the living room, all of which I had contemplated many times since, as I tried to believe—desperately believe—that some deeper instinct told me it was a good idea to keep this person alive.

Again, Shade seemed to detect the course of my thoughts. Breathing that familiar hot tartness into the side of my face, she spoke.

"Even if you somehow avoid a fatal wound, which you won't, or if it's a slow leaker, giving you time to wrestle the blade away, you face another problem. Do you remember what it is?"

Uncertain if the rules of silence still applied, but not wanting to shake my head with the knife so close, I ventured a quiet, "What?"

"The problem, you fool, is that you can't kill me. You're such a soft-hearted little boy, you can't bring yourself to kill Shade of Night. You couldn't even let your creep do it when he had a passing chance. Imagine that? I had tricked my way into your home to butcher you, to carve you into choice morsels, that I might serve them to the man you hate, and you were unable to so much as harm a hair on my head. What does that say about you, Vazeer the Lash?"

For a moment I tried to come up with an answer that would aid me somehow, that might stall her, or facilitate what was feeling like an increasingly suicidal counter maneuver, but I couldn't think of anything, so I just muttered the thing that was actually in my head.

"It says that I'm a hopeless half-wit. That you might as well start the carving, because I'm getting thoroughly sick of being me."

There was no response at first, and we continued to lie there in our brutal stack, Shade's stomach bathed in my blood, that honed edge pressed against my most critical artery. Her mouth was so close to my ear I could hear the little oceanic roars of her breathing, feel clammy moisture settling on my face. The smell of her had grown strong—citric and damp as it invaded my nostrils. Then at last she spoke, in a low, throaty grumble.

"It's answers like that, you fool…"

And the hot, citric ocean roared a few more times.

"It's answers like that which make you so irresistible, my sweet Lash. You are just so horribly irresistible."

And then, to my stunned amazement, I felt her fulsome lips on the side of my face, kissing the scarred flesh of my cheek.

"I know you told me to stay away," she breathed, "to give you a little time to work your scheme, but I couldn't. Watching you here each night, meeting with your creep, making plans to banish boredom from Shade's life…the whole thing has been very arousing. I simply couldn't help myself."

Now I felt her writhing against me, rubbing around in the wounded grease of my naked back, and the entrapping fingers in my hair began to massage my head, injecting a giddy alternation of pleasure and pain as the long nails intermittently scraped my scalp.

"I also came to chide you," she continued. "That was very dumb, the way you protected me from your creep. Especially the last part, when you blocked his throw. You looked ridiculous and desperate, trying to keep him from harming poor Shade, willing to endanger everything just to set me free. How silly of you, but… I must say, very romantic."

My pulse was slamming, thudding against the knife, my body undergoing a hectic fluctuation between suffocating heat and frigid chills. There on my stomach, with my face angled to the left, a new storm of humid kisses descended.

"Roll over," she commanded.

And I complied. The strategy I'd been concocting—to affect some sort of reversal—died inside me, as she no doubt knew it would, and though the stiletto did come off of my neck for a heartbeat during the turn, I did nothing about it. Once I was on my back, she settled her rather insignificant weight back on me, and the blade returned to its vigil against my jugular. But this time I could see her. I could fully absorb the sight of that face, and those weirdly breathtaking features, savage and carnal—a slender, dusky oval with lavish red lips, dotted by moles, inset with the speckled, almond gemstones of her eyes—and any hope of fighting back was lost. As she levered down, her raven hair spilled forward and sheltered us in a piquant cocoon, the ends tickling my shoulders and neck like insect legs.

"My targets are all very amorous before they know who and what Shade is," she huffed from inches away. "But once they learn, they squeal and plead, and, if for one second they think they have the upper hand, they turn nasty. I can see that they would happily kill me, if only they could. But not you. You saw it all. You might even, possibly, have been able to kill me, kill me only because you had help…but still it was possible, and yet you chose not to. You did this knowing full well that it would guarantee your death later on. In this way, my sweet Lash, you are so very, very different."

Dipping her head farther, her mouth opened, and with a sort of impulsive gluttony, she swathed my lips in hers, nudging my teeth apart. I could have kept them closed, but the relief I felt was visceral, and if my compliance was the very thing that was stopping her from murdering me, then so be it. In came her hot breath and that long, sedulous tongue, and while no part of me was truly ready for this, let alone in the mood, I played the role of the receptive vessel.

"Shade," I said, when we had momentarily unlocked, "was it really necessary—"

"Shhhhh…" And her mouth came back over mine to muzzle my question.

When this was done, she pulled her face back a few inches and shook her head.

"You are not to speak unless I tell you to. But yes, it was necessary. It was necessary to show you how easily I can finish you, do it even when you are armed and prepared for trouble. You must always remember that Shade is in charge. Me being in charge is one of the rules of our engagement."

Her free hand came out of my hair and found its way down to my chest where, fortified by a glossed armory of magenta nails, she scraped happily over my pectoral muscles like a child tracing her name in the sand. That soft color of purple was picking up a similar tint in her eyeshadow. Upon further study, it was clear that she was amply made up, with a gentle rose gloss of lipstick, a dabbing of rouge, and some obvious attention paid to her eyelashes, which, almost to a comical degree, had that long, wispy quality sported by her alter ego, "Jisselle." This was one hell of a pretty fix-up for a backstabbing.

"And here comes another one of the rules," she went on, her tone husky and very much the "Jisselle" voice. "Regular payment will be required."

I would have liked to speak then, for excuses were at the ready. I had money in this apartment, a rather ample supply, for such things as procuring food, paying Cad, bribing whoever. But not exactly "Shade of Night" numbers. I had promised her this, and since I meant to uphold my end of the deal, some stalling was required until I could retrieve my stash. To signal this, I began to point down towards my purse, which had been sucked into the twisted mess of my trousers.

"Nooohhhh…" she said, shaking her head and tapping the

little magenta spearheads against my chest. "You can pay me money later. I need a different form of payment now."

And with that, she slid backwards and went partially upright, so that she was straddling the area that she had clutched so rapaciously earlier. Her blade was still at my neck, but somewhat loosely, and she actually began to tap the tip against my jaw playfully.

"I came prepared," she said, smiling. "Which you can probably feel."

Oh…yes. Now that she mentioned it, I could. Shade was wearing a short, tailored black coat, and underneath that was a belted emerald tunic, which hung down close to her knees. Her legs were swathed in finely knit black woolen hose that descended into similarly colored, laced shoes, but somewhere between the top of those hose and the bottom of her, there was apparently a clothing gap. My skin felt a smeared warmth beneath the skirted section of the tunic, and she quickly maneuvered this moist part of herself into position.

My opportunity to launch a counterattack had certainly arrived. The problem was (and it was becoming more of a problem with each deviant undulation) I just couldn't kill this woman. In no uncertain terms, killing her was the only solution if I wished to fend her off, for anything less was going to turn into an organ-poking, blood-splattering disaster. I had seen her fight; I had felt her honed strength and expertise. Only a full-scale clubbing, rending, throttling campaign would get the job done, and on the most essential level, I was incapable of that.

As it turned out, I was incapable of other things too.

"What's happening down there?" she asked, frowning, then she wiggled and ground herself into me as she tried to get a physical response.

The answer was: nothing.

She craned around as if to look, though all was obstructed beneath the flared portion of her tunic. The frown deepened.

"What's wrong with you?"

What's bloody wrong with *you*? I wanted to say. I'm a man, not a piece of siege equipment that can be levered into readiness at will. Go find somebody who could do this after almost losing his genitals a few minutes earlier. I said none of this and instead cleared my throat, before replying politely.

"Shade."

"Yes?"

"I think maybe this isn't the right moment."

"It isn't?"

"No, I really think it would be much better if you—"

"Listen, you!" she snapped, and suddenly she was flattened upon me again, those pretty fingers abrading up the side of my face into my hair, as the stiletto blinked back to the jugular. "You don't get to tell me when it's the right moment. You don't get to tell me anything. Did I not explain to you the rules of our arrangement?"

Not all of them, I guess. At least the bit about silence had sunk in, so I stuck with that.

"You must understand," she said from but an inch away, a glittering thread of spittle starting a slow foray from her lower lip, "this whole thing is based on one important idea—you must entertain me. You must not, in any way, disappoint me, because the moment that happens, I'll find it tedious to keep you alive. A bored Shade is not a very nice Shade, and if there's any piece of you that's particularly disappointing, that will be one of the first little gifts I will send to the proffer."

I don't know if it was Shade's intention to certifiably ruin my libido, but she accomplished that now.

"Here's what we're going to do," she puffed, with sharp breath that I had finally decided was unpleasant. "Because you're still adjusting to our deal, I will give you a pass tonight, but only tonight."

And with that, she abruptly stood up. I watched her tan buttocks from below as she stepped over to my weapon's belt, which she shoved away with her shoe. She then systematically pushed the whole jumble of leather, buckles, and scabbards across the rug until it was lodged firmly beneath my sofa.

"Stay where you are."

I had started to sit upright but stopped midway, levered back on my elbows. Everything in me wanted to reach down and pull up my trousers, but I didn't dare.

"By the time I come back for the next payment," she said, brushing her hands over her tunic and straightening her coat, which was now streaked with my blood, "you better have fixed whatever's wrong with you. If you don't, then there won't be any need for a third visit."

That was a helpful motivator, and about as useful to my "problem" as an ice pick to the crotch.

"Also," she continued, now heading towards the door, "you are not to tell your creep about my visit. You must swear to me on this, that you will keep it a secret. Swear it now."

"I swear," I said, "though I can't promise he won't figure it out himself. He's quite perceptive that way."

"Yes, I'll give him that," she said on the threshold of my front door hallway. She reached up to tie the cascading blackness of her hair into a ponytail. "I have big plans for him, but they will take a little time to arrange. I won't bother asking you where he lives, since you don't have any idea, do you?"

I shook my head, because I sincerely didn't. A devious little kink appeared on her lips.

"No Finisher will ever tell you that. And this one knows I would happily torture you for hours to get that information, so he'll hide it from you. No matter. I will hunt him down when the time is right. You, my Lashy, have a very slight chance of living, if you satisfy all of my needs. He does not."

Through the dark glass of my living room window, we now heard the muffled quartet of Fourth Bell. Shade stared that way thoughtfully, her eyes, in their flecked sharpness, scanning the dimensions of the barred portal that had once given her passage.

"You still haven't brought our plant back to the apartment," she said, with an almost meditative lull. "Make sure to remedy that by my next visit."

For a moment we just stared at each other, she in her nicely smoothed, suitably bloodied, urban travel wear, me naked to the ankles on my twisted rug. Finally, she smiled, and it was a strangely sweet expression, with just the pearliest peek of white exposed between the lips.

"It is nice to see you, though," she said.

And with that she disappeared down my front hallway, where she clunked away at the locks and bars, before releasing herself quietly into the night.

6

BURIED TREASURE

The next morning, Cad arrived at my apartment just after Eighth Bell, which was a full hour earlier than we had agreed upon, and (if I was being realistic about my sleep needs) three hours before he should have come. The young carpenter looked well-rested and perky. Lieutenant Constable Vestién D'jaen had released Cad from the Imperial Garrison a couple days after the events at The Crossbiter Tavern, and since then, he had been visiting my apartment at least once a day. I provided Cad a key to the building's exterior door, so that he could come straight up to my apartment and knock. His face was freshly shaven, and he wore a tan, woolen shirt beneath his usual leather vest.

"Where's your rug?" he asked, as we sat at the kitchen bar, eating boiled eggs, toast, and cheese, along with an oversized pot of strong tea.

"Needed a wash," I said.

Cad stared at the empty swath of hardwood flooring in the middle of the living room, where, a week earlier, we had enjoyed a rather memorable evening of intoxicated camaraderie.

"It did? Must've got dirty real fast, because it looked fine yesterday."

"I spilled something."

"What?"

Now I glared at him.

"What the hell does it matter what I spilled? It was late. I was tired."

Cad, immune to my grouchiness, pursed the flushed block of his mouth to a thinking man's pucker.

"Interesting, Zeer, very interesting."

"What? What's interesting, you prodding little prick?"

"It's just that I know all your habits. You told me that when you're alone, having a bite, you can never be bothered to leave the kitchen. That's why I'm having trouble picturing you sitting there in your living room, all by yourself, late at night, spilling something. Maybe it was a glass of wine, but you would have said 'wine,' and you said 'something.' I'm just saying, it seems interesting."

This, unfortunately, was part of what came with Cad. Irritatingly observant, maniacally driven to jest, his nose for provocative items of this nature was like that of a bloodhound. Today, there was fresh carrion in the space.

"Leave it alone, Cad," I said and poured us each some more tea.

"Yeah, okay, I get it, Zeer," he replied, gnashing down on a crumbling square of toast. He crunched noisily for a few seconds, then his rusty hairline raised slightly and he smiled.

"I'm just wondering, did she help you clean the rug, the property manager? It was her, right?"

"For hell's sake, Cad! Why do you always have to push these things?"

"I don't always, Zeer," he said, sliding back a little on his stool but otherwise unperturbed. "It's just that I've seen her, and I still can't get over that you bedded a gem like that."

Indeed, Cad had seen "Jisselle." It was during the two-day stretch when he was helping me set up in this apartment, and then hunting for Sebastien, that he spotted what he considered a "precious gem" doing odd jobs around the building. Because of the all-consuming distraction that followed, he didn't mention this until he was released from the Imperial Garrison, at which point, as befitted his bloodhound instincts, he caught me in the act of feigning disinterest in Everine's new assistant. His merciless prodding eventually yielded a disclosure. Only a partial disclosure, presented as a frivolous tryst, since the one thing I knew I had to avoid was revealing the Finisher's true identity. That might turn into a death sentence for Cad.

"I don't know why you don't use what you got more often, Zeer," Cad went on, trying to break through my irascibility. "Can't figure out what they see in you, but they see it, whatever it is."

"Not lately. You wouldn't be saying any of this if you knew what an epic losing streak I'm on with women."

"Could've fooled me."

"Appearances can be deceiving."

Cad's shaven cheeks pinched into a special breed of droll suspicion, which was his *you can't fool a ladies' man* look, and I knew I hadn't heard the last of this. Cad was, in fact, a ladies' man. Handsome from the start (something I never was), he had been successful with the opposite sex since about the age of twelve. Now, as a young man, he was considered all but irresistible; however, he still held me in a special veneration, and this was on account of one simple fact: I had, at one time in my life, been the lover of Terza Falconbrow. Cad could never get over that.

"She's gotta be the biggest jewel of them all!" he would say.

This reference to precious stones and treasure, vis-a-vis female beauty, seemed a piece of Dockside slang that I had missed over the years.

"You hardly knew me then," I would respond. "Or her."

This was only partially true. Cad had barely entered puberty by the time my relationship with Terza ended; however, he had lived in enamored awe of the striking, tattooed Contract Blade whenever she came down to the docks. As he grew older, Terza began to treat him with notable affection, mostly because he reminded her so much of her departed younger brother. To this day, Cad semi-worshiped Terza, and the warm feelings were mutual. With the safe buffer of their age difference, my ex-lover enjoyed Cad's romantic devotion, which she viewed as uncommonly sweet.

"Listen, horndog, I need you to go visit your favorite tattooed goddess and deliver a message."

As expected, Cad's already upbeat disposition turned bouncy, and he popped from his stool with a feverish jolt.

"Okay, what's the message?"

"Sit down, will you? Your enthusiasm is making me nauseous."

Cad took his seat once again, but the giddiness remained, and he drummed the bar and tapped his feet, and in several other ways thoroughly annoyed me.

"You need to set up a meeting. Between me and her. Plus, Adelyn and the Seer. Those three in a private place, as soon as possible."

Cad's "thinking man" pucker returned, but this time it was polluted by a skeptical undercurrent.

"I don't mean to piss on your party, Zeer, but does Falconbrow even take meetings with you these days?"

"She took one recently. It didn't end well. Which is why I need your charm to set up the next one."

"Alright," he said happily. "Finally putting me to good use on this job."

That was hardly accurate; Cad had been extremely useful already. From the moment Lieutenant Vestién D'jaen released my assistant from the Imperial Garrison, he had come home with a head full of attitude and big demands of ongoing transparency. He deserved this, though I tried, rather unsuccessfully, to retain a degree of opacity. Presenting my current activities as a vague, nonviolent bid for Labyrinth stability, I ran straight into Cad's instincts for the truth, and eventually I had to lay the whole thing out for him. He was astonished at first, then unsettlingly enthralled, for he now imagined himself part of a Narrow Bid.

"There's no way you'll be part of the ambush itself," I declared. "But I'll need you to do a lot of things leading up to that moment."

We both knew that Cad had every intention of being part of the ambush, and I had every intention of stopping him. But we had a ways to go before that point, so it wasn't worth rocking the boat this early in the planning. Plus, he was really thriving in his new role. I had already paid him a hefty bonus for bringing the constables to the Shadowbiter duel, thereby saving my life, and he seemed immensely focused and enthusiastic with each new task I gave him. He also (and this was a promising development) took reasonably well to Radrin Blackstar. Given that Nascinthé of Levell had intensely disliked Radrin, Shade referred to him as the "creep," and Selene detected the Finisher as a frighteningly cold wraithlike presence, the fact that Cad viewed him as an actual person was encouraging.

"I think he can get the job done, Zeer," Cad said when we

were alone together after their first meeting. "The man means business. You can feel it."

Yes, I could definitely feel it, and I sometimes wondered why the Finisher had chosen a vessel such as myself to act as the lynchpin for his plans. I was, after all, prone to those "foolish diversions" that Radrin often referenced, a proclivity that—based on the prior night's encounter—wasn't likely to end anytime soon. Still, I did bring some things to the table, and looking to make good on those, I returned to the day's coming errands, starting with Cad's all-important task.

"Alright, Ladies' Man," I said, ushering him towards the door. "Go get me my team. Call them every pricey bauble from the Imperial treasury…whatever it takes. Just get me in a room with them."

A half hour later, I finished readying myself, then finally made it out of the apartment. As usual, I took one of my inconspicuous routes, winding through the harbor-adjacent portion of Dockside and eventually into the southern boundary of White Hill. From there, I crossed the soft, damp field of brush that led to the ocean cliffs, where a couple weeks prior I had dumped three corpses into the sea. Shuttling to the west, I made my way along a pleasant footpath that eventually intersected the main road to Lothrum.

The autumn morning contained a hint of winter's exploratory bite, but it felt noncommittal, softened in the face of a coastal breeze and the hazed-over ascent of the late season sun. Below me was the smeared glimmer of the Derjian Sea, about a mile of which was visible in front of the fog. That stretch seemed peaceable enough, with sedate ripples inching towards the land and perishing with a muted rinse in the rocks. Up ahead, where the coastline bent to a point, some spray jetted off the boulders, while sea birds circled the area, eying briny things swimming or crawling beneath the silver crust of the waves.

When I reached the road to Lothrum, I found it puddled and flecked with debris. I seldom took this route since my primary use for our closest neighboring port was as an auxiliary smuggling drop. (Inadequate law enforcement was Lothrum's only recognizable virtue.) Therefore, I generally always made the journey in a small cargo sailboat, which I am reasonably capable of handling if winds and seas cooperate. But today I walked. I walked because I wasn't actually traveling to Lothrum, which was a full ten miles away and held no attraction at the moment (or ever). I was simply heading one mile down the road to a nondescript section of the track with only the mile marker to identify it. Something of great significance awaited me there.

A modest number of travelers were present as I made my way along the heavily furrowed highway. A group of laborers were walking several hundred feet ahead towards Lothrum, and a series of mud-spattered carts filled with goods sloshed and skidded past me en route to Sullward, complete with private soldiers on horseback. This was a welcome sight, for in addition to bringing much-needed supplies to our city, the merchants were smart enough to hire armed guards. I had seen a few haphazard city watch patrols in the last week, but nothing equaling standard levels of law enforcement.

The one mile marker was a simple affair—a round stone on the side of the road, painted white with a single black vertical line. I paused there to take a sip from my waterskin. As soon as a wagon headed to Sullward had passed around a curve to my southeast, I ducked off the road into the thick grass to the south. Making my way down a steep, foggy embankment, I wove through scrub bushes and boulders. Eventually, I reached a large outcropping of granite, the far side of which offered excellent visual protection from the road. In that sheltered spot, I could hear the ocean's respiratory rhythms but caught no sight of them. All in all, this was a rather clever hiding place for buried treasure.

Before we parted on the Elena's Guile, Nascinthé of Levell had given me precise instructions on how to recover her contract payment. In the last year, she had thought through the logistics of storing her various bid fees, and also the means by which this money would make it to her family in the advent of her imprisonment or death. This current location was one of three repositories she used, and on the handful of visits to her parents and sister in the last year, she had provided them clear directions to her secret caches. The spots had all been selected with her family's safety in mind—outside of the city proper and located in areas where militia patrols discouraged highway robbery. Since she had emptied the caches and carried a decent sum home three months earlier, I didn't expect to find much additional money here.

But the contract payment itself was a fortune, and I needed it. Failure to secure advance funds from Count Tygean meant that Radrin and I had to pool our resources to pay the operatives for our coming bid. Having given my own contract payment to Nascinthé, and by extension her beleaguered family, I was now dependent on hers. In fact, I was desperately dependent on it, in more ways than one. Shade of Night would eventually expect the back-half installment of my assassination contract, and the mere thought of coming up empty-handed in that moment gave me a shudder straight down to my most defenseless parts.

The problem was, the treasure hunt itself gave me shudders. This anxiety centered around one disturbing question: was it possible that Nascinthé of Levell had deceived me? She had joked darkly about this aboard the Elena's Guile, the idea that she might depart with my contract payment, then lie about where hers was hidden. In a few months, she could easily return in some perfect disguise, retrieve her money, and become as rich as a Tergonian merchant.

This narrative didn't really match what I had experienced in her arms; however, self-doubt is a rather permanent fixture of my inner landscape. When it takes this particular shape—questioning my worthiness for even the most base-level affections—I have struggled mightily over the years to dispel it. Count Tygean's talk of the majestic "Spellbinder" really hadn't helped matters. The thought that Nascinthé of Levell might, in fact, be a figure of almost mythic stature in the Tergonian Empire only compounded the sense that I was unworthy of her affections. Add to this my humiliating failures with Terza Falconbrow and Shade of Night and suffice it to say, I wasn't exactly my most confident self as I started my search.

I knelt down next to the largest of the overhanging boulders, and my hand scrabbled around below. Nascinthé had supposedly wedged a loose rock here, covering the sack. I didn't see anything obvious, so I began poking at every stone within reach, my troubled fingers flailing at the underside of the outcropping, scratching for looseness, probing for validation. I tried to reassure myself.

"It's just not possible," I said, stabbing at yet another rock. "I may be a romantic imbecile, but I couldn't possibly be that wrong."

Then something moved.

It was a wide, flat stone, turned on its edge, jammed back a couple feet beneath the looming weight of the outcropping. It seemed too large to dislodge at first, and a potential load-bearer, but it was neither. When I got my fingers around it and pulled, I found it to be an improvised door, obscuring a hollow.

For several long seconds, I was overwhelmed with relief. My hand explored a little farther and touched the soft bulk of a sealskin sack, the felt-like smoothness seducing my fingers into a gentle stroking motion, as if it was a kitten. Then I dragged the bag from its burrow. Exposed to the light, I could now see that this sack was well made—properly cured and stitched, and likely capable of staving off ground moisture and even limited submersions. The silky gray surface was dirty, but I detected no rips or bald spots, and it was tied, folded, and strapped at the mouth.

Once the bag was open, I quickly found the pouch containing the Gosian Diamonds. Peeking inside, I saw the familiar tinted sparkle, like flecks of rosy ice, and my initial impression was that few, if any, of the stones had been removed. I also slid out the brown bag that Merejin had given me, containing the two reference books on the Tergonian aristocracy. Nascinthé hadn't known that I would be the one retrieving this sack; however, she had been wise enough to clear all of the valuables from her rented apartment prior to the Narrow Bid, and these books were among the items she hoped to return to their rightful owner.

Additionally, there was another large pouch filled with coins, plus some pretty candlesticks, writing implements, and a case that I quickly identified as Nascinthé's makeup kit. Inside was a round mirror, the collapsible cane she had used when we met at Marzan's Emporium, various pads to go under clothing, some colored charcoal, and an assortment of glass vials filled with liquids, powders, putties—all of this presumably to assist with her disguises. I also found a leatherbound journal, and just a cursory scan revealed that this was a private log, probably left for her family, in case she never returned. I would leave everything except the contract payment and Merejin's books. I carefully tied and strapped them back up inside the sack and then returned the bag to the hollow. Wedging the rock into place, I slid backwards on my hands and knees, smoothing over any scrape marks or footprints.

With the diamonds stowed away in a buckled pocket, I opened the gaping mouth of my satchel to receive Merejin's books. It was only then, as I hoisted the brown felt bag off the ground, that I noticed it was heavier and thicker than it should have been. Untying the drawstring, I pulled the books out into the foggy light of day. *The Codex of Noble Tergonian Lineages*, and *Splendors of the Tergonian Court* were both inside and seemed no worse for the wear. However, I now saw that the bag contained something else.

It was a box. It was a low, wide, mahogany container, exquisitely crafted and inlaid with lovely swooping rose gold patterning and triangles on the corner of a similar material. While the box lacked a keyhole, there was a delicate gold clasp at the front, currently hooked. I was quite familiar with this genre of item and knew this to be an expensive piece, possibly a commissioned work, straight from skilled hands of one of the three or four finest craftsmen in Tergon. Jewelry boxes of this quality arrived at our docks from time to time. In fact, my most notorious conflict as a Grell Runner, the one that had left me both scarred and named, had been fought over a cargo that contained solid gold versions of these. Hefting the box, I didn't hear any tinkling or rattling, but it was heavy, so I knew something was in there. Whatever it was, it apparently deserved its own little home.

I had a peculiar moment just then. The most recognizable quality of this so-called "moment," paradoxically, was the fact that I was so aware of having it. Kneeling in the vicinity of Nascinthé's secret cache, holding that mysterious box, I knew, beyond the shadow of a doubt, that I was going to open it. Which I shouldn't, something I also knew. But here it was in my hands, retrieved from hibernation by accident, an elegant piece of collateral discovery, and in the same way that the clear sloshing reverberation of a breaking wave forced its way to my ears, despite a barrier of living brush and deadening fog, inevitably to be followed by another, and still another, so too did I know I would open that box.

Many years ago, I had an oddly similar experience, though the details were entirely different. I was talking to a Contract Blade named Gerard, and he was recounting to me a series of entertaining drunken episodes, which, in his life, were a constant. His discourse meandered to the subject of Cojis, which was the single most powerful drug known to man and was only available to Sullwardians in select establishments in the Lower City. So addictive was this drug that even people with the strongest of wills took a terrible risk just to try it, and here was Gerard, possessed of no such will, mentioning how he had never smoked Cojis but wanted to. I distinctly remember having the following thought:

"Isn't this interesting. Here's this moment in time *before* Gerard has tried Cojis. I'm going to note this."

Which I did. And it *was* interesting, for a few days later, Gerard ventured into the Lower City, smoked his first pipe of Cojis, and within a year he was dead from an overdose.

It wasn't really the premonitory aspect of the experience that stayed with me; after all, I frequently worry about things that never occur. Rather, it was the fact that I was so piercingly aware of its temporal quality—a small, illustrated page in the picture book of time, teasing before an opaque future. Which is exactly how I felt as I squatted there holding Nascinthé's mysterious box. It was closed now, a custodian of untold secrets, but soon it would open. In a matter of seconds, it would yawn wide and reveal some hitherto unknown thing that might, as with Gerard's latent drug addiction, start a slow but inexorable tumble into the realm of unintended consequences.

Or it might not. Perhaps it would be just another in a sequence of events that ultimately signified nothing.

I slid the clasp aside and opened the box.

What I found inside was a book. It was a relatively small, light blue volume, nestled within the purple velvet interior as if snoozing in a cushioned bed. At first this seemed a strange item for a jewelry box. Until I read the title.

I, Asadeissia.

From my throat emerged an incredulous burst of air, and for a second or two my fingers trembled. I gawped around my private hideaway, just to make abundantly sure that nobody was watching. Which was ridiculous, for I was entirely alone.

What instigated this? What would lead me to gasp and tremble? Let me put it this way: I would probably struggle for a while determining which of the items in my possession—a full pouch of Gosian Diamonds, or this book—was more valuable. The diamonds, ultimately, but only because they were transferrable as currency, whereas the book would first require finding an appropriate buyer, which might prove to be a risky drama in its own right.

This volume was none other than the personal memoir of the Empress Asadeissia, the most consequential Tergonian ruler of all time. There were only five known copies in existence, though it could be less at this point. The original was permanently housed in the Emperor's palace. Of the four scribed copies, each meticulously reproduced under Asadeissia's direct supervision, one was known to reside in the Capital Library, another in the ancestral home of one of the top aristocratic families (possibly the Odels, or a house of that stature), and the other two were out there somewhere. Actually, just one, because my ever-surprising Nascinthé of Levell had somehow managed to procure the other.

According to my friend Merejin, no copies had ever passed through Sullward in the many decades that she had lived here. There were inferior reproductions of the work, one of which I owned, but all of these had been composed centuries later by authors who were not in possession of the original manuscript. As such, I had carefully schooled myself on how to spot an authentic copy, just in case some arriving captain was too stupid to grasp what he had in his possession. For instance, I knew that all the legitimate versions had been produced on the finest pure-grade vellum and were calfskin bound. Additionally, Empress Asadeissia had personally branded her own mark into the soft leather of each cover, and this was not an easy emblem to duplicate. I stared at it now—a scripted "A," set over a balancing scale, meant to represent the Dawn of Reason, the philosophical movement with which she was most associated.

Oh, how Merejin would coo when she saw it! Or rather, *if* she saw it, which, I realized rather quickly, she'd better not. My dear friend would lose her mind if this volume entered her bookstore, and under no circumstances would I be permitted to walk out of that building with it still in my possession. Asadeissia, on account of her role in the banishment of organized religion from the Empire, had earned the lofty stature of being Merejin's favorite human being of all time. Having read portions of the memoir in her youth (hunched in the vault of the Capital Library, glowered at by guards), Merejin pined endlessly to acquire a copy of her own. This book was supposedly a treasure trove of all things political, and reading it was like a direct transmission of the brilliant ruler's mind.

I was pulled from these thoughts by the sound of voices on the road above. A group of travelers was walking past, and while I was in little danger of being discovered, it was just enough to remind me to be on my way. I quickly closed up the jewelry box and slid it into my satchel. I waited until the sounds were gone, then I crept back up the hill, and when I was confident nobody was looking, I popped back out onto the muddy road and started towards the city.

My first errand of the day was behind me, and while I felt a touch of guilt to be ferreting away Nascinthé's personal treasure, this was where some small inaccuracies would come in handy. Perhaps I hadn't noticed the obvious extra bulk inside that brown sack until I was already home, at which point it would hardly seem prudent to venture back out in public with such a treasure, returning it to a dank hole along the side of the road.

And, on a deeper level, I needed it. My own judgement was sorely lacking, and if this book could help me, even the tiniest bit, then it was worth the transgression. Beyond that, the treasure felt like a little piece of Nascinthé herself. I still didn't know if the magnificent actress would ever return here, but the simple fact that she had left behind something so precious certainly raised the odds that she would.

7

UNPARALLELED GENIUS

It's not like I feared being mugged, or not much, since those who had tried in the past had always come away empty-handed (or, in some cases, broken-handed). Still, by the time I reached the alleys of Dockside, my satchel was starting to feel heavier than a bag of rocks. Never in my life had I moved this much wealth through the streets of Hell's Labyrinth.

I skulked out of Dockside, into White Hill, and eventually to the rear entrance of 27 Fletcher Street. Of late, I had been avoiding my townhouse, and this was ostensibly to circumvent the Raving Blade's men, who might be staking out my home, but probably weren't. After all, if Count Ulan Gueritus went to the trouble of hiring the top Finisher in Hell's Labyrinth to eliminate me, freeing up additional resources should be one of the benefits.

I quickly worked the locks on the back door and slid into the kitchen entrance. Once inside, I lit no lanterns and was careful not to disturb the curtains, then I conducted a quick survey, spending a few extra minutes in my art gallery. I felt especially happy to visit with my gorgeous, bronze statue of the ancient battle queen, Giradera, who—courtesy of my duel with Coljin Helmgrinder—was still mine. At last, I made my way to the hidden panel in my library, behind which lay a thick steel safe. This customized home vault was heavier than an anvil, and bolted into the framing, so I felt confidence in the security of Nascinthé's contract payment as I locked it away. However, *I, Asadeissia* would not be stowed there yet. I needed the book immediately, and I brought it, still housed in its exquisite box, down to my first-floor drawing room, where some highly vexing problems were about to be solved.

With the exception of my second-floor guest room, the first-floor drawing room in 27 Fletcher Street was the part of my home that saw the least use. I'm just not much of a host. The wine cabinet lived in one of the corners (I'm not much of a drinker), and the room, as a whole, had become the designated storage space for frivolous purchases that never should have made it to my home (I have a damned hard time throwing things out). It was here that I displayed a small gallery of my impetuous purchases from the year after Terza Falconbrow and I broke up. They languished on the back shelves: numerous ornate candleholders, eight vases without a single cut flower between them, several overly embossed (thereby useless) dinner plates, and an entire battalion of mismatched figurines, acquired without rationale or strategy, each tactile enough to insert substance into my emotional void.

Additionally, the room housed another unsettling occupant. In one of the windows facing Fletcher Street lived Shade of Night's deadly houseplant. Originally foisted upon me like an orphaned demon, this plant had now become a privileged tenant of my building, and a proud spawner of her own poisonous progeny. The purple flowers and berries bloomed to excess, so that I had to put down a tray to catch the ones that fell.

Discerning people don't generally furnish the most public room of their house with the most disquieting possessions from their past, but I've never been especially discerning, and there's no such thing as a public room in my house. With the exception of Cad and my late housekeeper, Dessie, I essentially bore witness to these relics alone. But today would be different.

Bringing Nascinthé of Levell's splendid treasure into this space felt, weirdly, like an antidote. Despite my cavalier instructions to Cad, I was nervous as hell about my upcoming meeting with Terza Falconbrow. I didn't think she would actually harm me, but she might humiliate me again, and I didn't feel like my nerves, or pride, could quite survive a repeat performance. Sitting in this small emporium of rejection-induced trinkets felt like the proper space in which to ready my defenses. But there was more, for if I was nervous at the thought of facing her, I was absolutely terrified by the other woman now plaguing my life. Shade of Night had demanded that I port her leafy little monster all the way through the streets of Sullward to my rental apartment, transplanting the past as a form of appeasement.

Radrin Blackstar had wryly informed me that my targets on the upcoming Narrow Bid would all be men; however, before then, I would be *negotiating* with quite a few women, and these would be tough negotiations, particularly this deadly dance I was doing with Shade of Night. To arm myself, I felt the need to seek council with the most esteemed negotiator of all time. I flipped the hasp on Nascinthé's jewelry box, then reached out across the centuries to a mind that had solved far bigger problems than mine.

The Empress Asadeissia of the Besidian Dynasty was not a fabled warrior like the mighty battle queen, Giradera, nor was she known to possess her forebearer's frightening self-assurance. Instead, Asadeissia was simply a genius, a political savant on a scale unmatched by any who had come before, or since. Somewhat plain of feature (I have seen several paintings over the years, and none have stirred me), she was nonetheless uniquely gifted at swaying others, capable of delivering speeches that, through a subtle brilliance in her rhetoric, cajoled even the most determined political opponents within striking distance of compromise. To the populace she also spoke, often directly, in words that were simple enough to be understood and yet which hid, deep within the folds of their syntax, intricate messages of persuasion.

It was for all these reasons that my dear Merejin so loved her. While it was hard not to be awed by Giradera's brutal charisma, not to mention her skill in battle, plus—perhaps most significantly—the grand stature to which she briefly raised women, my friend simply could not abide the theocratic nature of what was accomplished in the ancient world, or its lack of longevity.

"Of the two, lad, it was Asadeissia who achieved lasting change in Derjia. Change for the better, none can dispute."

And so, with a palpable shiver, I placed the precious book in my lap. The cover was of fine grade leather, dyed soft blue, and as I carefully fingered the material, I could tell at once that this copy had been read extensively. There were saturated oil smudges at the edges, along with copious fraying. I turned the cover and looked inside. I had no idea how long Nascinthé had owned this book, or how she had been wealthy enough to purchase it.

Of course, there was always the possibility that the revered actress had received her copy as a gift (perhaps from her infatuated duke, the man who eventually brought about her downfall). I looked inside both flaps to see if there was an inscription. Nothing had been engraved into the binding board; however, when I turned to the next page, I did find a piece of high-grade parchment, with a note composed in pretty, fluid script. Strangely, the handwriting seemed familiar to me.

Your performance was magnificent again last night, my dear. Here are the words of our favorite Empress to show my admiration. You never disappoint!

My eye scanned down to the signature, and when I read it, I almost dropped the book.

Your very own,
Shaeyin

My gaze slowly traced over the elegant swirling "S," the long-stemmed "Y." My eyes had followed the exact same pattern a couple weeks earlier in the boathouse, when I read the transcribed letter from the Countess Shaeyin Odel. That version of the signature had been a forgery; however, the scribe had clearly done a very good job, for this appeared a perfect match—a match to the hand that had unwittingly ignited a Narrow Bid, that had passionately clutched the High Lord of Hell's Labyrinth, that might soon grip the scepter of the Tergonian Empire, if Merejin's predictions were to be believed. I felt a queer lightheadedness just holding it.

And yet, didn't it make sense? How astonished I had been by Nascinthé's theatrical performance on the Narrow Bid. While there had been a brief, dazzling masquerade as Lave Kaszivar, the bulk of the acting had been an impersonation of the Countess Odel, and it had been so utterly convincing that our entire party had been allowed into the compound. I had no doubt that Nascinthé was capable of concocting a personality straight from her imagination, but still, there was something so remarkably authentic about her portrayal that I felt I had actually met the aristocrat herself. Now I knew why.

Nascinthé of Levell and Countess Shaeyin Odel were friends.

On board the Elena's Guile, Nascinthé had told me some details about her life in Tergon, but she certainly didn't describe it all. In fact, there had been a general reticence to flesh things out beyond the story of her exodus. Holding that letter in my hand, I found myself wondering about the full extent of her fall from grace. Shaeyin Odel, heir to the family title, and possibly the realm, had gifted this sort of treasure to Nascinthé. The Countess referred to her as "my dear" and mentioned "our favorite Empress," as if this were a familiar discussion between them. She also signed with "your very own," followed by just her first name, all of this suggesting a rather intimate relationship. It seemed incredible to me that Nascinthé would not have mentioned this.

Unless there was pain surrounding this memory, just like all the others. Nascinthé did convey, in a broad sense, the way everybody turned their backs on her in Tergon. Might this have included Shaeyin Odel? The only thought I had given to the Countess since the night of our Narrow Bid was the fact that she probably still lived. Even if she did undertake her ill-advised journey, her ship's captain would have pulled into a protected harbor before the winds grew too strong (the Swell Driver's slow onset time was one of its only maritime advantages). However, now that I considered her again, it did occur to me that perhaps she was not the beneficent woman whom Merejin described. Countess Odel had, after all, carried on a protracted love affair with the High Lord of Hell's Labyrinth, and it seemed likely that there were some darker dimensions to her personality.

Seeing no further notes, I turned to the opening paragraph

of the work itself. This book was a scribed version, but in keeping with Tergonian protocols, Asadeissia's secretary would have made every effort to duplicate her Empress's handwriting. Thus, as I gazed at the tight, sharp script, with its meticulous letters, I did feel I was observing the fabled ruler's own hand.

> *I was born Nirabella of House Besidian, in the year 379 of the Imperial calendar. I was the youngest of three children, and my brothers, Asagenjus and Désian, were much beloved by me. When later, I lost both to the hateful blades of the zealots, my heart never fully healed. From the combining of their two names, I derived my Imperial title, Asadeissia. From their dreadful sacrifice, I derived the very purpose of my life.*

My eye skimmed down the page, and I saw that Asadeissia had devoted the next paragraphs to her upbringing. This carried on for several pages, and while the material interested me, I would return to it later. Right now, I wished to get further along before the needs of the day drew me out of this peaceful interlude. When I thumbed through the core of the work, I was surprised to see that small marks had been made in the margins on many of the pages. The ink had already begun to fade, which suggested that it was relatively new, since common inkwells did not include oxides. The notes appeared to be bracketing meaningful lines and paragraphs. One of these drew my eye.

> *I have been accused of being cold-hearted, manipulative, two-faced, ruthless. These terms don't capture the half of it, for I am all of that and more. When a ruler wishes to exert her will upon the people, great reservoirs of ambition are necessary.*

How much more so when an Empress seeks to change the very face of the world.

I kept skimming, looking for the terms "negotiation," "deal-making," "appeasement," or anything along those lines. At last, I stumbled upon a series of starred paragraphs that seemed relevant.

> *I have found that there are only two types of political opponent: those who are weaker and those who are stronger than I. To the former I bare my teeth, to the latter, my lips. The weak can, and should, be cowed. Like children, or pets, they need a firm hand. These opponents believe they seek power, but it is submission they want, so do not deny them this.*
>
> *But the strong are different. They cannot be bullied from the outset, should not be met with a show of force. Clang shields with them too early and all hope of finding their weakness disappears. But it is there, the soft, vulnerable underbelly, always findable, ready to be stabbed.*
>
> *Singular is your mission, Empress. Charm, smiles, gifts, friendship—offer all of this as you conduct your search, but never, all the while, imagine yourself the weaker. You are simply a cunning blade in search of a wound.*

I paused, my finger pressed to the page. There was a fair amount to digest here, and it would take time to organize it into actionable ideas, but already insights were coming. The concept of "gifts" was swirling in my consciousness, and I began to see a tricky but clever path forward. Keeping my finger in place, I jumped close to the end and found a section that was boldly bracketed and starred for emphasis.

Woman, they will love you as never man can be loved, but so too will they hate you to the brink of madness. As woman, you are their last best hope, the stainless citadel that exists no true place but in their dreams. When it falls, it emits a horrible stench. So, pamper their love to bursting, be a mother and daughter and wife to their famished needs. And from such love, wheedle compliance before your final audacity grinds the illusion to poisonous dust.

Finally, I thumbed on to the last page.

My two brothers, Asagenjus and Désian, I know not where you have gone, and whether you wait for me in a world beyond. I fear you do not, so I write these words before Time the zealot comes for me too. Know that you gave me my purpose, know that you shaped the entirety of my life.

And to those who come after, I would say this: expect the hatred, expect the blades in the dark, but do not fear them. Time is a blade that will claim us all in the end. Before that day comes, let the sharp steel of your own dream razor a pathway to the light.

I closed the book. For a few moments I simply sat there, staring out the far window. There was no way to know for sure who had written in the margins, but I felt in my heart that Nascinthé was responsible for some of the marks. Perhaps Shaeyin too, a sort of reverential discourse between them, brackets and stars to affirm the enormity of a shared vision.

And these things—the vanishing ink in the margins, Shaeyin's kind note written during a kinder time, the profound and affecting words of an Empress who grasped, with searing clarity, the wistful brevity of her days—all of this suddenly made me sad. I closed my eyes and sank back into my chair, feeling the weight of exhaustion, along with other, less definable things, all of them connected to loss.

I did not quite fall asleep. I drifted, instead, into some sort of hazy in-between place, a miasmal waystation en route to true slumber. Here, the sluggish current of sorrow churned with fragments of past wisdom, and I found my mind in an odd place of remembrance. I had been in just such an in-between place recently. I could dimly remember it, this realm of churning vapors and sludgy cognition, of seeing nothing fully but knowing many things deeply. Where and when was it? And who was there, for, indeed, someone was. Someone speaking.

And then, quite suddenly, it came to me. It was Radrin Blackstar, conveying things to me as I sat on my horsehair couch, following my first violent encounter with Shade of Night. He spoke possibly in the room, or possibly inside my head, or possibly not at all, for maybe I made the whole thing up. I couldn't remember what was said, nor could I remember much of what I saw. But one thing I did remember—that twirling shape, gyrating before me like the creaking blades of a rusted windmill. The symbol I had seen drawn in Dockside.

The Summoner from Darkness.

Just then, there was a loud knock on the front door of 27 Fletcher Street, a sound so concussive it felt like being struck on the side of a metal helmet with a club, and my eyes snapped violently open.

8

THE PAINTED WALL

The gods only know why I have a front door knocker. Cad always came the back way, and we had a secret code of raps and bumps that lent themselves to knuckles on hardwood. My late housekeeper, Dessie, also used the rear entrance. On those days that I was so grotesquely inconsiderate as to be anywhere but the kitchen in the hour she was due to arrive, she would assault that back door with tireless rounds of incensed hammering, driving her wage-earning fists into the stiles like a gorilla. A genteel device on the back door, or anywhere, would have seemed unequal to her indignation.

Therefore, when somebody set to work on my knocker that day, I was practically launched straight out of my chair. Careening upright, the precious memoir still in hand, I ran into the vestibule prepared to answer the summons of the constables. When I stared through the peephole, I was met with a shock.

It was Merejin.

Old, rotund Merejin, my dear friend, who never left her bookstore, which also happened to be her home. What the hell was she doing here?

I glanced down at the blue, leatherbound rectangle in my hand, clutched in bleary unconsciousness, separated by a mere four inches of oak from the city's most tenacious academic predator. Had Merejin smelled the book? Did she have scholarly spies who waited in every crevice; who were posted, of all places, along the worthless road to Lothrum, just in case her favorite customer happened to go digging for intellectual treasures beneath a rock? None of this made sense.

I opened the drawer of my console table, shifted the flint lighter to the back, and slid the priceless *I, Asadeissia* inside. I closed the drawer securely, then set to work on my locks.

When I opened the door, my first impression of Merejin was that she seemed much sturdier than the last time we met, her coated form showing no hint of an elderly stoop. In our prior discussion, Merejin had recited a couple of arcane Oulmaen phrases describing the Summoner from Darkness. This had ignited within me a frightening, superconscious maelstrom, disgorging all manner of internal wreckage. I couldn't tell to what degree Merejin grasped the effect her reading had on me, but she certainly appeared alarmed at the time.

But today she looked determined. Very determined, with an almost martial erectness, her face unsmiling.

"We are going for a walk," she said, and the intonation of her words had much in common with her knock.

Merejin had only been to my home on two occasions in the past. Those visits I had relished, for they were replete with full house tours, discussions of art, history, and thorough perusals of my library. Today, I was less enthused about the sudden drop-by.

"Would you like to come in, Mera?" I asked tentatively. "I can prepare some tea."

"No time, dear."

The molasses color of her face had the tiniest hint of raspberry nuance from makeup; her burgundy coat and matching shoes accentuated it. Her hair was done up in a smart, graying bun, with no escaped coils, and she looked prepared for travel.

"Where are we going?"

"Where do you think, lad?" She tossed her head forward in an emphatic nod. "We're going to see your mysterious Dockside symbol."

Here, I really had to collect myself. Merejin was referring to the strange wall mural I spotted in the streets of Dockside. It was her conjecture that this image represented the Summoner from Darkness, whatever that was exactly. There was some logic to her seeing the cryptic wall mural with her own eyes, observing its swirls and hooks in the original form; however, the complications this presented were many. So I stalled.

"At least come into the vestibule," I said. "It will take me a few minutes to ready myself."

She came in.

"Such a lovely dwelling, lad," she said once she was standing in my front hall. I locked the door and attempted to shuttle her towards one of the two settees; however, she remained close to the entrance, which, by nerve-wracking extension, kept her within easy reach of that console table. I tried not to look at the drawer.

"Mera, some of the items I need are upstairs. Would you please take a seat somewhere as I fetch them? The drawing room is more comfortable."

"Go fetch, lad. I'm fine where I am."

And with that I jogged upstairs, uneasy for at least three reasons. One, the "items" I needed to fetch were weapons, and plenty of them, strapped and buckled and scabbarded all over my body. How was I going to avoid looking like I was escorting Merejin into a war zone? Two, I still hadn't decided what I was going to do regarding the potted nightshade; however, based on what I'd read from Asadeissia's memoir, I probably needed to view Shade of Night as a "stronger" opponent, thus in need of gifts and appeasement. So, add to my payload of steel a cumbersome houseplant, festooned with its own toxic weaponry. Finally, there was the memoir itself. I sure didn't like leaving Merejin alone in that vestibule, so close to the book, just one curious drawer-opening away from a massive, diversionary hubbub, or (let's not pretend here) a theft. Would I peek inside the drawer before we exited, just to make sure it was still there? Would I give her a pat-down?

Perhaps there was a way to excuse myself from this field trip entirely, which is what I really wanted. However, five minutes later when I came back down, fattened to shapeless bulk by wool and leather layers—under which lived two stilettos, three jacks, and a throwing dagger, along with the smallest and thinnest of my spades—I still hadn't figured out how to escape this errand. The timely ringing of the First afternoon Bell presented an opportunity.

"We need to get moving, lad," she snapped. "I left a note on my door saying I'd be back by the First Half Bell. This is already taking too long."

"Then, perhaps, Mera..." I ventured.

"Perhaps we do it another time?" she asked. "Out of the question. There is a real problem here, one that may demand action. The drawing of that symbol is not some innocent or harmless act. I will need to explain this to you as we walk."

And here, with this dangled enigma, my interest in this expedition grew. I wasn't entirely sure what we would find at the end of our walk, given that trash was starting to be collected again, so it was possible that the sweepers, or even some residents, had scrubbed the wall clean; however, the prospect of getting a more thorough explanation was certainly a motivator. And this new suggestion that we were dealing with something dangerous only added to the intrigue.

I grabbed my cloak and hat, and then, pausing at the drawing room doorway, I threw a final glance at the room's deadly denizen.

Sorry, Shade, I thought. *There's no way I can haul that plant through the streets now.*

At the front door, I ventured a stealthy glance at my console table, which elicited another mental apology.

I did my best, Nascinthé. If that book isn't inside that drawer when I return, I'll stoop to burglary to get it back.

After that, we were off, whisking out into the lucid crispness of a fine autumn day. In the time before my many troubles began, when the Underlords still valued me, when contracts had not been put out on my life, I loved taking a stroll at this time of day. All was relatively bright and cheerful, and you might pretend to yourself that you were walking the fine streets of a town in the Midlands. It's not like those places held any architectural advantage, but they sure beat us on weather. During the midday hours, however, the discrepancy wasn't so pronounced, and though the sun rarely penetrated that final marshy lacquer, soft shadows were thrown by balconies, swans and griffins picked up flinty highlights, and brass railings went creamy gold at their crowns. The city became quite a treasure to behold. I felt elevated as Merejin and I coursed rapidly down the gentle off-white bend of my street.

"There is much I haven't told you about my past, my dear," said Merejin, once we had achieved a rhythmic pace. I was impressed by her jaunty stride.

"As I mentioned last time," she said, "I was—many, many years ago—a student in the Tergonian Academy of Scholarly Arts."

"You didn't say which academy. I've actually heard of that one, which means it must be prestigious."

"The *most* prestigious. By far."

We crossed Gale, and there we neared two pedestrians whom I recognized from the neighborhood. One of them, a fastidiously attired elderly man, waved to Merejin and appeared set to approach. But the combination of Merejin's brisk, no-nonsense gait, plus my unneighborly scowl, killed that reunion in its tracks.

"Anyhow," she continued. "After dithering about with an assortment of subjects—I was very young then, mind you, much younger than you are—my adventurous spirit had me falling in with a small rebellious crowd who made a habit of flirting the perilous legal line regarding religious study. Understand, I had no belief in the stuff, even back then. I am a Gosian after all, and you won't find a more militantly practical people anywhere in the Empire."

I thought of Coljin Helmgrinder in that moment, and this assertion checked out.

"This crowd," she went on, "led me to a professor who was viewed with suspicion by the rest of the faculty. Which I couldn't fathom, for he seemed as harmless as harmless could be—anxious and polite and endearingly self-conscious, but ever so smart. Brilliant, really, and I took to him instantly, and he to me. He was hardly a dashing figure, but he was young by scholarly standards, and I do think I developed quite a crush on him. Which was unfortunate, for I followed him rather blindly into a line of study that eventually doomed me. Doomed us all, including him."

We now arrived at Stenneck, which was the western boundary of Dockside and the potential start of danger. I didn't particularly fear being accosted, but it was certainly better that I not be seen walking about, so I cut us right on Stenneck. I steered for a preplanned route that was not exactly one of my rodentesque alley crawls but was definitely less than scenic.

"There is a complicated story about how I decided on my curriculum," Merejin continued, neither breaking stride nor conversational flow. "But for now, you simply need to understand that learning the Oulmaen language is, by its very nature, an exploration of the Summoner from Darkness. I didn't know this at the time. None of us did. Several students dropped out early, for the language was just too difficult, but six of us continued. Of those, four reached an advanced level, where the truths began to reveal themselves."

"What truths?"

Here Merejin stopped and turned to me. We had just turned off of Stenneck onto Gutwalk, which was one of the least travelled, and (as the name would suggest) least appealing Dockside streets. Gutwalk was really more of a broad back alley than a street, of which Netter's Way was the main thoroughfare. The butchers and fishmongers who lined Netter's often tossed their excesses out onto the cobbles here, though today the smell was manageable, and Merejin seemed oblivious anyway.

"These truths are subtle, dear, and don't simply lend themselves to casual discourse. The things we began to discover in our study were not a 'philosophy,' as such, but a direct understanding. It was a peek at something that probably should not have been seen, an underlying material: the intrinsic component from which all causality is derived."

I signaled for her to continue, as I was now thoroughly engrossed.

The tinted planes of her cheeks flattened, muting some of the wrinkles, but in no way supplying youth. She seemed grave.

"It is as I explained to you on your last visit, lad. The substance, as best I can describe it, is *wanting*."

This word was uttered in a hoarse whisper, and when she added a few more for clarification, they were spoken the same way.

"*Desire* on a primal, dangerous scale. A terrible, terrible craving. It is a feeling so deep and violent that the human heart should not attempt to hold it."

This matched what I had experienced in her study: a vehement, febrile need that seemed strong enough to blow my head off its shoulders.

"I felt it," I murmured. "When you read to me."

Merejin nodded, still in her grave aspect.

"I could see that," she said. "I could see it in your face. You are highly attuned, lad, for with just one viewing of a crude wall painting, you have become receptive to these truths. That is so very, very rare. It also tells me that an advanced student was your Dockside artist, and this raises even more dangerous prospects."

Just then, one of the back doors opened, and a thick woman stepped out and spilled a barrel's worth of glistening fish heads out onto the cobbles. There wasn't much blood, and this load did not seem to include entrails, but it was definitely a signal to keep moving.

"Let's go, lad," Merejin said brusquely. "How much farther is it?"

"Not far."

I ushered us down Gutwalk, skirting the slimy pile.

"What dangerous prospects?" I asked, picking up where we had left off.

Merejin didn't miss a beat.

"The prospects of one of the students coming here, coming and doing such a ghastly thing…after all we went through. It's nothing less than unconscionable, and rather frightening."

Up ahead, two young men strutted a weaving path towards us through the dingy canyon. I marked them quickly as local toughs, possibly from Breaker Tabard's crew, which meant they represented the least threatening form of trouble I might encounter today. Still, I shuttled Merejin over slightly, putting myself between her and them, and I lifted the brim of my hat. One of the bastards spoke anyway.

"Hey, ya got any…?"

And this sentence died on his lips. He didn't seem to recognize me (too young and stupid), but his partner did, and a quick yank aside coupled with a fierce hiss to the ear got the message across. We were gifted with a cordial nod as we passed.

"I still don't understand, Merejin," I said once we were out of earshot. "Who has come here, and what, exactly, did you go through?"

Merejin, who seemed unmindful of my little exchange, released a pronounced breath, and replied in a tone suffused with regret.

"I'm afraid my time in Tergon did not end well, as it so often doesn't for the unwary. Ultimately, I must blame myself, though I really was quite young, and my professor did not properly estimate the effect his studies would have on people my age. I was affected, certainly; however, I am cerebral by nature, as was my professor, while the other students were of a more passionate persuasion. Three of them perilously so, which became obvious in the latter stages. They wound up crossing the line."

"What line?"

I wanted to get an answer before we turned off of this track, and since I could now see the cross alley I planned to use to get us to Trader's Way, I slowed our pace. Unfortunately, the First Half Bell rang just then, and this made Merejin impatient.

"There is too much to tell here," she said. "We need to keep moving."

"Your customers can wait an extra half hour."

"It's not only that. This is a hard thing to explain, even under the best of circumstances."

"Try me. I'm receptive, remember?"

Merejin adjusted herself slightly, waggling her burgundy form as if driving away an unpleasant memory or smell, both of which were assailing her on this street.

"The principle itself," she said, "doesn't actually have a word to describe it. There is no good equivalent in the Derjian tongue, apart from the descriptions I have already used."

"The desire?"

She nodded.

"However, when this hidden substratum takes a *form*, here in this world, it is called Summoner."

"Like the symbol?"

"That is one of the forms…and not the most likely. Very little is written about a shape like the one you drew for me. I read you the most compelling bit. Far more often, the Summoner from Darkness takes a human form."

The mouth of our alley was a few feet farther on, but I stopped before we reached it. A door opened noisily behind us, and a butcher emerged, his leather apron running red, his expression trending angry. Mercifully he did not dump some repugnant payload out into the street, though he did come our way rather hurriedly, and in defense of our apparel, we scampered aside to let him pass.

"What could that mean, Merejin?" I asked once the butcher was passed. "How the hell does this thing take a human form?"

I hadn't meant to be so curt, but this talk was starting to unsettle me.

"It's a theory, lad," she replied. "Developed primarily by my professor, though it is supported by many clues dotted throughout Oulmaen literature. There are multiple references to this concept—that here and there, throughout human history, these figures emerge. They are the ones called the Summoners from Darkness. The changes they cause are disruptive and violent. Some do benefit humanity, but many bring dreadful things, cruel and destructive events, that the world would be better without. All of this was meant to be an academic study, mind you. We were hoping to more fully understand the tides of human development through this lens. We sought inflection points in key historical incidents and tried to see if we could tie a Summoner to that moment."

"Could you…tie them?"

"Sometimes. I had some aptitude, poring through old records, looking for clues. However, the other students had different ideas. It is hard to tell a young person to simply observe the actions of others when they are, themselves, at an age when action beckons. And the readings began to infect them, to stimulate feelings in their own hearts—just as you felt yourself stimulated in my home. They tried to consciously evoke the wanting. They tried to turn themselves into Summoners."

This was a terrifying notion. The very idea of deliberately unleashing that force inside, of allowing it to rip like a rapacious hurricane straight through the psyche, seemed insane. I couldn't even imagine what would happen.

"Did it work?"

"It worked to draw the inquisition down upon us. But before that occurred…"

And her voice dangled like a provocative thread, causing me to pounce.

"Before that occurred?"

"Before that…things revealed themselves, shocking things, which, had they not been so threatening, so dangerous to us all…"

More dangling, followed by more pouncing.

"What things, Merejin? Just say it."

"I do believe they were, at least to some degree, successful, lad," Merejin answered in a thin voice, "because something became present in our midst, not a seeable thing, but palpable, and this palpable thing was somehow…alive."

There was now an increase in foot traffic moving down Gutwalk, from both directions. To the east it looked like a delivery—a train of three laborers hoisting wet sacks, which were likely filled with newly arrived fish. The other way, I saw a man and a woman and two children approaching, seeming, to all appearances, like a poor family who had the misfortune to live on this street. We had only a little more time and privacy before both parties squeezed past us, so I gestured forcefully for Merejin to finish.

"It was an entity of some sort," she continued. "Bigger than the three, but somehow their collective, joined by the alignment of wills, or at least that's how one of the students explained it. He was the leader, directing the others on some unspoken level, possibly through dreams. He made it clear that they needed to align themselves to the same purpose."

"What purpose? What were they trying to achieve?"

"That's just it," Merejin replied anxiously. "They did not seem to know what to do with it, for they had no shared goal, apart from the discovery itself, and possibly power. So, they fractured, fractured badly, and once that happened, everything came apart. You see, a person isn't meant to carry this thing alone. The wanting is too strong, and it turns into violence and other forms of destructive behavior, all of which eventually became known to the university provost. At that point, the Oulmaen studies department was shut down, and my professor was locked away in an interrogation cell. Terrible things must have been done to him, for he never returned. One of the students committed suicide, another was sent to prison, and I don't know if he ever got out. The final one fled."

"And you?"

"Me." Merejin smiled sadly. "I got off quite easy. I cooperated with the inquest and expressed equal parts remorse and girlish ignorance, which was ultimately viewed sympathetically by the authorities. A mere slap on the wrist, plus expulsion from the university. That was enough, however, to make me a pariah in Tergonian academic circles and, by extension, destroy the life I had tried to build for myself."

The laborers finally arrived and shuffled past us, forcing us towards a grimy wall to avoid the teeming bundles. A moment later the family also slid by, the group of them giving us some curious looks.

"Lad," said Merejin in a drained voice, "I think I have been more than generous today with information…information that is painful for me to relay. Can we please get along now and see the wall painting?"

"Follow me."

We started down my chosen shut. This was not the worst of my skulky little alleys, for it was rarely stuffed with garbage, though there was one section that required turning sideways to get through. Elderly or not, my companion would simply have to make do. At this point, she had to be wondering why her architecturally obsessed friend was dragging her through the literal intestines of the city; however, at least I hadn't followed through with my original plan, which would have had me jostling her right now with a poisonous plant.

We emerged onto Trader's Way a short time later, and I directed us roughly fifty feet down the street to the mouth of my secret courtyard. I'll confess, I was more than a little concerned that we would arrive to the space and find a plaster wall that had been washed, scraped, or painted clean of the offending mark. Merejin had concerns of her own, for she grabbed my sleeve as we skirted down the musty entry passage, tugging me to a stop. We were a mere dozen feet from the sheltered space, but her eagerness was now replaced by something else.

"Vazeer," she said, taking the rare step of using my name.

In the dim, downward glow of a hazed sky, her martial briskness was gone. The pains and regrets of a distant past seemed to have welled up behind the shine of her spectacles, and her voice was less than steady.

"Please understand, dear, that I have rejected this thing we are about to see. I have come, over the years, to agree completely with the authorities in Tergon, to feel I did the right thing to cooperate with their inquest. The Summoner from Darkness should not be taught. Nor do I even believe the premise itself—that figures have appeared throughout history possessed of it. Instead, what may have happened in generations past was something similar to what my fellow students experienced—misguided, self-inflicted attempts, which wound up unleashing dangerous forces. The point is, I don't believe this power arises spontaneously, that it somehow chooses a vessel for a greater purpose. In the end, I found no proof of that, just scattered clues, which a zealous mind can twist."

"But I felt something very strange in your study, Merejin, and I haven't undertaken some misguided, self-inflicted attempt… not that I'm aware of."

"I know," she said. "Because you had already seen the image at that point, an image that never should have been drawn. I'm not saying there isn't a certain power to it, a power in all of the writings, but this falls more into the category of occult hypnotism, not a view into reality. Over time, I have arrived at this conclusion, which I felt the need to say, before we look at whatever is drawn here."

Beneath her timorous confession, I detected another concern, and I did my best to address it.

"Merejin, do you fear that one of the students has come here to threaten you? To take revenge for the role you played in the inquest?"

She paused, then twitched forth an anxious nod.

"It has occurred to me, yes. The shape you drew, if one stretches the imagination a little—it could be seen as a provocation: the three arms representing the three students, and the circle in the center possibly suggesting the greater entity."

I put a hand on her shoulder.

"Well, you can rest assured on that point," I said. "Because you have definitely picked the right man to be your favorite customer. Anybody who thinks they can touch my Merejin is in for a very unpleasant surprise."

Now a grateful smile broke out on the wrinkled terrain of her face.

"That has also occurred to me," she said. "As it did to those young fellows on Gutwalk."

"You noticed that?"

"I notice everything, dear. Haven't you realized that by now?"

I hadn't, actually, but going forward I would. I also noted that I felt better already, playing this role of protector, which is somehow where I always wound up. The last two women I had tried to "protect"—Terza Falconbrow, then a disguised Shade of Night—had not exactly stuck to their damsel roles. However, I felt pretty sure that Merejin would not pull some awful reversal on me, and I did relish the fact that she trusted me with her safety.

"Okay then," she said, looking relieved. "Let's go and see if we can figure out who drew this forbidden thing."

Scooting the last ten feet down the narrow crevice, we emerged into the retreat where I had found safe haven from looters a week earlier. This accidental courtyard, likely the result of poor coordination between builders, was also the place that I had conducted a clandestine meeting with Radrin Blackstar on the eve of the Narrow Bid. Now, however, there was only one relevant memory associated with it: this was the place where, breathless and unsettled, I first spotted a swirling, mesmeric shape painted on the wall.

And, as fate would have it, it was still there. After but a moment of searching, I found it again on the tan plaster rear wall of a building, obscured from the brightest rays of daylight, but infinitely easier to view than the last time. Nobody had scrubbed at it or written their own crude graffiti over its circular dimensions. It remained very much as it had been that night—a whirl of three curved black arms, hooked at both ends, spinning dizzily inward towards a circular center.

"It's still here, Merejin!"

I strode to the wall and took up a position a little to the side, trying not to obstruct her view. There, I began my presentation.

"You see how expertly this thing is drawn?" I asked. "With no mis-strokes or drip marks. It would have taken a great deal of time to achieve this, likely with a stenciling of some sort first, which might explain why such an obscure location was chosen. They must have used a drop cloth, for nothing spilled."

Merejin had come forward several feet, affording her a reasonably good vantage as she strained and squinted.

"Note, in particular, the perfect symmetry," I said, returning to the image. "This was painstakingly measured out and executed. By a skilled artist, not some doddering classmate of yours, who's been hiding under a rock all these years. It would have required an incredibly steady hand and eye."

In my peripheral vision I saw Merejin take another step forward, and it seemed to me that she was trembling as she gazed upon it.

"This is your first viewing," I said. "So, you are feeling its strange effect. But, interestingly, I'm not. Not this time. I think I've grown acclimated to it, which probably supports your theory that this painting is a trick of some sort, not a peephole into the dark heart of things. The more I stare at it, the more I think there is nothing much to fear here. A mystery, yes, but not a particularly dire one."

Now I turned to look at her, and she at me, for she had torn her straining gaze from that wall. The sight of her abruptly halted my presentation.

Merejin appeared, idiomatically put, like a woman who had just seen a ghost. It was worse than that, for she hadn't *just* seen one, but was rather seeing it now, as she stared at me. And "ghost" was far too quaint a word. The dumbstruck alarm on that aged face, the pasty, appalled horror smeared like bleach across her cheeks, required words like "fiend," "monstrosity," or "nightmare" to encapsulate how frightened she appeared. Her whole body was wracked with a palsied tremor.

"Vazeer," she said, her dry, brown lips quaking like dead leaves. "There is nothing painted on that wall."

9

FREAK

I've always known I was weird. I recognized it as far back as the orphanage, when, for reasons unknown to me, I felt that this life should offer me more, transform me into something remarkable, allow me to be part of some grand, extraordinary thing exceeding the ambitions of a cast-off piece of human waste. This latter I knew myself to be, but still, there was that other thing—the improbable sense of mission, an aggravated notion that I did not fit into any appropriate receptacles.

As orphans, our primary job was to make ourselves presentable to the shoppers who came looking to traffic in human wares. The brothel madams and pimps would arrive first to sweep up the pretty girls (and some of the boys), though a fair portion of these buyers came seeking young beauty for their own consumption. Luckily, my homely Flerra was immune to such purchases. Then came the press-gangs, who sought the biggest, dumbest lads for a life at sea, living under the whip of any number of entities—smugglers, merchants, pirates, occasionally even the Imperial Navy. Droden, who might have actually enjoyed this, was just too wiry and brittle at that age, and I wasn't exactly a strapping specimen myself.

Finally, there was the real prize: childless couples, hunting for that perfect, obedient vessel into which to dump their unspent parental capital. Rarely did this so-called capital involve love, but it did usually mean mastering a trade, or being brought into a local business at the lowest levels, presumably to learn it from the ground up. This is what we were all after, or should have been. But not me.

When the desirable shoppers arrived and we were lined up for appraisal, it was me who conducted the interview, not them.

"When will I be taught to read and write?"

"Never, you hoity little bastard. You're going to be a mason, not a scribe."

"How much will I be paid?"

"Just be glad you'll eat. You look like a scraggly, malnourished rat."

"What might I ultimately expect from this life you are offering?"

"If you ask another question, you can expect a bludgeoning from my forge hammer. I didn't come here to be interrogated."

This was the sequence, give or take. Until, one day, a scary man named Holod Deadskiff showed up, and every one of the responses shifted.

"If you don't learn to read and write by the second year, I'm going to gouge out your goddamned eyes."

Excellent answer.

"You'll be paid more money than you'll know what to do with. But you probably won't live long enough to spend it."

I'll take those odds.

"Here's what you can expect from the life I'm offering: ten years of brutal, soul-crushing training, followed by a career that will have you negotiating with—and frequently being attacked by—cutthroats, spending huge portions of your life squatting in cold, miserable places, and then almost certainly spending several years in prison, with a good chance that one day they'll lock you away for good. However, in your free time, you'll get to live whatever life you want and be whoever you want to be."

I only heard that last sentence. All the other stuff went in one ear and out the other.

It was there in that next phase, at the infamous Broodhouse, that my strangeness finally consolidated into a discernable thing. I was, on every level, a freak.

"You're so bloody extreme, Scuff!" my new criminal father would snap. "I show you how to kneecap a man, and you're looking to rip off the whole leg. I teach you how to read, and you want to learn the entire history of the Tergonian Empire. I train you to endure the elements, to withstand pain, and here you go falling into some kind of demented trance, coming out with your eyes slicked over like a Cojis fiend. Why can't you just do things in the proper measure, like the others? What makes you such a goddamned freak?"

Yes, the "freak" question, which was first asked by Holod Deadskiff, then Flerra, and then—eventually—everybody. Now, it was being asked, or implicitly implied, by my dear friend Merejin, as we stood together in front of a blank Dockside wall.

Only a few seconds passed in silence, but in that span, I watched Merejin's expression squeeze through a foreseeable cycle of bad reactions. What had started as naked horror mingled rather quickly with a degree of deliberation, and just after that, a subtle but unmistakable mien of disgust. That demoralizing chute (the gutter down which the *freak* progression flushed) had a reliable composition: at the top of the chute stood horror, at the bottom, disgust.

"I must go," Merejin croaked, and her face, still sour, picked up a measure of her earlier determination—determination to get away from me.

"Merejin…we must discuss this."

"No," she said, already shuffling back the way we had come. "I need time to think, to think about all of it."

"Let's try together—"

"Do not!" she snapped, jabbing a finger at me. "Do not follow me. There is too much I must consider. I need the time and space to consider it."

And away she stumbled, slipping briskly down the alley that led to Trader's Way. I wanted to follow, to ask more questions, and of course to look after her, but that last, pugnacious finger stab did not lend itself to casual disregard.

So, instead I simply watched her go. All the while my mind discharged a natter of explanations. I tried to educate her, mentally, about a subject they had never taught her in the Academy: the incalculable weirdness of Vazeer the Lash.

"Understand, Merejin," I would say, "while I can't explain why I, alone, am seeing this Oulmaen thing, you must disregard any concept that I am some momentous agent of change. All of those elevated notions of purpose, all of that grandiose crap that has bothered everybody, forever, is in fact built upon a firm foundation of delusion. The real explanation is that I'm a freak; that's all. And freaks, you come to learn, often bumble blindly into things, stagger about in so many discordant directions that somehow, somewhere, they might pick up a small shred of an ancient Oulmaen philosophical system, and then project it onto a Dockside wall. That's what freaks do, among other things."

But none of this was said. And Merejin was gone, off into the early afternoon streets of Dockside, which were probably safe enough to accommodate her, as long as she stuck to the main tracks. The question was, which place was safe for me? The threat was inside, and while I didn't really understand anything about it, or truly believe it—not in the manner it had been presented—I did grasp that I had a problem.

In that vein, I turned back to that large section of wall, wondering if the offending party might have something to say on the matter. Lo and behold, the symbol was gone! My maelstrom of black swirls and hooks had departed into the ethers, scrubbed away by a cerebral sanitation crew, and I was left standing there in the quiet dankness, feeling as deluded and confused as a man could feel.

I meandered out of the little courtyard, leaving by a different route. A dozen feet or so down the connecting shut, I hooked right into a wider alley that would eventually lead to Broad Street. I passed a side door that was propped open a few inches for ventilation, and from inside, the stinging smell of varnish emerged. Glancing down, I saw that wood shavings had been swept out into the alley, and I recalled that there was a carpenter's shop on the corner of the main thoroughfare.

Some voices emerged from within. Usually, I don't care what other people talk about, especially these people, but for some reason I felt intensely interested in what might go on inside such a place—in a tradesman's shop—with a residence above and a homey domestic life within. Just the sort of life I could have had, were I not so maladjusted. What do you know, I caught wind of the homey domestic life immediately.

"Ya clumsy dumbass litt'l shit!" a man yelled. "I ain't taught ya ta hold it like that, did I? Give it here, before ya gouge the rest!"

Some scuffling, then the man barked again.

"See, ya litt'l bastahd…see how that feels? That's what ya damn well just done ta tha stile."

And a young voice shrieked, a boy's voice, then he shrieked again.

This clearly wasn't my business. Episodes of this sort probably occurred all the time, in all of these buildings, but today, owing to seminal revelations, I reacted differently; not to mention, the man really shouldn't have left the door ajar if he wanted to carry on like this. I pushed it just wide enough to slip through, then passed down a small hallway into the workshop itself.

The space beyond had a low ceiling and was preposterously disorganized, with tables at jumbled angles and assorted woodworking projects piled everywhere. The whole place was lit by sooty ceiling lanterns, dangling at headbanging height, while the reek of varnish was overpowering.

Visible to me dead ahead was my eavesdropped vignette, with the pre-pubescent boy's back before me and his mentor-tormentor, possible father, gripping him by the wrist. This "father," typical of carpenters, was hefty, and he sported a balding crown and a bushy mustache. He also, inopportunely, was staring in my direction, as he gripped his chisel.

"What tha hell?" the man muttered. He seemed too surprised to marshal suitable levels of hostility for this trespass.

"You'll be releasing the boy and giving me the chisel," I said as I came forward. My eyes were shaded by my hat, and that, combined with the bad lighting (I sure wouldn't want this cretin doing precision work on my stuff), made it unlikely he would recognize me.

"You'll also want to tell me which arm you'd rather put out of commission for a couple days," I continued. "Because that's the one I'm going to gouge with the chisel, just like you gouged the boy."

This aroused the hostility, and he pushed the boy aside and took a step forward, the sharp tool raised threateningly.

"Gods, ya really must be a—"

But I interrupted that proclamation, mostly because I wasn't interested, but also because mid-sentence (theirs, mine, the words of some ranting drunk in the next alley) was my favorite time to attack. I lunged, extending both hands towards that chisel, glaring at the implement intently, which was more than enough misdirection for this fool. He raised the threatening arm, getting ready to stab over my reaching hands, which made my sweeping kick to the side of his knee a legitimate surprise. It didn't quite drop him, but it was a shock, which then opened him for a palm to the side of the jaw.

The man did, in the midst of knee buckling and head jerking, manage to jab at me with the chisel, but I anticipated its compromised trajectory, so it was easy to bob out of the way and catch his stabbing wrist with my free hand. After that, it was a small matter to hook my instep behind his ankle, shoulder him in the chest, and send him toppling straight onto his back. I went down with him, landing with my knee in his abdomen, which expelled all of his air, and his chisel at the same time.

"Since you didn't make a choice, I'll go with the left," I said, sweeping up the flat bladed tool and pressing it into the meat of his forearm. I chose the arm he hadn't used, presumably his off hand, since I didn't want to imperil this family's ability to earn. And I didn't stab very deep—no damage to tendons or prospects of infection—but it did win me a nice howl, plus some genuine fear, which was the real prize.

"I work for Breaker Tabard," I said, spinning something on the fly. "And he doesn't want any of the children in this neighborhood suffering abuse."

There were so many things wrong with this, I don't even know where to start. However, a varnish-addled wag like this might possibly overlook my nice clothing, my lack of a Dockside accent, the fact that Breaker Tabard's influence didn't extend to this part of the neighborhood, and, most of all, the reality that the big, foul-mouthed racketeer would sooner sell kids to the press-gangs than protect them from abuse. However, happily, this inspired horseshit seemed effective, since the man garbled out a series of apologies, and he assured me, when I demanded it, that he would be better to his son going forward.

I stood, straightened my clothing, and turned to the boy. He was a wiry little fellow, about Ichod's age, but of paler, North Derjian stock. Since I blocked his father's view, I was able to slip a couple tolgens into his palm unseen, and when I put a finger to my lips, he smiled, gave me a discreet nod, then stuffed the coins into his trousers. And with that, I was on my way.

See, Holod, I thought as I stepped back out into daylight. *I can do things in their proper measure, act like all the others. I'm not always such a freak.*

I threaded my way back through the streets and alleys of Dockside towards White Hill, where I hoped to finish what I had started. I would retrieve Shade's plant from 27 Fletcher, mitigating that particular threat. I would also open that console table drawer and confirm that Nascinthé's book was still inside.

Given all that I had learned today, I needed to make sure that my meddlesome librarian friend, with her heretical past and haunted freakshow philosophy, wasn't a common thief, on top of everything else.

10

THE SEDITIONISTS

I finally arrived back at my Dockside apartment around Fourth Bell, carrying the nightshade plant and a lot of money. Shortly after I returned, Cad showed up, bearing good news.

"They'll meet with you at Eighth Bell tonight," he said when we were seated together at my kitchen bar, eating an early dinner of mutton stew and sourdough bread.

"Who'd you speak with?"

"My future bride," Cad said with a smile. "And Adelyn, who was also at Terza's shop. There aren't two richer prizes in the whole Labyrinth, Zeer, and if Terza somehow turns me down, Adelyn wouldn't be a bad runner-up. You really blew it there too."

"She was never mine to begin with, you ass. The meeting will be at the store?"

Cad took a moment to finish a thick section of mutton. He even went to the trouble of patting his lips with a napkin, drawing this out.

"Well, that's just it," he finally replied. "Terza won't let you come directly. You need to be brought. Someone will pick you up in Westward."

"What?"

"Those were the terms."

Cad stretched back, extending the wooly blue arms of his tunic.

"Seriously?"

Cad nodded, a smirk infecting his face like a rash. Somehow, I couldn't help feeling that this was actually Terza's smirk, which—through the asinine mechanics of his infatuation—he had somehow caught from her like a venereal disease.

"This is getting to be too much. I should have brought that goddamned book here."

"What book?"

"Nothing," I said, a bit alarmed that I had muttered this out loud, my mood plainly affecting my judgement (indeed, I had found *I, Asadeissia* still in the console table drawer). "Just a political volume from 27 Fletcher. There're no pictures. You'd hate it."

Cad quickly lost the smirk, and he shifted forward a bit on the stool. Usually, he rebuffed my condescensions with a storm of "ain't's" and "ya's," though those were now graciously in abeyance. However, he had a much more sophisticated counterattack at the ready.

"I'd hate the book 'cause it's politics, not 'cause it's got no pictures," he said. "I don't need politics to talk to women. Maybe you do."

That was a superb comeback, and spot-on. Since I really had no interest in continuing this tit for tat, I steered things back to the night's meeting.

"I'm assuming you learned where I'm supposed to be 'picked up' in Westward?"

"Corner of Gobein and Tradesman. There's a deep door well on the southwest corner you can wait in. People rarely use that door. Try not to be followed."

After finishing our meal and going over a few additional errands, I sent Cad off and then began to prep for the night's meeting. I set out just before the Seventh Half Bell.

It was a cool evening, with a diffuse, chilly mist sheathing the streets. My boots emitted a dull clocking on the stones, and there was a muffled quality overall to the city's noises—warped catches of conversation and occasional raised voices. These came from partially open windows, adjoining streets, amiably glowing taverns, serviceable at last, and irresistible to those seeking a return to normal life. I spotted clusters of individuals out and about, some gathered for their own safety, others for less benign purposes. I passed several of Breaker Tabard's men, who clearly recognized me, so I was given respectful dips of the chin. In fact, one of them actually smiled, and it suddenly crossed my mind that perhaps Tabard and his closest confidants had gone ahead and stolen the treasure I'd disclosed. I would have to look into this, for I had promised Cad I would find out what the take was and then reward him for giving me that information.

Not long afterwards, I crossed Seafinder and entered the insipid stucco grid of Westward, which made crafty routes more difficult. I didn't hear any accidental scuffles behind me, feel that extrasensory tingly thing, usually in the neck, sometimes on the backs of my arms, that would tell me the eyes of others were upon me. In fact, given all that I had been through, I felt surprisingly little. Reflexively, I scanned the sides of buildings, looking to see if my Oulmaen symbol would make another appearance. I tested my psychic feelers (first checking to see if I had any of those, which, as my banal, internal garble would suggest, I didn't), and then I tried to stimulate some sort of connection to the Summoner from Darkness. I achieved nothing. My mental activities were what they usually were, my perception of the world without interest. All of this confirmed that I had simply had some sort of aberrant, hallucinatory episode, instigated by... who the hell knew what, but clearly short-lived and ultimately of little consequence.

Eighth Bell rang just a minute or so before I arrived at the corner of Gobein and Tradesman, and when I made it to the appointed door well, I found my escort waiting for me.

"It's been a long time, hasn't it?" she said, stepping out of the recessed shadows and into the shine of a nearby streetlamp.

"Too long," I replied. "If it had been up to me, we wouldn't have been apart at all."

Adelyn came forward another step, her high, narrow boots moving lightly over the slick street, her camel-colored shawl fanning out as she approached.

"So you say," she replied, with a warm smile. "But you would've grown bored of me, Vazeer. I'm not as exciting as your other women."

"Boring is good, Adelyn. These days, female excitement is killing me."

"So I've heard."

Her mouth dipped in an expression of sympathy, which she was able to project to uncommon degrees. I was charmed, as always, by Adelyn's covert allure, that mysterious composition of facial features, which were pleasing to the initial glance and then harder to pin down through isolated inspection. Her face was a bit round, removing the possibility of high cheekbones or more defined sculpting. Her brown eyes sparkled with intelligence, though they lacked the drama of color, and her lips, while shapely, were not particularly lush. Her curly, shoulder-length brown hair was clean, but here, too, there was a dearth of luster or sumptuousness; and yet, undefinably, none of this made her drab.

Just the opposite, for each piece of Adelyn's puzzle fit together with a sort of augmenting logic, so that the roundish face did not want for more chiseling because of the placement of the lips, and the eyes did not crave more vibrancy since the warm toffee glow of her skin accomplished this. The net result was a diffused appeal, like visual perfume.

"Come," she said, hooking her arm in mine. "Let's walk."

We started together down the straight, gleaming course of Tradesman. Up ahead, I saw a city watch patrol coming our way, which was a welcome sight, though I did wince through an involuntary personal survey, checking to see if I was doing anything wrong.

"We're fine," Adelyn breathed quietly. "Unlike the last time you ditched us in Westward. Remember?"

That was in the aftermath of the Gaff saga, when Adelyn, Terza, and Heshna confronted me in the streets of this neighborhood. At that time, I spotted an approaching watch patrol and I beat a hasty retreat, leaving the trio of women to face the half dozen soldiers on their own.

"I never did ask what happened after I left," I said, as we passed the watchmen. This group was a team of four, and we both nodded to them politely, which was met with impassive stares.

"Oh," said Adelyn. "It was a real mess. A full twenty minutes of being questioned: why were we armed like that, what were we planning, who was that we were talking to…and why did he run like a fugitive at the first sight of the watch? Things like that. Terza almost slugged the commanding officer. I had to talk her down."

"You do a lot of that, don't you?"

"It's one of my jobs in life," she said, and she looked up at me with her lips tweaked.

Adelyn was shorter than me by several inches, though she wasn't actually short. Her build, like all of her physical traits, was somewhere in between—height that was average for a North Derjian woman, and a slender figure that stopped shy of being skinny.

"I could have used your presence at Terza's shop a week ago," I said. "I went there to warn her, and…well, it could have been a warmer reception."

"I heard, and I wasn't happy about it," she said. "Nothing like that's going to happen tonight, I promise."

"Always looking out for me, Adelyn."

"Just another one of my jobs."

I felt then, as I did always, just how much I enjoyed Adelyn's company. Perhaps she was right, and I would ultimately need more stimulation than she could provide; however, in this moment, strolling with my arm hooked in hers, nothing felt absent, and a sense of calm overtook me. I didn't know if I could ever love her (or any woman), but I was certain that I could fall deeply in like with her.

A short time later, we arrived at our destination. To my surprise, it was Adelyn's home—her *original* home—a visit that was about to prove enlightening, as such things always are. The building itself was sturdy, but it was a homogenous stucco creation, indistinguishable from its neighbors. There were four units, and two of these were composed of her parents' cobbler shop and the apartment above, while the adjoining pair were similarly stacked.

I knew the basics of Adelyn's story and was aware that her father, in the first of several ill-considered moves, had bought the whole building when Adelyn was a child, thinking that he could rent out the other apartments and help offset the tremendous debt he incurred. But the man wasn't a good businessman, and the terms of his loan were so usurious that he wound up selling off years of future profits just to keep the lender from seizing the building. Seeing that she would never get her family out of debt by being a cobbler, Adelyn headed to Dockside in her late teens to take advantage of the hungry need for contract operatives that was expanding at the time. In those days, inexperienced recruits were joining the Shadow Bidder ranks by the skiffload, then shipping off to prison or the graveyard almost as quickly. The fact that Adelyn managed to avoid both fates meant that she was either very good at her job or very lucky.

"Back here," she said, leading me into the alley next to the shop.

She unlocked the building's side door, and we found a staircase inside.

"I took over the whole upper floor a few years ago," she said as we climbed. "It's difficult for my parents to make it up the stairs now, so I moved them into the unit next to the shop. They still work a few hours a day, though they don't have to."

Creaking our way up the heavily scuffed steps, my hand brushing the palm-worn banister, I couldn't help but put myself in the perspective of young Adelyn. Compared to my own upbringing, this seemed palatial. Additionally, there had never been any mention of drunkenness or abuse in Adelyn's family, so she had that over the rest of us too, and it was my understanding that her relationship with her parents remained close to this day.

We stepped off onto the upstairs landing into a broad space with clean plaster walls and functional, if pedestrian, furniture. A couple of oil flames twitched inside of glass sconces, and in between these, there were two framed sketches—one a beautiful charcoal study of a dove, the other a moody rendering of the Harborway skyline. These pieces, elegant and expressive, had nothing in common with the bland decor, and I knew at once that they were Terza's work.

Adelyn crossed the heavily tracked carpet, heading for a door that looked like it had been framed out recently. This clearly led out of her family's original dwelling, and I did some hurried surveillance to see if I could spot Adelyn's childhood bedroom before we left. There was an open door leading into a small space containing a plush rug and a narrow bed. Was this where young Adelyn had plotted her family's salvation; were those the snug sheets where she had dreamed of being a Shadow Bidder? She must have been out of her mind.

"Why a Blade?" I suddenly asked, stopping her before she grabbed the doorknob.

Adelyn was a Masque now, but she had begun her career as a common mercenary, which seemed a weird choice.

"It was the only thing I knew how to do," she answered, her hand hovering. "I couldn't pick locks, I wasn't stealthy enough to be an Eye. I had the temperament to be a Masque but no training, so I did the one thing I was remotely good at."

"Fighting?"

"On rare occasion. More often, bluffing the ship crews into thinking I could."

She smiled, then reached forward and opened the door.

The space beyond was warm, pleasantly lit, and furnished with some real taste—a lovely green and yellow Testhian rug on the wide plank floor, standing braziers in the corners, low comfortable couches along two walls, and a round dining table off to one side. Here, too, Terza's artwork brightened the walls, but these were clearly the more up-to-date pieces, for the common theme wasn't subtle. All of them appeared to be studies for *Fall of the Patriarchy*, Terza's masterwork. Several were pencil sketches, a few were rendered in colored charcoal, and one was an oil work on canvass, focused exclusively on the nine heavily armed female figures who dominated the foreground.

Terza and Heshna were waiting for me. They were sitting at the dining table, staring my way, and my pulse did a little throbby thing at the sight of them. While it was Terza I was most afraid of (as any sane person would be), Heshna was a close second. Above and beyond my Brood sister's role as my life's designated hobgoblin, she somehow—insidiously, creepily—always knew everything. The last time I had seen her, she was fully aware that a Finisher had been hired to kill me.

"It figures you would survive," Heshna said as I approached. Her flat, toneless voice was not entirely toneless, for she spoke with a distinct crabbiness. She was dressed in her standard muddle of nondescript cloth; however, Heshna's face was less dreary than usual today, imbued with both life and color. There was a slight vibrancy in the wan flesh (possibly spurred by hatred of me), but at the same time, her dirty blond hair had a certain fullness, which definitely had more to do with grooming than loathing.

"Disappointed, Heshna?" I asked.

"Of course she's not disappointed, Vazeer," said Adelyn from behind. "We're all very happy you're alive. I think Heshna's just a little surprised that you wanted to meet with us, and curious too."

I glanced at Terza, who sat stiffly in her chair, her hands fiddling on the table. If I didn't know better, I'd say that the fearsome Falconbrow was nervous. She seemed reluctant to meet my eye, and she definitely wasn't frowning. My ex-lover was wearing a silver, collared blouse, which matched and accentuated her eyes, as well as slimly cut leather pants descending into shiny black boots. Seeing this, I had a sudden hope that this novel attention to personal appearance was simply Terza's new look—her "sedition look"—and that it didn't represent the presence of a lover in her life.

"I'm here for two reasons," I said, arriving at the dining table and offering myself a chair, since nobody else did. "The first is to try, once again, to stop you from getting yourselves killed."

"We don't need your protection, Brood brother," said Heshna, her flushed scowl all the more vivacious in these close quarters. "That point was stomped into your face the last time."

Oh! That was good, and surprising. Heshna's newly assertive demeanor, with her lively skin tones and uncommon loquacity, had yielded a clever joke, one that put me in my place. The use of the word "stomped" was a skillful way to reference Terza turning me into a human carpet, though the woman who had done the actual deed did not appear to be gloating. Terza looked almost chagrined. The metallic flicker of her eyes, taking furtive refuge below her growing bangs, seemed like the gaze of a woman who was happy to see me, who, quite possibly, was sorry that she had treated me so roughly the last time, and now felt intense relief that she hadn't sent me off to my grave with that final "stomping."

"Maybe so, Brood sister," I replied, settling into my chair. "However, the situation has changed, and I bring news that even you don't know."

"Tell us," said Adelyn, taking a seat at our conference table.

And so I did, at least the relevant details. I explained how I had teamed up with one of the surviving operatives from the Narrow Bid, and that the two of us were hatching a plot to bring down the Raving Blade. I also went through the salient points of my meeting with Count Tygean, rounding things out with the Underlord's pledge of full support.

"So, you see," I said, after I had laid it all out, along with the fact that I now needed the three of them for my coup, "this is really a much better way to achieve your aims than what you've been doing with your graffiti. In fact, Tygean knows all about your project—who you are and where you live. He'll let it go, but only if you stop right away and get on board with the plan."

Now, that other, more intimidating side of Terza Falconbrow appeared.

"How?" she asked in a cold voice. "How does he know?"

"It was bound to happen, Terza."

"No, it wasn't. We were careful. Somebody must have told him."

"Tygean has a lot of spies," I replied. "One of these, apparently, lives on the Virtuoso."

Terza shuttled this information somewhere, ushering it along a mental pathway for several seconds, then suddenly she slammed her fist down on the table and stood.

"It's Marzan!"

The reverberant crash startled me, forcing me into immediate damage control.

"We don't know that, Terza."

In reality, we kind of did. Terza had made an astute guess, one which I should have made myself. Jaspar Marzan, who owned Marzan's Exotic Emporium of Fine Collectibles, ran the most successful store on the Virtuoso, possibly the most successful store in Sullward, and I'd always wondered how he secured such prime merchandise. The man had obviously worked out some sort of astonishing deal with the Underlords, which allowed him to siphon off the best items from the Ripening Halls before the Southern Traders and the auction houses got a hold of them. Working as a spy for Count Tygean could definitely accomplish that.

"I've always hated him!" Terza ranted. "The way he looks at me…like I don't belong on his street, the fact that I sell my own work instead of stolen crap."

Point of information, Terza also sold "stolen crap," just like everybody else, though not nearly as much as Jaspar, who happened to be her main competitor.

"He dies tonight," she said with finality. "There will be nothing left of him to open the Emporium tomorrow."

"We don't have proof, Terza," I said.

"It's him. I've seen him looking in my direction a lot lately, though I thought he was just gloating at the bad condition of my shop."

"Jaspar's obviously under Tygean's protection—"

"I don't give a damn, Vazeer!" Terza said, and that striking face became the very image of reprisal.

"Yes, dear, you do give a damn," said Adelyn, and she reached out to pat Terza's arm sympathetically.

Terza started to pull away, but Adelyn's gentle patting became a firm grab, and she held her friend securely.

"The old Falconbrow would storm over there immediately and take her revenge," said Adelyn. "But not the new one. Our warrior general is a much craftier creature now. We'll get Marzan, but not tonight."

And what do you know, Terza listened. She listened entirely to these few mollifying words, which never would have happened had I delivered a hundred of my finest speeches. This was that strange Adelyn power, which had stood Terza down all those years ago on the Gaff, and which had achieved similar results with the worst captains to crowd our docks. As a de-escalater, Adelyn was second to none.

"I'll bide my time for now," said Terza, taking her seat, "but when this thing is done, Marzan's done at the same time. There's no talking me down from that."

Adelyn offered no dissent, which meant Jaspar was as good as dead, unless, of course, he could be convinced to flee the city, something I might try to facilitate.

"You really think this Underlord is different, Vazeer?" Adelyn asked.

"I do. I've now met the three senior figures, in quick succession, plus a bunch of their vassals, and this is the only one who seems like a normal person. He's actually married and has a family."

This was met with some interest, and possibly appreciation, which stood in marked contrast to the cynicism of Radrin Blackstar. Of course, I neglected to mention that Tygean's "family" included his son, Devlan, who was among the huffiest, snottiest little bastards I'd met in years. But I was making progress, so I proceeded with the best news of all.

"I would go so far as to say Count Tygean and I see eye to eye. We share dreams in common."

"Oh?" This produced a lift in the tanned spheres of Adelyn's cheeks. "What dreams?"

My eagerness now expanded to some finger tapping, which really rounded out the juvenile look.

"That the artistic city-state might be restored. Not immediately, obviously. But eventually, through a careful process that he and I discussed at length."

Terza snorted softly.

"That old obsession of yours," she said, though this was uttered more with amusement than derision.

"Very old," said Heshna, all derision and no amusement. "He was caught up with this ailment even as a child."

And just like that, my mood, which had been drifting pleasantly upward, took a sudden nosedive.

"Ailment?" I spat at her. "Who was the sick one? The young boy who had dreams…or the vindictive little troll who stalked him and tried to sabotage everything he did?"

"You were never a *young boy*, Brood brother," Heshna replied, her drony voice quickened strangely, her lackluster face lit by emotion, though I couldn't begin to tell which emotion it was. "You were always this sick thing, or in the grip of it. I didn't understand it then, but I could tell it was a problem, a problem for the rest of us."

Terza and Adelyn both looked mystified, and they turned to Heshna, seeking clarification.

"Go ask his librarian friend," Heshna continued. "I tailed them earlier, at a distance, so I didn't hear what was said. But the old woman left with a terrible look on her face, which I recognized. It's how he has always made me feel."

I could tell that Terza and Adelyn had no idea what Heshna was talking about, which was fortunate. Everything else, however, was unfortunate, namely the fact that my childhood nemesis had tracked me on an errand that had nothing to do with her, one that included Merejin, who, if I could somehow orchestrate it, would never come within a mile of my Shadow Bidder existence and a hundred miles of my disgusting past.

But there were worse things going on here. Heshna's accusation held deep, frightening implications that deserved further exploration. What the hell had the uncanny Seer *seen*? What had she always seen in me that would disturb her so much, frighten her even as an unsociable little girl? I would have to pursue this, but now was not the time or place, for I couldn't afford to have another word said on this matter in present company. Terza and

Adelyn were both key components of my upcoming plan, and last thing I needed was for them to think of me as some cursed freak who sees symbols where there are no symbols, except where they actually live—in the twisted theater show of my own head. I needed to move us quickly away from this topic.

"Listen," I said to the group of them. "We must put our past dealings behind us. All of us. There's a quiet war underway, which will soon grow very loud, and if it doesn't go our way, the life we all knew will be destroyed. The three of you are the key to this thing turning out right."

I then laid out their precise roles in the coming operation. I explained exactly who would do what and when, and I did not neglect my sour Brood sister, whose extraordinary talents could make all the difference in this gambit. My tone, I felt, was magnanimous, since I was setting aside grotesque insults that I had received from two of them recently, and this allowed me to be persuasive, as best I could tell. To that point, I pulled a small pouch from my belt and spilled the contents out on the table. It was time to put my latest political reading to the test.

"A great deal more will be coming once Count Tygean can access his vaults."

In the cheery radiance of braziers, one-third of the Narrow Bid contract payment glinted in a reddish-purple glow on Adelyn's dining table.

"For now, he wanted to show you his good faith and reward you in advance for the services you will render."

It was risky to tell a blatant lie to a trained Masque, not to mention a Contract Eye who had known me my entire life; however, very quickly, I could see that the Empress Asadeissia was right. The "gifts" approach achieved the proper effect. None of them could lift their eyes from the small pile of Gosian Diamonds, which, factoring in an equitable split, was enough to take care of them for a long time to come. And they needed it. None of these Shadow Bidders had received contracts in weeks, and their future employment prospects were, at best, uncertain. Terza's shop had suffered significant damage in the storm, and Adelyn had her parents to look after. I had no idea what Heshna's financial needs were; however, she seemed just as transfixed by the twinkling treasure as the others.

At last, Terza looked up from the pile, and her steely eyes were concentrated but not disagreeable. While Adelyn was the diplomat and mouthpiece for their operation, Terza was the true leader, about which I'd never had any doubt.

"I'm not promising anything, Vazeer," she said. "But I suppose there could be some value in this. And maybe, just maybe, we will take a little break from the writings…just a short break. But you need to understand something, our campaign is about more than self-preservation. It's a vision."

She was referring, specifically, to the cult of Giradera, a conception of the ancient battle queen as an avatar of the goddess Yisva. Giradera's reign had existed centuries before the rise of the Tergonian Empire—over six hundred years before the time of Asadeissia—and it signified a powerful (albeit brief) period when women dominated the top of the religious and political hierarchies of the day. Embracing this philosophy was, in addition to its radical religious implications, a call for female leadership in society.

"I understand that, Terza," I replied. "And I am not opposed to your vision, and never have been, which is why I fought a huge Gosian killer in front of a crowd of other killers, just to keep them from taking my statue of Giradera."

"Not very smart of you."

"No, not very."

And then, right there—for the first time in what felt like ages—an undeniable pulsation of warmth passed between us. On that wind-burned, gray-eyed face, beneath her flawless bird, something tender appeared, reminding me of days long past when Terza Falconbrow might conceivably have loved me, had I not been such a stubborn fool. And I, in those same distant days, might conceivably have loved her too, if not for the same reason.

"Give us some time to gather the others," Terza said by way of completion. "And please, Vazeer, try not to do anything stupid in the meantime. There are a lot of killers in this town. For some reason, you have a bad habit of attracting them."

11

AFFECTIONS AND AFFLICTIONS

I arrived back at my apartment after Tenth Bell, and there I found one of my killers waiting for me. It was the good killer, whose job it was to protect me from the bad killer, and this made me uncommonly happy to see him. Radrin Blackstar stood at the door of my apartment, looking as he always did—neatly groomed, nestled in his high-collared black cloak, his features billeting equal parts alertness and composure. I could easily have gotten there a few minutes earlier and not caused him to wait, but the thought of arriving home alone after dark literally made me queasy. That other killer had really done a number on my nerves.

"How did they react?" he asked once we were safely inside.

The two of us had settled in at my small dining table, where we had been holding our council of war of late. As was my ritual, I first fixed myself a light snack of crackers, smoked sausage, and tea, and I made sure to offer some to Radrin. Predictably, he refused. In the first few nights of our planning, I had gone to absurd lengths to get him to eat or drink something, mostly just to see if he could; and while I did eventually learn that he was capable of this normal human process, I wouldn't call anything about his relationship to his basic needs "normal." There was something fanatically ascetic about him.

I bit into a cracker and crunched down too hard on the left side, sending a hot eruption of pain straight up my jaw and into the side of my face. It took a few seconds to recover, and I glanced at Radrin to see if he noticed, though I don't think he did. This scalding agony was one of the enduring legacies of the Gaff, which I definitely didn't feel like recounting right now.

"They reacted well," I finally replied, in a pain-muffled voice. "Especially when I dumped a fifth of my contract payment out on the table."

"A full fifth?" Radrin asked, and he looked perturbed. "I thought we agreed to a single diamond apiece."

"I had to read the moment, and that's what the moment called for."

The real tally was a third, and I had prepped it in advance, my strategy being to temporarily blind the trained Masque in the group to the fact that our new Underlord employer didn't have a pot to piss in. However, explaining this to Radrin now would merely bring up my own failures from the negotiating process with Tygean. Also (and this was none of his business), I was secretly happy to give two of those women a small fortune; the third I viewed as collateral benevolence.

"They'll stop the writings?"

"Umm-hmm," I garbled, for I was engaged in a very delicate chewing process, one that kept my mouth a little slack. This had the unfortunate effect of spilling several crumbs onto my map of the city. The vellum diagram now lived in an open position on my dining table, and while I could see that it was taking some damage from being used in this manner, it wasn't the priceless beauty from my Fletcher Street bedroom.

"I'm surprised," Radrin mused. "I would have thought this was a matter of principle with them."

"It is. But so far, the campaign isn't working very well. They've apparently attracted some female Shadow Bidders; however, few of these are Contract Blades, for there aren't many female Blades, apart from Terza and, once upon a time, Adelyn. So, this group isn't very warlike. A team of Masques, Eyes, and Locksmiths doesn't exactly constitute an army."

"She was onto something then," he replied.

"Who?"

"Shade of Night. She must have known the movement was going nowhere."

I avoided responding and hoped he would quickly move on. I was always uncomfortable discussing Shade in Radrin's presence, primarily because the whole subject was an embarrassment; however, there was something else. In contrast to almost every other topic that crossed our war table, I noticed that Radrin Blackstar always exhibited a strange preoccupation when it came to the female Finisher, something in the genus of obsession. I couldn't tell where this came from or what it signified, but I didn't like it. His earlier proclamation that the two of them were headed for a lethal showdown had stayed with me, and Shade's own words had reinforced this.

Tactlessly, I glanced over at my new, bushy tenant. Radrin hadn't commented yet on the nightshade, which lounged in verdant contentment on the same windowsill where it first appeared. He probably didn't recognize the species, and my guess was he viewed it as just another of the various keepsakes I had brought over to make myself feel at home.

"Falconbrow has good standing with Shadow Bidders of both genders," I said. "She'll be able to find some Blades. The problem is, the Seer indicated that most have either been recruited by Gueritus already or decided to retire. It remains to be seen how many will be *allowed* to retire, but that's another story. As for Helmgrinder, I've got the Seer looking for him, and once she finds him, Adelyn and I will offer our proposal. I can't tell you what will come of it, but as promised, I will try."

Radrin provided the faintest of nods, then went back to studying the map.

"One way or another, Gueritus will be crossing canals as he moves through the streets," I continued, "which presents our best opportunity. I'm going to secure a couple of specialty craft from the man who used to rent me my skiffs, though he's going to be even less happy to see me than Col."

Radrin did not look up from the map. He did at least make a low throat noise, which might have been agreement, or maybe a desire for more clarification, or (this would fit tidily with past discussions) an admonishment for ever giving a damn who was happy to see me and who was not.

"I've asked Terza to recruit a Grell Runner. A tough one, because the group of us are going to crawl like trolls from beneath the bridge and surprise Gueritus's soldiers that way. Underlord retainers always meet people like me at the end of the run, when we're no longer being stealthy. They have no idea what sneaky bastards we can be."

Now, at last, Radrin did raise his eyes, and the unscarred quietude of his face held a distinct look of approval.

"That's a good idea."

"Isn't it?"

"You're good at this."

"Who would've thought?"

"I thought."

This drew my own noncommittal pharynx noise, which, as it so happens, did mean something: that I was absurdly gratified to hear this. Living as I had been with my needling doubts, most of them centered around the possibility that I was too internally wayward to pull any of this off, I found his expression of confidence welcome.

A short time later, we finished our strategizing, and Radrin stood to leave, at which point something odd happened. I found that I didn't want him to go. Radrin and I had engaged in several exhaustive strategy sessions in the last week, and in every instance, I'd found myself listening to the successive night Bells with rising exasperation, hoping he would soon make motions to wrap things up.

Tonight, I felt otherwise. I didn't know to what degree my earlier meeting with the sedition gang was influencing me (strolling amiably with Adelyn had ignited a remembrance of companionship, and being unloathed by Terza had done something even more profound). Nevertheless, my main consideration at the moment was the fact that I was scared to death of being alone. I couldn't shake the feeling that somehow, despite my many precautions, Shade of Night would find a way to penetrate the defenses of my apartment. She had done this before, and I suspected that she would eventually do it again.

I now had plenty of money to pay her, but the bigger threat came from my inability to compensate her in other ways. While shortcomings of this nature could, on occasion, afflict me, the specter of impotence in this situation was literally a matter of life and death. My anxiety about it was so acute that I came close to confessing my situation to Radrin, which would quickly undo any sense that I was "good at this," plus it would wantonly violate the oath I had given Shade when my pants were twisted like macramé around my ankles. Only bad outcomes could result from such a disclosure, so I kept my mouth shut, and Radrin soon left. Adding to the desolate feeling was the fact that our farewell would encompass the next several nights, since we had decided there was no additional value in these meetings until the team was assembled. While I did finally fall asleep, I woke no less than five times in the night, falsely imagining that my stalker had returned.

The next morning, I was out of the apartment early enough to see the dock crews setting up for work. Wispy, blunted figures arrived in groups and began to load and unload the five mid-sized ships currently in port. That was less than half of what we might expect during normal times, but the numbers had been growing each week.

I reached Droden's patchwork section of docks as the sound of Eighth Bell penetrated the moist carpet of fog. At the head of what was essentially a construction site stood Cad, garlanded in the implements of his trade.

"The sins of the past are forgiven?" I asked when I arrived.

"For me, maybe," Cad replied. "Can't say anything about you."

My plan, clever in concept, was to send Cad down to Droden Sailwain's marina covered in carpentry implements, which would be my first peace offering. I knew Droden would have trouble turning this down. My former Broodmate's docks had been largely destroyed by the Swell Driver, along with most of his skiffs, and he simply didn't have enough staff to fix it all. Cad, in addition to being one of the better carpenters in the city, had once worked for Droden and therefore knew all the ins and outs of these repairs. While that employment had ended badly (Cad's teenage indiscretions with Droden's daughter being the cause), many reformative years had transpired, and in recent times, Cad and Droden had taken to gruff but civil greetings in the streets of Dockside.

Therefore, patching up that relationship didn't seem like too big a challenge; however, friendship between those two was of no great interest to me. What I wanted was to fix my own relationship with Droden Sailwain, which had been defunct since the catastrophic events of the Narrow Bid. Just prior to that, as a worrying harbinger of my new addiction to lying, I had spewed a string of falsehoods to Droden in preparation for the job. I misrepresented the target, the true objective of the contract, the terrible possible backlash that might affect all who were directly involved, or were foolish enough to lend assistance. Droden wasn't foolish, but he had been trusting, and I betrayed that trust in an overt way.

Leaving Cad, I walked alone to the end of the new dock, and there, at the slowly unfurling rug of wooden planks, stood my Brood brother. He clearly wasn't thrilled to see me, though he didn't make a threatening gesture or turn his back. Droden's long hair hung ungathered around his shoulders, which was his custom, and his mustache was a little bushier than I remembered it. He made a cutting gesture to the two dock boys at his feet, who were fitting planks, and they promptly got up and left.

"So, this is the strategy then?" he asked, once we were alone. "Send the kid that rutted with my daughter to pave the way for the bastard who spat lies in my face? Dangerous lies that might have brought an Underlord army to Eastcove? You really must think I'm desperate, Lash."

Droden probably was a little desperate, since he had quit his insurance policy several years back and was paying for all of these repairs out of pocket, though I couldn't see how it would help my cause to agree with him.

"I was in a jam, Droden," I replied. "And probably not thinking too clearly that afternoon."

"And how many times am *I* in a jam, Lash? How many times do I get pressure from all sides—the constables, the watch, the Harbormaster…all manner of solicitous bastard who would pay me a small fortune to sell you out, which I never do?"

"You know how much I value that. And what I did wasn't selling you out, just covering my ass. I never would have let them track me to you."

Droden now looked me up and down a couple times, as if searching for the gaping fissure out of which all of my reason had drained.

"It wasn't you that came to Eastcove that night, was it?" he asked. "Did you teach your Midland girlfriend how to avoid being tracked?"

As usual, the ever wise Droden Sailwain had found his way to the flaw in my argument, a rather pronounced flaw. On the night of the Narrow Bid, I had given Nascinthé directions to the Elena's Guile, and while I did join her two days later (for the most wonderful romantic interlude of my life), she had originally made her way to the boat alone. Not only didn't I teach her how to avoid being tracked, she actually went out of her way to put as many Underlord soldiers on her trail as possible, and only escaped pursuit by means of a miraculously timed storm surge. But that last part I would skip.

"I had originally thought I'd be with the passengers," I conceded. "I didn't consider the danger of sending one of them to you alone."

"There's a lot you didn't consider from what I hear. What's this nonsense you've got Habard spinning around the docks—Habard, of all people—that you didn't know what you'd gotten yourself into? That you thought you were actually doing a 'service' for Sherdane? What kind of crap is that?"

I'd largely forgotten about the twenty-tolgen favor I'd asked of Droden's Eastcove guard, Habard. For that considerable sum, I'd requested, first, that he forget that he'd ever seen Nascinthé of Levell at Eastcove, and second, that he make a sincere effort to spread the word that my motives on the night of 28 Dekharven had been innocent. Obviously, Habard had done this, and while I didn't know to what degree it had helped my cause, it clearly hadn't hurt, for nobody in the general populace had accosted me.

"I'll tell you about it, Droden," I said. "Everything, which you deserve."

And so I gave it to him, or most of it, sparing only the goriest, blow-by-blow details on the Narrow Bid. I actually conveyed more to Droden than the others, for there would be no hiding my "Midland girlfriend" from the man who had allowed her onto his caravel.

"You really let her go?" Droden asked when I had finished.

I had to hand it to my Brood brother. Having just heard an entire disastrous tail of treachery and murder, of a transforming Labyrinth that would soon involve a great deal more bloodshed, and possibly an end to his business as a service provider to Grell Runners, the first question he asked was about my relationship.

"This is supposed to be a temporary separation," I replied. "For her safety. But if I'm being honest about it, I'm not sure she'll ever return. I'm not sure she *should* return, given all that's coming, and all I might need to do to survive it."

It took Droden a little spell to respond to this.

"I don't know why I'd bother to help you at this point," he said, with just enough warmth that I sensed he did know why. "But you should take my advice on this. When a woman like that walks into your life, you've got to recognize the moment for what it is. You need to act, not just wait around to see if she comes back."

This was something he understood personally. Elena Sailwain was, to use Cad's expression, a "gem," a woman who was not only intelligent, charming, and splendid looking, but who hailed from a social class that should have categorically rejected a man like Droden. Born *Elena Gromwell*, Droden's wife had come from the same family of landholders as my tailor, Osvert, but—just like Osvert—she didn't own any land. The fortunes of the regional gentry had been slowly declining over the course of the last two centuries, and most of the children from those families had been forced to learn trades. Elena had been a governess when Droden hired her to teach the dock boys at his new marina to read and write.

Too busy with his fledgling enterprise to undertake this task himself, Droden was nonetheless committed to doing what Holod had done: dramatically improving the skills of the young people in his charge. He was also loyal to the idea (again, through Holod's example) that women inherently outclassed men, and that Elena, who was highly educated, born of a named family, and possessed of a lovely temperamental grace, deserved more than he could possibly offer. But offer he did, and at the same time, he made a solemn vow that every day from that moment forth—should he be so lucky as to win her—would be a sacred altar dedicated to her happiness. Elena, for reasons that Droden still doesn't understand to this day, but which I do, took him up on this proposal, and I would have to conclude that my Brood brother has more than lived up to his end of the bargain.

Decidedly wealthy by northern standards, Droden and Elena lived happily together in a huge tasteful Dockside apartment, as well as the complex at Eastcove, which was quite enchanting on the inside. Plus, they owned a bunch of expensive sailing craft, which, in between rentals, they used for their own pleasure. In addition to this, they had three fiercely intelligent children whom Elena took extraordinary care in molding, along with the dock boys, whom she saw as an extended family. So, all in all, Droden's story was an exemplary tale of love, and a model that any man would be wise to follow.

Which is exactly why my spirits now pointed their sights towards the bottom of Sullward Harbor. I knew Droden was right. I had also known that Holod was right when he told me to take my money and run away with my "little Masque," leaving all this treachery and mayhem behind. But I couldn't do it. My ensemble of mad dreams had just taken a stratospheric leap skyward and were now holding uninterrupted court in my consciousness. I had it that killing the detestable Raving Blade would, of a glorious piece, resurrect a past that had come to mean more to me than anything in my present. This definitely wasn't the proper order of priorities, but I couldn't let go of it, and the more I pondered this obsession of mine, the more I sensed that Heshna the Seer was probably right. This *was* a sickness. This was a problem for everybody around me, but me most of all.

Droden and I spoke a while longer, and in that time we reconciled nicely. As anticipated, he did have an assortment of streamlined Grell Running craft tucked away at Eastcove, and for two of these I gave him a single Gosian Diamond, which was a ridiculous overpayment. However, that sum was actually an underpayment to fix my sticky mass of guilt, which was what the money was really about. Droden recognized this, but sometimes one just isn't in a position to turn down a windfall, no matter what drives it.

After that, I gave a few additional instructions to Cad, then I was on my way north, heading to the Wags. I didn't know it yet, but I was about to run smack into another ailment, delivered from an unexpected source.

I arrived in the vicinity of the Broodhouse sometime after Tenth Bell. I hadn't quite reached the fat, black rectangle of granite, when a small shape called to me from an alley.

"He's not going to want to meet with you, Zeer. Nothing's changed since the last time you were here."

When I turned and saw the nonchalant angle of her waifish body, leaning against the nonchalant angle of a misshapen hovel, I was, in no uncertain terms, delighted. Selene's face was grimed somewhat, which was her standard makeup policy, and her dark hair had that tousled look that had been present when I first met her. Even so, I could see the wiry poise underneath her pleated gray dress. I could also see that little sterling rod of intelligence running right up the core of her.

"What makes you think I'm here to see him?" I asked. "Maybe I came to see you."

"What for?"

"Oh, I don't know, possibly for saving my life. We could start with that."

"Pfffff, it was nothing," Selene replied. "I was just doing Ichod a favor."

She took two steps out of the alley, moving with nimble efficiency, as was her way. A week earlier, Selene had deftly sped through the Banks, following me and Col on our trip into the Lower City. Ichod, Selene's enamored sidekick, had trailed behind her, and in that interval the boy's already besotted esteem of her had expanded manyfold. When Ichod told me how Selene effortlessly maneuvered around every danger in her path, I became convinced that she would soon be one of the Labyrinth's top Contract Eyes.

"Ichod tells me you really outdid yourself that night."

"I outdid *him*, is what he means," she said with a vaguely crooked smile, revealing her vaguely crooked teeth. "I also outdid Helmgrinder too, I guess, and those mud people in the bushes, and those nasty men in the Lower City…but other than that, I didn't do much, Zeer."

"Did I give you permission to call me that?"

"No, but it's going to be pretty hard to stop me."

True, I supposed, so I simply shrugged and smiled, and meanwhile I tried to keep down the spontaneous, embarrassing thing that was arising inside of me—an overwhelming desire to take this girl in my arms. I wanted to squeeze her, to kiss her head, to treat her like a daughter, which (with a lurching emotional spasm) I suddenly wished she was. For three or four seconds I was throttled with the feeling, felt it hot and dizzying within me, waylaying my common sense.

Then it passed. It passed quickly because I squashed it down, though I still felt a faint tremor moving inside.

A trio of neighborhood laborers were carrying boards and other repair items towards us down the winding lane, and as they skirted our conversation, they gave me a wide berth. I ignored them, but Selene's dark eyes panned their faces, their possessions, other features big and small, which I couldn't begin to guess at, but which she silently snapped up and digested like a plover pecking mites from the sand.

"Where's Ichod?" I asked once they were gone.

"Grounded till the spring. Maybe longer. He took the blame for the whole thing, which was very brave of him. He said it was him that went and tracked you into the Lower City, along with Cad."

"And Holod bought this?"

"Uh-huh…can you believe it? Ichod really did good, and he even knew to say I was involved, just a little, because Holod wouldn't believe it otherwise. I'm on probation for a month, which means I have to stay in the Wags and check in at the Broodhouse every two hours."

Well, that was something. In my last interaction with Ichod, he had desperately confessed to me his love for Selene, and I, most hypocritically, dished out guidance on winning her heart. Among my instructions was a commandment that he stop simpering around like a craven poodle and never snitch on his Broodmate. Ichod had clearly taken this last bit to heart.

"The kid will grow up to do impressive things," I said.

"You think?"

I studied Selene's delicate cheeks to see if they contained sarcasm, if her abiding cockiness would quell the moment, but this did not seem to be the case. It appeared to me as if she genuinely wanted to know.

"I'm sure of it," I said, not really so sure. However, my optimism was growing, for if the boy could funnel courage, in such short order, to the places within himself where it was most needed, what else was possible?

Selene was silent for a bit, her chapped lips bunched to the side as if pulled there on a tiny string. Quite possibly, she was imagining her young suitor growing up to do impressive things, whatever those might be. Finally, she smiled broadly and assumed one of her insouciant postures.

"He just might, if he stays close to me."

Then she came forward another step and poked me in the stomach.

"You didn't really come here to see me, did you, Zeer? You came for Holod."

"I hoped to see you. But yes, I have a message for him."

"You'll have to give it to me, because you're not allowed in the Broodhouse. Holod's even angrier now, after what you got Ichod involved in."

I had been expecting this, and I knew to prep a veiled statement in advance, since it might be delivered via one of the urchins guarding the door.

"Tell him to wait before he goes spreading information that might cause him problems," I said. "I'm going to take care of matters personally, so there's no reason for him to get involved."

This was a reference to Holod's plan to spread the truth about Ulan Gueritus's role in the Narrow Bid, something that would likely get my mentor raved or killed. Since I now had a clear plan to eliminate the Raving Blade, I didn't want Holod doing something reckless in the meantime.

Selene's pale lips returned to their chaffed sideways wrangling. "I'll tell him, Zeer, but I don't like it."

"What do you mean you don't like it? You don't even understand it."

"How dumb do you think I am?" she snapped. "I saw what it looked like the last time you 'took care of matters personally.' I'm not allowed to leave the Wags now, and Ichod's grounded. How are we going to rescue you?"

Oh gods! This girl. For a second time I found myself jamming down the bizarre emotional rush, a slushy fountain that was getting ready to swamp my insides. I took a half step forward as a spastic hug impulse jerked through me, which I quickly converted into an ungainly stretch. I needed to get away from this kid.

"I'll just have to find someone else to rescue me this time," I mumbled, already starting to enact my retreat. "You definitely deserve a break from that job."

I shuttled away down the twisted lane. Selene didn't make any moves to follow, though she did bark out a piqued goodbye, to which I simply threw a backhand wave.

From there, I retreated quickly from the damaged neighborhood, and a short time later I found myself at the head of the Virtuoso. I had come here, as I so often did, to solve mysteries, to get to the murky bottom of it all, but today I was out of luck. As I stared up at Merejin's Books, a reproachful "Closed" sign hung in the dark first-floor window.

This never happened. Worst case, Merejin left a note on the door stating she would be back at such and such time, a promise she always kept, give or take a few minutes. She never simply *closed* during normal store hours. I found the sight of that heavy white sign ominous.

"You've got a couple days to figure out what's wrong with me, Merejin," I muttered as I turned and started towards the other stores on that street. "After that, if the sign isn't gone, I'm busting down that goddamned door."

12

THE HOLE

I didn't return to my apartment until evening, for I spent hours wandering the length and breadth of the Virtuoso, conversing with my favorite shopkeepers, sympathizing with their losses, celebrating their recoveries, many of them heroic, and in this way, I whiled away a pleasant afternoon. Only Terza's shop remained boarded up, which was mostly a ruse to keep attention away from her team-recruiting activities.

I paid respects to Annaliese at Wind and Strings, Havlec at Jain's Furniture Market, Osvert at Gromwell's Finery, and finally, Jaspar Marzan at his fabled Emporium. Conversing with Jaspar, something I never much enjoyed, took on a new, awkward resonance, for I couldn't help feeling that every word we exchanged would eventually be conveyed to Count Halsin Tygean. Additionally, it was always uncomfortable speaking with a dead man, which is exactly what this snitchy storekeeper would be if I couldn't talk Terza out of her vendetta, or Jaspar out of the city.

When, at last, I completed my tour, I had only purchased a brass ice chipper, a set of matching tongs, a pair of large cheese plates (for my late-night snacking), and a lovely ceramic wall medallion (for absolutely nothing), at which point I ambled into the Marquis, one of the few taverns in White Hill. There, I had a savory late lunch, which capped off the sense that normalcy was returning to my city. While normalcy had not returned to my life, it did feel good to move about town like a regular citizen, not a condemned man.

Returning to my apartment as night fell, however, I became present to the fact that I *was* a condemned man, and probably shouldn't have pushed things so late. Radrin would not be coming over tonight, or anytime in the foreseeable future, so I felt acutely alone as I entered the back vestibule of 44 Masthead Lane. This time, I had a stiletto drawn. I listened carefully, sniffed the air for perfume, peered into the dark recesses where light from the hall lanterns hit obstructing corners and left behind shadowed geometry. My deadly stalker was nowhere to be seen. As I made my way slowly up the creaking stairs, I heard sounds of life in the various apartments—the brisk clinking of dinnerware in one of the kitchens, the scratching of paws near a front door, a young boy complaining about something, then an adult voice telling him to shut up. I also ascended through an array of cooking aromas, which included baking bread, assorted peppery spices, and, on the third floor, unmistakably fish.

I recalled all of this pleasant domesticity from the days when I used to live here, and I felt just a little comforted by my unseen neighbors. Still, I was cautious right up until the moment I finally slid inside the door of apartment 16, and threw the locks and bolts into place. I had left tiny scraps of parchment hidden in the door cracks, and none of these had been dislodged, telling me that nobody had gained entry.

After that, I hung my cloak, hat, and weapons belt on hallway wall pegs, felt around in the dark for the flint lighter, then made my way into the kitchen. A hint of luminance filtered in through the living room windows, and by this glow I found my way to the lamp on the counter. It wasn't until I was striking the lighter, my eyes flash-blinded by the snapping white sparks, that I detected the subtlest trace of lilac perfume. By then, it was too late.

She came at me from behind, as was her way. I did hear the predatory patter of sprinting feet, but it only arose at the last second, so I couldn't spin in time. A vicious thrusting kick took me in the back of my right knee, instantly buckling my leg. Forward and down I went, my chin cracking the surface of the bar, the lamp arcing from my hands and crashing to the floor.

I crumpled like a sack of potatoes below the counter, half senseless from the blow to my chin, my eyes still compromised from the flint lighter, and I swear my heart convulsed so violently it was ready to splatter in my chest. I did also, shamefully, feel the hot, clammy creep of moisture at my groin, as that expensive glass of wine from the Marquis found its way into my trousers. Then she was on me, her itinerant arms and legs hooking into position like shackles.

It was always a question with her, where would she stick the knife, and tonight, much to my anguish, I felt the needling tip of it jabbing inside my left ear. It didn't quite poke the eardrum, but it was so close that the slightest jiggling would deny me hearing from that side for the rest of my life. Of course, the Derjian stiletto could do much worse things if pushed a little harder.

"This thing goes straight through your brain if you so much as twitch a muscle, you blundering fool," Shade spat, tart flecks from that piquant mouth raining on my cheek.

Her teeth were jammed so close to my ear that she was in a fine position to bite it off entirely if she happened to get bored with poking. As usual, this cunning killer had attained a strategically grisly advantage, for when I fell on my right side, she had lunged in behind and got her left leg hooked over my hip with her heel in my crotch, while her right arm had snaked through the narrow space beneath my neck to come up into a choke hold. Being strangled was a slight concern, but the far bigger problem was the fact that the arm had made it all the way up and around so that her right hand capped itself on the stiletto-wielding left, and there the two of them exerted steady pressure into the vulnerable receptacle of my ear. Not only did she control the flow of air through my windpipe, but she had only to clench her arm muscles and that blade would drive itself straight through my skull.

"What the hell were you thinking strolling around like a prissy, sightseeing ass!" she snarled. "You think it's a good idea to take your hundred-year-old librarian out for a walk? And today, how many hours did you spend shopping for baubles and dinner plates? Do you think this makes *me* look good? I'm supposed to have diced you already and sent the bits back to the proffer. Every pointless errand you run in the city has me looking like I failed at my job!"

"Shade, I—"

"Shut up!"

She exerted a little squeeze, and the tip of the knife went deeper into the flesh just to the side of the ear canal. My hands were in front of me, more or less, the right arm partially pinned beneath my body, but I really didn't feel confident about my ability to grab her arm in time to stop that needle point from penetrating my head.

"Oh, what the hell is this?" she hissed, her voice fuming against the side of my face. She kicked my crotch hard with her heel, and I sagged forward with a groan.

"Did you piss yourself, you miserable infant?"

Shade's feet, I now gathered, were bare, and she had apparently detected the wetness below.

"That's just perfect!" she snapped. "Not only does the worthless thing go limp when I need it, but tonight it's squirting all over the floor. I came here to cut off some pieces to keep the proffer at bay. Now I know which part comes first."

With that, I'd abruptly had it. Gruesome and humiliating, this utterance marked the moment when I was officially done with this nightmare, and whatever it took, no matter which parts of me suffered permanent disability, I was going to make a move. In fact, I was now ready to kill her, and though I might feel conflicted about the whole episode later, I would deal with it then.

I was in the process of prepping my maneuver when I suddenly heard the quietest and tartest of whispers against my cheek.

"Yisva help me," she murmured. "Please get this fool to fight back."

My hands had been creeping up to grab that imprisoning arm, with the primary aim of escaping her stiletto, but I paused. Something about the intonation of this little prayer, bordering on desperate, got my mind working in a different direction. Into my mind sprang the words from Asadeissia's book, specifically her admonition that one should, while acting compliant, search relentlessly for the enemy's weakness, which I sensed that I had just found.

"How did you get in here?" I asked. I relaxed my body, so that she wouldn't think I was about to counterattack.

"Quiet!" she growled. "I didn't tell you you could speak."

"You didn't have the front door locks picked," I continued. "I would have known it if you did."

"Shut the hell up!" And she kicked me in the crotch again,

even harder this time, but my body was braced for this, so I took a deep breath and continued.

"It must have been clever, whatever you did. I'm truly stumped."

For a moment Shade just lay with me in her cruel snuggle, the little bellows of her breast advancing and withdrawing against my back.

"I cut a hole in the wall," she finally replied. "Or, the building staff did, under my supervision."

"What?"

"It took Everine's carpenters about an hour," she replied, and her voice lightened somewhat. "I put on my property manager's dress and went to inform the neighbors that there would be some repairs on the fourth floor, so they shouldn't be alarmed by the noise."

"You're joking."

"I'm not. Mine is the adjoining apartment; it butts up to your guest room. I had them clean up the dust and finish the edges so that the little hole is very usable. You and I now have a double suite."

I spent a moment trying to picture this, feeling the poke of her blade in my ear and muggy wetness surrounding my groin. The slightest whiff of frying cod travelled to me from the third floor, and outside somewhere I heard revelers singing badly, or possibly arguing.

"I guess the lesson in all this," I said, "is that our landlady is more afraid of you than me."

The sound that emerged from her was a hoarse, disorderly rattle—that same weird laugh which I had heard before, and which always distinguished itself by seeming so genuine.

"Naturally," she finally replied, and I felt her body soften against my back.

For a few seconds we lay together in awkward, painful silence, then I heard her suck in a sizable draught, and I sensed that she was about to resume her tormentor role. This I nipped in the bud.

"You know, this does solve one important problem for me going forward," I said.

She seemed to briefly totter on the brink of hostility, then slipped forward into curiosity.

"What?"

"I'll probably be away for several days when I conduct my operation. I've been wondering who would water our plant."

It wasn't quite a laugh this time but a gusty, croaky pant, drafting into my pinioned ear, unmistakably a sound of pleasure.

"Also," I continued, creeping into what I sensed was an opening, "you mock me for buying tableware, but did you happen to notice I purchased two plates? Two is perfect, and now I can rest assured that my dinner date will be on time."

The blowy sound continued, but it picked up a skeptical timber.

"You lie. One of those is for your Finisher creep."

"Nope. You clearly haven't been watching all that closely. If you had, you would know that my creep never eats."

"Never?"

"Never."

Again, more drafty, throaty silence. Finally, she spoke.

"You think I'm going to fall for this? You doting on my plant? And this talk of romantic dinners…as if I could care less about such things. Shade of Night does not fall prey to sweetness."

I have always thought that I could have been a Masque. I concede that I lack the temperamental balance; however, I do think I came into this world with at least some of the pieces in place. Shade of Night, by contrast, whose frightening reputation had at times held insinuations of being a Masque, was anything but. Stated plainly, the woman was a horrible actress, and her inability to disguise her feelings was even worse than Terza's. Up until this point, her advantage had been the capacity to keep me terrified and on the defensive, conditions that do not lend themselves to spotting vulnerabilities. Now, in this little reprieve from the cycle of ambushes and pokings, fear and urination, I had nudged some crucial responses out of her, and these told me everything about what was really going on here.

"I'm going to get up now, Shade," I said, starting to shift my weight forward. "I've had a long day, filled with all those annoying errands, plus, thanks to your energetic greeting, I'm now drenched in my own piss."

"What!" she barked. "You're not to move even an inch."

"Sorry, but I'm going to move a lot more than that."

I pressed my hands down on the floor and started to heave myself upright, battling the weight of her, which wasn't much.

"I'm not counterattacking," I wheezed through the constriction of her tightening arms, "or making that sudden move you were hoping for. I'm simply getting up, so that I can wash myself, then boil water for tea."

Shade resisted my move the whole way, squeezing the hell out of my neck, slamming her heel into my crotch as if I was a truculent mule. She did not, however, drive that blade straight through my brain, which I viewed as progress. Finally, when I had gotten myself to my knees, her foot still whacking away, the rest of her squeezing and puffing as if she was giving birth, I finally took hold of the strangling arm and cinched it far enough away from my windpipe that I could speak, and also breathe.

"Can we stop this charade now?" I coughed. "I'm onto you. You overplayed your hand."

She paused in her efforts, then lay there panting on my shoulders like a living fox cape.

"What do you mean?"

"The act went too far," I said. "It got too mean-spirited. I should have seen it the last time."

"I'm very mean-spirited; it's no act."

I shook my head, which caused her, quick as a blink, to retract the blade from my ear, as I knew she would.

"You're mean, but not this mean," I replied. "I know the sound of somebody trying to convince themselves."

With that she swiftly, and unambiguously, gave up her assault. Sliding her weight off, she allowed me to slowly regain my feet, and once I was standing, we faced each other. The room was still unlit, and though my eyes had largely recovered from the lighter sparks, we were, to each other, little more than faint sketches upon the canvass of gloom.

"I think there's something wrong with me," she mumbled, sounding both disturbed and perplexed.

"There's a *lot* wrong with you. But this thing happens to be one of your few virtues."

"What is it?"

"The same condition I have," I replied. "We're both incapable of killing each other."

She took a long time to contemplate this, her svelte outline expanding and constricting many full cycles in breathy muteness. Finally, she asked:

"Can it work?"

"Can what work?"

"This." Her dim finger joggled back and forth between us.

"You mean intimacy...based solely on the inability to murder each other?" I said. "It doesn't sound promising, but when it comes down to it, it may be all I'm good for."

And that was it, a single wry comment, a careless red scarf before the bull, and the launching of a new, mad paradigm was upon her, upon me too, for that's exactly where she hurled herself. Like a murky smudge against the even murkier backdrop, Shade of Night leapt forward, her hands grabbing my collar, the sheer determination of her charge causing me to stumble straight into the bar out of fear. No matter what the circumstances, notwithstanding any niceties that may have preceded it, the sight of this woman flinging herself in my direction was, ever and always, a thing of dread.

The lean fingers of her left hand fastened on to my shirt, jagging the neckline up to my chin, as her other hand came around to claw the hair on the back of my head, and these fierce appendages, now blessedly stiletto-free, went to work imprisoning me in new ways. She had hopped off the floor so that her knees clinched my ribs, and with the petite power in her upper body, she slammed our two mouths together. There was a boney clacking of teeth, also a broken fingernail (discovered later in my tunic like a shiny, magenta beetle), but the intended objective was achieved, for that wild tongue of hers penetrated straight through my defenses and began to worm around inside my mouth.

I tried to push her away, succeeding only in a brief decoupling. She clung to me throughout, her knees pinching, her hands scrabbling.

"I have my own terms…" I sputtered, my head turned sideways.

"What terms…?" she breathed as she continued to ram that mouth at me.

"You can't abuse me anymore. No more terrorizing."

She directed the force of her lips against the side of my face, puckering away at my cheek.

"Maybe just a little...?" she asked.

"No, no more. I'll probably have to seek counselling as it is. Plus, my chin is going to swell like an egg, and I can feel the blood dripping inside my ear."

"I know," she whispered huskily. "Shade was very wicked tonight, but she'll fix it."

And she kissed her way to my exposed left ear, at which point she thrust the dubious healing properties of her tongue straight inside, licking the blood and jabbing at the wound like a new, fleshy stiletto. I found the sensation revolting, and I turned my face back towards her to make it stop.

"So...you promise to stop attacking me?" I gabbled through a new mouth-on-mouth offensive.

"I promise," she gabbled back.

"And you'll be nice to me instead?"

She aggressively kissed a bit longer.

"That's going a bit far," she murmured, "but at least I won't hurt you."

And these, I'm afraid, were the terms I accepted. I tried to free myself so that I could head to the bath chamber and wash up, but she wouldn't hear of it.

"I'm the one who made you wet yourself," she said, unbuckling my pants and yanking them down, "so I must do penance for my sins."

And with that, she unleashed her frightening mouth upon me. My initial reaction to this was muddled. Above and beyond my acute embarrassment about my unclean condition, and also the memory of this woman's erotic trances, which might, at some overly stimulated juncture, result in dire consequences involving those teeth, I had been trained not to expect this from a woman. Terza viewed it as categorically demeaning and even went so far as to instruct other women not to engage. (I did find it interesting, though, that Terza had no problem when the roles were reversed, which is how I spent at least a quarter of my time making love to her.) Shade, too, I came to learn, rarely assumed this position, though tonight was "apology night," so everything was on the table, including me.

She tugged me by my vulnerable parts up onto the surface of the bar, so that she wouldn't have to kneel down. I complied, after which she quickly got back to work, and all the while this dreadful thing started to happen. Slowly but surely, I began to enjoy myself. My lustful partner in crime felt this, which encouraged her all the more. Paralyzed by flaccid anxiety the last time, I was, this night, unhindered by the threat of castration and death, and I can't tell you what wonders this did for my libido. Apart from my initial carnal encounter with Shade's alter ego, "Jisselle," every moment I had spent with this woman, or even thinking about her—which was quite a lot—had been thoroughly contaminated by fear. To suddenly have that removed was nothing short of a panacea.

But there was more going on here than that. I could palpably feel Shade's happiness, could detect—in her touch, her sounds, the buoyant motions of her brow—how relieved she was to stop making war, both with me and herself. Her emotional surrender was a tangible thing, and her desire for me even more so, to the point where it swelled straight up my body in a wave of delicious warmth.

And the fun didn't end on the bar. Unafraid Vazeer was an astonishingly virile Vazeer, and when the first round was done in the kitchen, we moved to new locations—the sofa, the guest room bed, the living room floor, and then, on a stimulated whim, we slid together through Shade's secret hole. Small and round, with plaster edges filed and coated with clear varnish, the passage into the next apartment seemed like something a fairy-tale gnome might use (or maybe a cobra). Through we went, giving me a chance to observe the sparse dimensions of my dwelling's new wing, but only briefly, for Shade wanted to take full advantage of my revived faculties.

Our night eventually ended there, in Shade's bed, a narrow but comfortable iron-framed piece that squeaked a bit but was otherwise serviceable. And I must have done an adequate job, for I sent her into screaming, moaning fits that guaranteed multiple tenant complaints in the morning. Dawn was getting set to break when we finally finished, and thoroughly saturated with each other, we collapsed in an entwined heap. From there we drifted off into heavy slumber, and I feel confident in saying that neither of us feared we would wake up alone the next morning, or dead, at the hands of the other.

And in this way, I began my sordid and wildly erogenous affair with the Empire's most notorious contract killer.

PART

II

13

FERAL THING

I've got a problem with women.

Over the years I have attracted some exciting ones, and sealing the deal at the critical moment lies within my skill set. However, the statement stands. When all is said and done, when the romantic ledger is picked over, there's no way to conclude that I make good decisions when it comes to love.

All those years ago, standing in my smuggling skiff on the night of the infamous Gaff, I can't pretend that I didn't know what I was doing. With just the slightest pivot away from selfishness, I would have recognized that Terza Falconbrow needed—desperately needed—for me to be just a little bigger and more evolved than I had yet been in the three years of our relationship. Had I been capable of this, I might this very day be the proud father of a rambunctious little Selene.

After that came Adelyn: appealing, levelheaded Adelyn, madly likeable at the very least, and possibly lovable, who broke with her fellows to come to my defense. There, she joined the growing ranks of benevolent Vazeer rescuers, a society that has far more members than its namesake deserves. It's true she turned me down, but shouldn't I have selected that occasion (and not all the others) to display some obstinance? Why didn't I keep at it, woo her endlessly until she finally gave in? Instead, I became the perfectly differential gentleman, at the perfectly wrong moment.

This topic troubles me: how a virtue becomes a vice if poorly timed, and a character flaw a benefit, if the opposite occurs. I wasn't an appropriate match for Nascinthé of Levell, I knew that. Every new piece of evidence—tales of the mythic Spellbinder, the woman's friendship with a future Empress, stars and brackets upon the pages of *I, Asadeissia*, which possibly reflected some broader life plan of which Sullward could only be a brief, criminal hiatus—these things only confirmed that she was better off without me.

And yet, why did I choose *this* moment to be such an altruist? A little self-interest might have gone a long way. Droden Sailwain was right, you don't just leave it to chance that a woman like Nascinthé will return. You go and get her, you make sure she doesn't slowly forget or rethink you. Exchange her contraceptive herbs with parsley, make it so that, plump with child, terrified of the broader world, she would become desperate and needful, incapable of navigating the many threats that were everywhere, and against which you were the sole defense. A craftier emotional schemer would have come up with a plan like this.

Let the record show, I did none of those things, with any of those women, and what was the result? I wound up in the deadly arms of a contract Finisher, of whom I was one of the contracts. Lest you think this was but a single, ill-considered incident, it wasn't. Shade of Night and I became a thing, an actual thing, and while it's very hard to tell you what sort of "thing" it was, we did, both of us, become deliriously infatuated with each other. And the logistics of the affair were ideal. I, who had never managed to exchange keys with Terza during our three years together, was now essentially living with Shade. My former tormentor had become my suitemate, and with the exception of the two and a half magical days I had shared with Nascinthé of Levell aboard the Elena's Guile, I'd never spent more uninterrupted time with a woman in my life. I'd definitely never had intimacies more often, since Shade and I literally couldn't get enough of each other, and for several days running, my new double suite became the soiled fairgrounds of an intoxicated carnal derby.

All rooms were permissible, no swatch of upholstery safe. We behaved like adolescents; we were, on a very real level, out of our minds, and my use of the word "intoxicated" was not figurative, for we spent more than a third of the time drunk. We were other things too, since Shade was a regular user of nithrin, and also kettle dust—a narcotic that shared some of the euphoric qualities of Cojis, without quite the heavy load of addiction. Both of these I tried and, somewhat disturbingly, liked. Many hours I frittered away in numb-lipped, enraptured sprawl, studying wall cracks and wood knots as if they were Oulmaen hieroglyphs, pondering deep riddles such as, "if a man can find contentment right now, flopped in this chair, without restoring anything, is there any purpose to struggling so hard?" and, "why don't wash basins come with little grills on the drain to keep women's hair out?" The latter pertained to the new reality of having a housemate with long tresses; the former was a reaction to having anything resembling common sense, and when I caught myself thinking it one afternoon, for literally hours on end, I promptly swore off the kettle dust.

But, when all was said and done, the real intoxication was Shade herself, who, in very short order, I came to crave to a degree that was even more frightening than the narcotics. It reached the point where, if she was gone from the apartment for several hours, possibly not to return that evening, I came to miss her horribly. I'm not even sure where this was all coming from. Why did I desire this particular woman so intensely, when I had managed, to one degree or another, to keep all those others at bay? Possibly, it was no more complicated than the fact that Shade wanted me too. She violently wanted me and was willing to go to extreme lengths to keep me, effectively placing me under house arrest early in our sensual proceedings.

"You are not to leave this apartment unless I give you permission," she said. "My nice streak will end if you defy me on this."

Ostensibly, this rule was to protect me, and also Shade's reputation, for she was now willing to commit the most egregious breach of Finisher protocol of her entire career. Shade planned to find a swarthy-skinned corpse somewhere in the waring Lower City, or else create one, and then chop it up and bring several choice pieces to the proffer's people. At that point she would receive the back half of her contract and, far more importantly, make me officially "finished" in the eyes of the Labyrinth.

"Do you understand how much you must mean to me, Lashy, if I would do this disgraceful thing?"

I absolutely did. After weeks of thinking I'd made the dumbest mistake of my life by sparing Shade of Night, I now began to wonder if it wasn't my finest masterstroke. Above and beyond my personal need for her—details coming—she had now given my operation the perfect cover, for with the most defiant of the Shadow Bidders presumably dead and diced, and with Terza and company laying off of their slanderous scrawlings, Ulan Gueritus was likely to remove his sights completely from the world of contract operatives. He had already recruited a number of the men. The others had scattered, and (as he had explained to me at length at The Crossbiter) he did not trust the women enough to employ them. His attention would now be fixed entirely on bringing Count Halsin Tygean to heel, plus putting a fair amount of effort towards retrieving sunken merchandise. Both endeavors would probably take a couple weeks at the least, thereby creating a wonderful recess—time in which to ready my team, but also to lose myself in the wiry arms of my eccentric lover. That one became a top priority.

As a sensual being, Shade of Night was unmatched, even by Terza, who did not lack for passion. It was no exaggeration to say Shade was ravenous for me, and I for her, and I quickly attuned myself so completely to her needs that I could send her into states that could only be described as rapturous. My own rapture was largely a function of pushing her across those boundaries, since it's hard to quantify what this did for my self-esteem. The net result was startlingly erotic exchanges that left us both panting and sweating and crudely entangled, like a huge, squashed insectoid, its dusky feelers and appendages twitching helplessly.

However, carnal pleasure was only one piece of the puzzle. I actually came to like her, or more accurately, I was fascinated by her, for she really was a unique creature. That weird inauthenticity I had experienced when she was playing "Jisselle" (terribly, now that my official review is in) and also the psychotic sadism she mustered in her efforts to want to hurt me when she didn't really want to hurt me, or not much, were both gone. What was left behind wasn't exactly sweet, but she was appealing, for her emotions were raw, her mind sharp, her needs intense, and she did, for some strange reason, consider me a kindred spirit.

"We are a pair of misfits in this world, Lashy," she said to me in one of our post-coital, perspiring heaps. "None can define us. None can tie us down."

Actually, Shade did once tie me down to her iron bed, and though she ran her blade over my naked form much of that time and claimed that this had been her plan all along—to get me helpless so that she could carve me for the proffer—she was, as I have stated, a dreadful actress. I wasn't particularly fooled, though I did spend several hours in that condition and was not untied until I fully satisfied her three times, which was, for some unstated, superstitious reason, the magic number of release.

As for the particulars of this arrangement, they were, again, ideal. The only one privy to my new relationship was Cad, who was officially introduced to "Jisselle" on one of his stop-byes, and who couldn't have been more teased by the situation. Shade and I covered our secret hole with a tapestry, but Cad saw the trappings of our dual existence everywhere in my messy apartment, plus smelled the nithrin, as well as subtler, more provocative odors, and the whole thing was clear as day to him—the whole thing, minus Shade's true identity, which he must never know. He was also instructed not to tell anyone about us, especially Radrin Blackstar, who would likely attempt to end our relationship in every sense of the word. Cad swore this to me on his life.

As for Radrin, and the rest of my team, they were hard at work. According to Cad, Blackstar was busy scouting the Lower City and trying to gain information on the status of the simmering war. The word was, full-blown conflict had not yet erupted, while at the same time (and this may have been connected to the prior observation), the Raving Blade's staff had been seen moving most of the furniture out of The Crossbiter Tavern. As to where they were headed next, Radrin told Cad he wasn't sure, but he had noted a great deal of activity lately in the old Kaennamin Academy building, perhaps my favorite edifice in all of Sullward. It was unclear whose men were in there, but whoever they were, they appeared to be working around the clock.

In the meantime, Terza and Adelyn were out recruiting

Shadow Bidders, while the ever-slippery Heshna was discreetly trying to locate Coljin Helmgrinder, to whom she would pass an even more discreet meeting invitation. And Cad, perhaps the busiest of the bunch, was managing it all. How he enjoyed this role, my protégé—playing point on a burgeoning Narrow Bid, coordinating the activities of Finishers, Blades, Masques, Eyes, whisking between Terza's store, Adelyn's apartment, prearranged meeting sites in Dockside where Radrin gave him updates, and finally back to my smoke-choked den of hedonism, to which he shuttled a steady flow of food, wine, and nithrin. There he got to flirt with Jisselle, who knew just how to reduce him to salivating fits. My new lover often invited the poor lad in to share a pipe or a drink with her, and when she finally sent him on his way, she made sure to deliver a slow, sensual kiss, just off his lips, which no doubt had him rethinking his fantasy marriage with Terza Falconbrow.

As for my own coming proposal, a hateful marriage of convenience, there was at last a positive development. I had promised Radrin I would make a genuine effort to recruit Coljin Helmgrinder to our cause, and I now learned that the huge Blade apparently wasn't ingratiating himself with his new family. Helmgrinder (soon to be "Baron Ujendus," of the Gueritus line) had managed to enlist a half dozen other Contract Blades, but he had taken little part in the war himself. That vicious puncture wound I had given him in the Shadowbiter duel, along with his already injured leg (aggravated during our fight), made him resistant to engage in battle until fully healed. Having known Col for many years now, one thing the man *wasn't* was brittle, or squeamish about his injuries, so I had to interpret this resistance as something deeper. My guess was that Col didn't like the idea of being used as the Raving Blade's attack dog and was wondering at what point he would be granted his fancy title, and the command of troops, and, most of all, a new, shiny Ripening Hall, filled to the brim with plunder. What did he *think* his new responsibilities would entail? When I said the man lacked imagination, I wasn't kidding.

Needless to say, all of this worked in our favor, and on the third day of my sensual sequestration, Cad brought me the news I had been waiting for, and also dreading. Heshna had finally been able to approach Col unseen, slipping him a message that directed him to a secure locale where he was met by Adelyn. Draped in the sultry disguise of a prostitute, Adelyn laid out just enough to make Col interested—hints of heavy financial renumeration, along with reclaimed dignity and autonomy—if he would only listen to what I had to say. To this he agreed, and our meeting was set for the next morning in a portion of the Lower City that was always deserted in the early hours.

It was set, then, the heinous chore I had been anticipating for over a week, and to take my mind off of it, I threw myself wholeheartedly into my new source of repose. Shade and I really pushed the limits the evening before the Helmgrinder meeting, and when we were finally exhausted from our endeavors, we lay together in a gratified embrace.

"Tell me about this one," I said, tracing my fingers down the sweaty freckles of her back to a set of writings that ran straight into the crack of her buttocks. I had, in our time together, elicited a handful of divulgences about her past contracts, which were recorded in swirling fragments of foreign letters all over her flesh. The script itself was a language called *Ojodszik*, a remote Western tongue used primarily by desert traders, and which Shade had modified into her own shorthand code. She was never too specific about her targets, though from the bits I had gleaned, these men were generally criminals, quite a few concentrated in Sullward, but just as many in the Midlands and Kaszia.

I prodded the back tattoo a second time, trying to spur an answer.

"Ummnnnhh," came a deep larynx noise as she shifted to lie with her head on my chest. "To tell that one, Lashy, is to tell everything. Are you sure you're ready for everything?"

"I feel ready."

"Be careful what you wish for."

For a while we lounged in silence, and in that time, I pondered the hazards of probing too deeply into this person's past, which was likely to uncover things that I would wish, later, had not been uncovered. Still, suffused by the warmth of the moment, I craved closeness, and I continued to encourage her. At last, toying with the hair on my chest, she hoarsely breathed it.

"The name running out of my ass is *Uzgjeet Nuzrin Tzangmat*," she said. "A smuggler, just like you, who happened to be my father."

Another period of extended silence followed. In that interim I recalled my first meeting with Shade in Landry's Tavern, when one of my offhand comments sent her plunging into a brief, moody withdrawal. "Your mother will certainly warn you about fascination with men like me," I had said. To which she responded: "Doubtful. I myself am the product of just such a fascination." This reply, mysterious and burdened, was obviously a reference to the name tattooed ignominiously in her posterior.

"Remember the things I threatened to do to your manhood a few nights ago?" she finally said. "I did those things to him. That's how Uzgjeet died, prickless and drooling into the muddy soil of the grasslands. I even kept the member, desiccated in a pouch, until I decided it would be difficult to cart such trophies around.

After all, I was only sixteen, and I planned to have a very long career, so the writings were the more practical choice."

Now Shade slid up to my face, softly kissing my neck and cheek along the way.

"Having heard that," she whispered, throatily, "do you still seek these tender confessions?"

I'll admit, I didn't love the story so far, though I knew there must be more to it than she had told.

"Did he abuse you?" I asked. "Is that why you chose that particular revenge?"

"Not me," she answered. "He seduced and raped my unwed mother. I came into this world as a bastard thing, tossed out of a wealthy family into the nomadic wastes where my mother and I fell prey to all manner of wicked men. So many wicked men... and all had their way with us."

More silence, onerous and swelling. I couldn't tell if Shade was done talking or just getting started. Either way, I did have to wonder if this was the first time she had ever shared these things.

"We were finally captured by a rich warlord," she said at last. "My mother was placed in his harem as a concubine. I was too young, and also my body was covered in freckles and birthmarks, which my new master detested...the polluted legacy of the rapist. The warlord tried to turn me into a household servant, but I was angry, such an angry little girl. So, he came up with a different idea. I was trained in the Finishing arts, starting at that sweet age. No childhood for me, Lashy; by the time I was a teen, I was a practiced Finisher. *His* Finisher, to kill his enemies when they were drunk and half-naked, running their hands up my dress. That became my specialty."

"I've seen you do much more than that."

"When I have to. My education was thorough, including

all forms of combat, though it is better to play to one's strengths. I do not have the size to take on a large man in a sword fight. I must always skew things in my favor."

Again, we mutely lay, entwined and now involved, and while I could feel the charring glower of her indignity and, below that, an even hotter hatred, I also sensed the suffering presence of the victimized girl. Like me, she had been robbed of her childhood, though her robbery had been much worse than mine, and it had spawned darker things.

"All react differently to pain," she murmured. "The warlord's instructors could not control me, turn me into an obedient killer. When I grew older, I was ready to slit my master's throat and flee with my mother to the East, to the shores of the ocean where we might start a new life; however, my mother did not wish for this. She had grown comfortable in her silks, bringing pleasure to her lord, and she begged me to spare him. So I did. I left them to each other, and from what I hear, they are together still. Fat and happy, my mother has become madam of the harem, reigning over the household like a queen. All the while, her sweet daughter wanders the world as a vengeful ghost, writing a tale of death across her flesh."

Now Shade went up on an elbow and gazed down upon me with those dark oblong eyes, flecked and brooding.

"So, you tell me, Lashy. Between my mother and me, who's the wisest? The woman who meekly submitted and found her way to happiness? Or the girl who can submit to no one, forgives nothing, and finds her only satisfaction in toying with wicked men before she sends them groveling to the grave?"

I allowed myself some time to truly contemplate this.

"Was it ever a choice for you?"

"Never."

"In that case, there's nothing left to ponder. Have you ever shared this with anybody?"

"One person…never a man."

"Why me, then? Why tell it to this particular man—spare him too—when all the others have been sent from this world?"

"Oooooohhhhhh," Shade moaned, and she flopped back on the bed, raking her fingernails through the sheets. "Yes, Lashy, *that* is the real question, the great mystery, to me as well as you. You must help me solve it."

"I can't."

"Yes…you can."

And now she crawled back on me, all the while breathing warm, fervent air into my face, scented, it seemed, with desert tartness and remembrance.

"When they contracted me a decade ago," she continued, "your colleagues, to put an end to you after the Gaff, I thought 'This one is perfect for Shade: a cocky smuggler like my rapist father, someone I will seduce and then humiliate before he dies.' But then the contract was cancelled, and afterwards, as I kept watching you, you did not play your role. You sweetly tended my plant, you sat alone at night, reading, and in the daytime, you went shopping for pretty trinkets on your favorite street. At the same time, the deadly stories about you piled up, and I could not make the two things match.

"When this latest contract came, I again had trouble; each of our meetings provoked me. I could not get you to strike me, or abuse me, which is what I wanted, so that I could take my revenge. When we lay together for the first time, it got worse. You were a sensitive lover, who went to endless lengths to please me, thinking little of your own needs. You were not being Uzgjeet—whose final act was to try and rape his anonymous daughter when she wandered as a young stranger into his camp.

"I pride myself in being a professional, Lashy, and I was determined to complete your contract, even though it was going to bring me terrible grief. But then something strange happened. Your Finisher creep arrived, and when he gave you the upper hand, you let me go. You did not retaliate, as all those other wicked men would have. Knowing what I was, knowing that I would surely come back and try again, it was more important that you free me.

"You, Lashy, are nothing I have ever seen. There are plenty of harmless boys in this world, like your Cad. They are useless to me, for no one ever puts out contracts on them, and they bore me to tears. But you are not harmless. You are a killer like me, a savage who will fight anyone, face any odds. I have heard every one of your stories, including your famous duel with the big Gosian warrior you are going to meet tomorrow. Even *I* would not accept a contract on that one, and yet you fought him to a standstill. There is no man that can beat you, yet despite that, you won't harm a hair on my head. You are always looking for new ways to satisfy me, which you do better than anyone ever. Why is all this the case? You must explain it to me, what makes you this impossible thing that you are?"

For quite a while I just lay there, lolling beneath the acute glare of that irresolvable question. Finally, I shrugged.

"I like freckles, I guess."

The laugh that exploded from her was as unbridled and uproarious as anything I had heard, a mad drumroll, pounding out into the cozy quiet of the bedroom air. It was not now, and never would be, a melodious sound; however, I relished it—its clouting racket—and I felt my spirit swell with the noise. In no uncertain terms, I was besotted with her, which made two of us, for she literally clamped herself upon me, unleashing such a storm of covetous affection that my whole body shuddered beneath the assault. And, surprise, surprise, my spent resources were not totally spent, her satisfied needs not entirely satisfied, and we threw ourselves again into another round of amorous athletics.

But something was different this time. A new dynamic was present, spawned of confidences shared, burdens unloaded, an implausible amity between the dazzling spider and her delicious prey. We felt things for each other. I truly cared about this damaged, dangerous woman, and I palpably grasped how much she cared for me. Shade of Night wasn't my soul mate. She wasn't any man's soul mate, and I suspected, somewhere in the very back of my mind, that I was hoping to defy the odds with a feral thing, that I might turn it into a family pet. The beast would surely revert one day and devour its owner in his living room, then lounge contentedly by the carcass, waiting to be scratched behind the ears.

Not tonight, however. The claws retracted, the teeth were sheathed, and I felt myself pulled ever deeper into a warmth and fondness that no man, especially one with a history like mine, had any business refusing.

14

HATEFUL ALLIES

I met Adelyn the next morning at the northernmost boundary of her neighborhood. There, just past the point where MidRiven made a sharp, upward turn and narrowed, a small slice of Westward abutted the Outer Ring. Without needing to cross a canal, we wound our way into the fringes of that old, heavily damaged artists' district that Radrin and I had traversed after my meeting with Count Tygean. These days, nobody had a particular name for the place, though back in the time of the Old Calendar, it had been wryly called "the Cacophony." Musicians, opera singers, and orators practiced for hours on end in these quaint apartments, as did playwrights and actors who spewed all manner of imperious verbiage. Their noises could not eclipse entirely the thumping of dancers, or the grinding squeak of pottery wheels; and only the poor painters, glassblowers, and sculptors had to suffer all of this in silence, though perhaps they tossed down a heavy implement or two, just to earn their place in the confederacy of noise.

This morning, the area was as quiet as a crypt, as it had been for two centuries. In preparation for this errand, I had made elaborate vows to my beautiful jailer that I would take the most covert route possible, and that I would not, under any circumstances, engage in frivolous side errands (I still hadn't been back to Merejin's shop, and didn't anticipate solving those esoteric mysteries any time soon). I was officially "finished" now, so it wouldn't be good for either of us if I was spotted walking about. The prior day, Shade had located what she believed to be my perfect stand-in corpse, and from this body she had offered choice pieces to the proffer's agents. Additionally, she had brought them the same hat I wore on the night I met Gueritus, and, as far as she could tell, this confirmation package had been accepted without suspicion.

"But that is not to say they were happy with me," Shade had said, clearly agitated. "I should have gotten it done sooner, they said. They think I'm off my game, which I am, in so many ways."

"I know," I replied, "and I have promised to compensate you for what you have done. Not only will I match the back half of your contract, I'll match the whole thing, earning you double on this job. And the proffer will be dead within a week, along with his agents, so none will know."

"I'll know."

"What will you know? That you got to collect all that money and collect me at the same time? That sounds like a good deal to me."

"You better continue to make it one."

And with that honied sentiment, I was ushered out the door, hatted and cloaked and dressed in the most uninspired garments from my limited apartment wardrobe. When I arrived a half hour later at our rendezvous point, I found Adelyn garbed in her own unobtrusive apparel—a dark brown cloak with the cowl pulled up and tall leather boots of a matching color. She was rather brown overall, as her outfit pulled forth her Gosian skin tones, which I found lovely. "Dark," in my world, had always meant exotic, and now, on account of my domestic situation, it was ravishing.

"You should have gone with gray," I said by way of greeting. "Brown is too flattering."

"And you should have gone with 'Hello.' Your flattery is too obvious."

Adelyn took my arm, withstanding my flirtations, as was her way.

"Come, let's see if we can go double our army," she said, pulling me in the direction of the meeting site, which was several blocks away.

"Is it that bad?" I asked, stepping onto the first of the heavily damaged Cacophony streets. Over a quarter of the cobbles were cracked or missing entirely, making careless strolling a hazard. The flood waters had largely receded, but because of recent rains, oily rectangles of water glinted in the many granite gaps.

"Well, we have a total of three Blades at this point," she replied, making a careful leap over a bad section. "We also have the toughest female Runner in the Labyrinth."

"Getta."

I didn't bother to inflect it as a question, for there was only a small handful of active female Grell Runners, and, among them, Getta Reed was the only true bruiser in the bunch. Adelyn confirmed it.

"Col is probably equal to that entire group combined," she continued. "Which is why I consider today's task a double."

"Should I even ask who the Blades are?"

"Best if you don't. Terza will be offended if you criticize her list, and I'll be obliged to tell her how you reacted. Some faith at this point would go a long way."

Up ahead, a sizable deposit of detritus had collected, including a long, rotted ceiling joist, a mound of roof tiles, and a heavily chipped statue leg; and then suddenly, out of this jumble, I saw a small, gray form emerge. Heshna the Seer deposited herself in front of the pile, looking, for all intents and purposes, like a heap of debris herself.

"He's in there," she said, pointing towards one of the ruined buildings. "He's alone, and the area is deserted."

Now that we were close, I saw that there was a contemptuous little scowl on those shrunken lips.

"What?" I demanded. "What is it today?"

Heshna was remarkably well camouflaged for this outing, her gray cloak such a good match to the surrounding stonework it might easily have been peeled from one of the walls. She had her hood up, obscuring the dismal stream of her dirty blond hair and throwing murky splotches across her eyes.

"As if you don't know," she said.

"Know what?"

I probably shouldn't ask this. Adelyn was standing right there, and I had no clue what might come out of Heshna's mouth; but then again, I assumed she told Terza and Adelyn everything anyway.

"All these years," Heshna said, "and never once have I seen it happen."

All these years certainly sent my mind spinning back to days of spiteful yonder, and I prepared myself, at this most inopportune juncture, to receive some gross, childhood denunciation, possibly with occult undertones. But Heshna meant something else, a rather surprising something else.

"Why?" she continued, her flesh worn and colorless but her mud-like eyes strangely enlivened. "Why is it that she finishes all her other targets perfectly, never with a problem. But you...she not only spares you, but now you become her lover. How does this sort of thing happen with you?"

This was a shock on several fronts, and not just for me. Adelyn displayed some perplexed fascination, coupled with a "what's this talk of lovers?" forehead hike. Her confusion made it clear that Heshna the Seer did not, in fact, tell her everything. The question was, how the hell did *everything* keep winding up in my Brood sister's head?

"Even with all the damage you do, people like you, Brood brother. They always like you, and I wonder why that is. It seems like a relevant question."

"They don't always like me, Heshna," I responded, to what I didn't feel was even remotely a relevant question. "The man inside that building doesn't like me, which is why I brought Adelyn with me this morning. And, how the hell do you know so much about my personal life?"

"They do like you, though," Heshna went on. "You need to work hard to make them *not* like you."

"So do you, Heshna. You work harder at it than anyone I know."

"Okay, okay," said Adelyn, and she stepped in between us, hands diplomatically raised. "There's a lot here, obviously, but now's not the time."

Around us the realm of deceased noise remained quiet, in spite of the commotion we had brought. The two sides of our broken street were a ravine of glassless windows, fractured statuary, and bleeding rust stains. In several places, there were holes in the granite walls, beyond which lay dim, mildewed nests of clutter. This had never been a promising neighborhood for beggars, so I had to assume our sibling spat went unobserved. But who really knew, since our vaunted lookout on this operation had exchanged her talents as an Eye for a new aptitude with her mouth.

"Where's this all coming from, Heshna?" I asked, pushing up against Adelyn's cautioning palm. "You've said more to me in the last two meetings than you did in the last four decades."

"Heshna's just cautious, Vazeer," Adelyn said, resuming her diplomacy role. "Remember, she's never worked with you before."

Technically, this was true. Heshna had done preliminary work on a couple of my bids, but we had never been active in the field together. Still, there was obviously so much more going on than that, and I found myself struggling to identify the inciting moment for this new verbosity. When Terza had humiliated me on the floor of her shop a week earlier, Heshna's spoken contribution, threatening and prescient, had been uttered in the same aloof monotone that had marked all of our previous interactions. Since then, lively self-expression had ruled, with years of implicit resentment bursting forth. I could think of only one relevant change that had occurred in that time, and quite suddenly, the whole thing started to make sense to me.

"The two of you work together?"

Adelyn, still wedged tactfully in the middle, pivoted her gaze back and forth, clearly wondering if "the two of you" and "work together" included her. But I wasn't looking at Adelyn, and neither was Heshna.

"We do."

"That's how come she knows so much about me?" I asked, starting to feel a bit queasy. "Knows when I'll be out of the apartment, when I'm taking a walk, a nap…a piss?"

"All of that and more," Heshna responded, her nasty scowl picking up a trace of derisive humor. "Shade of Night is good on her own, but with me she becomes unstoppable. Finishing skills are most effective if you know everything your target is going to do ahead of time."

"Were you aware of this arrangement, Adelyn?" I asked.

"Yes."

"And you, Brood sister…you're happy playing a Finisher's role in Hell's Labyrinth, because that's what you essentially are."

Heshna shrugged.

"Shade and I refer to it as 'taking out the garbage.' If I'm ever uncomfortable with a target, I recuse myself."

"Did you recuse yourself last week when *I* was the garbage?"

Here my Brood sister took a moment, an unnerving moment for all of us, and I saw Adelyn shift fractionally closer to me, with her body tensed in anticipation of violence.

"No, I didn't recuse myself, Brood brother. Do you want to know why?"

What I *wanted* was to clamp my hands around Heshna's little neck and throttle her like a chicken. But Adelyn was in the way, and I was purportedly on this mission to turn enemies into allies, not the other way around.

"I think I get the gist. You hate my guts, always have, and you relished the idea of having your vicious partner toss me out with the rest of the trash."

"I don't like you, brother, that part's true. But I stayed with the contract because it was the only way to warn you…which I did. I've never warned anyone before, not once in the thirteen years of working with Shade. She still doesn't know, though you'll probably tell her."

Oh, this was a lot, a whole hell of a lot, and I found myself desperately trying to corral my anger before it went into a bloody frenzy, like a pit bull.

"That was a deliberately misleading warning," I said. "If you could have brought yourself to utter just one more word that night at Terza's shop—'female' comes to mind—you would have alerted me to the actual threat."

In fairness, Heshna didn't realize the degree to which I had believed that Radrin Blackstar was the one on my tail, so the gender distinction may not have seemed as relevant to her.

"Maybe it was an incomplete warning, but it was enough, enough for anyone else. As Terza keeps telling you, you're stubborn. And stupid."

"Alright now," Adelyn said, intervening a second time and swinging her whole body in my direction, possibly ready to tackle me. "Seer, please do another perimeter. We can work all this out later."

Heshna, likely sensing that she was now in danger, suddenly whisked away with that preternatural quickness that I never quite expected from her. I noted only the direction she started in, but she dodged behind Adelyn and moved at such a startling pace that I had trouble determining if it was a doorway or hole in the wall that had finally engulfed her. All of this reminded me that Heshna's slovenly, shapeless appearance was part of a greater trickery, since she—like all members of Holod Deadskiff's Brood—was an assiduously trained specimen who could be quite dangerous if backed into a corner. Of course, with allies like Terza Falconbrow and Shade of Night, all Heshna needed to do was escape an attack, and retribution on her behalf would soon follow.

I would have liked some time to collect myself. How useful that might have been: just a few friendly moments alone with Adelyn, her calming hand on my arm, those magically balanced cinnamon-colored features filling my gaze. But something very different occurred, and I lay the blame squarely at the feet of my hateful Brood sister for fouling up my mood at just the wrong moment.

"You make one hell of a racket for a dead man, Vazeer the Lash," he said, stepping out of the ruined doorway, his dark volume filling the space behind Adelyn. "I try to imagine how peaceful this place might be if only that foolish tongue of yours would stop wagging."

Sometimes, you forget how much you hate somebody until you lay eyes upon them again. This is how it was when Coljin Helmgrinder stepped out onto the broken cobbles of our little ghost town, and I'm certain the feeling was mutual. Attuned as I was just then to being hated, it was really no trouble to detect Col's fuming cloud as it rolled over me.

"What makes a tongue foolish, Col," I replied, "is when it spews all sorts of boastful trash but can't back any of it up. Your last attempt to silence me was a failure."

"But the next one won't be," he said, and now he came forward from the ruined building, forcing Adelyn to spin and square up against the new, larger threat to her diplomacy.

"Col, stop," she said, in a voice that wasn't loud, but which, in contrast to her customary affability, sounded harsh. "We're not here to settle old scores. We're here to forge a new partnership that will benefit all of us."

Col showed no sign of listening, but when he reached Adelyn's outstretched palms, he didn't swat them aside and instead allowed her to slowly press his chest to a halt. There he stood, staring at me from a few feet away.

My erstwhile dueling partner looked even scarier than usual today, and this had much to do with my own contributions. The wound I had delivered to his left cheek was quite a wicked thing, a chasmal gash from the dark, peninsular front of his cheekbone all the way down to the very back of his jaw, and even across a small section of neck. He hadn't stitched it, though I could tell from the oily sheen that healing liniments had been applied. Irony of ironies, this wound charted the exact opposite course as my own notorious facial décor, though his was straight as a stiletto and mine a hooking claw, to match the two implements involved. If I was feeling generous towards him, I might have told him that this injury was soon to be one hell of an impressive scar, which would only enhance his powers of intimidation. Instead, I said the following:

"Have your whores started charging double yet, to put up with that ugly face? And how's the puncture wound? I'm guessing that's why you're here…looking to offset the costs of the injuries I gave you."

"Vazeer, stop it!" Adelyn said.

Col, whom I sincerely thought might use this as a pretext to attack, smiled instead, which must have stung like crazy, or at least I hoped it did.

"No, I'm having no problems with money, Vazeer," he said, with a hefty shake of his colossal head. "Remember, I was paid a small fortune in Gosian Diamonds recently."

Adelyn, seeing that Col wasn't quite ready to attack, angled her body so that she could look back and forth between us. This allowed me to observe Col's form in its entirety and note that he was dressed in a full regalia of black leather armor with steel plates woven in at the chest and stomach. He also wore a voluminous, dark green cloak, with a silver brooch at the collar, shaped like a hammer.

"Come to think of it, Vazeer," Col continued, "you were also paid in Gosian Diamonds. When Adelyn told me about Count Tygean's offer, she showed me a couple of similar stones, just to entice me. I am very familiar with these gems, since I worked in a Gosian mine as a boy, and it is interesting to me how much this new batch looked like the ones you and I were given—the exact same cut and size. Strange, that Count Tygean is paying people in this currency when we're certain that the only money he has is a pile of tolgens he found in Count Donblas's coin vault."

Ohhhhh. That was damned clever. When I said that Col lacked imagination, it didn't mean that the man was stupid, which he wasn't. These are some subtle distinctions—imagination versus intelligence—and someday we'll explore them, but not now, because the big, unimaginative, but highly clever bastard had just created a real problem.

Adelyn, in her oblique, intercessor posture, continued to swivel that calming face of hers between us, and now, on one of her reconnoitering sweeps, I spotted discomfiture. It was a hasty cramp above those soft eyebrows, which also infected the bridge of her nose, wrinkling it into a tan carpet. Clearly, she got it. She was starting to figure out that the diamonds I had paid her had *not* come from Count Tygean, that our powerful Underlord ally didn't have enough money to pay any of us. The question was, would she confront me on my deception now, or could it possibly wait a bit, because I had a little more hating to do.

"Lucky thing, Col, that you haven't blown your entire contract, since I hear your new paymaster has been all master and no pay. Without that fancy title, you're just a common slug with a sword...and apparently not a very active sword."

"Yes, I've kept almost the entire payment, Vazeer," Col responded quickly, as if he'd been ready for this. "But I've really got to wonder how much *you've* kept, since not only did Adelyn show me those diamonds, but another development has made me curious about your finances. How many diamonds does it take, for instance, to convince the top Finisher in Hell's Labyrinth to cancel her contract? Did you match her entire bid fee? Did you double it? I know the woman isn't dead, because she brought us some select body parts, which didn't quite look like your skin tones, though I may have been the only one who knows you well enough to realize that."

Oh boy, Col's new clever streak really had some legs. Again, I glanced at Adelyn, trying to determine if uncomfortable nose wrinkles had descended to sneering mouth pleats, which might be my first warning of a bad turn. Perhaps this had occurred already, but Adelyn, who was a Masque, after all, had brushed the agitation from her face.

But my agitation was getting worse. Sometimes, when an opponent stuns you with a clever play, as Col had just done, you can't but feel a certain grudging respect, and this, under the right circumstances, leads to reconciliation. Good-natured comradery might even ensue, after much ribbing and jousting.

That's not what happened here.

"Just to save ourselves some time, Col," I said, "why don't you tell me if you actually came to consider our offer, or if you're more interested in taunting me. Or, maybe you want to pick up our duel where we left it."

Col appeared to be working his mind through these three choices, as he twisted his lips for a couple seconds; then he pressed them in the equivalent of a facial shrug.

"Probably option two or three," he said. "Your offer doesn't look very good."

"In that case, let's just jump to number three. I want your treacherous ass out of the way by the time the real Shadow Bidders take back the Labyrinth."

And with that, I abruptly moved our meeting in a different direction, a direction that Col was ready for, because he drew his spade at the same exact moment I drew mine. Then the stilettos were in our off hands, and just like that, the igneous feud between us was in a state of full eruption.

It's probably time to reveal something. I came to that meeting secretly hoping that I might get a chance to kill Col. This was mostly because I couldn't stand him, but also because our attack on Gueritus would be much less viable with this huge obstruction in the way. However, I also can't rule out a third possibility (likely the real motivator), and that was the fact that a substantial, manhood-sized hunk of assertiveness had been stolen from me recently, spirited away by the beautiful warden of my apartment prison. Since I had no real plans to get it back from her, I turned my attention to someone from whom I expected no benefit, with whom I desired no future, expect perhaps a joint trip to Hell, which is exactly where I was prepared to take him.

"Halt!"

The sound was shocking. I'm not even certain it *was* a sound, though I unquestionably heard that word, and can even recall the tone of it—mid-range, feminine in the loosest sense, penetrating in every sense—but the audible component seemed the least relevant part. I tangibly felt a blow to my chest, even though nothing hit me, which was weird. All I know is that I was certifiably stopped in my tracks, and whatever happened to me also happened to Col.

There we tottered, the two hulking hotheads, weapons drawn, teeth bared, flesh and musculature strained, but, at the same time, with a peculiar, limp mystification around the eyes. In the middle of this frozen combat stood Adelyn, her two hands outstretched towards each of us, palms open, her face angled down, staring at no one directly but offering both warring parties a section of profile. And it was one hell of a section: rumpled eyebrows collapsed into severity, round jaw extruded forward into a taut openness, as if she had just released a lion's roar. Never had I seen my sociable, pleasant-faced friend look like this.

But I had heard the stories. There were rumors about "Adelyn the Allayer," a phenomenon that had manifested on a handful of hostile buy operations, but which, given the moniker's serene connotations, seemed to suggest something different. I can't say that I exactly felt "allayed." Though I will concede that crouching in bewilderment, angry but effectively halted, was quite a bit more peaceable than gouging lengths of sharpened metal into another man's body and having the same done to me in kind.

"Now listen, both of you," Adelyn spoke, with grim impatience, raising her chin and glancing between us. "Here's what's going to happen. You're going to sheath your weapons, because they have no place in this negotiation."

When Col and I both hesitated, Adelyn snapped.

"Do it!"

And so we did, reluctantly.

"Haggling at this point is useless," Adelyn continued, "because I can see that Col doesn't have enough faith to switch sides. But here's a deal that even he can't turn down, because there's almost no risk involved, with a lot of upside."

Col gaped at her, the puzzlement still present. Finally, the stony darkness of his brow creased.

"Go on."

"All you need to do," Adelyn said, "is stand down during our operation. Simply stay out of it, and if you can convince the recently recruited Shadow Bidders to do the same, all the better.

Tell them during the attack, not ahead of time, since I don't know if they can be trusted."

"Don't know if they can be trusted, Adelyn?" I spat. "What about trusting *him*! And what kind of deal is this anyway... letting him sit back and watch who wins, then join sides afterwards? There's no way—"

"Silence, Vazeer!"

Adelyn slammed me again with the verbal equivalent of a punch, and, what do you know, I shut up. I was acutely present to that strange Masque power, encountered intermittently in my life, dredged up from the depths of some hypnotic hinterland.

"The second question answers the first," she went on. "Col can be trusted because this is very easy for him. All he has to do is stay out of it, which costs him nothing. He can then join the winning side, which means he wins either way."

"Do I, though, Adelyn?" Col asked. "I am in a favorable position right now, set to reap rewards as soon as this war ends. How do I know that a coronated High Lord Tygean would place me in a similar position?"

"He will, if you still want it then," Adelyn answered. "We will make your role look a little more proactive than it actually is—"

"Adelyn!" I gasped because I really couldn't take much more of this.

She simply raised that palm of hers, and while I didn't feel any kind of subtle shock, the intensity of her sideways glance was just sufficient to stay my tongue. Still, I could tell that her peacemaking powers were not unlimited, which meant that her skills at diplomacy were going to need to fill the gap.

"Col, don't pretend that your current situation is so great," Adelyn continued. "We have the Seer on our side, remember?

Plus some others; and they tell us that you are not a happy soldier. You probably thought that your boss wasn't as bad as the rumors said, but he is, isn't he? Vazeer told us, and you saw it yourself. You don't belong there, Col, and you know it."

This little speech, to whatever extent I agreed with it, appeared to shift the dynamic, bringing out Col's more amenable side.

"Okay then, I accept," he said. "I won't tell the others, but I need advance warning, to make sure I am in a position to influence them, and also to stay out of it myself."

"We will give you that warning, but only if you give your word that you won't rat us out."

Here, again, I had to bite back commentary, though even I had to admit that snitching wasn't exactly Col's thing. His *thing* was what he did next.

"I'll give that word, for a price. I demand a small pouch of Gosian Diamonds, since I have a feeling that Vazeer possesses one of those…given to him by 'Count Tygean,' of course."

I'm going to take a moment to make my case here. My antipathy towards Col was not merely an irrational thing, for his capacity to jam me into a corner was of such a practiced quality, reflexive even, that his role in my life had become akin to a grossly unpleasant weather pattern (something on the order of sleet, mixed with viscid chunks of humiliation). While I don't love being compelled to look at my failings, most of the time the compelling parties would prefer that I change. Holod pressured me this way, Flerra too, and Terza. It's not like I enjoyed it, but I knew that each, in their own way, was privately hoping that self-reflection would lead to self-improvement, which it sometimes did.

But Col was different. Col wasn't interested in seeing a new, retooled Vazeer the Lash; he wanted only a weaker version of the one that existed, and he'd dredge up anything, reflect back everything, as mere additions of his eviscerating weaponry.

"I'm paying you nothing, you shitbag!" I smoldered. "All I'll do is let you walk away from this meeting alive if you agree to the plan. If you don't, you're a dead man."

"Vazeer, no!" Adelyn cried, seeing me again reach for my spade. This time, her words had no effect.

"So much damned yapping from such a little dog," Col spat, and he also drew his weapon. "You think you'll get lucky a second time?"

We had both gone into fighting crouches when a new voice inserted itself into the fracas.

"People are coming, two blocks away. Time to go."

Appearing from the unexpected left—pretty much opposite from where she had disappeared to—Heshna the Seer manifested with the suddenness of a dingy rucksack that had been dropped out of a window. She was simply there, grayish and uncustomarily intense. It only occurred to me later that perhaps nobody was coming, and this was a prearranged maneuver that the women had concocted in case the men lost their wits. We'd definitely lost those, though just enough of them remained that we knew it was hazardous to be spotted in this gathering. De-escalation commenced immediately.

"Col, take this," said Adelyn, and she jammed a little cloth sack at his stomach. For a moment he just stared down at it, then slowly, he took it from her.

"It's a small pouch, like you wanted," she said. "And it comes from Vazeer, which is also what you wanted. There are eight stones in there."

"Don't give him half of your goddamned payment, Adelyn!" I barked.

"I'm not, Vazeer," she shot back. "You're going to replace the diamonds later, after Col leaves, which he's now going to do. It doesn't serve any of us to be seen."

Col, who still looked angry, did at least manage a grim smile, for that was one hell of a brilliant sequence from Adelyn. Col got his payment, and while it was smaller than he wanted, and he didn't get the satisfaction of taking it from me directly, he could still walk away with a victory. Which, of course, I needed to spoil.

"To answer your question, Col," I said as he started to ease away, "if you screw us, I *will* get lucky a second time, because we won't be having a duel. I'll catch you in a tight space somewhere, where you can't swing that broadsword, and then I'll rip your guts open like a beached whale. You'll die choking on blood and tripping over your own entrails. That is a solemn promise."

Col just stared at me a moment, the grim smile still present, then he rattled the little pouch of diamonds.

"I'll honor the deal with Adelyn, Vazeer, but not with you," he said. "When this is over, there's literally no amount of money you could possibly pay to keep me from killing you."

15

WOMEN OF THE WORLD

"Okay, so that didn't go so well."

We were back in the northern reaches of the Westward neighborhood, standing in an alley that the Seer had scouted for us. I thought the sheer size of the understatement would at least win me a smile, but Adelyn wasn't budging.

"You scare me sometimes, Vazeer," she said.

"Only sometimes?"

Still no smile, which was unusual, and concerning.

"For me, it's all the time," said Heshna.

The Seer, who had just left to do a perimeter, was back again, sudden and drab. In the misty dimness of our little stucco canyon, the two women flanked me distrustfully.

"We don't need Col for this job," I said. "All we're looking for is a distraction, which the current team can provide. The Finisher will do the rest."

"The Finisher who tried to kill Shade?" asked Heshna.

"Shade, who was trying to kill me."

"Because she had a contract. Your Finisher created his own contract, which is not what a Shadow Bidder does. What's his real goal, this person I have never seen or heard of?"

"The Seer's right, Vazeer," said Adelyn. "We're hinging everything on this one member of the team, and we still haven't met him yet. Terza insists we fix that immediately. Tonight, at her store."

And with that we parted. There were no warm smiles or hand squeezes from Adelyn, and Heshna was simply gone. So, I started my evasive journey back to 44 Masthead Lane. When I finally entered my apartment, I was disappointed to find that my shadow wife was absent, even when I went fumbling through the secret hole into the sparse confines of her unit. What I did see were the trappings of a woman readying herself. Several pairs of shoes and boots were scattered about, her emerald dress and another black one were tossed over the foot of the bed, and on her vanity I noted a full spread of colorful little bottles, brushes, and jars, all unlabeled and possessed of the dainty extravagance that men find confusing. There was also, most beguilingly, a vaporous hint of the lavender perfume that Shade had been wearing on our first night together. I wasn't sure which of the little receptacles had produced it, but I closed my eyes and felt myself slipping back into a reverie of our maiden encounter, my mind and to some degree my body returning to a moment before I knew who and what Shade really was.

Not long after, while I was back in my apartment tidying things, Cad arrived. I informed him about the night's meeting, and I also asked when and where Radrin would be providing his next report.

"Second Bell, behind the Gilded Razor."

"When you tell him about the meeting, let him know he should wait for me in the alley just to the east of Paintings and Prints. Seventh Bell."

Cad agreed, then he started craning about, sniffing conspicuously.

"Where's Jisselle?"

"Doing her job, I assume."

"I didn't see her in the property manager's office."

I said nothing, returning to straightening.

"She's never in that office, I notice," Cad continued as I grabbed two dirty plates from the tea table. "And I don't see her moving around the buildings, like you'd expect with a property manager."

"I'm not sure exactly what category of annoying innuendo this is," I said, "but drop it, please. Everine needs a lot of errands run. Jisselle does the purchasing for all six properties."

"That's what I told Blackstar, because he's been asking about Jisselle. A lot."

I froze, the plates jutting from my fingers like dirty court fans.

"He has?"

Cad gave a somber nod.

"I didn't mention anything about you two being together. I didn't mention her at all, but Blackstar brought it up…asked if that western woman was still the manager, and if I ever saw her around."

"And you told him?"

"I couldn't lie. He'd figure it out himself, then he wouldn't trust me with anything. So, I said I see her occasionally, here and there, but that she's gone a lot, probably doing errands, like you said."

I put the plates in the sink, then leaned back against the chopping table.

"Anything else?"

"Yeah, one thing," Cad replied. "You know how I said Blackstar seems like a man that means business?"

I nodded.

"Well, when he talks about Jisselle, that's when he *really* means business. They got some history, those two, and whatever it is, it isn't good. I gotta tell you, Zeer—and I know I'm playing with fire here—but I'm not sure Jisselle is exactly who she says she is. Blackstar doesn't seem to think so. The last time I saw him, he said he'd 'take care of it.' Not sure what 'it' meant, but…kinda seemed like it meant her. I just thought I should tell you."

I remained motionless against the chopping table, likely blanching.

"Zeer…?"

"Thank you, Cad. That's enough on this subject for now."

We discussed a few additional logistics, then I sent him on his way. An hour or so after that, I became aware of some furtive noises in my apartment's other wing. When I came through the opening, I saw that the scattered pile of footwear had increased by two—a pair of tan lace-ups with elevated heels—though I didn't see any other additions to the general mess: no coat, dress, leggings or undergarments, which seemed strange. I heard water sloshing about in her bath chamber, so I knocked politely.

"I'll be out soon," she called through the door. "Wait for me in your apartment."

A full half hour later, Shade slid through the tapestry into my unit, uncharacteristically stripped of makeup. She was wearing a pale blue silk housedress, with matching tasseled slippers, and her face, her hair, even her teeth looked like they had all been scrubbed to the point of abrasion.

"You look very clean," I said.

She strode over to my pantry, fixing her hair up in a bun as she walked.

"A girl tries."

She set about rummaging through the shelves until, after much fumbling and shifting, she found a jar of crackers. This, along with some cheese and a knife, she brought over to the sofa.

"How did your meeting go?" she asked when she had slouched back on the couch. The soles of her slippers were pressed against the edge of the tea table, with the jar in her lap, and I watched with some interest as she prepared a snack for herself. Balancing a cracker on the shiny top of one of her knees, she carefully sliced a piece of cheese on it, then crowned it with another cracker.

"It went wonderfully," I replied. "About as good as a meeting could go."

Shade paused as her little sandwich was just about to enter her mouth. Beige and lightly freckled, her unglossed lips hung open.

"It did?"

"Definitely. I was practically a Masque."

She allowed the swaddled cheese to continue on its way, and as she crunched the thing around in her cheeks, a few white crumbs found their way out onto her chin. She swiped at them and frowned noticeably as she chewed.

"Right about now," I said, "you're thinking to yourself, 'If he would lie to me so brazenly about this, what else might he be lying about?' That's what you're thinking, right?"

Shade stopped chewing, then nodded.

"And me, I find myself wondering, 'Why would my freshly groomed bedmate have reason to think I'm lying? Why, in fact, does she always seem to know exactly how my day went, even when I'm not so sure myself?'"

Shade finished her chomping, swallowed, and reached for my cup of mead to wash it down. She took a small sip, wiped her mouth, and looked at me squarely.

"She told you?"

"Only after I'd figured it out myself. Siblings sense these things."

Shade fetched another cracker, which went straight to her mouth with no cheese embellishment. She bit off a small piece, chewing thoughtfully.

"So, the meeting did *not* go well," she said. "Mostly because you were terrible, or so I'm told. How do you plan to deal with it?"

"I was terrible in just that way you love. And the main objective was achieved. Let me worry about those details, and you can tell me about a few of your own. For starters, where were you this morning, and why did you bring all of your clothing into the bath chamber?"

Shade looked away. When I continued to wait for the answer, watching carefully, she finally sighed.

"I had business in another part of town. And that outfit needed a wash."

"Dirty business, then?"

Now she was bluntly glaring. Her eyes had reclaimed some of that livid fire from ambushes gone by; however, I didn't sense total conviction here, which told me I was onto something. I suspected that Shade's "business" elsewhere was not some errand on behalf of Everine Agaedus, for whom she had never really worked. I also surmised that when a Finisher comes home with clothing so filthy it needs to be washed before she can exit the bath chamber, chances are, mud stains aren't the problem. The question was, did I care? It wasn't a question, because I knew I did, mostly on account of Shade of Night's tactics. I hated the thought of what might have proceeded the final act (not to mention, I wasn't too crazy about the final act itself). On the plus side, this kept her infidelities brief.

"So, you're close with her?" I asked, trying to shift to less incendiary territory.

"Her?" The accusatory snap told me she wasn't aware that I had changed topics.

"My Brood sister."

Shade took a moment to shake off whatever needed shaking, but at last her expression lightened and she shrugged.

"In a sense."

"What sense?"

"In the sense that I've probably shared more with her than anybody else. Even my own mother doesn't know me so well, which isn't saying much."

I really tried to fathom this relationship, which I found close to impossible.

"I didn't know Heshna had any real friends."

"She doesn't. The Seer is difficult to befriend."

"Like you."

"Oooooh, why would you say that, Lashy?" she asked, her fiery eyes cooling quickly, as her expression warmed. She slid towards me on the couch.

"Are we not the best of friends?"

"I'd like to think so."

"Then think so," she said, "until I give you reason to think otherwise."

"When will that be?"

"When you keep asking too many questions about my dirty laundry."

After that, the clothing started to come off—the clean clothing—which became a crumpled range of hillocks around the couch. Soon we were again putting Everine's sofa at risk, and I found myself, as always, amazed by how totally I could forget my troubles with this person, which was fascinating, given that she was one of my troubles. However, there was something so consuming in her clinches, her vehement kisses, that I simply lost myself. Despite her petite stature, Shade covered large swaths of territory in our lovemaking. She crawled all over me like a spider monkey, and she took us places (to the floor, in this case) where we knocked the tea table so hard that mead spilled and drenched us.

The gods only know where this wellspring came from in me. Even as a younger man, I don't think I had quite this capability, but the astonishing depth of her appetites seemed to unleash my own. After our lovemaking, we sprawled on the living room rug, passing the nithrin pipe. Having witnessed Shade's creative snack skills, I put her in charge of cheese sandwich production, and the two of us went through a quarter wheel of Lothrum goat and most of my crackers. There was something profoundly relaxing about these interludes, which were novel in my world. On occasion, Terza and I had lounged about post passion, though because we generally met following bids, we often passed out shortly after that. And then, the next day the ever-restless Falconbrow was up and active, eager to get on with things—some painting she was working on, her stall during market days, or just life itself, which (if I wanted to be part of it) required I tag along. Terza was open to this sometimes, other times, not.

Shade was different. Her life now very much included me, and while I didn't know exactly how to classify this life of hers, with its sinister peripheries and dubious laundry, I did feel strangely flattered to play such a central role. When we were together, she was more apt to cling to me than to cast me off, and I had yet to sense her growing bored. Yes, she laid down the rules in our little fiefdom, and when she demanded things, it was understood that I would provide them, which I mostly did. But for some reason, I did not feel suffocated by this arrangement.

"I have been meaning to ask you something," I said, as we slumped together on the damp, crumb-infested rug. "You talk about all the wicked men that you've targeted. What about the wicked women?"

Shade, who was picking at her fingernails, crumpled her nose fussily.

"I don't deal in those."

"Never?"

"Once. But I regretted it. I've vowed never to do it again, except in self-defense."

"Interesting," I said, lying back and staring at the ceiling. "This is yet another handicap you and I have in common."

Shade abandoned her cuticle task and rolled over to slump half on top of me, which seemed to be her favorite position.

"That is a dangerous weakness, Lashy. You must get over it."

"I'm not sure I can. Your friend, Heshna, figured it out, which is why she hired you after the Gaff."

"In that instance, you got very lucky, but with the next woman, you won't. And believe me, there is a woman coming for you… coming for all of you wicked men, so you better not have this handicap when she arrives."

This was just startling enough that I levered upright, causing Shade to do the same. If she was irritated at being dislodged, it was offset by the pleasure she took in my alarm.

"Your girlfriends with the paintbrushes don't understand the trouble they are stirring up with their graffiti," she said. "Lave Kaszivar will see those writings as a sign that her moment has come, which it probably has. I warned Falconbrow about this, but she is stubborn, just like you."

This elicited new shock.

"You spoke with Terza?"

"Mmmm, recently, when I was asked to join their group. She is one of Giradera's Storm Maidens, that one, so I can't help but like her."

"I think she fancies herself Giradera."

"No," said Shade with a definitive shake. "Falconbrow knows better. However, Lave Kaszivar doesn't know better. She's convinced that she is the second coming of Giradera, and it's just possible that she's not wrong, for never in my life have I met anyone with greater confidence. When I picture your puny Underlords trying to stand up to her, I can only laugh at the thought."

"You actually met the Red Siren?"

"Several times."

"When?"

Shade blew a few strands of hair from her face, looking off to the side in thought.

"Here and there, throughout the years. The dates are all written on me somewhere. The last time was a year ago, when she hired me to take care of this pig."

She pointed down her leg to a place where a small section of writing encircled her lower calf.

"You contracted bids for her?"

"What else do you think I was doing, serving cheese and crackers?"

"There was no Sketcher buffering her?"

Shade snorted.

"Why would the Red Siren need that? She doesn't hide in a hole like an Underlord roach."

Now I was the one who rolled on top of her, working my fingers into the feathery sumptuousness of her hair. Her bun had fallen to pieces during our intimacies, so the silky blackness spilled on her freckled shoulders and breasts.

"What's she like?"

Shade again stared off in thought.

"She is everything the rumors say and more. I have read some of the tales of Giradera, how men would fall to their knees before her, how her command was uncontestable, and these descriptions work for Kaszivar too, almost. I am not easily intimidated by anyone, but around that one I watch my step. She has a strange power. All of Derjia should be afraid."

My mind was whirling now, pulled into my own musings about Giradera of Azmoul, but also, much closer at hand, by my personal fascination with Shade of Night. How many exotic worlds had this intrepid Finisher visited?

"Have you been to Tergon?" I asked.

"Been there? I was a citizen for years, and I still return often. Those of high birth have a lot of work for people like me."

I remembered Nascinthé's story, and how a Finisher in the employ of one of those aristocratic houses had splattered the blood of a kindly theater director across her startled face. That contract, with its martial brazenness, didn't sound like Shade of Night's handiwork, but I had no doubt that there were plenty of other jobs that matched her skill set.

"You were familiar with that society, then?" I asked.

"Of course."

"Have you ever heard of an actress called 'the Spellbinder'?"

Shade now went silent, and she squinted at me in a strange way, like I'd made a joke, or possibly lost my mind. Then she spat out a laugh, which did not have the appeal of her spontaneous ejaculations, rife instead with derision.

"Why are you laughing?" I asked.

"You Sullward rubes, how insular you are in your little rat maze."

When I continued to gape, she shifted up on an elbow, separating from the warm interweave of my fingers.

"Asking if I have heard of Spellbinder is like asking if I have heard of the Emperor. It's that stupid a question."

"It is?"

"Of course, you fool. There is nobody on the entire eastern shoreline of the Derjian Ocean who has not heard of her, except perhaps in this backward place, where you know nothing of art that is alive. Here you deal in things long dead."

This was unfortunately true. The older our stolen items, the more valuable they became, and we obviously had no way to capitalize on works of performance art in our smuggling empire.

"Then again, not all who have heard of her were lucky enough to see her," said Shade, and she slid back with an arm behind her head, a puckish smile on her lips.

"Were you so lucky?"

"I was more than lucky, Lashy. There were long stretches when I did not miss a single production, sometimes several repeat performances, and I refused to sit in the plebian seats. I paid up for the front section, which is where a large percentage of my money went. If Nirabella was the lead, and she usually was, then I was there."

"Nirabella?"

Shade shook her head and groaned.

"What the hell do you read for so many hours? Nothing current. Her name is Nirabella Spellbinder, and never has our world known one to match her."

Now I also lay back, and together we stared at the knotty boards of the ceiling. *Nirabella*, I repeated inside, for I had recently read that name. Nirabella was the birth name of the Empress Asadeissia, which I had learned a few days earlier while perusing her autobiography. It was a detail that I had probably encountered years ago, in some other work, but not until I read Nascinthé's prized tome in my drawing room had it made an impression.

Nirabella of House Besidian. The girl who grew to become the Empress Asadeissia, the greatest ruler of all time. What other name would Nascinthé choose?

"You know, Lashy," Shade said in a quiet, pensive voice, "I have often thought a strange thing. I've not shared this with anyone, not even the Seer, but I will tell it to you, because you have raised it. I used to think to myself, if I could ever become close with Nirabella, if she and I could become friends…or perhaps more than friends, then it might fix me. It might heal whatever is wrong inside of me. This thought started on the very first night I saw her, up there on stage, spinning her spells, becoming a poor prostitute who overcame impossible problems and then achieved glory. The story itself was ridiculous, but the performance was not, and it touched me in a way that I cannot put into words. And this did not wear off with all her many other roles, whether she was young or old, dark skinned or light, titled or slum born, because my strange feeling only gained strength.

"'Win her heart, Shade,' I kept saying. 'Win it, then maybe your own heart will be repaired.'"

For quite a while I continued to lie motionless, unsure how to respond, unsure even how to feel, but at last I asked, "What makes you think she'd be interested in a woman's heart?"

"There were rumors. They flowed throughout the Capital for a time."

"What rumors?"

"About the Spellbinder and Countess Shaeyin Odel. They were very close, those two, and though they went places I could not follow, I would see them together briefly after a show. I have never wanted to be a frilly noblewoman, but sometimes when I'd see Countess Odel laughing and whispering with Nirabella, I burned with a terrible envy. How I wished I could enter the elite halls where they walked, flirt with her behind those fancy doors."

I knew this was the moment to keep my mouth shut, or at the very least offer some pleasantry. But instead, something different came out.

"I don't know if the Spellbinder would be interested in a woman's heart, Shade, but I do know for sure that she doesn't want a Finisher's dirty soul."

That was a bad one. These sudden, punitive statements were among my unfortunate trademarks in life. They had caused uncountable injuries during my relationship with Terza, then became my only means of communication with her after we broke up. How compliant I can seem for long stretches, until something truly vulnerable is revealed, and then—instigated by a rebuke or a smug sense of dominance—in slides the emotional knife. In Shade's case, I don't know what set me off exactly. Possibly it was all of her barbs about my ignorance, or maybe it was remembering the role that a Finisher had played in Nascinthé's past, but most likely it was petty jealousy that this little devil should pine so adoringly after the angel that had briefly been mine.

There was a sharp intake of breath. It did, in fact, sound like pain—a wracked gasp, as if I had delivered a stomach wound—and I feared to even look sideways. But I didn't need to, for Shade suddenly sat up, her black hair dancing out on fibrous currents, and she pivoted to glare down at me. All of a sudden, I was afraid. My heart banged about, as my imagination was invaded by that stalking fiend, Shade of Night, who had possibly been reawakened, and who might have a stiletto hidden somewhere nearby just in case I ever said something so stupid.

"What did you say?"

"Nothing, I didn't mean it. My soul is just as dirty."

"No, you fool. Not that, the other part. You said you 'know for sure.' How do you know for sure? And why are you asking about Spellbinder?"

Now, in an effort to make nice, I said more stupid things.

"I don't know, I'm just being theoretical, based on all you said, because I obviously don't know anything personally…"

…yak, yak, yak. I disgorged a couple more sentences of this crap, and in that time, I watched Shade's speckled eyes shift, her naked lips twitch, and I could tell that my utterances went largely unheard. She was using that interval to work something out in her mind.

"Oooouuuuaaaiiiiiihhhhh!"

It was one of the strangest sounds I'd ever heard. Shade may have largely easternized herself in the last two decades, but in that moment her howl was some dreadful, primaeval thing bellowing straight out of the western wastes. It scared the hell out of me. But not quite as much as when, a moment later, she threw herself on top of me, with all of the coiled acrobatic savagery that had marked her less friendly visits.

"It's her!" she shrieked.

Pinned below, unsure whether I ought to defend myself, I was at least sure that I should have gone to the privy, for I was now in danger of another urinary accident.

"It was Nirabella!" she shrieked again. "The mystery woman they all speak of in Dockside, the one pretending to be the Siren, who I know wasn't the Siren. It was a Masque, and not just any Masque, it was the greatest Masque of all time. And you were with her, Lashy! That's what they're all saying. You escorted her… you were with my beloved Nirabella Spellbinder!"

Shade had gone into one of her ferocious grapples, one hand reaching up to clutch my ear, the other squeezing vice-like at my throat, while the muscles of her thighs started a steady, anacondic contraction around my ribs. Her hair shrouded us, leaving me in sultry proximity to that harrying beauty.

"Did you lay with her?" she asked.

My mind went into a panic, my body readied itself for a stabbing. Shade had just expressed a terrible, burning envy at the mere sight of Shaeyin Odel laughing with Nirabella; how much worse would her reaction be when she learned what I had done?

"Answer me," she pressed.

There was no getting away from her. That face was too close, my freedom too compromised, and I simply wasn't able to fabricate anything convincing.

"It was just a brief affair," I sputtered. "Only a few days. I think she was simply grateful—"

"Oooouuuuaaaiiiiiihhhhh!"

That terrible sound again! Shade suddenly rose up, vigorously astraddle, and the only thing that prevented another privyless discharge was the fact that she didn't look angry. Just the opposite, for she appeared positively triumphant in that moment. While I had never witnessed the successful completion of one of Shade of

Night's contracts, I imagined that she might look something like this when she sent another pig squealing to his grave.

"Shade knows!" she cried, her face barbarously happy. "She knows when a thing's worth having, and though she doesn't doubt herself, sometimes she wonders. She says: 'Shade, why don't you just dice this Grell Runner bastard and honor your Finisher's code?' At such times there is a conflict, but no longer. Never again.

"If my favorite woman in all the world could see fit to give you her heart, even for a short while, then I know I have not entirely lost my way."

16

THE KNOCK

"You're not jealous?" I asked, still shaken but also, as only Shade of Night could make me, heaving with relief. How many times had the threat of stabbing, strangulation, castration, or death turned into sensual kisses? Which she was doing again now, her moist lips working their way all over my face and then sucking onto my own mouth, as if trying to absorb the lingering essence of Nirabella.

"No, Lashy," she softly breathed. "I'm not jealous. You are my own Lashy, the one that belongs to me, and, for a brief time, Nirabella belonged to you. In this way I have almost had her too."

This didn't seem like perfect logic, but if it kept the kisses flowing and the stilettos out of my flesh, I was all for it.

"You don't understand this impossible thing you accomplished," she said. "You probably think little of it, which is all part of what I find so irresistible about you."

Shade had not dismounted, and her new intentions, evidenced with some gentle writhing, were obvious, but I was still trying to get over my frayed nerves, plus my resources weren't limitless. Some pleasant chatting seemed a better idea.

"What, exactly, have I accomplished?"

"You bedded the Spellbinder. You simply can't imagine how many tried and failed. It became a thing—how impossible she was to win. The nobles in Tergon tumbled over themselves to woo her, to get her to even look at them, and she would not. 'Nirabella the Untouchable' they called her, and where such self-possession came from, for a woman lower born even than me, I do not know. When Lave Kaszivar walks into her audience chamber, she has followers ready to lay down their lives for her. She has galleons and armies, she has wealth beyond imagining. But Nirabella had only herself. Still, she thought herself better than everybody around her, which she was."

I closed my eyes and tried to evoke this picture. I thought of my painting, *Late Day over Imperial Square*, set in Tergon's enormous central plaza. There, at the nexus of the Emperor's Palace, the Capital Art Gallery, and Nascinthé's own workplace, the Tergonian Imperial Theater, a spectacular yellow fountain spit ever skyward. Could I picture my beautiful Masque clicking over those balmy marble flagstones, the world swooning before her? I could, for I would surely feel that way myself; however, outer appearances can be deceiving.

"She has fallen a long way from what you remember, Shade," I said. "Life in the Capital didn't ultimately agree with her."

"Yes, I know," she replied. "That disgusting duke, I never believed any of what was said. I even thought of seducing the haughty cock afterwards, then slaughtering him, but to do such a thing is worse than a death sentence. They wouldn't just send one Finisher after me, or two, or even three. A small army would come, and when they had me, they would do things to Shade that even I couldn't stomach doing to others. Such are the costs of targeting a man of that sort."

I sighed in affirmation.

"That's a good instinct. The Finishers did follow her, all the way to a town in the north, and though it was a theater director they killed, to keep her off the stage, the brutality of it haunts her to this day."

"Ooooh, the roaches!" she hissed. "I hate them, I hate them all."

And just like that, the loathing ignited, a scalding spark hitting the tinder of her past, and I needed to rush in to douse it before it caught fire in earnest.

"Don't worry," I said. "Nas…Nirabella is alive and well, reunited with her family and very rich. Good things lie in her future, so there is no need to take revenge on her behalf."

But Shade's resentment was not an easy thing to cool. That eccentric western face, glorious and smoldering, reminded me again of how volatile she was, how precipitously unstable, and yes, definitely in need of heart repair, though I doubted Nascinthé of Levell could achieve such a healing.

"…And she was brilliant on the bid," I continued, hoping to further entice her mind away from anger. "I have worked with many Masques, but she was something entirely different."

"Yes," Shade said, shaking off the remnants of her distress. She slumped down upon me, her warm mouth fuming softly on my cheek, and she murmured in a voice that was almost vaporously weak.

"Tell me, Lashy. Tell me everything."

And so, in keeping with my new, unwanted role in life, I found myself telling the tale yet again, or at least the parts that interested Shade. Strangely, the very elements of the story that had most titillated others—the Narrow Bid itself, the objectives, the target—seemed of small consequence to her. I couldn't tell whether this was a Finisher's instinct to disregard the contracts of others, or whether such details simply bored her, but either way, the only thing that fascinated her were events directly associated with Nirabella. No, there was one other item that drew her attention. In order to convey Nascinthé's genius, it was necessary to explain that she arrived at the bid site as Shaeyin Odel, and in order to explain that, I had to reveal the Countess's love affair with the High Lord. Upon hearing this, Shade clucked her tongue and smiled viciously.

"The dirty tart," she said. "What a fine, highbrow show the Heir of Odel puts on for the world, but I have never fallen for it. She will probably rule us all one day, and when that happens, the Empire will surely collapse."

I avoided all but the most cursory talk of Radrin, though even that little bit was enough to send a demonstrable shiver through her inscribed flesh. If Radrin Blackstar was grimly obsessed with Shade of Night, then the same was even more true in reverse, leading me, once again, to vow to keep them apart at all costs.

Aside from these two deviations, I held to adoration territory, paying special attention to the theatrical performances.

"Describe it again, Lashy," Shade whispered, after I had reenacted the incident in the High Lord's entry vestibule, where our Masque performed her extraordinary *displaced seduction*. "She really ran her fingers down your cheek, in front of them all?"

"She did, and there wasn't a single soldier who wasn't riveted. They wanted to be me, I think."

"I know, I know," she cooed. "The Spellbinder can do that, I have seen it myself. But always the little details are different, one show to the next."

"This was no show, Shade. This was a real threat, with real soldiers, ready to kill us all, and she handled herself with almost impossible poise."

"That's true, Lashy, that is so, so true. I have always imagined she could do great things, great things in the world, and now I know it is so."

From there I described our violent flight from the Ripening Hall, though I made sure to skip over Nascinthé's paralysis, and how she and the Line Man endangered the group. This was easy enough to accomplish, because Shade really didn't care how things came apart, nor did she concern herself with what it all meant for the Labyrinth as a whole. She didn't even seem interested in Nascinthé's real name, which I found perplexing; however, given that Shade had lived her entire life using an array of false identities, she probably didn't put much stock in names. Nirabella Spellbinder was the only way she wanted to know this woman.

When we reached the latter portions of the tale, I gave oversized attention to Nascinthé's brave and rather foolhardy antics in the marsh, and the way that she drew a whole garrison of soldiers out of the compound by leaving little clues behind. Shade veritably lost her mind at this, clapping wildly and then rolling over to kick her feet towards the ceiling, a maneuver that she reserved for our most impassioned moments. And yet, for all of that, there was one disclosure that moved Shade beyond all others: it was the fact that her own Lashy had rescued Nirabella Spellbinder from death. This was, in her mind, the pinnacle of all things.

I really don't like playing up details of this sort, as they depict my own savagery, and I simply can't view myself as a hero, no matter how hard anybody else tries to portray me that way. But with Shade, there was no escaping either issue. She, who couldn't be bothered to ask a single question about Ripening Halls, command structures, number of troops, now drilled me over and over again about every heinous act I committed in defense of my damsel.

"Oh, Lashy, is that when you bit off a man's fingers?" she asked.

"Was it here that you boiled a man's face down to steaming blood?"

"This man, Lashy…this was the one you stabbed straight through the eyeball, was it not?"

And so it went.

"I honestly don't remember it all, Shade," I said. "The surviving soldiers could tell you more than I ever could."

Which they had, obliquely. When I first met Shade, while she was posing as a provocative stranger named "Jisselle," Everine Agaedus had hinted at all sorts of grotesque behavior on my part, which she herself had learned from a Lower City contact. While Everine didn't list the gory particulars in that conversation, evidently Shade had pushed for clarity afterwards.

"You were so heroic, Lashy!" she sighed. "You did all of that for her."

"For myself too. I was just trying to survive."

"Nooooooo! You can't fool me. I know you now. I have felt your touch, the way you please. I have also seen you stop your Finisher creep when he wanted to hurt Shade, and I know that when my Lashy defends a woman, he will lay down his life, lay down his very soul for her. This is what you did for Nirabella."

I had no counterargument, so I tried to move on. But she couldn't let it go, any of it, and she pushed for the most exciting details of all.

"Tell me about the reunion on the boat," she whispered. "I want to know every word, every touch, every kiss."

If, by temperament, I'm opposed to dramatizing episodes of violence, then I am triply so when it comes to items of this nature; however, I can't begin to convey how much relief I felt that my companion had skewed in this direction, not towards jealousy. You would need to spend time with a partner like this (I don't recommend it) who drags your psyche from warmth to desire to mortal terror, then back to warmth again to understand the lengths I was willing to go to keep her in that final phase of the cycle. So, I told; I told quite a lot. However, I pretended to recall it all as if it were a dream, which was somewhat the case, but in this dreamlike rendering, I suggested that specific details escaped me, when in truth they did not. I remembered everything that happened aboard the Elena's Guile—the lyrical timber of Nascinthé's voice, the supple whiteness of her body, the clever wisdom of every word she uttered—but I saw no advantage in revealing it all to Shade.

And she was more than content with my telling, for in my ethereal version, I focused heavily on the closeness and warmth that Nascinthé and I shared, and also the staggering relief we both felt to have lived through such an ordeal.

"It was gratitude towards life itself," said Shade, "that your hearts should find each other."

I was startled then, to see moisture glistening in the almond rims of Shade's eyes. Her face, mere inches away, had become an extraordinary picture of loveliness and innocence, neither being words I would ever use to describe her, or wouldn't have until that moment. If the purity of youth had been stolen from this woman, then it was possibly being restored now, for the floodgates continued to open ever wider.

"Again, Lashy, again…" she sobbed after I had taken her through the entire reunion, tears beginning to crawl like quicksilver down her gently pocked cheeks. Over and over, she had me describe that moment when Nascinthé first spotted me walking the floating gangplank in Eastcove, and how she let out her rapturous shriek, then started a mad dash down the deck of the Elena's Guile.

"It's the most beautiful thing I've ever heard in my life," Shade heaved, her whole body shuddering. "Nirabella's happiest moment, and you were the one who gave it to her. Her only audience…and now I can see it too."

Shortly after that, Shade and I became intimate again, kissing and caressing and warmly entwining, though we went no further than that. There was really no need, as we were already sharing the tenderest possible union, at least for two Shadow Bidders.

"I'm sorry about the unkind thing I said earlier, Shade," I whispered. "I was being spiteful and jealous."

"I am the queen of spite, Lashy," she whispered back, "so you are allowed, this one time. Let us have no jealousy between us. We can share everything."

Truly, it seemed we could, for in that sincere joining on my shaggy rug, bathed in the enduring smell of nithrin and spilled mead, we shared, on some profound emotional plane, the essence of a woman who was not even in the room. I did not close my eyes and pretend to myself that Shade was Nascinthé of Levell, and I doubt that Shade was able to fool herself either, but the beautiful, spellbinding Masque was somehow interlaced through every one of our affections, which only made the experience more profound.

Who knew where this relationship with Shade of Night might have gone? Locked compartments that I never expected to open had already started to break their seal, and the prospects of a longer-term union with her felt both enticingly possible and desirable. But such is not the way of things in my world.

Elusive forces close doorways at these moments, shatter unions, and there is always some catastrophic mistake that I am ready, willing, and able to make. So it was that afternoon, with just a little help from someone else.

The knock on the door was not the sneaky "rap, rap" of a co-conspirator, nor was it the impatient "crack, crack, crack" that Merejin deployed against the knocker at 27 Fletcher Street. It was something in between in terms of volume, but lower, meaner, and longer: "*Thunk. Thunk. Thunk. Thunk.*"

It spelled trouble; I knew that immediately.

Shade looked snoozy and unconcerned. There was, after all, a heavily locked and barred door between us and the source of the knocking, not to mention we had a convenient escape route through her apartment if a real problem developed. So, there she lay, sumptuously sprawled, the innocence and loveliness still glazed upon her. I got up, threw on a silk house robe, and moved cautiously down the front door hallway. I grabbed one of my spades from the console table, then leaned in close to take a peek.

The orbital constriction of reality, as viewed through a peephole, is a meager and stifling thing. At best it's practical, sometimes comical, never exposing much beyond a visitor's basic identity, except in the rarest of instances, like today. I saw the posture first. In most situations, I see the side of someone's face, or sometimes their forehead as they stare down at the floor, and usually there is an overall fidgetiness, indicative of one of life's classic in-between moments. This figure was different. He glared directly at the peephole, unmoving and solemn, and the backlighting from the hallway lanterns created a pool of blackness upon his face, with a strangely fiery perimeter. I could see the kindled dark blonde of his hair, and the shining black blades of his upturned collar, these details converging to produce a circular portrait, balefully alive.

"*Thunk. Thunk. Thunk. Thunk,*" came the next round of knocking, though the figure didn't even seem to move. *I* definitely moved, spasming away as if I'd burnt my eye on the door. My pulse began to crash madly, and I slowly backed down the hallway, my spade leveled towards the knocking, my other hand tickling unsteadily along the bumpy planes of plaster. When I reached the open space of the living room and Shade saw me, she registered her first look of concern.

"What?" she mouthed silently, her brow rumpling.

"You've got to go," I mouthed back, tiptoeing towards her with the creak-avoiding awkwardness of an adulterer.

Shade looked both mystified and alarmed, and she sat up hurriedly, her arms hugging her naked breasts. At just that moment, I heard the faint noise of a Half Bell, droning its single note through window glass. I was quite certain it was the Fifth Half Bell, which was a full hour and a half before the designated meeting time—a meeting that was to be held in the alley outside of Paintings and Prints.

"*Thunk. Thunk. Thunk. Thunk.*"

This set was particularly thunderous, and I saw Shade's freckled shoulders visibly flinch. Suddenly she started to look around for her clothing, but I was ahead of her, sweeping her skimpy dress and slippers from the floor, then thrusting them into her hands. I literally hauled her up by her armpits.

"Go," I breathed from close.

"Vazeer the Lash," came the loud voice, echoing down my entry hallway. "I know you're in there. Open the door."

The sound was somehow magnified. The overall tenor of it—including the knocking—was almost impossibly threatening, and when I looked at Shade, those gorgeous features, so often in command, or at least spirited, with her little bundle of clothing clutched up to her chin like a stuffed toy, she did, for the first time, look afraid.

"Your Finisher creep?" she whispered. "What does he want?"

"Move," I hissed, and I started to shove her towards the guest room.

"But why…he's not coming in, is he?"

"Go. Go through your hole, get dressed quietly, and when he comes in here, leave your apartment."

I continued to shove her towards the guest room, and then, once inside, I drove her straight towards our secret tapestry. Finally, when we were a few feet away, she turned on me bitterly.

"What the hell is the matter with you?"

Her expression was a new mix, reflecting visible efforts to regain assertiveness, and even more visible failures to achieve it. Her eyes still had puffy elements from her crying, and the glaze of exposed softness pervaded. On every level she appeared undermined—undermined by her own doubt, by this dissonant threat rattling her at such a vulnerable moment, by the fact that after days of devoted, obedient Vazeer, she was suddenly faced with a rude, domineering version of the man, one who was more than willing to shove her naked from his apartment. These things all coalesced to rob her of a fitting "Shade of Night" response.

For me, there was little in the way of uncertainty, though much in the way of fear. I was haunted by Cad's comment that when Radrin Blackstar spoke about Jisselle, "he meant business," that Radrin had said he would "take care of it," meaning *her*, no doubt. The forbidding sight of the man, bleakly encircled by the bronze of my peephole, seemed a prelude to exactly that sort of business. I do believe I was interested in protecting Shade, more than anything else. I was now quite familiar with the varying dispositions of Radrin Blackstar, and that malevolently knocking version was on the most martial end of the spectrum. I remembered the sight and feel of that icy killer from the first time he came hunting Shade, and while I had been able to stop him then, that was merely because I caught him off guard.

Shade was right about one thing, though; I didn't have to let him in.

"He knows I'm in here," I said quietly. "This man is a key part of my plan."

"No, he's not!" Shade hissed, starting to push back. "It is *you* who is a pawn in his plan. You're too blind to see it."

"Just go through the hole, and be quiet in there," I said, and I pulled back the tapestry.

"*Thunk. Thunk. Thunk. Thunk.*"

The sound came to us easily from two rooms away, and again I saw the jolt in Shade's shoulders.

"You're so ignorant, Vazeer," Shade breathed, and now, at last, a little whiff of her menace was present. "You don't have a clue who and what your creep is and where he comes from, but I do. I know who he is—*what* he is, and I pity you for being such a fool, for falling into his wicked trap."

And then she slid through the opening, still clutching her clothes, and as I watched those taut, camel-colored buttocks retreat from view, I did have a mournful sense of having been at this doorway before. There was a disturbing similarity to the water door out of which I had shoved Nascinthé of Levell during the Narrow Bid. There was also, in a less tangible sense, something analogous to the bind into which I had thrust Terza Falconbrow on the night of the Gaff. My motives were worse then, but I can't say they were entirely pure today. I was absolutely mortified at the thought of Radrin Blackstar catching me in the arms of this woman, the one he had literally risked his life to rescue me from, and the idea of him witnessing my overall condition—cozily sprawled, alcohol saturated—was simply too much for me to bear.

Once Shade was gone, I made my way into the living room and called out in a mumbly voice, "Give me a second. I was asleep."

I then started a frantic effort to straighten up. I hid the nithrin pipe and mead, fixed the rug area, opened a window, and then finally headed down my entry hallway, with my robe cinched tight. I put the spade back on the console table and unlocked the door.

So often in life, my paranoid precautions turn out to be overblown. There is much that I dread in this world, and while the world is, habitually enough, a dreadful place, rarely do the things I fear most turn out to be the real problem. A strange law tends to make expectation an antidote to manifestation, at least when it comes to specific troubles. Therefore, I was more than a little taken aback when, upon opening the door, I soon learned that my precautions possibly undershot the threat, for Radrin Blackstar brusquely pushed past me, a long fighting dagger in his fist.

"Is she here?" he demanded without looking back.

"Is who here?" I asked, scrambling to follow.

Radrin reached the living room, and he entered with the slightest crouch, obviously prepared for combat.

"Is she here, Vazeer?"

"No."

He turned to me halfway, but he did not expose his back to any of the unseen areas of the apartment.

"You swear this?" he demanded. "I will not take well to a lie at this moment."

"I swear."

"But she *was* here?"

"Yes."

Radrin now fully angled his posture and glared at me more directly. He was standing just inside the living room, and as I came to join him, he adopted an expression—contempt, possibly; judgement, definitely—which interrupted the smoothness of his face.

"You're in a relationship with Shade of Night?"

I sighed weakly and nodded.

"I thought we were done with this sort of behavior," he said.

I tried to smile disarmingly, but my face felt stupid.

"Understand, Vazeer, I will end this thing," Radrin said, in a voice that was all the scarier for being so composed. "With or without your consent. I'm giving you fair warning."

"But why? Why does it matter?" I sputtered. "She's helping us. She told Gueritus I was dead, which, I don't need to explain to you, is a severe breach of her code…just to protect me."

Radrin absorbed this, doing something analytical with it, while his eyes became dense like green marble.

"The woman's instinct to break her codes does not increase my confidence," he said, "especially when she's been contracting bids right under your nose. Did she tell you about those?"

"I don't ask those sorts of questions."

I had asked *exactly* those sorts of questions; it's just that the response I received ended the discussion.

"You could probe all you wanted, and I doubt she would tell you what she's really been doing."

"What…?" I asked, and I inadvertently swallowed at just that moment, making my reaction absurdly hyperbolic.

"Killing the very men that Count Tygean will need if he is going to make this grand restoration dream of yours possible.

Your new lover has been taking bids on the lesser Underlords that will eventually underpin the plan. So far, she's finished one of Tygean's sub vassals—a very smart administrator from what I hear—one of Count Donblas's direct vassals, along with his Chief Legate, who almost certainly would have come over to Tygean's side. For all I know, Shade killed Donblas himself. I'm not sure exactly how she's managed all of this, but I definitely know who hired her."

Now a revolting glaze infected my panic, as if I'd just learned that my lover was sleeping with a family member (mine, or possibly hers).

"She's bidding for Gueritus?"

"There's nobody else that would want that specific array of men dead and could also afford her fees. Shade is one of his principal weapons in this war. He has plenty of money but insufficient manpower, so he can't send his remaining men all over the Labyrinth on lengthy searches. I can't quite fathom how Shade has such good intelligence, but she has it."

Oh, I could fathom it, and this new realization only made me sicker. Radrin was clearly unaware that Shade of Night's finishing operation included the greatest Eye in the history of our city. This wasn't something I wanted to reveal, since I had already promised him that this particular Eye was now working for us.

Radrin turned away, imbued suddenly with the scent-catching bristle of a predator. He began to walk slowly through my living room, the dagger tapping lightly against his thigh, and as he came close to the guest room, he stopped. I had left that door open, thinking—possibly wisely, possibly not—that a closed door would look suspicious; however, this presented a new problem, for Radrin stared inside with interest.

"Shade was here recently," he said, without looking back.

I don't know what he saw, or smelled, or sensed to tell him that, but it definitely wasn't a question.

"But I did not see her leaving your apartment," he continued, "and I observed your unit for some time before I knocked. I also heard you talking to somebody."

Now he entered the guest room, and I tried to decide whether I should follow him or run back into the entry hallway and grab a weapon.

"This is a curious new wall hanging," came his voice from inside.

I abandoned the weapon idea and jogged to the doorway, just in time to see Radrin arrive at the tapestry. The room was dim, but there was enough light filtering in from the living room for him to study the purple, green, and gold print. It was a complex Inland Kingdom piece, a weave of hexagons and stars, bordering a garden scene. In the background, a great range of mountains crossed the image, while in the foreground, two lovers were intwined in sensual embrace. This had been Shade's decorative contribution, provided the day after she knocked a hole in my wall. I could clearly see the fabric rippling lightly on air currents from behind.

"So, this is how she did it," Radrin muttered, and he reached out with the other hand, grabbed the tapestry, and tore it violently from the wall.

17

GRAND DISPATCHER

The tousle of colorful silk twanged to the side like a woman's delicate undergarment, and there revealed before us was the vulgar little aperture through which all of my credibility had been sucked. Radrin glared at the dim opening for a moment without moving. I couldn't tell if he saw something beyond, but his militant carriage suggested that Shade might, in fact, be standing on the other side, ready to face him. And I, with no weapon in hand and teeming with confusion, tried to formulate a plan. Was I prepared to defend her again? Would I risk it all to save the life of this woman who had been loyal to me personally but a traitor to my dreams, though of course she knew nothing of that, and likely wouldn't care.

Crouching slightly, Radrin pushed off and launched himself through the hole. The sight of him disappearing into darkness with the long dagger gleaming before him snapped me out of my indecision, and I knew immediately that I was prepared to do whatever was necessary to keep him from harming her. Shade of Night was certainly capable of defending herself; however, I knew that Radrin Blackstar was a different species entirely than her usual targets, and when I stepped through a second later, it became apparent that she knew this too. She was gone.

A quick search of the unit confirmed it. The infinitesimal rippling of the tapestry that had alerted Radrin had likely been caused by a cross-draft when she exited her front door.

After checking all the rooms carefully, Radrin made his way back into Shade's bedroom where the opening was located, and there, her untidiness was on full display. In fact, it had worsened, for two of the bureau drawers were open, with blouses and stockings spilling out. I looked at the chaotic scattering of footwear on her carpet, thinking, perhaps, that I might determine which pair she had selected for her escape, but I soon learned that I had a limited memory for such things.

Radrin toured somberly through the clutter, kicking through her boots and shoes, lifting her emerald dress from the bedframe, studying it, then tossing it aside. His glower was equal parts magisterial scrutiny and disdain.

"Risky, Shade," Radrin muttered at her vanity area, where he was systematically opening each of her little vials of perfume. Upon uncorking a nondescript gray bottle, Radrin twitched his head back and scowled. "Lathrin oil."

The name was familiar, but I couldn't remember what it did.

"Just a few drops of this in a target's wine," Radrin explained, "and temporary paralysis ensues, making them an easy kill. To even possess it within the confines of the Empire results in a ten-year prison term."

Radrin tried a few more bottles, and eventually he reached a small purple one that he sniffed, then recorked quickly, turning to me with a severe look.

"Discovery of this one would be an automatic death sentence."

"What is it?"

"Colyrox."

Even I knew what that was. Colyrox was the most lethal contact poison ever created, derived first from serpent venom and then mixed with herbal compounds that enhanced it and allowed its deleterious qualities to survive on a blade for a couple of hours. Some Finishers allegedly smeared it on their weapon just before an attack; however, between the prohibitive cost, legal ramifications, and the dangers of accidentally wounding oneself while applying it, Colyrox wasn't considered a popular option.

"These two alone justify what I have to do," said Radrin, and he took the bottles and stuffed them into a pocket inside his cloak. "My apologies in advance, Vazeer, but this woman has had plenty of opportunities over the years to stay in my good graces, and she never seems to take them."

Set in the context of this uncivil room tossing, following on the heels of Shade's dire warning, this comment brought me to the moment beyond which cryptic reticence was no longer acceptable.

"Who the hell are you, Radrin Blackstar?" I asked. "Or rather, *what* are you, because I'm having more and more trouble believing that you're just another Shadow Bidder."

Radrin paused in his inspection, his measuring glance telling me that a degree of frankness was coming.

"I'll give her this," he said. "For someone so willing to jettison her codes, she does a reasonable job of holding her tongue. She hasn't said anything to you about me?"

"Just that she loathes the mere thought of you."

"That hatred is a thing of her own creation. I was originally quite accommodating, going so far as to offer her a job."

"A job? Working for whom?"

Now he offered a small, open-hand gesture, as if acquiescing to the fact that this conversation could no longer be avoided.

"Some time ago, you asked me if I had a secret proffer on this undertaking. You wondered if maybe somebody was contracting me to kill the Raving Blade, to kill the High Lord too. Do you remember?"

"Of course I remember."

"Well, the answer is I do have a proffer. But he's not anonymous."

The impulse towards a follow-up question arose, but it couldn't advance, for something else intervened. Every once in a while, I get such a bad case of goosebumps that it feels as if I'm having some sort of medical emergency, a circulatory rash that attacks the back of my arms, my neck, and even my skull. So it was when Radrin Blackstar dangled this provocative thing before me.

Gliding just beneath the goosebumps was the weirdest of thoughts, harkening back to the dream I had experienced at the height of the Narrow Bid. At that time, as the frigid waters of the Swell Driver gripped my body, a wild hallucination laid hold of my mind. During its culmination, Radrin Blackstar had appeared to me, and in both language and gesture, he had implied that *I* was the proffer on the Narrow Bid, and while I had more or less relegated the memory to fever dream territory, I had never entirely forgotten it. Just now, awaiting the thing that was about to come out of his mouth, I was momentarily terrified that he would pick up that same bizarre thread. It made no sense, obviously, this idea of me being the proffer, but nothing about this man made sense, and several things about me also made no sense, and I was provisionally terrified that this was the exact moment it would all come together.

"The name of the man who employs me," said Radrin, "is Marcus Reldus Besidian. Otherwise known as Nesabedrus II."

"What?" I said.

Radrin nodded. "You heard me."

"It's a joke."

"No, it's definitely not. I work directly for the Emperor himself. I am here on his orders."

There are those revelations in life that are horrifying, and then there are those that are merely shocking, and this disclosure, ironically, was the latter, providing a strange swill of relief.

"You're an agent of Tergon?"

Radrin nodded. "You could call me that. I am the man that Nesabedrus sends to take care of the Empire's most difficult problems. I answer to nobody but him, and no others hold my position."

"A spymaster?"

"The formal title is 'Grand Dispatcher,' but it is never used, for only a handful of individuals even know that I exist."

I eased over to Shade's bed and sat down, the flouncy motions unleashing a small chorus of squeaks. Associated as they were with more pleasurable circumstances, I found the sound a risible mismatch to this moment.

"The Emperor sent you…to do what?"

Radrin leaned against the vanity, causing it to rock and clink the little glass receptacles. With the dagger still in his right hand, he used the left to slide open one of the drawers and peek inside. I don't know what he saw in there, but it didn't interest him enough to shuffle around.

"My mission for many years now has been to carefully monitor, and at times influence, the activities of the Underlords. I come and go from the city, but when I am here, that is what I am doing."

"You influence them…how?"

"The same way I monitor them. I have cultivated key informants in the Lower City, and through them I disperse useful information that helps the Imperial cause. Donblas's Chief Legate was one of those men, so you can see why I am not well disposed towards your paramour at the moment."

This, I suppose, did make sense. However, "monitoring" and the simple dispersing of information did not entirely describe Radrin's recent activities.

"Has your mission changed?"

"It has. There are problems facing the Empire that will soon weaken our position in Sullward, and other Imperial holdings. I have visited assorted locations in the last year, neutralizing threats where I found them. However, this city is complicated. It has taken me a while to determine the greatest problem that might arise here as Imperial power wanes, and I have come to the conclusion that it is Count Ulan Gueritus."

"Whom you have just effectively made High Lord."

Radrin now leaned all of his weight against the vanity and stared up at the wide plank ceiling for a few seconds. Finally, he whistled out a long exhalation.

"Not all of my ideas work out as planned," he said. "I should have suspected that the Narrow Bid was too good to be true."

I thought back to that fateful night, remembered the sight of Radrin clutching his head in that underground pantry, coming to grips with the identity of the target. His shock then had seemed genuine and intense. Nonetheless, the "Grand Dispatcher" had quickly jettisoned our original mission and pivoted to the new, far more treacherous one: murdering High Lord Beranardos Sherdane.

"You sure reacted quickly to the surprise," I said.

"I had to make a swift judgement call. I decided, in that moment, that I would never get a better chance to bring the entire system down than to kill Sherdane. For decades now, Tergon had been benefiting from the activities of the Underlords, but those benefits are certain to end, one way or another."

I shifted my position on the bed, releasing more squeaks, and also, I could have sworn, the softest hint of Shade's smell. I was again acutely present to the crude violation of this break-in. Radrin eased off of the vanity and now began to walk slowly through the room, continuing to kick lightly at the items in his path, at one point stepping directly on a pair of Shade's white stockings.

"Regarding the blackmail story," he continued, "that information tracked closely with my own intelligence, which is part of why I believed the Narrow Bid was real. For quite some time, I have been aware that Countess Shaeyin Odel was up to something. She was often sneaking away from the Capital, concocting improbable excuses. I assumed it was an affair with a married noble, or possibly a man of disrepute, or even a woman, for there had been some rumors along those lines. Rumors that I have subsequently dismissed, since I now believe them to be a salacious falsehood spread by the Countess herself. She was simply diverting attention from her real secret, and also trying to drive off the legion of noblemen who were forever seeking her hand. In any case, I found it plausible that a scheming man like Count Ulan Gueritus might have uncovered Shaeyin Odel's affair and was using it to blackmail her. This made the Narrow Bid an almost irresistible lure for me, since it accomplished two critically important objectives at the same time."

One of those—dealing a fatal blow to the Underlord power structure—I could see immediately. Beyond that, I wasn't sure what Radrin might have been after. He quickly clarified.

"My second priority was freeing Countess Odel of her bind," he said. "I thought it might restore peace between us."

He had now arrived at the room's closet, and he drew back the curtain and began to explore. He swept a bunch of Shade's dresses aside, knocking one off the hanging bar, and then he probed the space beyond.

"Restore peace? Did you go tossing her bedroom too?"

"In a sense," he said from inside the closet. "I did some digging, which wasn't much appreciated. Shaeyin Odel is one of the few people in the Capital who know I exist, and I am one of the few people who do not think highly of her. However, such feelings can never be expressed to the Emperor, since he is entirely taken with her."

A moment later Radrin emerged from the wardrobe, carrying the thing that he had presumably been looking for. In his arms was a purple leather travel trunk, studded with brass rivets, which he ported to the bed and plunked down heavily. Opening it, we saw Shade of Night's tools of the trade—two dozen small blades of different sizes and shapes. Additionally, the case contained several garotte wires, assorted sharpened hairpins, and a few fascinating novelty pieces, such as ornate metal claws, a decorative pen that was actually a reinforced stabbing implement, and a pretty narcotics pipe that was, upon closer examination, a means of blowing darts. I had always wondered if there was such a cache in her apartment, though, as a general rule, I try to respect a woman's privacy.

"At least she was smart enough not to keep the poison in this case," said Radrin. "Still, a constable might go checking the blades and eventually find one with residue. That should be more than enough evidence for the magistrate."

"Blackstar," I said in appalled amazement. "I hardly have the feather touch with women, but next to you I feel like chivalry's steward. I don't know what job you offered Shade of Night, but I can see why she didn't take it."

"My manners weren't the problem. Neither was the fee, because I offered her a good portion of the Imperial treasury."

"To do what?"

He slid the darts he had been inspecting back into their holder and turned to me.

"To Kill Lave Kaszivar. It was achievable back then, or at least I think it was, and Shade was in a unique position to accomplish it. But she refused out of principle. Fear too, I assume."

Faintly, Sixth Bell came to us through the bedroom window glass, and Radrin, perhaps remembering that we had more important matters to deal with tonight than Shade's use of toxic substances, closed the trunk. He left it where it was and made his way slowly towards the entrance to my apartment, though I sensed that he had not entirely abandoned Shade's vexing presence. There was a palpable animosity here, an almost cardinal opposition between these two.

"Listen," I said, stopping him before he stepped through. "I wasn't just being droll earlier, when I chided you about women. I'm about to bring you to a room full of them, and they are going to have to like you, or, at the very least, trust you enough to go along with our plan. These aren't easy women to impress."

Radrin, still possibly affected by his admission of a failing, smiled and shrugged.

"They may not like me, but they seem to like you. So, if you want your grand restoration dreams to come true, you'd better figure out how to sell me to them."

And with that, he stepped through the aperture back into my apartment.

I followed, and when I had made it to the cusp of my bedroom, I faced him. He stood in the center of the living room, composed and alert, as always.

"Tell me something," I said. "Is this talk of 'grand dreams' a mere mockery? You laughed at my ideas before."

"I'm not mocking you. Though the chances of it all coming to pass seem remote at best."

"I don't deny that, but would Tergon stand in our way, if the restoration of the Lower City started to work?"

"No. Tergon would support the effort, if it meant the eventual end of the fencing operation and continued allegiance to the Empire."

"It would mean both," I said. "To whatever degree I have a say in the matter, it would mean both."

After that, I entered my bedroom and turned my attention to getting dressed. As I rummaged through my wardrobe, selecting the proper apparel for the night's meeting, I found that the earlier chills had transformed into warm prickles. Tergon was on our side. The Emperor Nesabedrus II, ruler of all lands from Eastern Inlands to Western wastes, from the northern reaches of the Derjian Sea to the islands of the distant South, had sent his best man to help us. There he was, standing in my living room, the most capable and deadly agent in the Empire.

I pulled out a dark green tunic, a pair of charcoal gray pants, boots of medium height, sporting dull metal buckles. As I made myself presentable (and hopefully appealing) to the night's discriminating audience, I tried to fathom what had just happened. It was a dangerous development, to be sure. Figures like Radrin Blackstar—anonymous to the world, mentioned only in passing in the annals of history—had wielded ruthless, obstacle-clearing blades since the founding days of the Empire. The fabled

Asadeissia had supposedly made generous use of such men as she eliminated the most zealous opponents to her Dawn of Reason. These "Grand Dispatchers" were so much more than Finishers. One didn't need to read an extensive treatise to grasp why an intimidating figure like Shade of Night would slink half-naked from her apartment, leaving the bulk of her weaponry behind, just to avoid a face-to-face confrontation.

Fully dressed, I strapped on my spade belt and began to slide home my many implements, fitting jacks into hidden folds, stilettos into secret sheaths, a throwing dagger into my right boot; though, I didn't anticipate needing any of it. The Grand Dispatcher was my escort. Which was not to say that all of my problems were solved. Weird symbols lingered, unsettling, premonitory dreams and ancient philosophies continued to haunt the peripheries of my existence. The details Merejin had explained on our Dockside stroll were not entirely dismissible; however, at least I could now remove one thing from the mix. The enigmatic, calculating man standing in the other room, with his high-collared cloak and fiendishly quick dagger, could be shifted into the "known" column.

He was merely the Emperor's Grand Dispatcher. That's all. And while this was not a small thing, it was better than the many identities I had projected upon him, ranging from a physical incarnation of caustic human needfulness to an ambassador from Hell. Tergon's Grand Dispatcher was much more manageable. And all that other weird stuff? I would simply have to sort it out later.

I approached the doorway, largely ready, my mind and body primed for the task that lay ahead, which I knew would not be easy. I would sell them. I would convince Terza and Adelyn and even Heshna that this was the man for the job, and I would make this pitch without revealing who and what he was, since, it went without saying, this was not the sort of thing that should be revealed. Not yet, at least. Not ever, possibly, for he might never allow it, and I would simply have to be okay with that. Sometimes that's what you had to do in service of a dream— carry it inside, manage the intensity, the feelings, the truth. A mad dreamer did this. A mad dreamer could hold it all within himself, simmer with solitary understanding, burn broodingly in the conflagration of a secret.

I stepped into the living room, and there my companion stood, gazing at me. However, something was wrong. Something was very wrong, for, though I was staring at Radrin Blackstar, the erstwhile Shadow Bidder, standing right where I left him, cloak on, collar up, waiting casually, he was accompanied, horrifyingly, by something else.

Blazing in the soft jump of the room's lamplight, framed by the orderly sweep of his dark blond hair, a circular thing was visible on his forehead. Sharp little arms emerged from its core— spiraling, reaching, hooked and grasping. Its searing clarity made it a thing not of the crust but the core, abruptly emergent, like a tunneling troll that had clawed its way into the light.

More visible than Radrin's face, more tangible than the floor beneath my feet, was the Summoner from Darkness, whirling its way back into my life, arriving just in time to make havoc of my dreams.

18

TOUGH AUDIENCE

"Vazeer," he said in a cold, startling voice. "The Half Bell just rang, we must get moving."

Still standing in my living room, him in the center, me near my bedroom, I found that I'd lost all grip of time. What did he mean 'Half Bell'? Wasn't it Sixth Bell just a couple minutes ago, in Shade's apartment?

"Vazeer," he snapped again, as if I had fallen asleep during a watch shift. "You need to focus. It's time to go."

Scouring his forehead, I saw only smooth pale flesh, with no hint of a symbol. Had this happened? *When* had it happened, since there was no lingering trace of a nascent thing, just a cool plane of unscarred skin.

"Come now," he said curtly, and he started down my entry hallway. I followed listlessly, and once he opened the door, he swept his arm to usher me out. I locked up, then we were gliding down the stairs and out the back door into the streets.

Full night had fallen, and as we threaded our way through the darkest of alleys, peering through a dense layer of mist, I tried to return to the task at hand, which wasn't easy. My mind was disoriented, but it couldn't stay that way. The hours from Sixth to Eighth Bell were busy in Dockside, and simply escaping the neighborhood with minimal human contact was a challenge. Several times, Radrin pushed me to a standstill at the head of a tight intersection, as he waited and scanned, and then, after some figures had walked past, he had us resume. At the northern reaches of Stitcher's Way, a wide street where the bulk of the cloth vendors, tailors, and sail merchants set up shop, I became aware of something flashing conspicuously in the corner of my vision. I turned and was stunned to see a hooked little whirlwind, reflective in the steamy gloom, coiling. It was my Oulmaen symbol, beckoning from the murkiness of a shut.

"This way," Radrin said, and he tugged me towards that exact alley. He didn't say why, he didn't say what, if anything, he saw, or knew, or sensed. He just led, and as he did, I recalled his behavior in the latter portions of the Narrow Bid when, with chilling accuracy, he had directed us back into the compound, always knowing where to go and how to avoid the next threat. Did it appear to him too? Did it spin before his eyes in the darkness like a devilish pinwheel, calling him away from one danger towards another, moving us ever onward to the execution of the bid?

"Wait," he breathed as we neared the end of our constricted route; and, sure enough, the image was there—pulsing, back-illumined and crisp, the dark cyclonic lines grinding against an even darker backdrop. It was clearly communicating. In its own way, it said "Stop."

Pressed back against a wall, a musky compost smell making our urban runnel feel like a battlefield trench, we waited in silence. A group of men suddenly filed past, the hilts of their weaponry dully glinting, the quiet scuff of their boots steady enough to suggest they weren't drunk. I couldn't tell who they were, whether they hailed from one of Dockside's gangs, or were possibly men from the Lower City, doing the gods only knew what here, but I did know one thing: Summoner didn't want us to meet them. Summoner did not find it advantageous for us to be seen by these men, to exchange words, to be threatened by, or possibly attacked, by them.

"Let's go," Radrin said a moment later, and lo and behold, the symbol had started to move onward, a gyrating black signal torch flickering its way through the foggy night.

This was certainly my chance to ask him. I could come right out with it, demand to know what, if anything, he saw, and if this was his creepy secret; but I didn't. I didn't, because I sensed it should not be asked, and the part of me that knew this was the same part that understood what Summoner meant when it moved forward and what it meant when it stopped, and what it was telling me when it spiraled briefly and blazingly upon Radrin Blackstar's forehead, identifying him, so obviously, as something much more significant and dangerous than a Grand Dispatcher.

We arrived at Paintings and Prints a quarter of an hour later. While I was still finding it difficult to get my head back in the mission, I was aided by a visceral memory of the last time I had entered this shop. As I rapped on the side door, I could recall the weight of Terza's shoe pressing down on my face, relive the shameful moment when I realized that all my efforts to be her savior had turned into a farce. Adelyn would never allow anything like that to occur tonight; however, as irony would have it, it was Adelyn that I feared most.

The "Allayer" could read people. She might even be able to read Radrin Blackstar, which would be a major accomplishment, though more plausibly she would find him unreadable, which wouldn't help our cause. It was also possible that she would react as Selene had, sensing dark, murderous things about the man that made him seem like a moral and emotional vacuum. That, too, would be unhelpful.

A moment later the door opened, and I was a bit surprised by the brawny, weatherbeaten face that greeted me, about a half foot below my own. Grimacing inhospitably, she observed me as if I was a vagrant she had just caught pissing against her building.

"I swear, Lash, I can see Terza's footprint on yer face, clear as day. Improves the sight of ya, I think."

"It's nice to see you too, Getta; you're also looking well."

"That's crap, and ya know it. I look like shit, always have."

She stepped back a pace and made a muscly arc of her stubby arm, granting us entry but no welcome, which was all you could hope for from Getta Reed. Amply decked in the dark padding and strapped leather of her trade, this grouchy Grell Runner looked every bit the thick-skinned, coarse-mouthed brute she prided herself in being. She had a bristly tangle of formerly dark hair that was going silver in places, and her squat, heavy-jawed face was a grim, North Derjian classic. Adding to the overall effect was a small tattoo of a snarling badger on her right cheek, which somebody other than Terza must have drawn, because it was uglier than hell. That said, it did represent her perfectly.

None of this was to suggest that I disliked Getta Reed. At a minimum, I respected her, for she handled a skiff extremely well, had an excellent working knowledge of our waterways, and she could hold her own in a fight. Her artifact appraisal skills were a different matter, and our contentious moments had come when she tried to cover up for ignorance during negotiations with sarcasm, which is always a dead giveaway that a Runner has no idea what something is worth. You only feared you were being cheated when you didn't know whether you were being cheated, and throwing on a snide load of histrionics at such moments achieved nothing except to endanger a deal. This is what had happened on two occasions, and after that, I made it known that any bid of mine that included Getta Reed required that she remain in the skiff and not come on board the buy ship. This hadn't done much to endear me to her.

"Who ya brought with ya, Lash, another smartass that thinks he knows better than the rest of us?"

Syntax notwithstanding, that wasn't the worst characterization of Radrin Blackstar I'd ever heard. I made a quick introduction between them, which received a dour sneer from Getta and a small, cordial nod from Radrin.

Beyond our delightful greeter, I saw that the main gallery remained sparse, with no tables or furnishings of any kind. It did, however, contain the three people I had been expecting, standing back a little ways, watching. Sicking Getta on us was a deliberate goad, and possibly a prelude to further entertainment along these lines. My gaze was drawn first to Terza, as it always was. She wore a long burgundy, silver-trimmed tunic, crisscrossed at the waist with two black weapons belts, and she had swathed her long, muscular legs in a pair of dark silk hose, which descended into oxblood-colored boots. It seemed she was allowing her gradually lengthening brown hair to tousle naturally about her face, as opposed to jabbing irritably with the assistance of hair oils.

Flanking her were her de facto lieutenants, and they, too, didn't have quite the martial bearing I expected for this meeting. Adelyn, always an appealing sight, was even more so today. Her curly hair was pulled back loosely in a ponytail, and this allowed many wispy tendrils to escape in the front, creating a distinctly romantic effect. She wore a clean, belted white blouse, with a sparkling gold pin at her throat. Even wicked little Heshna was just a bit more presentable than usual. Her dirty blond hair was combed and had been parted on one side, with a clean, sweeping bang offering useful coverage of her pasty forehead.

"Aren't you going to introduce us to your guest, Vazeer?" Terza said, in a tone that was not unfriendly.

"Yes, of course," I said. Then I went back and forth with names, which felt ridiculous, because all parties were well aware of each other. I ushered Radrin into the middle of the space and started to explain, as if they didn't know already, that he and I had been working together closely on everything, and how confident I was in his capabilities…etc., etc.

"That's fine, Vazeer, we can take it from here," said Adelyn.

Thereafter, they did just that.

"Will there be an Empress in Tergon?" Terza demanded, striding right up to Radrin and stopping a mere foot and a half away. Their eyes—his green and dark, hers gray and fervid—locked on an equal plane, for they were essentially the same height.

"Terza," I said, "Radrin is a Sullward Shadow Bidder, like us. He doesn't—"

"Quiet, Vazeer," she said without looking at me. "There are some snacks in the other gallery, so go help yourself. I'm going to speak to this man for a few minutes without you butting in."

And now the four of them surrounded Radrin, Terza taking the point position, Adelyn standing just to the side, and Heshna and Getta closing in on the rear. This wasn't, I imagined, a position a Finisher was often in, but Radrin reacted to it calmly, continuing to lock gazes with Terza.

"Yes," he answered after a moment. "If the current trajectory holds, the next ruler of the Empire will be female."

"A young female, too," said Terza, "who might have a long, influential reign. Right?"

"Or a very short one," he replied, "that ends with a knife in her back."

"Your knife?"

"That is not my intention."

"Terza," I interjected again. "What does this have to do—"

"Vazeer," she snapped. "Either go stick a piece of cheese in your mouth, or keep it busy some other way. This man knows things that are important to me, important to all of us."

Heshna glanced over at me from her flanking position, and despite the nicely brushed exterior, she delivered one of her withering stares.

"Shade told me he's some sort of Imperial officer," she said. "Or maybe a contract agent who bids only for the Emperor. Either way, he's not just a Shadow Bidder, Brood brother. If you didn't realize that by now, you're even dumber than I thought."

So much for Shade of Night's impressive code of silence. So much too for my sales job, which wasn't going even remotely according to plan.

"Which one is it, Radrin Blackstar?" Terza prodded from her threatening proximity. "Are you an independent, or an Imperial agent?"

It was an uncomfortable thing to watch, this crossroads, brought on by Terza Falconbrow but observed assiduously by Adelyn the Allayer. Which, by the way, was exactly what was going on here. I was present to another tandem, like Heshna and Shade, with Terza standing at the fore—intimidating Terza, always right up in it, forcing any person into a moment of unavoidable reckoning—while the ever-discriminating Adelyn passed judgement on it all. I couldn't imagine how my cohort was going to handle this.

At last, Radrin flicked his chin towards the back wall of the gallery.

"You are asking that question because you wonder if I will take personal offense at the Imperial emblem on the slain priest's surcoat. More to the point, am I interested in punitive action against you?"

I now glanced at the large, vibrant painting on that wall, *Fall of the Patriarchy*, Terza's masterwork. My gaze was drawn to the nine female shapes in the foreground; to the diaphanous purple ripples of the Storm Maidens' robes, dancing on antiquity's winds. Then I found my way to the piece's more gruesome elements—the high priest's leaking head in Giradera's fingers, the crimson runnels gliding down the radiant length of her sword. Finally, I observed the other half of the ancient queen's murderous act, the very thing Radrin was referencing. Visible through the women's legs was the headless body, wearing, anachronistically, a surcoat (these hadn't arrived in the Midlands until two centuries after the fall of Azmoul). On this surcoat was painted faintly, but unmistakably, the gold tower emblem of the Besidians. For some reason I had missed it the first time. For some other reason (but probably the same reason), Terza Falconbrow kept defying all my expectations of how goddamned stupid she was.

"So, will you?" Terza demanded, moving even closer to Radrin and shifting her body minutely, in that special Terza way. She was prepared to take care of this matter right here and now. So, too, was Getta, who was not so subtle as the others, but who sure could do some nasty work with that gutting dagger, which she had drawn halfway out of its sheath.

Radrin shrugged.

"I wish the problems facing the Empire were so simple that punishing a seditious painter would fix them. And while I do recommend that you change the emblem before you go presenting this piece to the world, matters of this sort are not my concern."

Without turning her head, Terza muttered to Adelyn.

"Is he telling the truth?"

Adelyn tacked her lips a few times and finally raised her eyebrows in a gesture of diagnostic surrender.

"He's a tough one to read. But if he's telling lies, it's not about this."

"Shade doesn't trust him," Heshna blurted from behind.

"Shade doesn't trust anyone," Terza shot back. "Including us. Which is why she isn't here right now, whereas this man is."

My Brood sister didn't have an adequate response to this, so she clamped her little mouth shut and returned to sullen glowering. Terza cocked her position again, a slight angling of the hip, a tip of the face, that moved her infinitesimally closer to parley, and away from a deathblow.

"So, these problems facing the Empire. You're here to fix them?"

"One of them, hopefully."

"And that painting on the wall behind me," she continued, "would you view that as a problem too? I'm not talking about the seal, which maybe, just maybe, I'd be willing to change, seeing as things could be moving in that direction anyway, but the rest of it. Do you have a problem with the vision?"

Here, Radrin undertook what, to all outer appearances, was an intense analysis of the artwork.

"There will indeed be a problem," he finally answered. "However, the problem will be for you, when you watch the new Empress take the throne, only to find that she does not share your vision. She will not be restoring the religious ideals of ancient Azmoul, nor its matriarchy."

"How do you know?"

"Because I am well acquainted with her, and while it's difficult to grasp what, precisely, resides in another person's heart, I am certain that your vision isn't one of those things."

"What does reside there?" Adelyn asked.

Radrin smiled bleakly.

"More problems."

For a time, nobody spoke. Then, when it seemed that either Terza or Adelyn might venture a follow-up, Radrin prodded things in a different direction.

"There is another woman, not from Tergon, whom I believe would be very taken with your painting. According to reliable sources, she is making preparations to bring her fleet here now."

"So I keep hearing," said Terza.

"However," Radrin continued, "when she comes, I fear you won't be any happier with her than the future Empress. At her core, Lave Kaszivar is a marauder. She is good at destroying things, but I doubt she will show much aptitude for building them. Or, as Vazeer hopes, rebuilding them."

At the mention of my name, Terza's face was colored by a cynical tint.

"He's spouted his obsession to you, has he?" she asked.

"He has. Another improbable vision, like your own."

"Like mine? You think our two ideas are similar?"

"No," Radrin answered. "Vazeer's idea is actually possible. Yours is not."

Radrin had been doing reasonably well so far in this interview, even coolly adjusting to the fact that his audience knew elements of his identity, but this was a misstep. I watched Terza closely, to see if her inspired painter's fingers reached for a different sort of implement, if muscles in her neck readied themselves to launch her avian artwork crashing down on Radrin's nose. I was prepared for anything, and Terza's bellicose scowl did nothing to reassure me.

"But I will say this," Radrin added, looking once more at the painting. "I have been to the Capital Gallery in Tergon many times, and while I am hardly an expert on art, I believe that this piece would not be out of place there, minus the seal of the Besidians. It is a very fine work. Quite possibly a masterpiece."

On the breadth of Terza's cheekbones, I saw some compacting, which possibly signified doubt, or maybe embarrassment.

"Addy," she mumbled, "is this Imperial spook merely honeying me now?"

Adelyn leaned in to examine Radrin with the squinty appraisal of a gemstone merchant.

"I don't detect any 'honey' in this one. I think he means it, including the parts we don't like."

And finally, with this exchange, I saw my opening. Having contributed nothing so far, I felt that this might be an opportunity.

"Let me say something you *will* like, Terza," I ventured. "*Fall of the Patriarchy* will hang in the center of the Arcadium, the restored Arcadium; this is something I have already mentioned to Count Tygean, and he is amenable to it. To all of it. We will reconstruct a Capital here, and you will be the first great painter to call it home."

"I'm not a great painter, Vazeer, and you know it."

"I goddamned don't. If there's one person who has always believed in you, it's me. And now there's proof, right on the wall behind you. That painting is just the first of many more still waiting inside you. You're going to fill the whole length and breadth of the Arcadium with them."

Terza was becoming agitated. She was also, I sensed, stirred, but she seemed incapable of stomaching it.

"Addy, tell me the turd's just adding horseshit to spook's honey…"

"He's not," Adelyn replied. "I keep telling you myself."

"But this crap about the Arcadium?"

"Who knows? Vazeer certainly believes it. He's always believed it, for better or worse. Even Heshna remembers him going on about it as a child."

I threw a sidelong glance at my Brood sister, to see if she would seize this opportunity to jab home a verbal knife, but she seemed vaguely disassociated from this discussion. Perhaps Terza's comment about Shade had rattled her. That blunt truth had either come across as an insult or a warning, but either way, it resulted in Heshna appearing withdrawn. I wasn't fooled, of course. The Seer observed everything, and no aspect of this interaction, ranging from spoken words, to gestures, to the least detail—a light fumy smell that always pervaded Terza's gallery, the fact that one of the wall lanterns had started to gutter slightly and was releasing a slow twirl of hoary smoke—escaped her. She simply didn't seem inclined to speak.

Next to her, the fourth and newest member of the team also seemed unlikely to contribute, though for different reasons. Getta Reed had at least figured out that she wouldn't be deploying that gutting dagger, for it was safely back in its sheath. However, that may have been the only thing she understood. Words such as "Arcadium" and "Azmoul" were apparently stumping her, and she had possibly even run afoul of "Besidians" and "Capital Gallery," which would explain why she couldn't appraise anything that had come from farther away than Lothrum.

Terza constricted her eyes into their own peering valuation, much like her counselor. There they stood, the problematic duo, the not-quite-opposing-team who were necessary for our Narrow Bid, but who might decide that our Narrow Bid ultimately wasn't worth the risk. Several long seconds passed, and I wasn't entirely sure how this would turn out.

"Well, what do you think?" Terza asked Adelyn. "Can we trust this man…either of them? Will their plan work?"

No gauging pantomime was needed, just a simple nod.

"I don't think they're lying to us, my dear," Adelyn replied. "They believe in what they're saying. As to whether they're lying to themselves…that's the part I don't know."

Terza pulled in a draught of air, swelling her a little above Adelyn.

"Okay, fine then," she said. "I'm tired of waiting. Let's get this damned bid underway."

19

THE BRIDGE

"The attack won't happen at this bridge," I said, feeling more defensive than certain. "I'll know the thing when I see it. Let's keep moving."

We were standing under the heavy, mildewed protrusion of a gargoyle, watching a canal flicker through a quilt of mist. This section of the Lower City was less desolate than others, evidenced here by many shuttered windows spilling needle slats of yellow across water and cobbles.

"How can you know such a thing?" she asked. "How can you know so many things, especially lately?"

I took in the sight of her, but just for a moment because I didn't like the look on her face. I didn't like the whole face, but the expression was uniquely bad tonight, as I knew it would be. She was sensing something.

"Come on, show me the next bridge" I said. "Get me closer to Gueritus's home."

Heshna the Seer grimaced irritably, but soon she turned and skittered away into the fog. She led us back down a musty street of the Outer Ring, and then angled us towards the inner core. The thoroughfares in this portion of the Lower City were a little easier to navigate than elsewhere, being neither so decrepit nor glorious as those to the north. One of the advantages of surveilling the Outer Ring was the fact that quite a few people not directly affiliated with the Underlords dwelled here. Perhaps as many as half the Shadow Bidder ranks owned or rented in this portion of the Lower City, along with seedier government officials. There were also others who sought anonymity for a whole host of reasons—those currently on the run from the law, or about to be.

"This is the best way through," Heshna said. She pointed down a tight shut, which I could have sworn led nowhere.

"You're sure?"

Her face converted to the more familiar "you're such a clueless imbecile," look, which I found reassuring. Under-expressed though she was, my Brood sister could convey quite a bit of contempt just by the way she stared. This particular gaze, interpreted more fully, said: "You miserable swamp vagrant, I have walked, slithered, and climbed over every square inch of this city for the last thirty years. Of course I'm sure."

I shooed her down the passthrough, finding some irony in the fact that my nemesis and I were finally working together. Our relations so far had been tolerable, if not friendly, and while I suspected that there was some bigger, more consequential thing that needed to be exchanged, that moment had not yet arrived. This joint reconnaissance mission had only been approved after wearing down the stiff resistance of Radrin Blackstar (and Heshna, for she did not like the idea of being alone with me). Eventually, I prevailed on them both by insisting that this was all part of standard Grell Running protocols, and I pushed to have it occur the night after our meeting at Paintings and Prints. Things were moving very quickly now.

Immediately following Terza's consent, I gave the "go" signal to Cad, who promptly gave it to Sebastien, who in turn passed it along to Count Tygean's people, still holed up in the dank, cavernous sepulcher of the Arcadium. We expected to wait only a day or so to hear if the Count's invitation to parley with Gueritus would be accepted, and if so, where the meeting would be set. Once we knew that, we could gauge the Raving Blade's path back to his current dwelling and thereby decide which canal bridge would be the spot for our ambush. Or so my companions thought.

I had a different idea. The phantasmal entity called the Summoner from Darkness had, on occasion, revealed itself to me in the streets of Sullward, and I sincerely hoped that this trend would continue. I wanted it to show me which was the right bridge.

And so, I had my Brood sister lead us on a canal tour, confining our expedition to Gueritus's most feasible routes. Because of the battered state of streets in the inner core, Radrin and I had concluded that Gueritus would make use of the far more serviceable streets of the Outer Ring to reach the meeting site. Moving a large, armed entourage through the Lower City was much easier, and safer, when the troop could employ well-maintained, semi-lit streets, rather than the gapped cobbles, dashed statuary, and rubblized sections of wall that composed most of the areas to the north. We didn't know which of the half dozen open plazas in the Lower City he would pick for the meeting; however, we could, I'm sorry to say, predict his general trajectory to get there.

Unsettling reports about Kaennamin Academy had now moved from speculation into reality, and it appeared that my least favorite person in Sullward had taken up residence in the city's best building. The intricate, iconic school of architecture had never been claimed by anybody in the 213 years since the Great

Storm, for which I'd always been grateful. The damage wrought by a cataclysm and two centuries of neglect had discouraged all who might find shelter there, yet who could deny that it had the potential to be the grandest residence of all? While any form of Lower City restoration was gratifying to me, I simply hated the idea of the Raving Blade inhabiting that space and carrying on his usual, sadistic activities. As it was, I would probably have trouble visiting The Crossbiter Tavern again, based on the horrors I had experienced there.

Heshna led me down the bending furrow, a route that was navigable, though barely, and we were eventually required to scale part of a jagged wall and then step through a little crevice that was the result of structural damage to one of the buildings. This wasn't a through-alley at all, but the depredations of time had made it one. Kudos to my childhood foe for being aware of it, for being aware of so many depredations and degenerations, fissures and cracks, proving that, if she was rodent-like in her manner, this was ultimately to my advantage.

"Next one can be seen a few feet ahead," she said, suddenly emerging from the dim naught. "I don't know what you're looking for, because there's nothing special about this one."

But she was wrong. When I crept to the head of the alley and stared out at the canal-spanning length of stone, humping grayly over silty currents, something distinct happened. My phantom reappeared. Concealed since my journey through Dockside the prior evening, it emerged again, tearing the night's shroud like a spinning blade. Back in the days when it was posing as a subversive wall mural, Summoner had remained stationary, but now the weird messenger had taken to pinwheeling around its circular axis and literally sucking my mind to one spot after another, like kitchen scraps whirled down a drain. My eyes were pulled first to the bridge, which I saw to be unremarkable, as Heshna had said. Its base was dirty granite blocks, like most of the others, and it had low sidewalls built of the same. Yet, Summoner did not linger there, and within seconds it was drawing my eye to the dark waters of the canal itself, off and away to the north. There, they slithered into a tall, lightless gulch between buildings.

Runner's ravines, we called them. There were a lot of them in the Lower City—towering canal canyons, with walls that hemmed in so tightly that you often scraped the stone with your oars. There were no pedestrian paths in the ravines, and seldom did the sheer stone faces feature windows of any sort. Passage at night was a sightless journey, though in the days of the Old Calendar, lanterns were spaced appropriately to make these snug, moody sojourns.

It didn't take me long to see the potential. The bridge itself was relatively wide, perhaps a full eight feet across, and this was going to make hiding below an easier prospect. There was currently about five feet of space separating the surface of the water from the underside of the bridge's crown, and about three feet at the sides. As long as the meeting took place at night, within the next few days, the tide cycle should be similar. All of this I deemed propitious, for it allowed enough room for us to shelter our skiffs, but not so much that we would be visible to anybody from above. A determined observer with a torch would need to hang down from the side of the bridge to see us, which they might actually do, and this was where the efficacy of the runner's ravine came into play. In that inky crevice, we would be invisible. Even with a brightly burning lantern, one could see, at best, forty, maybe fifty feet. Only once the troop had crossed, en route to the meeting, would we paddle into position, and then, on the way back, Gueritus would be too elated with his imminent ascendancy to bother having his men check below the bridge a second time.

"I need to look at the street itself," I said. "I'm going to walk the route that Gueritus will walk."

Heshna's crabby frown grew worse.

"This is just one bridge out of five, Brood brother. What makes you think it's the right one?"

"I should walk all the routes."

"You didn't ask to walk the others."

"My mistake. Let's start with this one."

I turned from her before she could make a fuss, though I did hear an ill-natured hiss behind my back. She had some justification. This was a widely used route in the Lower City, and the ever-watchful denizens of this neighborhood knew the difference between a skulking pedestrian, an Underlord soldier, and a Shadow Bidder. I had gone so far as to wear a cowl tonight to shield my identity, and I pulled it even farther forward as I circled around to the main thoroughfare.

King Benivus Boulevard was the street's true name, though there wasn't a single sign anywhere along its length, and nobody had called it anything other than Edge Winder in the last century. Edge Winder coiled tightly around the peripheries of the inner core, and the residents here, who were on the wealthier end of the Lower City spectrum, obviously had some sway with the state senate, for the avenue was replete with serviced streetlamps and well-maintained cobbles. Municipal attention seemed to have suffered of late, for as I stared down its mildly twisting warp, past the nibbled profiles of stone casings, I saw the faint glow of but one streetlamp, projecting its orange animation from around the bend. Additionally, debris removal had been less than perfect. Overt wreckage from the storm had been carted away; however, little had been done about caked mud, water stains, and a thin layer of mildew that was gaining a new speckled foothold.

This region of King Benivus Boulevard was notable for its liberal use of Old Calendar grotesques, deployed primarily as mortar-protecting rain spouts, but also as a form of architectural rivalry. An amusing rivalry, for some of these freaks really were hilarious. I gazed up at one that seemed to me like some kind of mix between a seagull and a cow, clutching a big spoon, I think. And what was that on its head? A hat or a helmet…or possibly some sort of crown? Across the way was another that was even weirder. This thing was definitely an ape, at least in body, but damn if that chipped old face wasn't a pig's face and those weren't crooked bat wings growing from its back. It didn't even appear designed as a rain spout, suggesting that its true function was retribution against the neighboring gull-cow.

I saw more than a few doors that looked operative. This was good, though some real discretion would be required to pick our spot. It was from one of these that Radrin Blackstar would emerge and perform the deed, and in order for the plan to work, the door needed to be legitimately locked, not just closed. Gueritus's men would try them all. They'd kick in the rickety ones, step through the door wells, poke their torches into every last crevice along the route, and make sure that nobody was hiding somewhere that was easy to hide. Our man needed to hide somewhere that wasn't easy to hide, so we'd put him behind a split locked door, in a place accessible only to the residents themselves. As long as we had just a little advance warning, we'd get our Finisher into position.

I ambled closer to the bridge, searching. I wanted a door on this side, since we would hit the entourage as they started to cross, thereby stalling Gueritus here. The question was, which one? Where was that perfect aperture through which the Grand Dispatcher would conduct his dispatch? Summoner did not make a spiraling appearance this time; it failed to materialize at all. But Vazeer the Lash can sometimes figure things out on his own. Having teamed with one Finisher of late, and intimately coupled with another—not to mention contracting two Narrow Bids in the space of three weeks—I was really starting to get the hang of this thing.

The door I found was a stout, iron-bound specimen, set back in an arched red granite frame As for the building itself, I saw no lights burning in any of the windows, so I slid into the door well. A firm twist of the knob and some forceful shakes revealed that it was securely locked by two visible cylinders. One can never know for sure if a door is barred, but my guess was that this one wasn't, for it had all the hallmarks of a place that somebody had locked and then left. There were some faded footprints in the caked mud, leading away, and there was a thin film of mildew on the knob. The owner had likely departed shortly after the storm and hadn't been back since.

Radrin would make the final determination, as would his Locksmith, but my gut told me that we had our ambush site. So, I approached the bridge itself, which wasn't a good idea. My one protection so far had been the packed proximity of buildings, ensuring that watchers needed to come quite close to recognize me; but this was not true on a bridge.

Bridges marked little breaks in the constriction of the Lower City. There, upon those elegant crossings, you received a limited but inspiring vantage, and with the soothing skate of the canal below, and the aimless drift of the mist above, the most interesting urban angles presented themselves. This was why I had brought Flerra Tellian to a bridge all those years ago on our walking tour. From that spot we could view both Nengriant Basilica, buttressed and towering, and the vaulted heft of Kaennamin Academy, along with a number of other buildings of note. Unfortunately, vantages work both ways, and the gaping profile of two entranced children was something that Holod Deadskiff spotted easily.

Despite the risks, I needed to do this. I needed to imagine how surprised an Underlord soldier might be to have some armed muskrat scrabble over the side wall and start poking him silly; a small pack of muskrats. While I knew Getta and I could get the job done, I was less confident about our Blades, so I strode to the top of the granite overpass, breathing the salty fog, lulled by the whirring waters. I adopted the carriage of one of Gueritus's men, hastening back to Kaennamin Academy to start celebrating.

I could faintly see the wrinkles of current, and when I gazed towards the black splinter of the runner's ravine, I tried to picture if it would draw the eye. In short, it wouldn't. In fact, nothing would make a person look in that direction, since this bridge, stable and dry, traversed a spot that was open by Lower City standards, and those prickly Underlord self-preservation instincts would be mildly assuaged here. That's all I was hoping for. Just enough negligence to allow us to slip over these sidewalls without getting our heads cut off. It wasn't even required that we kill these men, or at least not many, since distraction was the primary objective—something to heighten the impact of Count Tygean's arriving army. In the pinioning crush between two surprise attacks (one a surprise because we were, hopefully, surprising, and the other because it was an inconceivably duplicitous act from a man not known for such things), our Finisher would slide out of an agreeably decorated and locked doorway and run his blade across the Raving Blade's throat.

I spotted the movement as I was standing at the stony apex. It was down the street on the far side, a murky disturbance along Edge Winder, which, irrational as it seemed, I actually thought was Heshna. I had left her behind me, but damned if the slippery Seer didn't constantly find ways to approach from the strangest of angles. For all I knew, she had crawled along the underside of the bridge like a spider.

But a moment later I saw it was not Heshna, and then I noted it wasn't some skittish Outer Ring resident either. This figure had the distinct look of an Underlord soldier, with a dark gray cloak, the protrusion of a hilt at his side, and certain upright confidence to his gait. Furthermore, there were two others behind him, walking in a rough triangle formation, which certainly had a "patrol" look. Given that we weren't far from Kaennamin Academy, an Underlord patrol could really only belong to one group, so I quickly turned and started back the way I had come. Which was useless. Fully exposed on that bridge, I was a proverbial pile of coal in a ballroom, and I heard the scuffs of their boots making fleet echoes as they started to run after me. That's how things were done here, no words like "halt!" or "eh there, ya turd." Once the soldiers of the Lower City took an interest in you, they were coming.

I sprinted away, wounded hip and all. It was bad enough that these men had spotted a nameless Shadow Bidder in threatening propinquity to their home base, surveying a bridge, but should they happen to recognize me, our entire gambit would be compromised. So, I threw myself in the direction of safety. Once off the bridge, I beat a painful retreat towards the next curve in Edge Winder, and there I spotted a pedestrian—a slender fellow with thinning hair, who clearly wanted no part of this, for he immediately stepped down an alley. I glanced over my shoulder and saw that the soldiers had gained on me, and they had also drawn weapons, which appeared like steely smears in their fists.

I stumbled around the bend, trying to compel my legs into a faster rhythm. Up ahead, a small, cowled figure was loitering near the head of a pass. Thinking this to be another shifty Lower City resident, I was surprised when this person nodded in the direction of the opening, indicating that I should turn there. It was Heshna, her dull stare boring into me through the foggy gloom. For a second she simply watched, then she disappeared down the passage, and when I arrived, I followed.

Good old Heshna. Once hated, now needed, she would certainly know how to get us out of here. While I didn't enjoy tracking blindly with no real grasp of the plan, I could only imagine we were fast approaching some secret fissure, or hole in the ground, or hatch in the sky…any of my Brood sister's chosen shake points. Nobody knew this city better than Heshna the Seer.

But this hatch did not materialize quickly, and our desperate, reeling sprint down a clogged track was prolonged. We ran for what felt like half a minute, leaping piles of trash and tumbled architecture, but never turning from our straight course, which seemed a missed opportunity. I could just barely see Heshna's gray, diminutive back in front of me, gliding effortlessly through the warren of wreckage, while a mere thirty feet behind, the panting brutes came, kicking things as they ran, cursing and growing angrier. They closed the distance relentlessly.

Stupid Heshna. No longer so appreciated, was the miserable skulk going to get me out of this, or was I actually going to have to fight these animals? If they were the Raving Blade's men, then I'd be contending with the very worst that Hell's Labyrinth had to offer. I didn't want to deal with even one, let alone three.

Suddenly, I found that I could no longer see my guide. One second, she was there, fleeing through the faintest sections of dappled shutter light, a weaving blink in the dark, and then she was gone. Impossibly gone, and my only recourse was to press on through what seemed a final half-crumbled stony squeeze, opening into…I really had no idea. I jammed myself between the two ruined corners, spilling awkwardly over a broken quoin, and I all but rolled into what I now saw to be a small, dimly illumined quadrangle. A quadrangle that didn't appear to have a way out.

I whirled, looking for the trick. Maybe the Seer had left me one perfect escape route—a tight shimmy, through which bulky soldiers wouldn't hazard pursuit. No, my scanning yielded nothing but four stone walls, with two sunken doors, both of which looked locked. The vindictive rat had run me straight into a deathtrap!

I lunged at one of the doors and crashed it hard with my shoulder. It gave me only a loud, shuddery thud, and possibly a bruise. Wrenching the knob proved equally useless, and now I was out of time, for I turned to see the first of my pursuers coming through the tumbledown opening. There, at least, I might have held them off, using the tight pinch to my advantage, but I had squandered the opportunity. The second man followed, and then came the third, and before I knew it, I was faced with three heavily armed men in a confined space, with no chance of being happened upon by the city watch. The worst scenario of all.

There was a lantern in a third-floor window, rouging our space through a red curtain. By this bloodshot radiance, I observed them, and nothing about the sight gave me confidence.

"Screw a blighted whore!" the lead soldier said, his mustachioed mouth whistling, his dark eyes observing me from beneath the brim of a studded leather hat. "It's the goddamned Lash. How in hell's he not dead?"

"You know how," muttered the one on his right side, who wore nothing on his moppy head, but who had the most armor of the three, with some steel plates woven into his leather cuirass. "Both of us lost money against him at the Shadowbiter. Damned unkillable."

"Not unkillable," said the third, who was larger than the others, with hair that had been shaved down to the dirty sheen of facial stubble. He was starting to come forward in an obvious flanking maneuver. "We'll put him down. Bring his head back to the Rave, and we'll all be Urlords by daybreak."

Studying their getups, I now spotted something surprising. All three wore purple bands tied around their right arms, and while there were no insignias, this was a clear display of colors. Identifying marks of any sort were forbidden among the soldiery of the Underlords, except, I now guessed, during a war.

I drew a spade and stiletto and dropped into a fighting crouch. I also shook off my cowl, and though I felt nothing of the sort, I tried to affect an expression of savagery. I had already determined that sweet-talking these men wasn't going to work. They had been present at the Shadowbiter duel, so they were well-acquainted with my clever tongue. The better bet was to try and make them nervous, which they ought to be after witnessing that fight. Uneasy men could be induced to make mistakes.

"Maybe we should get some backup for this," muttered the moppy-headed one who had called me "unkillable." Good boy. Now I had my nervous target, the one I would try to force into a blunder.

"Maybe you ought to guard our backs, you craven cock," said

the one with the studded hat. "Make sure nobody comes at us through that opening."

Whether or not "craven cock" found this insulting, he seemed to relish the idea of withdrawing from harm's way, and he quickly stepped back to the tight entrance to the courtyard. There, he took up a watchful post, which didn't help my situation. Not only did this remove a potential weak link in the encircling chain, but it also precluded the faint possibility that my Brood sister had some ingenious plan to rescue me. Not sure what that might be, but it definitely no longer involved storming through that opening.

"Let's flank him," said the one with the closely shaved head.

The pair spaced themselves appropriately so that I had to retreat all the way to the back wall, and then they forced me to pivot back and forth as I tried to avoid exposing a side. These weren't neophytes. "Hat" bore the typical spade-stiletto combo, while "Stubble Head" wielded two spades, one being especially large by North Derjian standards. As they closed in from the sides, their movements were well coordinated, with a series of feints and jabs that I had to deflect with both of my weapons simultaneously. Also, Stubble Head, who was larger and bore that abnormally long spade, came at my left, and thus compelled me to use my stiletto to defend his significantly greater reach.

As this plight was on the verge of turning into a disaster, something fascinating happened. That locked door I had tried earlier, which happened to be directly behind Hat, suddenly swung inward. There was no screeching of hinges, no rusty resistance. It opened so abruptly that I didn't even have time to gauge how it might help me, though I found my body pivoting that way. From out of the doorway, with the flickering speed of a lizard's tongue, a hand with a blade came around the front of Hat's neck and pulled a slit across his throat. For a fraction of a second there was merely a dark line. Then it opened and spat, Hat crumpled, Stubble Head turned to face the new threat, and I lunged.

I came in low and mean, going straight for Stubble Head's nether regions, exploiting one of the few disadvantages that oversized combatants had. Catch them below the waist, especially if they happen to be distracted by something up a bit higher, and these heavies simply can't bring a block down in time. Not a block strong enough to stop an unscrupulous student of Holod Deadskiff from jamming his spade straight into the groin. There was a boil-hardened leather cup there, but I didn't need to hit the organ itself, just the region, and I drove my blade deep into the exposed space to the side of the cup. The big man squealed and levered down, and now, with his torso torqued forward, I jammed my off-hand blade hard into his ribs. The Derjian stiletto is such a terrible thing, and I had no trouble burying half its steel length through his relatively light side armor. A final, overhead cleave with my spade put an end to the fight.

By the time I looked up, I saw that the nervous, mop-headed one was already dead. He lay sprawled on the dirty ground near the entrance he was supposed to guard, though I couldn't see exactly which part of him was emitting all the blood. What I *could* see was a figure with a raised collar, standing over the fallen body, calmly wiping his dagger with a small black cloth.

"I suppose this is progress, Vazeer," said Radrin Blackstar, stuffing the cloth and the dagger away into the folds of his clothing. "For the first time that I can remember, you managed to kill a man without screaming."

20

POOR HARBINGERS

"This is your building?" I asked, as I helped Radrin drag the bodies through the open doorway. It was a back entrance, leading into a pantry. During the chase, Radrin had entered the building from the front, making his route shorter and craftier.

"The Emperor owns it," he replied, directing us over to a corner where we piled the bodies, away from the foodstuffs. "He owns many buildings in this city, and I have access to them all."

"Maybe you own the one I spotted near the bridge, with a red granite frame? That would make life easier."

Radrin stood from his task. There was, as usual, no evidence of his handiwork upon him—no crimson sprinkles, no rents in his clothing, not even the glistening polish of sweat. I couldn't even see that dagger of his, nor his soiled black cloth.

"You think that was the right bridge?" he asked.

An oil lantern was now alight, and by means of this softly palpitating glow, I could see Radrin hunting for things, sleuthing my face as if it was a drawer filled with sensitive documents.

"I do."

"Why, Brood brother? Why do you think that?"

Heshna, whose last instruction had been to surveil the surrounding streets, was apparently done with that, for she now seeped quietly through that doorway like a musty odor.

"You just made that bridge more dangerous," she continued. "You just made this whole thing more dangerous. Why would our target become complacent when his men are still being killed?"

My Brood sister stood on the cusp of the doorway. This was ostensibly to see outside, but it also facilitated an easy escape, which might be of interest to her. Her muddy gaze darted back and forth between Radrin and me, and I got the distinct sense that she was trying to decide which of her new, objectionable companions was most responsible for the night's fiasco.

"It might have that effect," Radrin ventured. "But then again, these casualties could prove to the Raving Blade that his strategy of slow attrition works both ways. Count Tygean can take credit for this, and it may give him a leg up in the negotiation."

Heshna did not look reassured. Whatever vatic analysis she was using to sum up her current state of affairs, she wasn't happy with the result.

"I was against this errand," she said, "and you were too, Finisher. My Brood brother does this sort of thing, always. He doesn't think first, and it endangers everyone around him."

"Yes, I'm aware," said Radrin, stepping away from the bodies. "But there is a strange efficacy to his improvisations. The rest of us must simply plan accordingly, as we did tonight."

I had just squatted down to inspect the purple war band on the dead soldiers' arms, but now I pivoted around to look at them.

"You couldn't have told me the plan ahead of time?"

"It was meant for only the worst of circumstances, Brood brother," Heshna replied. "Look how reckless you were *without* knowing it existed. Imagine what you might have done if you thought the Finisher was shadowing you."

"He was?" I asked her, then him. "You were?"

Radrin nodded. "I was prepared to intervene at several points along the way; however, the Seer was successful in drawing the chase all the way to the designated trap point. This location is ideal, as you can see."

When it came to maneuvers of this sort, Radrin had already shown his aptitude, but I was now mentally assigning a new range of capabilities to Heshna. Not only had my Brood sister brought this commotion to the prearranged ambush, but she had the wherewithal (and courage) to make a threatening noise in the alley outside the courtyard at just the right moment. This caused the mop-headed one to turn around and expose his back to the Finisher, putting a quick and relatively painless end to the affair.

Bravo, Heshna, your deadly side gig is really paying off.

"Go tell Cad what happened, and give him these as proof," I said to Radrin, handing him the three purple arm bands. "He'll give them to Sebastien, who'll get them to Tygean. The Count can decide how he wishes to use this incident. And Heshna, let the others know we're coming. It's time to meet Terza's team and see if they have any chance in hell of doing this thing right."

They didn't, which I soon learned. Radrin and I were introduced to the full company a few hours later, and (exactly as Adelyn had predicted) I reacted poorly. These Shadow Bidders were a rather likeable bunch, just the sort that I'd be glad to be teamed with for a routine buy operation from a known shipper, which, needless to say, this wasn't. I had anticipated that Count Ulan Gueritus would act swiftly to sweep up the best of the contract talent in the Labyrinth; however, what I didn't entirely grasp was just how many operatives would simply flee. That's what was happening, en masse.

Those who were given Underlord ultimatums either submitted or else quickly made themselves scarce, and those who were ignored, presumably because they were deemed useless to the Raving Blade's plans, either started looking for another line of work or, in a few select cases, joined us. That's who we were left with: Gueritus's rejects, who were too stupid to avoid our bid.

The gathering happened in a space where Flerra and I used to drink sometimes, back in the days when we did that. It was a small Dockside tavern aptly named the Mad Hussy, which belonged to Getta Reed's older sister, Dorcus, a retired Contract Blade and another chip off the brutish block. With the doors of the Hussy locked and the closed sign displayed, our team assembled around a series of tables shoved together in the middle of the tight, dimly lit space, and there I had unfurled my best map of the Lower City. Using a stick of red graphite, I had divided the huge territory into six zones.

"Blackstar and the Seer have surveyed all six of these areas," I said to the assembled group. "Only three seem viable for the meeting site, based on the presence of open space and how far the Raving Blade would have to travel to get there. In all three cases, his entourage is going to have to have to cross a canal at some point as they return home. It's at one of those that we're going to hit them."

I was standing at the head of the tables, feeling very much like a military leader. (Or, maybe, a highwayman.) This wasn't the first time I'd given a pre-bid brief; however, usually I was discussing the complexities of avoiding soldiers, not attacking them.

"This is a damned shit bath waiting ta happen, Lash," said

Dorcus Reed, her thick hands doing aggressive, knocking things on the table that were starting to annoy me. "How many of us can crawl up from under the bridge quick enough to do this? I'm not the climber I used ta be."

Dorcus was taller and broader than her sister, and definitely nicer to look at. The greater height seemed to elongate her features to her benefit, and the merciful absence of a facial rodent helped. During her years as an active Shadow Bidder, Dorcus's hair had been short and kinky, just like Getta's; however, in recent times she had allowed its silvery curls to spill around her creased face in a way that I found appealing. Back when we used to work together, which was often, she had been an exceedingly competent skiff mate, if an overbearing one, though those days were long behind us. While I did sometimes question Getta's intelligence, I never wondered about Dorcus Reed, who, in addition to being tough as hell, was also smart as a whip, and even mildly artistic in an offbeat way. She routinely wandered our rocky coastline, salvaging marine treasures—starfish, boat parts, conch shells, driftwood—and transformed them into clever wall collages that lent excitement to her tavern décor. Those pieces were poking and jutting all around us now, complete with the faintest hint of a salt tang, making me feel like I was in some kind of cloister of aquatic curiosities.

"That's what the job entails, Dorcus," I said. "Let Yurgen go up first, and you can follow."

"I'm not staring at Yurgen's ass for one second, Vazeer. I'm going up first, then Yurgen, then Getta."

My conciliatory gesture implied that it was all good, but it wasn't. The queasy feeling that had been present when I first met the group now assaulted me in force. Dorcus Reed shouldn't be on this mission. She was well past her prime and way out of practice, making her far less suited to the job than the man that she had just shoved into the number two slot. "Yurgen the Juggler," as he was unfortunately called, was a poorly named but duly skilled Contract Blade, who had picked up his moniker from assorted side talents that might garner applause in a cut-rate circus. I had watched some of his little magic shows, as well as his juggling act, and he really wasn't bad. Still, I didn't anticipate he'd soon be quitting his night job.

"You'll never see my ass, you old horndyke," Yurgen shot back. "I'll go up from my end of the boat. I don't need a ladder to climb a goddamned canal bridge."

Yurgen was a bit small as Contract Blades went; however, he was extraordinarily agile, which was a wonderful bonus in a profession that involved climbing on and off boats in the dead of night. He was also, as luck would have it, one of the few operatives I knew who had completed a Narrow Bid. I didn't know many details about that job, as well I shouldn't, but I had heard rumors to suggest that there was a good deal of fighting involved. The target was probably no more than a baron, but it was still a testament to Yurgen's reputation and skill that he had been hired for such a bid. The one knock against him (and this could either be a knock or a virtue, depending on the circumstances) was that he appeared to lack anything resembling normal human fear.

"What the bloody hell did you just call me?"

Dorcus had stood from her position at our muddle of tables, and her hand now dropped to one of several stilettos at her belt. She was wearing a cuirass, and she had adopted her "bouncer" expression, which usually preceded some sozzled fool getting pitched out of the Hussy on their head.

"I'm only calling you what I've heard you call yourself," he replied.

Yurgen's weaselly face was vaguely damp, which it always seemed to be for some reason. In keeping with his reputation, Yurgen wasn't cowed by Dorcus's bellicose posture, and this was probably because he knew he was right. I, too, had heard Dorcus use that name for herself, many times. It was well known that Dorcus Reed bedded women exclusively, and while there were a number of Shadow Bidders who shared her proclivities, Dorcus was one of the few who went out of her way to make the point.

"First of all, I can call myself that, not you," Dorcus spat back. "And secondly, I'm not even close ta old, you twitchy little carnival freak. I could still slam your head through a wall."

My gaze wandered away from this idiotic discussion, seeking refuge amidst the coarse whorls of a cargo net that stretched over two walls. Buoys, crab traps, lanterns, and a few rusty weapons were intwined in the bristly weave, and in the corner where the netted walls joined stood the tall, deranged-looking figurehead from which the place drew its name. The hacked grotesquery of its features did little to calm me.

"Dorcus, my dear, please take your seat," said Adelyn from her spot, midway down the improvised conference table. "And Yurgen, be mindful of your words. We're all going to have to work together."

Not surprisingly, Dorcus sat, and Yurgen shut his mouth, though both looked enduringly irritated. Adelyn then turned her sweet gaze to me and nodded, as if to say, "*See, Vazeer, all fixed.*" But was it? Was anything about this group fixable?

"I'd be happy to go in the Reed sisters' skiff and to let Dorcus lead. We've worked together so many times, it'll be second nature."

I pivoted to this volunteer, a rather venerable and courteous volunteer, and my feeling that the whole bid was going to hell magnified. He was near the end of the furniture logjam, tall, nicely dressed, and sporting his usual clean shave and neatly bound ponytail. It was Lethro—old Lethro, who had been a member of the predatory team that ambushed me during the infamous Gaff. He and I had briefly engaged in a standoff during my ensuing revenge campaign, though thankfully we never came to blows. In the years that followed, Lethro and I had made our peace, and we were even teamed together on a couple of bids before he retired.

Which begged the question, what was he doing here now? Even in his heyday, Lethro had always skewed a little too far in the direction of finesse, and away from the dark and dirty work of a Contract Blade. His best moment had come when he rescued Flerra Tellian from a floundering bid aboard a rogue schooner, and at that time his slender rapier, backed by his prodigious fencing skills, had been just the right tool to take out a bunch of thuggish mariners. Those sailors, wearing only padded armor and likely drunker than hogs, wouldn't have lasted fifteen seconds against Gueritus's hardened soldiers.

Since I was fairly certain that Lethro had *not* been given an Underlord ultimatum, my only explanation for him being here was that he saw it as a matter of principle. Lethro must have decided that the blame for Flerra Tellian's death ultimately lay with the Raving Blade, and if there was one last heroic deed left in him, it would be to avenge her. While I appreciated the sentiment, Narrow Bids were not the place to act out personal grievances, especially when one's skills were in decline.

"Why not team us women in one boat and the men in the

other?" said yet another member of our conference. "I'll go with Dorcus and Getta. Vazeer, you take Yurgen and Lethro."

Turning my attention away from those who were likely to fail me in the future, I focused on one who already had.

"For hell's sake, Terza, we've been over this already," I snapped. "The two boat crews were divided this way for a reason, so please don't mess with my lineup."

Terza looked suitably offended, for which she had grounds because it was Lethro who started this talk of switching lineups. But I was no longer attempting to be delicate with her, or Adelyn, since they were the ones responsible for this gaggle of whiners, has-beens, and circus performers. Was this really the best they could do?

"You keep saying that, but I don't get this all-important lineup," Terza shot back. "Maybe explain it better, because as it is, Dorcus is likely to crack Yurgen's skull on the way to the attack, and there's always a chance I'll crack yours."

The recent warming trend in the Falconbrow weather pattern was over now, mostly because Terza (perhaps more than anyone I knew) hated being condescended to, and I (perhaps more than anyone she knew) could be condescending. There was little to be done about it, seeing as my misgivings were overwhelming me, and this put Terza and I right back into the place where our relationship had been for the last decade.

In that spirit, I rattled off an exasperated version of what I had said before—that we would be facing Underlord soldiers, all-male soldiers, who did not think much of female combatants, and while this would certainly lead them to underestimate the likes of Terza, Dorcus, and Getta, the purpose of the attack was to achieve panic. For this reason, I wanted to mix it up and send a well-balanced group from each side…yak, yak, yak.

I had said this all before and received the same dissatisfied stares, because, while this explanation was in part accurate, it was missing some pieces, which people can sense. Here's the real truth: I didn't want to see anybody in this room killed, naturally. Among them, I definitely didn't want to get the Reed sisters killed, and Yurgen gave those two a much better chance of surviving than Lethro, whom I viewed as little more than deadweight. Admittedly, Terza gave the sisters a better chance still; however, if there was one person I could not accept dying, it was my erstwhile Gaff mate, intermittent antagonist, once-upon-a-time lover Terza Falconbrow. No matter how she riled me, the thought of her losing her life on this bid was something I couldn't live with.

So, I placed her in my boat, along with deadweight Lethro, because it gave me a slim chance of protecting them both. In Terza's case, I would literally drag her by her burgeoning tresses all the way into the salt marsh if that's what it took. Which could never be communicated, because it would result in my ex-lover putting me in my place again in front of all these people and destroying what remained of my credibility. Terza had never needed protection from anybody, and I couldn't help feeling that I was headed towards another one of my embarrassing miscalculations.

"Listen," I said to them all. "We are not fighting to the death here. We just want to shock the soldiers, and thoroughly confuse them, as Tygean's men come racing from the other direction down Edge Winder. Caught between two sets of attackers, they should be so distracted that—"

"Edge Winder?" Terza suddenly asked. "The bridges can't all be along Edge Winder. One, maybe two of them…but no more than that. I grew up there, remember?"

"I'm just using it as an example," I said, trying to repair the mistake. "It could be any of those streets, but the point is—"

"He's rusing you," came a flat voice from the back corner of the room, near one of the exits. "He thinks it will be Edge Winder. He's sure the attack will happen on that wide bridge over the King's Canal, the one with the block walls, just south of the target's home."

It has been my experience that you really can't send Heshna far enough away. No matter what task you give her—in this case, surveilling the streets surrounding Dorcus's tavern—she somehow always finishes the job too quickly.

"You do think that, Vazeer, don't you?" asked Adelyn, and she, to a degree that was even more insidious than the Seer, stared up at me with those intelligent brown eyes, drinking in the truth of the moment.

"I don't know for sure which one it is," I said ruefully, then I scrambled to head off the protests, which appeared ready to erupt from several mouths, "...but yes, I think it will be the one Heshna describes. It's just a hunch, but it has to do with my meeting with Gueritus, with the things he said to me that night, about coming out of the shadows, of holding his head up high. The man knows history, and after he receives Tygean's pledge, the Raving Blade will want to stride boldly along King Benivus Boulevard—the actual name of Edge Winder—and return to his dwelling like a true monarch. It's in his nature to do that."

That explanation was good enough to get Dorcus and Lethro nodding, and Getta at least shrugged, but I didn't seem to be doing quite as well with the other customers.

"You and your damned hunches," Terza muttered. "Why is it you always think you know people so well?"

While Terza appeared merely disdainful, Adelyn was something more, continuing to brush me with that investigative probe, and it was obvious that she sensed me withholding things. Our Masque had spotted many falsehoods in me so far in this undertaking—the fact that I was paying for this mission out of my own funds, my furtive relationship with Shade, perhaps even the fact that I was basing a key decision on the questionable authenticity of a phantasmal helper, something I'm sure she couldn't see herself, but which she possibly sensed. Neither she nor my Brood sister had addressed these falsehoods directly, but I suspected that a conversation along those lines was fast approaching.

"Ya looked at tha doors on Ed-winder, and foun tha one ya liked?"

This voice, coming from the very back of our patchwork crush of tables, was refreshing, despite its dissonant legacy of the Wags. There, at the end of the group, three mismatched figures sat near each other, one of whom was Benni Bones, a compulsive gambler, a notorious thief, and (now that Flerra Tellian was gone) probably the best Locksmith in Hell's Labyrinth. Radrin Blackstar's Locksmith, which really did seem like an odd alliance.

Radrin sat quietly at the end of the table, with a slightly overawed Cad on one side of him and disheveled Benni on the other. Radrin didn't wince at Benni's horrid accent or seem in any way perturbed by the Locksmith's less than appealing exterior, which included an uncombed bird's nest of graying hair and clothing that was always two or three sizes too large for his scraggily frame. Radrin tolerated him because he knew Benni was a dead-eyed professional when he set his mind to his work. The man was older than most Shadow Bidders, now well into his fifth decade, but he was still excellent at his craft, and he had even reined in his kleptomaniacal propensities in recent years. This had less to do with a change of heart, I think, than losing two fingers on his right hand. That sentence had been delivered by the magistrate about a decade earlier, and it did wonders to refocus Benni's efforts, for it limited some of his larcenous capabilities (climbing into windows, nicking items off of pedestrians) but still allowed for others (picking locks, which was more than doable for him, with just a little modification to the way he held his tools).

Nobody was quite as good at breaking and entering as Flerra had been, but Benni Bones, so named for his obsession with dice games, was more than capable of penetrating civilian locks, and even the occasional reinforced vault. He was also—and this always surprised me—a lot smarter than he looked, or sounded, plus he tended to avoid useless chitchat.

"Yes," I replied, happy to avoid engaging with either Terza or Adelyn. "If that does turn out to be the bridge, there was a door in the perfect spot, and it seemed to have the qualities you said you were looking for."

Benni simply nodded. The Locksmith didn't drill me about why I hadn't examined the other four routes, or why I was maniacally committed to one bridge in particular. At least somebody in this misfit team trusted me to do my job.

After that, I provided a few other details, including how long it would take to find out if Count Tygean's request to parley with the Raving Blade would be accepted (just a day or two, in my estimation), and then how long it would take to hash out a neutral site for them to work out their truce—about the same.

We shared a few more drinks as a group, and then, shortly after First morning Bell, the conference broke up, and we all headed our separate ways.

When I arrived back at the door to my apartment and began fumbling with my keys, I felt a hopeful little shiver at the thought that my suitemate had returned. Maybe I would happen upon her sleeping, ideally in my bed, or perhaps lounging about, waiting for me. She would be angry, no doubt. Our relationship had taken quite a hit when I shoved her naked through a hole in the wall, but the purpose of that was to protect her, and also my mission, the importance of which she should understand by now.

However, when I entered the space, I found only solitude. The vacant mess of our affections sprawled throughout the double suite like a sad tableau. Despite some earlier straightening, evidence remained: in my own apartment, the living room rug was still out of position and festooned with both crumbs and stains, while her apartment had been left largely in its former condition, with only her deadly Finisher's kit restored to its nest. I hadn't put away anything else, since I feared that in so doing I would appear to pass judgement on her untidiness.

Feeling her lonely absence, I crawled into bed and eventually went to sleep. Somewhere in the final hours of darkness, when a sliver moon was stifled by clouds and clock bells muffled by fog, my disaffected lover returned to me.

"Wake up, you slumbering fool," she hissed.

When someone rouses you from deep sleep, there's always confusion. Why have you been awakened? What time is it? Where the hell are you? (sometimes). But you generally recognize the person's voice and also, on some intrinsic level, their emotional state, because this gets conveyed easier than logistics. That night, long before any of the former questions got answered, I was clear about the latter, as I was immediately present to Shade of Night's unadulterated rage. She had climbed up on top of me, and the straddling buoyancy of her form, usually an inconsequential weight, was not entirely insignificant to a man enjoying a respite from gravity. But her mass was nothing compared to the vicious little slaps that began to rain down upon my face and shoulders.

"Up, you snoring jackass!"

"Wha…what the hell?" I croaked from my far-off place, still mentally stretched between this unpleasant thing and possibly some decent dreams.

"My fists aren't enough, you comatose bastard?"

I then felt the stinging nip of a blade jabbing the side of my face.

"Ow! Stop it!"

I swatted at her, but she was too quick, and she dodged out of the way, then climbed back into position with the jack pressed to my neck.

"How dare you tour your creep through my apartment and allow him to violate my private chambers, to take important things from me. Can you not see how humiliating that is? How degraded I feel having that man, the wickedest of men, soil my garments with his conniving hands? What a treacherous roach you've turned out to be. I'm finally going to carve you, like I should have done from the start."

"No, you're not," I mumbled, covering my mouth as I spoke, because I knew my sleeping breath had the potential to make her even angrier. "Put the damned blade away, and let's stop this charade."

But she wasn't done with the charade, for she promptly returned to one of her old tricks, and I felt a lancing burst of agony in my ear as she jabbed some miserable bastion of pain there. The ear, I have now learned (because of this relationship), possesses many sensitive little nerve endings, and is a splendid place to begin when inflicting torture.

"For hell's sake, woman!"

And now I swung for real, aiming for her stomach, but I barely grazed her side as she leapt away.

Up on one knee and clutching my wounded ear, I faced her across the craggy landscape of bedding. Illumed by a feeble shine from the doorway to the living room, Shade was a frowzy relief in the dark, her hair poking hectically, her clothing, to the degree that I could see it, poorly suited to a bed chamber, for she appeared to be wearing street attire.

"Why is it," I growled, "that of all the women in this city, I wind up with the deranged psychopath?"

Several heavy breaths followed, her untidy contour growing visibly, then contracting.

"Is that what you think?" she finally asked. "You think you *wound up* with me?"

"Seriously?"

"Yes, seriously."

"No, I mean, *seriously*, that's the part of the sentence you focus on?"

Shade took in another big heaping lungful of air.

"Those other words mean nothing to me."

"Well, maybe they should, if you want to repair the broken thing inside of you."

For a few moments, the face-off continued, the two of us glaring across the quilted battlefield. Finally, she spoke.

"I'm going to hurt you."

I absorbed this, then attempted to dismiss it.

"No, you won't."

"Yes, I will, because I need to. It's the only way I can fix it, fix the terrible hurt. By hurting you."

"You tried that already and it didn't work."

In the bleary darkness, I awaited a break in the deadlock, a slight release that would allow us to work our way back to where we had been. But that's not what I got.

"I tried the wrong thing," she replied. "I went after your flesh, but that's not the vulnerable part. The blade must be aimed at your soul."

Oh, I definitely didn't like that. I had no idea what it meant, but it was enough to send me into full appeasement mode.

"Shade, please, I can explain what happened—"

"Your sweet talk won't work anymore, Vazeer. Nothing will work, because I'm done pretending."

"Pretending what?"

"Pretending that this thing between us was ever more than a diversion to me. Pretending that I am a normal person, capable of normal feelings, which I'm not. You are going to learn that very soon, *Vazeer the Lash*. You are going to learn just how far I am willing to go."

The eerie veracity of it rattled me. However, I felt ill prepared to alter this trajectory, for all that arose within me were various species of groveling which—learned in the early days of our dealings—were not an effective approach with Shade of Night. So, I tried being assertive. Turns out, that wasn't a good approach either.

"Listen, Shade, I really don't have time for this," I said, mustering, with relative ease, a tone of fatigued impatience. "I'm right on the cusp of this thing I promised you, my big, 'exciting display,' and, being a man of my word, I'm prepared to do it, despite the odds. So please, go take off your goddamned clothes and come to bed."

Even in the dimness I detected her smile. Burnished drearily by the dying kitchen lantern, I could tell instantly that it wasn't the right smile, and that Shade of Night had just crossed over into some new, frightening place, from which there was little hope of extraction.

"I'm sorry, Vazeer," she said, continuing to use my given name, which sounded both threatening and indescribably cold. "Your vow means little to me now, nor am I interested in your exciting displays. I am about to put on an exciting display of my own, and there's nothing you can do to stop me."

And with that, she slid lightly off the bed, whooshed to the door of my room, and exited into the living room. I fumbled to follow her. Stark naked, still woozy from sleep, and smarting badly in my right ear, I wrestled my way out of bed and put up the semblance of a pursuit. But I had no confidence it would achieve anything, for I could palpably feel the depths of her wounded pride. Not to mention, she was still holding that jack.

When I reached the dim space of my living room, I didn't see her anywhere. I figured she had sped quickly to the guest bedroom, and then the secret pass to her unit; however, as I arrived there, I heard a jarring iron tumult elsewhere in the apartment. It was the sound of my front door locks being activated. By the time I reached the head of my entry hallway, the door was gaping wide, and Shade faced me in the illumined rectangle.

"I need to tell you something, Vazeer," she said in her new, cold formality. "I've figured out what matters most to you, the thing that's closest to your soul. I'm going to take that thing from you, just as you have taken things from me."

And with that, she pulled the door shut with an incensed slam, and I heard the chafing briskness of her footfalls as she sped away. I made no efforts to follow and instead simply stared at the door, trying, all the while, to neutralize the toxic trickle of fear that was seeping like Finisher's poison into my heart.

PART
III

21

NARROW BID

"You think she'll ever come back?"

The tiny wavelets slopped over the gray stones at my boots. Before me, respiring ever so faintly on the twilit mirror of the cove, the Elena's Guile sat in peaceful anchorage.

"I really can't say," I replied. "On some level, I hope she doesn't."

Droden swiveled.

"Don't say that. Don't ever say that, or even think it, Lash. You may be the Labyrinth's best Grell Runner, but you're still an idiot when it comes to this."

I gestured irritably.

"Is this the new rule? You get to lecture me and call me whatever you want because you caught me lying?"

"Pretty much."

On my other side, a low, froggy noise approximated a chuckle.

"Was that actually a laugh, Habard?" I asked, turning his way. "If so, the damned thing needs work."

Habard beamed, which was not the most attractive of sights. The squinting of those nature-bashed cheeks created all sorts of pocks and canyons, reminiscent of volcanic rock.

"Boss's right," he grunted. "Shud'a never let her go."

The three of us stood together a few dozen feet in front of Droden's Eastcove cave complex, staring at the exquisite vessel that had, several weeks earlier, shuttled away an even more exquisite passenger. Dusk was slowly coming on, and with it, a lacquering cover of mist.

"Thanks to you both for the relationship advice," I said. "But there's already too much blood in this city for a woman like that. Very soon, there'll be more."

"Blood out there too, Lash," said Droden. "After all, something made your lady come here in the first place."

This comment (like most of Droden's observations) was entirely on point, for it was indeed blood that had driven Nascinthé of Levell to our shores. When I had suggested to her that she move to some better place, with a better man, she had answered this way:

"Yes, that should work out well. Now that I'm fully acclimated to men's blood splattering across my face, I should do much better with the next one."

This apt and mordant remark underscored her nightmarish experiences in both worlds. Still, of the two, this one had to be a bit worse at the moment.

"Don't the two of you have something better to do?" I asked, gouging the toe of my boot into the shoreline and launching a spit of pebbles into the kelpy shallows.

"We did all that needs doing, Lash," Droden replied. "Your skiffs are prepped and hidden safely in the marsh. The rest is up to you."

Yes, up to me. Me and my suboptimal ambush team. The time had finally come to launch my second Narrow Bid.

Count Tygean and Count Gueritus had, this very day, agreed to meet, and so far, the preliminary news looked good. Per Sebastien's tongueless scribbling, Gueritus was quite open to his enemy's offer, mostly because Tygean had made some gains of late in the war of attrition (our recent mishap in the Lower City had actually served our cause, just as Radrin predicted). Additionally, the reports were starting to flow in consistently that the Derjian Sea was empty of red sails, for which there could only be one logical explanation. The entirety of the Red Siren's fleet was likely gathered in its hidden port off the Kaszian coast, readying itself for war. Since nobody believed Lave Kaszivar was foolish enough to attack Tergon, or any other port in the Midlands, that really only left us.

Therefore, the Raving Blade, in an effort to put a quick end to the internecine conflict, and to do so without losing any additional manpower on either side, had sensibly chosen to negotiate. Tygean's messenger had even dropped hints that Gueritus's ascension to the role of High Lord would be grudgingly tolerated, as long as he made the right concessions.

As for the meeting itself, it was to be held at midnight in a crumbling Lower City plaza known as Gessum's Cross, a spot roughly equidistant between the Arcadium and Kaennamin Academy. I was well familiar with this place, since many of my smuggling runs ended there, and, adding a dose of irony, Gessum's Cross had been the drop point for my cargo on the night of the infamous Gaff.

A few minutes later, I saw a skiff making its way around the rocky bend at the mouth of the cove. Cad, Heshna, and Radrin were aboard, my protégé rowing, and slowly the group made its way across the little bay. Soon the skiff pulled up onto the pebbly beach, and once it landed, Radrin Blackstar stepped out and came to speak with me.

"The Locksmith has created keys and is back in Dockside. Both doors of the site are now serviceable."

He was referring to the building I had discovered during our reconnaissance mission, and the keys had been created for him and Cad. Benni Bones had visited the ambush location on two occasions since my surveillance, confirming that the doorway I had spotted was a hopeful prospect. On the second visit, he had managed to gain entry and found the residence heavily storm-damaged and uninhabited. There was also a back door, which was going to be a crucial point of access and communication throughout the bid.

"I'd like to speak with Blackstar alone for a few minutes," I said to the others.

Droden and Habard quickly excused themselves, and Heshna got the hint, but Cad looked genuinely offended. He was wearing a coarse, brown tunic, with a cracked leather jacket over it (his "harmless pedestrian" disguise), and it was obvious that my protégé's conception of his role as messenger on this bid gave him a heightened sense that he belonged in all conversations. A little angry shooing finally got him to back off.

"We may have a problem," I said once Radrin and I were alone.

For an uncomfortable interval, Radrin simply stared at me, the chilly dampness of the stones exuding up from below, the liquid sounds of the cove enshrouding us.

"With your foolish diversion?" he finally asked.

This was a term Radrin had bandied about liberally on the night he broke into my apartment and rescued me from Shade of Night. It was an apt description of my idiosyncratic side endeavors, most of them involving women.

"*Our* foolish diversion," I replied. "I may have started this problem, but you did your part. Was it really necessary to go tossing her bedroom and to steal things…things that would require half a year of contract bidding to afford?"

"Not half of her year."

"Don't be snide."

Radrin now glowered. This was not a typical Blackstar expression, and I noted, yet again, how much Shade of Night bothered him.

"I will settle the matter," he said.

"I don't think that's necessary. If you just give me the toxins, I can return them to her, and while she'll still be angry—"

"Vazeer," he said, attempting to halt my efforts at mollification, but failing.

"Why pick this moment, Radrin, to be some sort of imperious enforcer, to punish her for being what you are, ultimately?"

"She and I are nothing alike."

"But do the methods matter so much? Are you so against…"

"Poisons?" Radrin finished for me. "To the contrary. I plan to use Shade of Night's Colyrox tonight, which is the main reason I took it."

And now I was the one who felt thrown.

"The stakes are too high on this job," Radrin continued. "We need a guaranteed kill. A toxin of that lethality can be useful under the right circumstances, and I have been on the lookout for it, though the scant supplies that exist in this city were ruined in the flood."

"But…have you not created a second problem, by trying to fix the first one?"

"That 'second problem' already existed, and has ever since you let her escape out your window. There's no point in retreading that ground now. As I said, I will handle it, but later, for I am certain Shade of Night will take no overt action to sabotage our bid. She needs Gueritus to die. She needs his vassals to die too, for if any of them survive, they will realize that she committed this egregious breach of Finisher protocol. Allowing you to live was bad enough, but by deliberately deceiving them, she has placed them all in danger. An ascendent Raving Blade is likely to innovate new, highly creative forms of torment just for her. She knows this."

On the surface, I had to agree. Shade had several reasons not to interfere with our operation, above and beyond the gruesome motivation Radrin described. For one thing, fouling up our bid would place her lone friend, Heshna the Seer, in direct danger. Additionally (and I acknowledge the vanity inherent in this), disruption would likely doom her own "Lashy," something for which she did not seem entirely prepared.

"The whole situation does continue to astonish me," Radrin said, his tone drifting from methodical to musing. This was just interesting enough that I crunched back slightly on the rocks to achieve perspective.

"What astonishes you?"

"This strange thing you accomplished. It defies many of my expectations, which is not the first time you've done that; or, I suspect, the last."

I really didn't know what Radrin was referring to, or what sort of new track we were on.

"A Finisher doesn't simply abandon a contract," Radrin clarified. "And unquestionably, she doesn't fall in love with her target, and then endanger everything she has worked for her entire career, including her life, just to protect him. Only when you are involved, Vazeer, do such things happen."

Here, I ran straight into a wad of emotional flotsam. I was confounded, first, by this idea of Shade being *in love* with me, which wasn't something I had really considered. And yet, among the pieces of whirling flotsam was the memory of the acidic conversation I'd had with Heshna the Seer in the Cacophony, when my Brood sister told me that Shade never, ever deviated in this manner. Only with *me*—irksome, baffling, grotesquely likeable— would such a thing occur.

"It is a strange power you possess," he said, "one that I may need to call upon soon."

"What power?" I asked. "To first draw women's interest, then to disappoint them to such a degree that they cast me aside, stomp me beneath their feet, jab knives into every vulnerable spot I've got? If you're in need of a power, maybe look for another."

He shrugged and turned towards the water, his immaculate profile set off by the cragginess of the surrounding rocks.

"A lady will be coming here soon," he mused, still looking away. "A lady that I, myself, will need to woo."

This one really tripped me up. So far, I had struggled to even conceive of Radrin Blackstar as a corporal creature, let alone a carnal one, so there was nowhere to stick a piece of news of this sort. He must have sensed my shock, for he glanced over and chuckled.

"You look like you have seen a ghost," he said with a smile. "But no, it's not what you imagine. This so-called 'wooing' is not for romantic purposes, and the lady in question is a political entity, one of immense importance. For us both, I believe."

Reorienting slightly, I now focused on a thing that had, on several occasions, crossed my mind. The possible arrival of Countess Shaeyin Odel.

"You think she will come?"

"I know she will. There is too much irresolution in this place, certainly for one with her political prospects. She will seek closure regarding past indiscretions, so that she can move forward with bigger plans."

"And this is relevant to me…?"

"Because, Vazeer," he said, pivoting fully back to me. "If there is one person who can make or break your grand restoration idea, it is Shaeyin Odel. She will become the Empress upon Nesabedrus's imminent death, since her father has made it known that he will decline the crown. Instead, he plans to act as her Chief Legate, giving her time to get used to her new role while he is still robust and able to guide her through the veritable deluge of coming threats."

"You actually think she might help me…and Tygean, with our plan?"

"I do. If you explain the value to her, present it as a great benefit to her reign and the Empire at large."

There was certainly space for this idea inside of me. However, it was a shared space, an unruly zone dominated by guilt, apprehension, and, most of all, the understanding that a thing of tremendous poignancy in this woman's life had met its brutal end on my watch. I remembered the nature of Beranardos Sherdane's cries the night that Radrin killed him, the raw, feverish quality of his love for the Countess. What extraordinary thing must have existed between them? What, if not reckless, unreasoning love, would have led them both to take such insane risks, and how bitter might be the aftermath?

"We may have liberated the lady from her indiscretions," I muttered. "But I'm fairly certain she won't like the way we did it."

It was generous of me to use the word "we." Radrin was the one who had made the decision to kill Sherdane, he was the shadowy agent who had chosen to weave his broader machinations into what was meant to be a local conflict. However, I had certainly helped set the stage for the act, had set the stage for so many acts (and was doing so still), so it seemed pointless to detach my culpability from his.

"No," he replied with what could only be construed as regret. "I imagine she won't."

There, standing on the pebbly shores of Eastcove, feeling the moist jacket of night dropping upon us, I sensed the new reality. *Alignment,* that illusive concept, had finally arrived. This was the idea that Radrin espoused, a notion also hinted at by Merejin, when she described the union of purpose that her fellow students had tried, and failed, to achieve. I was not failing here. For better or for worse, my rebelliousness was behind me, and I had dispensed with efforts to separate my own actions from those of this man. Yes, I would share equally in the blame for High Lord Sherdane's death, and yes, I would assist Radrin with his efforts to win the favor of the future Empress, to whatever degree I might be helpful there.

Why? Because, just before this talk of Shaeyin Odel, other words had been spoken, and those words meant everything to me.

"You seem to be treating my restoration plan with strange seriousness," I said.

"It has grown on me."

"Why?"

Radrin looked off to the side for a moment, his eyes shaded by dusk but sharpened by thought.

"When I first started visiting Sullward," he said, "my attention was focused on the principle of eliminating threats, and doing so with enough subtlety that it did not raise suspicions. I never truly contemplated the idea of this city becoming an asset to the Empire, above and beyond its role as a dispensary of bribes. But then I encountered you and your improbable ideas, and slowly it has dawned on me that the path you propose could, in fact, be the best of all worlds for Tergon: a Sullward that provides legitimate tax revenues—hefty revenues—and also serves as a boon to our traders, not a bane. There are many other benefits, broad, far-reaching benefits, which I will explain to you when the time is right. But yes, I have begun to embrace your dream, Vazeer the Lash. Your *mad* dream, that is."

And there it sat, quivering in the space, strangely alive.

This was the line that Radrin Blackstar had spoken to me on the night of the Narrow Bid, when he visited me in hallucinatory form and implied that his role in my world was to affect these changes, brutally affect them, as evidenced immediately thereafter by the arc of his dagger and the coming of the flood. How often did this confounding entity—the Grand Dispatcher, Blackstar, partner in shadow—deliver such moments, just when I was on the verge of once again ascribing esoteric weirdness to vagaries of the mind?

This time, I was ready to break the wall between us. I was prepared to ask him, to indeed *demand* from him, an explanation for this new paranormal turn in my life. But Radrin Blackstar saw to it that I could not.

"It is time, Vazeer," he said suddenly and incongruously. "We must get to the ambush site."

All meditative rumination was gone; expediency alone remained.

"Now?" I asked. "The others aren't even here yet—"

"I must be established inside that building well in advance. I have further preparations to make. Your team can come later."

And that was it. The ultimatum had been handed down, the code of silence restored, making my questions, even in their thought form, some sort of hideous breach of protocol. As to what this protocol was, and who had come up with it, I still didn't have the slightest idea.

A short time later, Radrin, Cad, and Heshna left Eastcove, each to ready themselves for their respective roles. The ambush team started to arrive soon after that, straggling in over the course of an hour, and once we were all assembled, we headed as a group to the secret pass that led to the marsh.

"If there's anyone that can pull this thing off, it's you, Lash," Droden said at the camouflaged door—the one through which Nascinthé of Levell had come, drenched and beleaguered, on the night of the Narrow Bid.

He and I clasped hand to forearm, in the traditional maritime manner, and then my team and I made our way through the weedy marsh to the place where our craft were hidden.

The journey to the bid site was easy. Getta Reed was a very capable operator, and she and I were able to stay in perfect sync as we silently directed our paddlers up the black, floodtide Grells. There was the ubiquitous mist to contend with, along with a streaky coating of cloud cover; however, neither was thick enough to fully impede the waxing crescent of the moon. That glowing sliver would be setting just past midnight, creating a useful beacon as it dropped through the vaporous western sky.

Shortly before Ninth Bell, we slid into the inky chasm of the runner's ravine. Having recently observed it from the limited perspective of the bridge, I didn't realize just how far back it extended, or rather I'd forgotten, since I'd paddled pretty much every canal in the Lower City at one time or another. As elsewhere, there was a fustiness to the air here, and something about the towering sheerness of the sidewalls seemed to magnify the cool, mossy smell of the water. That rippling floor made this seem a place spawned more of nature than of man—a ravine in earnest.

With no aid of torches, and little assistance from the moon, we gently bumped our way along the slippery walls, our quiet strokes releasing echoes up the cavernous flue. When, at last, we could see the hint of open space before us, we halted. Perhaps eighty feet ahead lay the break in the granite surround, where the bridge was located. When the time was right, we would glide out of our crevice, cross the final stretch of open water, then duck beneath the heavy stone arch. For now, we waited.

Shadow Bidders were well practiced at this. Often, we were required to sit or stand or crouch for hours, habituated to discomfort, alone with our thoughts. Veteran Bidders knew to be quiet, or at least they should have. Up at the front of my skiff, I heard a ruckus of creaking wood and flexing leather, and I detected a vague, disruptive shape in my limited field of vision. Lethro, who sat directly ahead of me, tipped to the side and then slid forward, to allow this creaky, disruptive shape to pass and then switch seats with him.

"I should never have let her go with those people," Terza muttered, the heat of her breath puffing my eyes in the chilly dark.

"She'll be safe," I muttered.

"But this was never part of the plan, Vazeer, the original plan. I didn't want her to have any part in the bid, just the run-up."

"Adelyn's a Shadow Bidder, Terza."

And I left it at that, or I tried to. We were sitting tightly abreast of Getta's boat, our paddles stretched across, and I could see that the others had leaned in to listen.

"She's a Shadow Bidder, but not a fighter," Terza continued after a brief silence, her low voice still loud in that place.

"She used ta be, girl," Dorcus chimed in, adding a most unwelcome assist from the dark. "Addy can wield a blade when she needs ta. Don't you worry about her."

"Not to mention the sweetest talker in the Labyrinth," Yurgen added. "One time, I heard her—"

"Shhhh!" I whispered harshly. "This isn't a goddamned garden party, you morons. You know the stakes here."

"Don't shit yerself, Lash, no one can hear us here." Getta's voice wasn't louder than the others, but it was definitely more obnoxious. "I've run this ravine a dozen times, and ain't nothing's heard on the outside."

"But why do they need her anyway?" Terza puffed again, even closer and somehow hotter, with a little finger jab to my stomach.

"Hopefully they don't, Terza. She's just there in case things get out of hand."

"Oh, they'll get out of hand, Vazeer. Your bids always do."

Terza had been uncommonly fretful since Adelyn had proposed her own singular role in this operation. Sensing, correctly, that a huge portion of the success or failure of the night's proceedings would hinge upon the Raving Blade and Count Tygean reaching some sort of amicable resolution (at least on the surface), Adelyn knew that she was well suited to overseeing the exchange. Yurgen was right in this respect: the so-called "sweet talk" of Adelyn the Allayer was a formidable force. It had, quite recently, kept Col and I from murdering each other in the derelict streets of the Cacophony. Before that, Adelyn's powerful influence had interrupted at least a dozen episodes of bloodshed in her role as a Shadow Bidder—forestalling bloody mayhem during buy operations, breaking up tavern brawls, and, of course, halting further carnage on the night of the infamous Gaff. This was her trademark.

Therefore, Adelyn had made her way into the Lower City earlier that day, with Heshna scouting ahead. An entourage of Tygean's men met her halfway and escorted her back to the Arcadium, where she was presumably briefed on the details of the coming negotiation. Her role, as agreed, was not to try and intercede as a Chief Legate, but rather to remain at the ready in case a sudden mollifying influence was required. She was also to determine if the Raving Blade was actually falling for the whole thing or if he showed signs of detecting a ruse. In the latter case, a signal would be given to the secretly watching Heshna, who would then convey that information to us. Finally, and I really didn't like thinking this, Adelyn was to scan subtly for hints that Count Tygean actually had no intention of coming to our aid, and that this whole endeavor was simply a risk-free assassination attempt, conducted entirely by Shadow Bidders. A different signal had been established for that.

"You're so damned ready to sacrifice people, Vazeer," Terza mumbled under her breath.

I'm not sure if the others quite heard this or, if they did, to what degree they understood it. For me, it was a lancing blow. Terza was clearly referencing the Gaff, the blame for which she laid squarely at my feet. My own zealous agenda, she asserted, had led to that tragedy, and more than once my ex-lover had declared that she would forever view me as a fatally selfish individual, incapable of subordinating my needs to those of others.

"And what about the kid?" Terza continued, switching subjects but not meaning. "How could you let him be involved with this?"

"Cad's tough. And he's a noncombatant."

"You think he knows that?"

"We've been over it."

"The gods help you, Vazeer, if you get another sweet boy in this city killed."

A second painful blow, targeting the same general area. Indeed, I was worried sick about Cad, and though I had done everything in my power to keep him buffered from danger, there was only so far away I could stick him. Cad's obvious use on an operation of this sort was as a courier of information, a real specialty of his, and for that reason I had made him the crucial link between Radrin Blackstar and the rest of us. Not only would he provide the Finisher the signal that we were in position, but he would also convey whatever last-minute information Heshna shuttled to us from Gessum's Cross. If the Seer indicated that things were going poorly between the two Counts, Cad was the one who would deliver this news to the ambush team, as well as Radrin.

Theoretically, this kept my young assistant away from the fighting, but there were no guarantees of safety in this plan. The Raving Blade might have men combing through the surrounding warrens, and while Cad, a pedestrian to all appearances, was not an overt threat, this whole thing was taking place on the cusp of the inner core. Loiterers of any sort would not be welcome.

We waited two more hours in our ravine, with periods of silence alternating with irritating bouts of chatter. Midway through this stretch, Yurgen pulled out a couple of flasks and made ready to pass them around the two skiffs, at which point I came close to losing it.

"You dumb magician!" I snarled, and I tried to swipe them out of his hands. But Yurgen was as quick as a springtime squirrel, and, lurching back in his boat, he started juggling the two silver containers high into the gloom with his back hand, while his other hand, operating with blurred suddenness, fanned open a half dozen playing cards right in front of my face. This had the horrifying effect of causing the entire bid crew to bust out in crackling echoes of laughter. Up the walls of our mossy crevice, the inane racket climbed.

It was just then, I believe, that I decided we were all dead. This flotilla of jackasses was as bad as anything I had commanded as a Grell Runner, on par with bids where I spent the whole night browbeating neophytes. These people weren't neophytes, but they were something possibly worse—experienced operatives who thought they had seen it all, acted like they knew everything, and had gradually lost touch over the years with how dangerous their line of work could be.

"I'm seeing light," said Lethro just after Eleventh Bell. He still sat in the boat's prow and was closest to the ambush site. "It looks like it's coming from the left."

"Left" meant from the direction of Kaennamin Academy, and we all stretched and craned so that we could see. Sure enough, it was soon obvious that a light source was moving along Edge Winder, starting to glitter the irregular sides of the chasm mouth. We began to hear the rustling of boots.

Then, out of the misty darkness, an entire entourage of armed men passed our slivered view. They carried torches, and in this jumping light we saw them rise up and over the now visible bulge of the bridge, two dozen at least. One of the men paused at the crown, pointing his sputtering wand down towards the water. He bowed out over the sidewall, clearly trying to see below, then he levered upright and extended his torch our way. It was futile. Even a directional lantern would not send its rays as far as our skiffs, and a torch would reach half that.

Behind him, the men clomped onward, a heavy parade of armor and cloaks, moving westward towards Gessum's Cross. Somewhere, lost in that barbed mass, was the Raving Blade. I couldn't tell which knot of men contained him, but I saw the focused intensity of the troop as a whole, their battle-readiness, telling me that this would not be an easy group to surprise. My only hope was that their primed condition would relax on the triumphant march home.

"No guarantee they will come back this way, Lash," said Lethro, once the soldiers were gone. "I would think that men like this would try to avoid being predictable."

Yes, that was a good point, and a rather veteran observation. Coupled with him spotting the approaching light source, I had to promote one of the jackasses back up to competent status.

"He'll come back this way," I muttered. "Our new 'king' won't feel like leaping mud holes and weaving through rubbish. Every other route is that, or worse."

When Eleventh Half Bell rang, we cautiously paddled the remainder of our rippling corridor and neared the open space beyond. There, at the mouth of the ravine, we paused to survey. All was still, with the moon's blurry crescent decorating the area with a dying light. A few minutes after that, we emerged from our crevice, traversed the final, exposed section of canal, then slid into the cool hollow beneath the bridge.

"I see Cad," Dorcus whispered. The other boat had taken its position at the far side of the enclosure, and Dorcus, in the vanguard, could observe the space beyond clearly. She waved her arm and then turned back to us.

"He saw me and signaled 'all's good.' Then he went back in his alley, Lash, so he's nice and hidden."

Well, that was a relief. The soldiers had passed, and Cad remained safe, which gave me my first measure of optimism since climbing aboard my skiff. Moreover, my jackasses were behaving professionally again, raising the possibility that it was me, not them, who was playing the part of the nervous neophyte.

Just after the Midnight Bell, Terza rose from her position, so that she could scootch forward to the point position, but I grabbed her belt buckle and pulled her back down.

"What the hell are you doing?" she demanded.

"It's better if you stay in the middle."

"You don't think I can handle the vanguard, you turd?"

"You can handle it, and everything else. I just need you here."

Now her shadowed face became a thing of confusion. Terza's lips closed, her fierce eyes blinked, and somewhere in there, behind the furrows and paint, lay the question: *"What do mean you need me here, and how worried should that make me?"*

We waited beneath the bridge until the Midnight Half Bell, after which we waited some more. A soft current flowed through the clouded depths, so we held ourselves in place by pressing paddles to the curved ceiling above. We had also brought small, lightweight ladders with us, to allow the first climbers to spring nimbly over the bridge sidewalls, and these we used to anchor ourselves to the edges of the canal.

When the First morning Bell sounded and there was no sign of Heshna, a faint draught of unease passed through the group. By the First Half Bell, the team as a whole began to shift about and mutter to each other uncomfortably. This was taking too long. While it was entirely possible that the two Counts would bandy back and forth for a while about cargo percentages, and how exactly Gueritus's new vision for the Labyrinth would work, this initial meeting was not meant to be a detailed affair. Its simple purpose was to convince the Raving Blade that the main threat to his ascension was neutralized, so that he could turn his sights towards outside forces.

It was nearing Second Bell when Heshna the Seer finally arrived. She did not, as planned, go to Cad first, that he might signal us from his side alley. She sprinted right up onto the middle of the bridge, bent over the edge like a spitting pedestrian, then dangled down in a warp of dull fabric and flopping hair. For a moment, she seemed too winded to deliver her message, with gusty heaves choking her, then out it came, in a thin, terrified retch.

"Scatter," she wheezed. "We are betrayed."

22

EXODUS

So little was understood in those feverish seconds, with Heshna hanging down before us like a tousled sack, and our rounded hollow reverberating with the word "betrayed." As to who had betrayed us, there was no time to figure that out. We first had to first deal with that other word, the one that had been pitched like a flaming brand into our humid hole:

"Scatter."

The effect generated by that single word was immediate.

Our skiffs, arranged side by side and each tucked just under their respective lips of the bridge, now separated by means of an aggressive team push. The boats whooshed sideways in a swell of dark water, and both parties, ejected suddenly from hiding, cast ladders aside and scurried frantically to deploy paddles. It was then that Gueritus's soldiers began to arrive. They moved in grunting disorder, blundering up onto the bridge, waving torches about as they searched for their next fight. There is a certain wildness in the faces of men who have just been battling, in the movements of their bodies as they interact with all things as extensions of a greater violence. For some, this creates a wary hesitancy; for others, especially those who have prevailed, a foolhardy madness, which was clearly the case here.

I had but a couple seconds to observe this throng on the bridge before the first one stepped up onto the sidewall and launched himself into the misty darkness like an ungainly bat. Forward and down he flew, aimed at the rear of our skiff, and with all my might I swung my paddle at the center of his descending bulk. I hit something—ribs, arms, head. Whatever it was, it was just enough to keep him from landing directly on me, and he crashed instead on the boat's back corner, which had the effect of dropping our stern and causing the prow to rise and crank around like a dock crane. This brought us once again roughly parallel to the bridge.

I jerked my paddle overhead and geared for a braining, and as I did, I became aware that more man-bats were preparing for flight. A pair had stepped up onto the wall, and with our skiff effectively lengthwise to them, a double jump seemed imminent. I also briefly saw the thudding tumult of men landing in Getta's boat, visible to me through the arch of the bridge.

Down hacked my paddle. My stowaway wasn't in a great position to defend himself, but a length of hardwood isn't exactly a durkesh. I really needed to hit the head, which was difficult to see under his hitched cloak. I whacked and smacked, beat and chopped, until at last there was a satisfying "whock, whock," which left him slumped to the side like a stunned seal. At just that moment, the next leapers went airborne.

This was a dubious strategy of attack. These soldiers had as much chance of capsizing our boat as landing successfully; however, nitpicking of this sort was best saved for later. At present, they were causing a world of problems for us as we attempted our escape.

"Thump, bump," went the next pair, arriving with such a shuddering boat-rocking that nobody was able to stab or brain or chop for several seconds. The bow, where Lethro was attempting to make a stand, dipped so badly that water slushed over the rail and Lethro was thrown wide. I did have a split second to see the veteran grab his attacker's cloak as he fell. Hanging aslant like a mountaineer, it appeared that he was using that interval and distance to carefully aim his rapier. But I saw no more than that, for there were problems closer at hand.

The other jumper had landed in the relatively narrow space between Terza and me, which was an impressive bit of targeting, and I had to hand it to him that he readied a spade in a matter of seconds. Terza was ready sooner, making use of one of the boat lurches to ram her shoulder into the man's thigh, sending him flailing overboard. That was my cue to shove my own attacker—the semi-conscious seal—right off the back.

When I looked around, I saw that Lethro had cleanly impaled his opponent, though how he had managed to avoid armor with that slender rapier is anyone's guess. The soldier now fell out of the boat, and this meant, unfortunately, that Lethro fell too, for he was still making use of that cloak as a rappelling cord. To the right, a dirty geyser erupted as Terza's swimming opponent hoisted himself over the side rail, launching himself straight back into the boat. This was a true feat of athleticism; however, Terza performed an even more impressive feat by dropping into the lowest crouch that an armored body might allow, giving her stiletto easy admittance to the man's throat.

Three down, but hardly a triumph, for the thumping, clunking army of fliers was just getting started. I even understood the reasoning, at least partially, for the moment our crew drifted out of range of that bridge, there was no ready access to us from the sides. We could slip away into the runner's ravine, ensuring, if not a full exodus from the Lower City, at least an escape from the ambush site. Besides, their tactics must have looked somewhat successful from above. Lethro had gone overboard, and Terza was crunched down in a flattened posture. I hadn't dispensed with my paddle as a primary weapon (still hoping to use it for its intended purpose), so this too could not have looked overly threatening from on high.

So, they came, the Raving Blade's reckless, bristling man-bats, ensuring a horrible experience for all below. Another crashed home, slewing and spinning us, and I knew he would soon be followed by others, since those on the bridge who had been initially wary now appeared to be joining the impetuous camp. I scanned the sloshing waters and couldn't spot Lethro anywhere. More immediately, Terza was in full combat mode, crouched and focused with a stiletto in one hand and gutting dirk in the other, and she was making the latest arrival sorely regret his awkward landing. Gouge, jab, thrust, jab, deathblow…that sequence, essentially.

The next concussion thundered just behind me, and I spun and chopped, going straight for the side of the knee. This fellow had suffered his own graceless landing, so cracking my wooden blade on that joint gave him zero chance of stabilizing. Paddles are quite good for this. In fact, paddles are superb weapons overall, something Holod Deadskiff had emphasized ever since I was a boy, drilling me on the fine art of breaking limbs, cracking skulls, flipping boats, and pinning drowning men below the surface of the water, all with this ever-handy tool, one that could propel a boat too, let us not forget.

"You can't paddle out of a shitstorm with a spade, Scuff," he had said many times in my youth. "Your job is to move cargo, not cross swords with degenerates."

In that vein, I promptly used that ever-handy tool on my degenerate, lifting him up and out of the boat. It was easy, for once the man had buckled sideways in leg-clutching misery, he clearly grew panicked that I would draw a blade and finish him off. This got him crawling, which allowed for a quick paddle thrust between his fleeing legs, followed by a crotch-levering maneuver to send him tumbling like a sack of meat into the drink.

"The next two are yours!" I yelled at Terza as a new pair drummed down hollowly into our hull. Demanding that she fight these two alone was asking a lot, but it was necessary, for if I didn't immediately return to paddling water, as opposed to legs, heads, and groins, then we were both as good as dead. Of course, there was one last thing I needed to do before we left the ambush site: search for our recently disembarked skiff mate. Normally, I don't waste time with men overboard. If a member of my crew is too clumsy to stay in the boat, then the bungling ass can swim home, or possibly to prison, or just as likely the undertaker's cart, which were the usual consequences of falling into the wrong hands on a bid. But this mission was different. Raving cells awaited the captured, and in deference to my dearly departed Flerra Tellian, who cared a great deal about Lethro, I would make one last effort to retrieve him.

Unfortunately, my man overboard was nowhere to be seen. I did spot two soldiers slapping about in the canal—the pair I had ejected earlier—but no sign of Lethro. However, as I threw one final look back at the bridge, I noticed a single head bobbing in the shadowed darkness beneath the arch. I was certain that I saw the fleecy hook of a ponytail sprouting from the back of this person's head, telling me it was likely him.

There was no retrieving him from there, and it appeared that he had plans of his own, for a second later that ponytail surged up, then went deliberately under. He was going to make a swim for it. Perhaps he was headed to the other skiff, where Yurgen and the Reed sisters were battling, or if his breath retention skills were strong enough, he'd slip away underwater, then secretly exit the canal somewhere beyond the lantern glow. Either way, there was nothing more for it, so I jabbed my paddle into the King's Canal and started stroking madly for the shelter of the runner's ravine.

Above and behind me, the enemy had started flinging things. A dagger stuck in the bench to the side of me with a twangy quiver. A second later, much more ominously, a durkesh went somersaulting down the length of the boat, deflecting off of one of the soldiers fighting Terza. The men above must have realized that they had equal chance of hitting their own, so they gave up on that tactic quickly, allowing me to paddle out of range.

All the while, I had to witness Terza's feral melee, which was not a pleasant thing to watch. It was, however, vintage Falconbrow, which meant these men were in for a very bad time of it. Terza and I had sparred often. As a fencer she outclassed me (not hard to do); however, what really amazed me was the fact that Terza was almost my equal when it came to close quarters combat. Her father had taught her this. He had insisted that it was sheer idiocy for a woman to trade strength for strength with a man and that the only way for her to even, and in fact skew, the odds was to exploit men's weakness.

"They'll come for you wide, Terzy," he had told her. "They'll swing and wrestle and choke you. Your job is to let them, then have a blade ready to open their guts."

Or their armpits, or their throats, or their genitals—all of these were specialty strike points for Terza Falconbrow, who could nail vulnerabilities in her sleep, and who (thanks to gifts from me, in part) kept an arsenal of vicious combat implements tucked into every inch of her clothing and armor. Such was our romance. While I couldn't identify every last one of the weapons my ex-lover used that night, I would like to think that at least one of them was a sweet gift from yours truly.

There was nothing sweet about Terza's battle with the last two soldiers, which turned into a horrific, grunting bloodbath. As I stroked towards the channeled blackness of the runner's ravine, I observed her putting an end to one of them. The man had started to pound and wrestle her, in just that way that male bullies, thinking to bludgeon, not stab, the woman, which he accomplished with the pommel of his spade and his free hand. This was a gross miscalculation, for Terza took this opportunity to slip inside and jam her gutting dirk straight into the man's larynx.

A gruesome burgundy swill rinsed across my boots, as Terza and the voiceless wretch toppled together into the well at my feet. The man gurgled and died while Terza, soaked and panting, slid to a crouch, awaiting the next opponent. That was my final vision before opacity engulfed us—a yelling, bench-leaping brute, coming at her with a spade-stiletto combo that looked ready to stab, not slash, to gouge, not beat, and I, with paddle in hand, seeing it all, had to force myself not to break my stroking rhythm. Then I saw no more, for even my sharp eyes could not penetrate the gloomy density of that place.

I could only listen, thereafter. The sounds were terrible—groaning and gagging, rasps of steel, slapping leather, and one reverberant boom as bodies fell to the vibrating boards beneath my feet. Around me, the darkness was a chilly drape. The odor of urban dampness invaded my nostrils, and all the while I kept up a ferocious, stroking rhythm.

Wasn't this, at last, the moment to relax my tempo? In the shelter of this city canyon, couldn't I have paused and come to my skiff mate's aid? I could not, or at least not if I truly wished to save Terza Falconbrow and myself, for the scoundrel in our boat was not the last threat we faced. Our enemies would soon figure out what I had known all along, that there was a perfect way to cut us off at the end of this ravine. Down where the long stifling trench ended, another bridge crossed our path, and then, beyond that, our final run of canal came complete with a pedestrian sidewalk, albeit a decrepit one. At either place—the bridge or the adjoining footpath—Gueritus's soldiers could attack us at will, with a distinct terrain advantage, essentially ending this.

So, that was the race I was engaged in. It was a tight one, since those men were sure to start running en masse to the next bridge. I did, however, have one thing going for me: I could paddle. I could *seriously* paddle—something I was better at than anyone I had ever met. I even outpaced Coljin Helmgrinder, who was almost as much of a monster with a wooden blade as he was with a metal one. But not as much of a monster as me. I'd raced other Shadow Bidders, local fishermen, and foreign sailors, leaving them all so far behind it was embarrassing. This talent is not something I could even teach, for it was bred into my body at an early age by Holod Deadskiff, who lurked tyrannically in the bench behind and would jab his own implement like a cattle goad into the small of my back.

"Faster, you little delinquent! Push yourself, dig…dig…dig, feel the goddamned water like it's part of your arms."

By the time I entered my teens, I could subtly time the forward explosions of the boat with undulations of water and current, I could harness every inch of power in my frame, avoiding wasteful motions, slicing through the fluid abrasion like it was air. Much attention has been given to the barbarism of Vazeer the Lash, to his unsavory fighting tactics; however, most of my Grell Running victories were the result of this thing in my hand, and not because I used it to brain someone.

And so, in cold, unsettling blackness, I deployed this crucial skill, scraping sidewalls on occasion but for the most part staying true to course. This was another thing I could do: sense obstructions. I could feel the little swell of my bow wave pitching off of granite edges, allowing for fractional course corrections that never broke my rhythm.

In the meantime, I had to endure the appalling noises of Terza's bawl. The fight had now reduced itself to a juddering rollabout, with the two of them snorting and wheezing down there below me, booting the sidewalls and presumably each other, as they did the gods knew what with their hands. Most likely, they had clinched in such a way that arms blocked arms, blades blocked blades, and sheer exhaustion made it difficult to deliver a blow strong enough to penetrate armor.

This was often the time when the larger combatant would dispense with weapons and instinctively descend into throttling. It was a primitive thing, born of the desire to dominate, but also mounting aggravation, for it was hateful to be stalemated by a physically weaker enemy. Surely this was coming soon, if it hadn't already, and once that happened, Terza's job was to withstand it. Against all preservation instincts, she must bare her neck to it, for those grubby male fingers, thick with encircling hatred, would leave ribs, kidneys, and the groin exposed. Without his arms blocking her, Terza would find a way past his armor.

You can live, Terza. You can live, and kill this piece of shit.

And that's what she did, as I knew she would. My warrior queen lived, and once again killed, rolling there in the filthy darkness, alone. I don't know what maneuver she used, or which implement accompanied it, but as we neared the head of the ravine, it was her sounds alone that I heard.

"Are you alright?" I demanded.

Inhalation, exhalation. A wheeze, followed by something close to a sob.

"No…I'm not alright."

We were drawing near enough to the end of the black channel that light was finding its way in—light of a concerning sort, for I was now aware of the faint skip of orange glow against one of the walls. Torches were coming.

"How hurt are you?"

"Very."

"Anything fatal?"

More breathing and wheezing.

"I don't think so."

"Can you still fight?"

"I don't know."

Twenty feet now separated us from that faintly glossy outlet, the distance shrinking at ferocious speed. Before us stood the arched silhouette of the next bridge, where, as yet, I saw no human shapes but heard the jostling commotion of their approach.

"Find some resource within yourself, Falconbrow," I said. "Because I might need you to kill again."

"I might need you to kill even one time, you turd!" she croaked. A second later we burst from the ravine.

There was but a single stroke of open water before the crumbling stone bridge imbibed us. I looked right, and down the ruined length of an inner core avenue, a band of men was coming fast. Only a couple torches dappled their armaments, unevenly revealing spades, daggers, and at least one durkesh. Then we were under and quickly past the bridge, starting down the final two hundred feet of open watercourse before the Banks. This was going to be the true contest of speed. Once the men crossed that bridge, they would have access to the sidewalk on the left, and abused though it was by time and human neglect, the path was certainly good enough to allow for a careful jog. We were about to find out what my paddling capabilities were made of.

Before me in the boat, I could now see my ex-lover's carnage. This was the sort of image that only Hell's Labyrinth could produce, a unique product of our vaporous, channeled metropolis, where anonymous boaters slaughtered each other beneath the ruins of fallen grandeur. The two dead soldiers were sprawled brokenly across the length of our skiff, their gray and black forms humped by benches. And there in the space between them, shuddering and gripping her leg, was Terza Falconbrow, a wet, anguished mound, whisking past a backdrop of vaulted doorways and crumbling gargoyles.

"Get ready on the left," I said.

This prompted her to start picking through the skiff's litter of bloody steel. In truth, hand-to-hand combat was unlikely, since the canal was wide enough that if I hugged the building on the right, they couldn't quite reach us. What they *might* do was throw things. Those of us in in the North—Sullward in particular—were not accustomed to distance weaponry, since the prevailing mists, the tight encroachment of buildings, and a general culture of throat-cutting intimacy did not lend themselves to attacking beyond the reach of one's arms. Still, I stayed as low as I could and warned Terza to do the same.

The first projectile was a dagger, and it breezed past my head from behind, then went clinking along the wall on the right with a flinty chime. They were having trouble keeping up, these men, and though my arms and chest burned excruciatingly, I kept us careening along our silty ribbon. Eventually one of the soldiers managed to puff abreast, a fleet and stringy son of a bitch, who ran faster than the others and looked like he might, in fact, know how to throw things. When he had gotten a little ahead of me, he suddenly wheeled, cocked back his arm, and unloaded the one implement I feared most of all: a durkesh.

The hinterland durkesh is a versatile and dangerous weapon, a short, nasty axe with a piked top and a serrated back edge, and while it isn't exactly a paragon of airborne sleekness, there are so many ways the thing can hurt you, it doesn't really matter which part of it makes contact. He targeted me, the paddler, and he did so at damned dangerous range—under fifteen feet. But I didn't stop paddling. I didn't dive to the bottom of the boat or raise my implement to attempt a deflection or do anything other than slouch a little lower on my bench and keep gouging those turbid waters, propelling us to freedom.

Then he threw. He aimed for the squat mass of me, directing the axe just fractionally ahead, where my momentum would thrust me into a collision. I didn't exactly see all of this, but I sensed it from his body language and the basic fact that it was the logical thing to do. As the durkesh whirled from his grasp, I pulled my body upright and back, sucking in my breath, and lo and behold, the spinning bird of death flew right past my nose and sparked against a granite column on the right. It chipped and ricocheted off of the front of the cylinder in such a way that the weapon was thrown clunking into the bow of our craft.

"Grab it!" I yelled at Terza as we left the thrower behind and barreled towards the edge of the city. "Get ready to cut brush."

The nettled mess of bushes, vines, and twisted oaks known as the Banks would slow our adversaries; however, there was always a chance that it would slow us too. I had not surveyed the head of the King's Canal since the storm (a stupid mistake, realized just now), and there was a very real prospect of a toppled tree, or a nest of woven limbs, halting our forward momentum.

Terza crawled to the bow on her hands and knees, releasing a painful cry in the process, but she managed to secure the durkesh by the time we went rasping through the gateway of thorns. At one point we were forced to duck as a clatter of hanging branches strafed us. But that was the worst of it. The remainder of the route was relatively uncluttered, and in under a minute and a half, we had sliced through the entirety of the Banks and were spit forth into the thick, dark flow of the autumn Grells.

In this way we escaped.

In this way, the urban storm maiden and her unkillable cargo hauler survived yet another bid that had gone disastrously wrong.

23

THE TREE OF LIFE

"You couldn't have stopped for one goddamned second and helped me?"

We were a full mile to the north of the King's Canal now, paddling ever farther up the Grells towards the place where the river became swift and shallow. Terza was lying in the front of the skiff on a makeshift bed of the dead soldier's cloaks (the bodies themselves we had dumped overboard). I had quickly checked the scope of her wounds, and while cuts, abrasions, and heavy bruises swathed almost every part of her, the only puncture wound was in her leg.

"No, Terza, I couldn't have stopped. You saw how close it was at the end."

"It was closer than that earlier. I almost died on the floor of this boat, no thanks to you."

She was slumped back facing me, or so it sounded, for neither of us could see anything. With the crescent moon set, all was a realm of fumy blindness, though there were still some faint lights from the thinning Lower City visible through the trees to the left.

"I trusted you to get the job done," I said.

"Well, maybe next time don't be so trusting."

"Would you prefer that?"

"Why not? You blew up your Narrow Bid for a woman… some foreign Masque you didn't even know. I'd like you to show at least half that much concern for me."

Oh, damn her, by whom I really meant Heshna. My Brood sister, in that bizarre way of hers, had apparently gleaned every last detail about the Narrow Bid, then fed it to Terza.

"Everything I did tonight was to get us *both* out of there," I said. "A little thanks are in order."

"For what, paddling a skiff? Paddling faster than anybody, as you always tell me? What a hero."

"Also, for believing in you. In knowing you would win, which is something I always know, whether you're wielding a weapon or a paintbrush…or even some crazy ideology."

This silenced her for a few moments. Around us, the sounds of the night river were a steady melody of shushed depth, unbroken by rocks. I was listening for the shallower timber of rapids, and, not hearing them, I knew I had to keep pushing on, despite my exhaustion.

"You've been saying that a lot lately," she finally said. "That you believe in me."

"I've been thinking it a lot."

"So, it's true then, what Heshna said that night in my shop… when you kissed me. That you want to win me back?"

"Are you winnable?"

Silence again. To the left, the lights of the Lower City had finally disappeared entirely, and the two of us found ourselves in a lilting cocoon of night, a place so shrouded with our respective thoughts they seemed like they might eventually conjoin in the muted blackness.

"Adelyn believes in me too," came her reply.

This didn't seem like an answer to my question; however, Terza spoke it with the sort of throaty significance that said she was trying to convey something.

"You're lucky to have us both, then," I finally said, unsure of where else to go with this.

Not long after that, I did begin to detect the murmurous duet of water and stone, making its way to me through the crisp air. In our world, it was always hard to judge distances based on sound alone, for the fog distorted things, sometimes dampening noises, other times enhancing them. This was often the case, for instance, with the rumbling of the sea, which occasionally sounded like the crashing of tidal waves, when in fact small breakers were simply echoing off of a low ceiling of clouds.

Tonight, I wound up having to trawl a full twenty minutes longer than the initial rocky strains seemed to indicate. At last, when the rushing sounds had risen to a steady, unmistakable babble, and I began to strike the chance boulder with my paddle, I directed my strokes out of the heart of the flow and towards the shrinking depths of the shore.

I pulled us up on a pebbly beach, and once the boat was secure, I drew forth a small, sealskin bag. In it I kept a flint lighter, along with some tinder and a tallow candle. Within a minute, I had produced a small light source and, leaving Terza temporarily in place, I ventured forth to find the markers that Droden's staff had left for me. It didn't take me long, and I followed the trail of tiny flags to a small clearing.

The prepared campsite was well situated. It was close enough to the river to allow convenient access to water, while still being nestled in sufficient evergreen growth to keep a fire largely invisible. I pulled everything out of hiding, arranged the space, then finally started a little flame in the pit. Once I had it burning steadily, I came back to help Terza out of the boat.

"We're both taking a bath," I said.

This led to a five-minute argument, since Terza, a bit cold already, and disinclined towards a plunge in the late autumn Grells, also hated being told what to do. But I prevailed, since she wasn't in a great position to fight back, and even she had to admit that she was dirtier than a hog. So, into the river we went. The water of the Grells ran swift and clean this far north, making it an ideal spot to bathe. We removed only our weaponry, then submerged ourselves fully, emerging a short time later, gasping and sloshing. I had brought a metal pot from the campsite, and I filled it to the brim with water. After that, I lugged it in one hand and used the other to support Terza, as we shuffled through the woods to the fire. There, we promptly descended into our next argument.

"Lie back on these pine bows, I'm going to undress you."

"You're not."

"Just do it, Terza. You've exerted enough energy as it is."

This discussion carried on for several minutes, until Terza, who was so exhausted she could hardly remain in a sitting position, and also starting to shiver, finally slumped back in the bows. From there I pulled off her boots and socks, then shimmied around to unstrap her armor, followed by her padded jerkin. Bit by bit, I took off all of the outer garments, which set us up nicely for our next conflict.

"That's enough."

"Everything's got to come off."

I'll spare you the back and forth here, but I was forced to remind her, repeatedly, that I had seen everything already, and that she should view me more as a physician than whatever she thought I was now.

"Your campsite better have something to drink," she muttered. "Give me that first."

I had instructed Droden's crew to leave two bottles of wine and a jug of mead, for I had anticipated that if I wound up needing this refuge, Terza, and hopefully Lethro, would both be with me. While I didn't want any of us dead drunk, this quantity would likely preclude that (plus, a host must always consider the guest list).

"You're also going to eat something," I said, producing a small basket with cheese, smoked beef, and some bread, along with one of the bottles. "But first, these two."

Terza stared at the small, pressed paddies in my palm: gummy green and yellow herbal composites that she obviously recognized.

"Gods, you really must've thought this thing would go to shit."

"It pays to be prepared. Now eat up."

Wincing with the taste, and demanding the wine to wash it down, she ingested both. The little green paddy was a composite of assorted sedatives and nerve-deadening herbs that had been combined into a mixture called Gaelax. It was expensive, but it was the single most effective painkiller available, shy of full-blown narcotics. Terza was still in a mild state of shock from her injuries, but the pain was likely to set in soon, especially as I worked on her. The little yellow disc was known as Movelin—even more expensive—and it was an extraordinarily powerful buffer against infection. I hadn't fully examined the puncture wound in Terza's right thigh, but I knew it posed the biggest threat, for injuries of this sort could lead to contaminants in the bloodstream.

After she had consumed the herbs, her portion of the food, and more than half the bottle of wine, I started to remove the last of her clothing.

"Take yours off first," she demanded. "You're still dripping wet."

This was a fair trade, and she was right. While the fire was doing a lot to warm us, remaining wet too much longer wasn't a good idea. So, I stripped off everything but my cotton loin shorts, then pulled from the bushes two pine drying racks. Droden's people had created these per my specifications, and I set them up near the fire and began to hang all of our wet garments there.

"You really did think of everything, didn't you?" she said, watching me intently as I performed my labors. "Were you expecting to take another one of your weird Grell dives?"

I continued to drape the last of the clothing over the rack, then I squatted down and put the pot of water partially over the fire. I was acutely aware of my ex-lover watching me as I engaged in these semi-naked actions, and I was in full readiness for some demeaning comment. It came as I was pivoting towards her to start the next round of care.

"You're wearing a lot of fresh scars, *Vazeer the Lash*," she said. "How many of these are from your new, psychotic girlfriend?"

Right about then, I came to the conclusion that trying to safeguard my personal life was a useless endeavor. This embarrassing transparency had to do, primarily, with the morbid reintroduction of Heshna the Seer into my life, though at least some of the blame lay with the fact that I now actually *had* a personal life, one that was salacious enough to gossip about.

"Oh yeah, don't think I don't know all about that," Terza went on. "I'm not sure which of your latest romantic choices is more ridiculous…the hoity Midland Masque, who got you to screw up an entire job, or that little homicidal lunatic who keeps taking out contracts on your life."

"Take off your goddamned undergarments."

"Take off yours first. They're still wet."

I started to reach forward to undress her forcefully, which showed just how stupid this conversation had made me. Before I knew it, one of those powerful Falconbrow feet was jammed into my naked chest with breath-jolting power. Terza had used her uninjured leg (or rather her less injured one), but this still caused her to yelp in corollary pain.

"See what you made me do."

"For hell's sake, I'm trying to help you."

"No, you're not…or maybe that's not *all* you're doing, with all of your 'win me back's.' Drop your own shorts, so that I can watch down there and see if you're just being a physician."

There was something sneeringly excited in the burned breadth of her face, telling me that the wine and the painkiller were starting to work on her in interesting ways.

"Here, take a swig yourself," she said, thrusting the bottle at me.

I took it, then sipped lightly.

"Finish it, you priss," she said, jabbing me in the stomach with her foot. "You were such a heroic paddler, right? You deserve a drink."

Terza definitely sounded drunk. She'd consumed almost three-quarters of the bottle, which wasn't a huge amount by her past standards, but her drinking of late had been so restrained that I suspected her tolerance had dropped. Plus, the Gaelax wasn't supposed to be ingested with alcohol.

Because she had issued a challenge, and also because her ongoing cooperation seemed predicated on mine, I turned the bottle upright and gulped away. It felt good, I must say. The warm wash of the liquid forging its friendly path down the internal piping was soothing. My own tolerance had been moving in the opposite direction, mostly on account of my "psychotic girlfriend," so I didn't do my usual tearing and sputtering with the oversized guzzle. When I tossed the empty bottle aside, Terza looked genuinely impressed.

"Go get another."

"Only after I clean and dress your wounds. Like I said, the clothing's all coming off."

Terza at last submitted, though not without enforcing her earlier demand that I first take off my shorts. She allowed me to put on a dry tunic from my stowed supplies, but she would not permit new clothing below, ensuring a half-nude (fully embarrassing) nursing operation.

"This will sure look intimidating if the marsh brigands show up," I muttered.

"Even with my tits jiggling and your prick dangling, they wouldn't touch us. We're Falconbrow and the Lash, remember?"

"I remember," I said, dipping a clean cloth in the hot water and starting on her legs. "Do you?"

Terza leaned her head back on the pine bows and stared up at the fire-lit sheen of the encroaching sky.

"Sometimes I remember."

I carefully rinsed the many cuts and scrapes on her legs, then started working my way up the rest of her body, making sure to keep the cleansing waters hot but not scalding. I must have achieved the proper balance, for Terza never protested, and a short while later she closed her eyes, and her breathing settled into a slow, steady rhythm.

The patchwork of slices, pokes, grazes, and bruises swathed virtually every part of her, making it look like she had spent the evening pretty much exactly as she had. And this fight had been against the Raving Blade's men, the worst of the worst, of whom Terza had beneficently purged the world of four. It was an astonishing tally by any measure, and I would see to it that the entire Labyrinth knew the extent of her heroics if we managed to live through this.

I could tell from the comfortable slump in Terza's posture, and the calm rise and fall of her breasts, that she was now fully relaxed, which would help with the healing. Therefore, I went on treating her. I gently rinsed each of Terza's injuries individually and patted it dry. Despite their disturbing quantity, and in some cases poor aesthetics (like the choke marks at her throat and a long strafing on her ribs), these wounds were not particularly threatening, apart from the thigh gouge. To this one I gave special care, washing it extensively, then, with plenty of advance warning, I doused it with pure grain alcohol.

Terza was stalwart as a rock, and while I saw her dense lips twist slightly, she didn't make a sound. After I'd finished all the rinsing, I began to apply the Nettledown poultices. Once again, I worked my way up her body, starting with the top of one of her feet, which had either been stomped on, or which she had bruised herself by kicking some hulk in his armor. I was exceedingly careful as I labored. I didn't want to cause her sudden spasms of pain or bring too much attention to the sheer number of hurts.

Meanwhile, I reacquainted myself with Terza Falconbrow's body. This was a landscape I knew so well, a muscly place of abrasive sensuality where, during key, formative years of my past, I had taken up residence. Tonight, I was but a tolerated guest, I knew that. Thus, with a brooding sense of nostalgia, I gently engaged in the return tour, traveling over the brawny reddish hillocks, the weathered dips, passing familiar landmarks, such as a weird, girlhood sternum scar, off-white and wormishly raised from her flesh, about which she would never speak. I also passed those sights which she referenced often, for she had created them: smartly curated tattoos, which—in contrast to Shade of Night's indecipherable scrawl of bygone murders—were objects of imaginative beauty.

On one of her shoulders was a silvery exhibition of exotic blades, swords distinct of outline and detail, overlapping near the hilt and splayed elegantly outward like a fan. On her upper chest was the wispy trapezoidal shape of an Azmouli temple. This piece, which rose from the top of her breasts all the way to the base of her throat, was back-illuminated and faintly glowing, crowned by the pale circumference of the moon. Both of these were striking; however, the true artistic crown jewel was on Terza's stomach. There lay a gorgeous tattoo of a Tundrian maple, one of the few deciduous trees to thrive in the harsh lands from which Terza's mother hailed, and to which she had returned when Terza was a teen.

Exquisitely rendered with golden branches woven through the fine hairs of Terza's stomach, and leaves drawn with such delicate, yellow dimensionality that you could almost hear them rustling, this feature of my ex-lover's torso was a masterpiece of ink and flesh. Terza had not only designed the piece, but unlike her falcon, she had painstakingly applied it herself. Several post-passion sprawls had seen my fingers tracing through the intricate architecture of those limbs. The stout Tundrian maple was a symbol of sacred importance to tribes to the north—the *Tree of Life,* they called it—and it was a specimen of some significance to me too, for I had spoken the most intimate and unrealistic of things wandering amongst those branches.

"Below this tree, our child will grow," I had murmured on more than one occasion, when wine and warmth had somehow converged into the perfect stupor of impracticality. At such moments, a future together seemed possible.

"A daughter," Terza would reply. "I want you to give me a daughter."

"Maybe one of each? A boy and a girl?"

"If you promise me a daughter, the son can come after."

"A daughter it is."

What might thrill me more, after all, than a feisty little Terza—a stunning headstrong creature, erupting with talent, immune to fear, gray-eyed (possibly), long-limbed (definitely), a mixed-blooded synthesis of our mix-minded proclivities. This was how it had looked to both of us back then, when things were going well, and we dreamed of a life that lay beyond Shadow Bidding.

I was still dreaming of a life beyond Shadow Bidding, and so was Terza; however, our dreams no longer felt the same. As I ran my hands once again over a tree that neither grew nor withered, which had tonight picked up a new scrape, but which would never shed a single leaf, I felt a dour regret about all that might have been.

"Hey, you," Terza muttered, startling me, for she had seemed asleep. "That doesn't look like a physician's tool to me."

I had, without realizing it, become stimulated while working in the region of the maple, and Terza had uncannily sensed this. Perhaps the excitement had transferred from the calloused ends of my fingers, or maybe my breathing had changed, but whatever it was that had alerted her, I was suddenly caught. Literally caught, for her hand thrust out and grabbed me below.

"I remember this fellow," she laughed, her voice garbled somewhat by drink and herbal compounds. "And it seems he remembers me too."

I tried to pull away, which was hopeless, for Terza had a grip like a carpenter's vice, and I had become highly grippable.

"You know what else I remember," she breathed, "…how crazy we used to be after bids. All dirty and sweaty, and we'd be humping the Black Hells out of each other. Remember that?"

"Obviously, I remember."

"You thinking to take advantage of me, Vazeer, now that I'm all cut up and soused? Just lying here helpless?"

"You're about as helpless as a bear with a bee sting."

"Yeah…but maybe I'm helpless in other ways. Maybe you've got me at another kind of disadvantage."

"What disadvantage?"

Terza gripped a little harder, pulling me closer, and this, combined with her congenial reaction to my unprofessional medical behavior, did nothing to make me less of a solid target.

"The fact that you're caring for me so nicely," she said with a bent smile that created a bulky pile up at one end of her lips, and minor darkness at the other. "I don't remember the last time that happened, or if maybe it ever happened."

She lay there in the pine bows, gazing up at me.

"And you know what…" she continued, letting the thought glide for a beat or two. "I kinda like it."

"I like it too."

"Feels like you do."

Clinched vigorously, but not unpleasantly, I felt I could see evasive things moving about in the saturated grayness of her eyes.

I didn't know exactly what was in there, for while the woman herself was deeply familiar to me, this moment wasn't. We had never been here exactly.

"Is this Vazeer the Lash winning me back?" she finally asked.

"I sure hope it is, Terza."

And then, what do you know, it was. She pulled me down so that we could slide our mouths warmly together, and this time those strong, decidedly unembellished Falconbrow lips opened wide to give me entry. I tasted, instantly, the hot fuminess—wine drenched and earthy—and in this condition, we carried on for some time, me crookedly angled, our inebriated faces locked.

Before we went further, I pulled back and asked if she was prepared for the consequences, and she cagily replied that she had been taking contraceptive herbs, which (most inopportunely) flashed within my jealous psyche the specter of that "other man." But I dispelled him quickly. After all, it was *me* here now—me, the one with longstanding history, the thoughtful care-taker, who, while not exactly the heroic fighter tonight, sure wielded a strong paddle.

And with that, I shifted into position, placing no real weight on her body, and we made careful, and uncharacteristically gentle, love to each other. The tenor of the experience was different than it had been with Shade of Night, since newness, and to a certain degree madness, had provided much of the excitement in that relationship, and neither were present here.

However, what I did feel was an overwhelming sense of healing. This was the therapeutic re-tying of a dangling end, a much-needed repair, leading, as the night flowed on into the wee hours, to a feeling of being set back on course again after so many years spent wallowingly adrift.

24

THE OTHER LOVER

The next morning dawned upon the marsh in a pink, steamy blush. Despite camping in the drier, northern reaches, where the ground was firm and the air less sulfurous, the close proximity of the cattail-choked realm to our south brought mist in good measure. Terza was still soundly sleeping when the sun rose beyond the blur, and I happily allowed her to continue.

Following our nighttime activities, I had re-applied the relevant poultices, then kissed her off to a deep slumber. I placed a cloth over her eyes so that the morning light wouldn't wake her, then I dressed and armed myself, settling into the role of night watchman. I'll confess, I napped a little here and there. However, I had seated myself uncomfortably upright against a tree, with a spade across my lap, so I never went out cold, and I don't think anybody but a practiced Eye could have crept up on me unawares.

I made a few careful patrols at first light and concluded that we were entirely alone. The brigands who usually haunted these woods were a seasonal lot, and when the winter came, they usually took shelter in the impoverished inland villages. The third month of autumn was a bit early for that migration, but the Swell Driver had likely decimated their ranks and reduced travelers (both on the river and the road that ran along the far side of the marsh) to the point where the predation business had become a meager affair.

I also made use of the morning light to clean out our bloody boat. I dragged it from hiding in the bushes and gave it a thorough rinsing, then lugged it even farther into the woods. When I returned to the campsite, Terza was still asleep, the improvised eye patch and the lingering effects of wine and Gaelax doing their job. I used this respite to restoke the low-burning fire and prepare some food. I chopped four potatoes into a skillet, and once they had begun to brown, I threw in some dried strips of venison. Smoked meat doesn't require further cooking, but it's tastier that way.

With the food crackling away, and the morning sun infusing our foggy little amphitheater, I felt strangely at peace. By any measure, this was inappropriate. So much had gone wrong with our plans, so many deadly unknowns awaited us, that a great bout of fretting should have been the next order of business. However, something delightful had also happened last night, and I felt inordinately pleased about this one development.

Staring at Terza's sleeping face, her neck newly tattooed in mulberry fingerprints, I saw only a snoozing angel. This is how it often was. Those whose minds have shuttled off in slumber leave behind the sweetest stand-ins, which is why I could watch women sleep for hours. I enjoy the docile ups and downs of respiring breasts, the whispering passage of ethers. Even a psychotic little murderer could appear like a visiting celestial while asleep, which is how Shade of Night had seemed at such junctures. And Nascinthé of Levell, a veritable fairy princess in the waking world, became nothing short of a goddess upon repose.

As I watched my no longer ex-lover, Terza, absconded on her restful holiday, I wondered what she dreamt about. Difficult things, perhaps, for these had been difficult days, but also, maybe, she pondered a few items of a softer quality. Could I send a missive to her right now, let the agreeable scents of breakfast reach her, reminding her of "Vazeer the Lover," not Lash, the "wound-mender," not maker…could I get all of that into the Falconbrow heart? I could not, I soon learned. The angel dozing before me bore no resemblance to the creature who eventually opened her eyes.

"What the hell did you do to me, you bastard?"

Those words, uttered like the wheezy snort of a mule, were my salutation upon the angel's return.

"Oh gods…you really outdid yourself this time, you lecherous turd. Drug and plug me, did you? This is a new low."

Terza looked less comely in the waking state. Those freshly opened eyes were bloodshot, and that previously genial mouth appeared puffy and chafed in ways that it hadn't when its only job was snoring.

"Get me some damned water."

"It's right next to you."

She tried to crane around, but the effort clearly made her achy, nauseous, or both, so instead she batted her hands against the earth at her sides until she smacked the canteen, then cursed when it fell over. This part I had anticipated, which was why I had screwed the lid on tight.

"Gods, I feel like shit," she gasped after she had taken a deep, glugging drink, releasing slick streams down the side of her face and around the hot humps of her jaw.

"I still have more Gaelax," I said, "if the pain is too bad."

"Not on your life, you toad. There's something wrong with the stash you gave me. You must've spiked it."

"*You* spiked it, Terza, by insisting on taking it with three-quarters of a bottle of wine."

She lay back in the bows and groaned.

"When have I ever *not* drunk three-quarters of a bottle, taking anything?"

That may have been true in the past, but she was thinking of the old Terza, when her tolerance was higher. Of course, this was only part of what was going on here, which she tacitly acknowledged in the least friendly way possible.

"Damn me for being a fool," she muttered towards the gently swaying pine branches. "I should never have gotten mixed up with your sick world again."

"Once you spit out your grievances, I want you to eat something."

"That's going to be a lot of spitting."

Terza did, at last, lever herself upright and then started to climb from her improvised bed. When I came to her assistance, she shooed me away.

"I don't need your help to piss."

She got herself slowly into a standing position, then limped with a blanket over her shoulders to a tree where she took care of business.

Standing there, attempting to brush aside my not insubstantial disappointment, I couldn't help thinking of Shade of Night. Even though the Finisher had reverted to untenable form in the end, she had been ever-so-tenable before that. Upon waking each morning, Shade had seemed more interested in me, not less, and putting aside my accidental violation of some decree or another (a bit scary at first, but I quickly learned her rules), she existed in a constant state of delight with me. Also, Shade was very much a feminine being, and she would never have wanted me to see her squatting like an ape, pissing against a tree.

"Help me get some clothes on," Terza said when she had returned to the fire. There followed a surly interval of hoisting, supporting, buttoning, and strapping. In marked contrast to the stoic reticence I had admired the night before, I was subjected to several painful yowls that were directed (purposely I would swear) straight into my ear canal. Afterwards, she limped towards the fire and the skillet of food.

"What did you make?"

She was hungry, which was my first useful piece of leverage. I had found a decent log to use as a backrest, and Terza finally allowed me to ease her down to the ground so that she could sit with her right leg extended and her back against the fallen trunk. I fed her on one of the small plates from the supply sack and encouraged her to drink plenty of water, and while I could tell she enjoyed the food, she went to extreme lengths not to show it.

"It's funny how quickly letting you back in my life has landed me in this goddamned marsh again, full of regrets."

At first glance, this is a pitiable scene. It includes attentive me, taking care of ungrateful her, which is a bit deceptive. The panorama is but a small segment of time, featuring "very nice Vazeer," waiting hand and foot on "very mean Terza," and it does not include other, peripheral characters. There was also this additional fellow, "acerbic, cunning Vazeer," who, as it so happens, was about to make an appearance.

"You know what else is funny?" I said, with a practiced smile. "How often the mighty Falconbrow needs to couch her own weaknesses in the blame she throws at others. I honestly don't think there's a bigger whiner in all of Sullward than you, Terza."

She stopped chewing, and her ruddy face blenched noticeably.

"What did you just say?"

"You heard me. I treated all of your injuries, and your ears seemed fine."

Terza now set her little plate aside and put her hands down near her hips. She had a pair of stilettos there, but she was actually testing her palms on the ground, to see how easy it might be to pop up and strangle me.

"You're lucky," she said, "that I am too banged up right now to come after you."

(Not lucky, really; I'd definitely factored that in before I picked this fight.)

"Good then," I said. "This way you'll have to face the truth, instead of covering it with all of your smacking and bludgeoning. When it comes down to it, Terza, you're one of the most insecure people I know."

I was really going for it today. But I was hurt. Despite being nominally prepared for some pushback, and my informal certification in "Falconbrow mood studies," I am human, after all, not to mention male, and egregious wounds to pride are still an excruciating business.

"Damn you," she hissed. "Damn you, you dog."

"Why? Because I occasionally hold up a mirror to your pathetic bleating? Because I'm reminding you that you went after me last night, not the other way around?"

"I was tanked up and drugged!"

"Not entirely tanked, Terza, and you know it. But that's a small matter to the queen of whiners, who can't square feelings for her ex-lover with whatever she feels for some new lover. That son of a bitch's presence is fouling up everything in this campsite."

Part of what made "acerbic, cunning Vazeer" a force to be

reckoned with was the fact that those wicked verbal barbs were coated with the acid of truth, or at least partial truth, which is something that Coljin Helmgrinder had experienced during the night of our infamous Shadowbiter duel. I'm always hunting around for this stuff, storing it up in my weapons cache so that it can be used at moments like this. Shade of Night, who had otherwise been in complete command during our tryst, had experienced this phenomenon briefly and acutely, and I'm sure, were it ever to materialize, a relationship with Nascinthé of Levell would eventually see the introduction of this cutting patten.

As for the target of the hour, she was beginning to display the telltale effects of the acid. The "whining" charge was a good one, because it reduced Terza's ornery bluster (a rigorous sham) to its fundamental composition (discomfort with the depth of her own needs), and when you add to this the shock of her "other lover," whoever it might be, and also the naked obviousness of her lingering feelings for me (I hope I'm not delusional here), you get quite a debilitating little impairment. Here's how it played out.

Stiff-legged and grounded, Terza glared at me across the low-burning fire as a stitch of uncertainty assailed her. She made slow, scrapy motions with her fingers in the dirt, and there was a notable shrink in the pastel expanse of her falcon, all of this telling me that my attack had changed the dynamic. The problem was, this also told me that I was right, specifically about the other lover.

"Okay, you can put away the knives now," she said. "You made your point."

Which point? I had made several. Also, this seemed an extraordinarily sudden de-escalation, making me wonder what sort of nerve I had hit.

"We've got to get the hell out of these woods, Vazeer," she said with hurried distress, "and start looking for the others."

"We're not going anywhere. I'm going to look at that leg in a moment, and you're going to rest."

"Screw the leg. You'll give me Gaelax, and I'll manage. We've got to find out what happened to everybody."

"They got attacked is what happened. Three Blades and one of the toughest Grell Runners in the Labyrinth. We have to trust they dealt with it."

"Not just them, Vazeer."

And now, acid-afflicted Terza, with her dirt-clenching hands and squeezy falcon, began to look distraught. My attack had broken through the noise, and with this muting, I was astonished to see a species of primal anguish laid bare. Again, which target did I hit? *Not just them* didn't refer to Radrin Blackstar, about whom Terza cared nothing, nor did it refer to Heshna, who, while breathlessly alarmed, had clearly managed to stay out of harm's way. Terza cared a great deal about Cad, but I was fairly certain that her terror wasn't on his account. That really left only one other party, the very person about whom my brave comrade had fretted terribly in advance of the ambush.

"Adelyn will be okay, Terza. She's very good at avoiding trouble."

"But we have no idea what happened at the negotiation site, Vazeer."

Vazeer, she called me, three times in a row. Not "dog," "bastard," or "turd." Something was definitely up.

"She was protected by some of the best soldiers in the Lower City. And she's not a bad fighter herself."

"But the Seer said we were betrayed. Maybe it was Tygean's

own men who betrayed him…which would mean they weren't protecting Addy."

"Never. Those soldiers are die-hards, and Adelyn would spot duplicity in advance."

"How do we find out? I've got to know, or else I'll go crazy just sitting here in this marsh."

"Heshna will tell us."

For a moment Terza stared at me blankly, so I clarified.

"Droden knows where we are, and Heshna will go to him to find out. She'll make it here eventually."

I had purposely avoided arranging a group rendezvous point, simply because we were facing an adversary who was a notorious torturer. I didn't want captured team members to give up the others. However, those who were clever enough to return to Eastcove would be able to find their way to us, which is why Droden had staffed his highly defensible refuge with extra guards. I had promised him that we would not be using Eastcove as our safe haven, however, since he had already taken enough risks on our behalf.

Terza eventually lay back, but only after I had fed her more Gaelax and wine, since she was starting to ache terribly. Before long she had transformed into "relatively nice Terza," though nothing close to the intimate being who had laid claim to me the prior night. I checked on all of her injuries, particularly the gouge in her right thigh, and everything was healing well. There were no signs of infection, and I had every confidence that she would make a full recovery. Still, just to be sure, I had her ingest more Movelin, and I insisted she stay reclined with her leg slightly elevated. To her chagrin—but also possibly pleasure—I proceeded to massage the leg in order to keep blood circulating, and, since

I was already in position, I figured I might as well massage both legs and feet.

"Your tricks won't work a second time in a row, you horny nursemaid," she said.

"You never know. I've also got a jug of mead, in case the wine, Gaelax, and foot rub aren't quite enough."

"Oh, Vazeer," she said with a dispirited expulsion of breath, her sturdy jaw pointed skyward. "You have to promise me you'll help me find her."

"I promise."

I went on rubbing and tending, and all the while I tried to put the pieces together, for there were definitely pieces here. I was certain I could build something tangible out of them, which, suddenly, I did.

"It's Adelyn."

Terza didn't look at me. Her face reflected no confusion or denial, or much of anything, beyond a general state of weariness and anxiety.

"Adelyn is your new lover?" I pressed on.

Terza offered the slightest shift of her shoulders to connote a shrug.

"Somewhat new. We're finding our way."

I was silent for a while, gently kneading, feeling the powerful substructure beneath Terza's warm skin. At face value, there was a certain logic here, and while Terza had never shown an orientation towards women, switching things up in this way was not uncommon among Shadow Bidders. The women seemed more prone to it than the men, starting with my dear, departed Flerra, who was interested in both genders but was more disposed towards her own sex. There were also a few men in our ranks thus inclined, including, I'm told, my skiff mate, Lethro. I'd always wondered if this was part of why he seemed more dignified than the other Blades—Lethro never displayed the rank braggadocio that marked so many of his colleagues, which was something I had always appreciated about him.

"Are you silently judging me?" Terza asked, breaking into my massaging reflections.

"I may judge a lot of things, Terza, but Looking Glass morality issues aren't among them. You two make a nice couple."

That was a vast understatement. Prodigiously talented, monumentally attractive, these two were among the most universally desirable Shadow Bidders in our city, and I had tried, at various times in my life, to woo them both. Which is where my next bout of mental rambling went—how viable was the whole "winning her back" plan now? Could I ever make headway with either of them, though I really meant Terza, for the quickest way to lose every woman in my life was to try to win them all. Also, while I wasn't exactly an expert in the science of human reproduction, I was fairly certain that Terza's claim that she had been taking contraceptive herbs made no sense.

"There's no one else?" I asked.

"Not at the moment."

We neglected to take the conversation further, as this had been a lot already. For my part, I didn't want Terza to mistake my questions for judgements, which they weren't, nor did I want her to think I was selfishly angling to get her back, which I probably was. Some sorting would be required here.

The hours passed relatively uneventfully at our campsite. I administered to all of Terza's needs—tending her wounds, feeding her, facilitating her state of semi-intoxication, and keeping a careful watch on the river and the surrounding woods. We remained entirely alone, visited only by a pair of deer, who didn't come close enough for me to contemplate hunting them. Our location was a little too far north to hear the Sullward clock tower, but I guessed it was somewhere around the Fifth afternoon Bell when night effectively descended over the marsh. There was still a semblance of twilight in the western sky, but the preponderance of fog ensured that darkness fell early.

About an hour after that, Heshna the Seer finally arrived.

25

UNSETTLING TALES

As always, she manifested out of godsforsaken nowhere and scared the hell out of me. Even when there was no cause for it, even when she was dealing with battered refuges, traumatized by violence (surprise violence inflicted when we thought ourselves hidden), even then, she could not help herself.

"I smelled this fire halfway up the Grells," she droned into my ear, as I was crouching to once again stoke the flames.

"Damnit!" I snarled, spinning on her, my spade already halfway around for a counterattack. Anticipating which hand I would use, she spoke into the other ear, then fleetly doubled back out of range, leaving behind a startled, enraged version of me—something she had been facilitating and manipulating since she was a girl.

"Why?" I growled. "Why did the Dark Gods rob me of the good sister and leave the shit one behind?"

Heshna, a leaden, fire-bushed bundle against the circle of night, absorbed this in resentful quiet. Then she replied.

"They didn't rob you, Brood brother. You simply abandoned her."

Oh, bloody hell.

"I'm not even going to bother to ask who fed you that shit, because that inquiry never goes anywhere. But I will ask, if you're so disturbed about me abandoning Flerra, why is it that you rejected her three decades ago?"

Muted in firelight, peevishly stewing, the face of the little nemesis glared back at me across a pool of shadows, across a chasm of time.

"I didn't reject her," she replied. "She just liked you better."

I glanced over at Terza, who had been lightly dozing before this family reunion got underway, and now she hinged upright in her bedding and raptly observed this interchange, no doubt trying to figure out the right moment to butt in and get the information she wanted. But even she, anxieties and all, could see that something of significance was transpiring here.

"Did you ever even try, Heshna?" I asked, my spade lowered but not sheathed. "Did you ever try to be an older sister to Flerra? Try to be more than a wicked thorn in her side?"

"I tried."

"I don't remember it. Flerra didn't remember it."

"She was too young."

"She grew older. Why not try then?"

"By then, you had taught her not to like me."

Within me, crawling down from the little brain cave where my most spiteful material dwelled, was a perfect stinging needle in the arsenal of *acerbic, cunning Vazeer*. It would be good, I think, for me to refrain from reflexively deploying these weapons, but character growth along those lines was still pending.

"Nobody needs to be taught not to like you, Heshna. It is an innate skill, granted spontaneously to all who meet you."

"Vazeer!"

Terza looked horrified. Just beneath her rubicund exterior lay the sort of reaction that suggested my ex-lover (the "ex" had disappeared briefly, but it was back again) sincerely wished that I wasn't habitually exactly who I was.

"Don't speak that way to her…that way to anybody. We are a team, and we need Heshna to tell us what happened."

We did need that. And the other part was also true, but at such moments there's always so much more going on than words. There's this thing called "history," a loaded phenomenon, unseeable to all but those who have added mass to it, and even then, not seen equally by contributing parties.

"Seer, please tell us exactly what happened," said Terza, who was now painfully getting to her feet.

I moved quickly to assist her, trying to prevent her from putting unnecessary weight on the bad leg. Heshna took this in, absorbing the sight of devoted Vazeer rushing to meet the needs of a needful Terza, laying his hands on her with conspicuous gentleness. What the Seer made of it, I wasn't sure.

"I will get the boy," she said. "Some of this should be told from his mouth."

When Heshna returned to our warm arena, she brought a visitor in tow, and that visitor was, gods be praised, Cad. I scanned him for injuries and didn't see any. But something was wrong. Cad was wearing a heavy, dark brown cloak, which was already odd, for jackets were his usual look, and something about the way this *boy* hunched within the clunky garment seemed like he was swaddled in a security blanket. And his face looked bad. In the random upward toss of light, I couldn't tell if those were droopy bags under his eyes or some kind of bruising.

When I came forward to give Cad a hug, he was less than receptive, turning away and returning the bearish grapple with two spiritless little pats. In closer quarters, I was now certain that there was a mild contusion on one side of his face; and yet, I was even more certain that the true injury lay in some deeper, emotional place.

Heshna did a quick perimeter of the campsite, confirming what had been true this whole time—we were entirely alone out here. She and Cad had come by skiff, and though they had beached the craft a quarter mile away as a safety precaution, there was no need for it. The Raving Blade did not appear to have enough troops to send them all over the city and marsh, hunting for a bunch of stragglers.

We sat around the campfire, passing the mead, as Heshna started the recounting. According to my Brood sister, the initial meeting between Counts Tygean and Gueritus went as planned. The two parties, backed by what remained of their soldiery, joined in the center of Gessum's Cross, and relations between them were tense but cordial, with a few morbid jokes and a respectable performance by Count Tygean, who displayed the proper balance of grim distaste and grudging resignation. Heshna wasn't a Masque, but she was certainly observant, and from her hidden vantage in the window of one of the neighboring ruins, she could see both Counts clearly. She could also see Adelyn, who would act as the bellwether for this meeting. Adelyn stayed removed from the direct negotiations, witnessing it all and, according to Heshna, showing no signs of alarm at first. Midway through the proceedings, however, Adelyn's face did appear to grow concerned, this on account of another, proximate party.

It was Adelyn who warned them. It was Adelyn who made the brilliant, split-second decision that transformed what might have been a slaughter into a true fight, for she spotted the problem as it was developing and passed the signal to the men directly around her. She also had the wherewithal not to cry out, thereby alerting the Raving Blade, as almost anybody else in her position would have.

"Betrayed," was the word that Heshna had used when she spat her breathless warning into our watery cave. Subsequently, I had speculated about who might have betrayed us, and my mind had rummaged through a worrying list of candidates, each with their own painful implications—Shade of Night, Coljin Helmgrinder, one of the Eastcove guards, Tygean himself, or, perhaps, the constitutionally duplicitous Raving Blade, who, not knowing of the broader plot against him, simply took this opportunity to kill his enemy when he was standing a few feet away.

No, none of those.

The young man who undid us was Count Tygean's son, Devlan. Devlan Tygean was not a traitor in the classic sense. What he was, was an obnoxious, glory-seeking hothead, a descendent of underworld nobility who had been relegated to a soldier's role, and likely felt humiliated at being excluded from the decision-making process. And so, to ensure that the night's great moment of avenging glory did not fall to some anonymous Shadow Bidder, he took matters into his own hands. Standing close to his father's side, Devlan suddenly drew a blade and attempted to strike the Raving Blade down midway through the negotiations. He did this in front of everybody, thinking, maybe, that with a clean dispatch, the mercenary-minded men of the Lower City would realize that only one king remained, and that it was pointless to carry on further conflict.

Quite possibly, Devlan was a half-wit. His theory, if indeed that was it, probably wouldn't have worked even if he had landed a killing blow, for the Raving Blade's men seemed strangely loyal to their sadistic lord. But he didn't land that blow, which was the most chilling part of the story. When I met with Count Ulan Gueritus at The Crossbiter Tavern, he had assured me that direct combat between the two of us, should it occur, would go extremely poorly for me. Per Heshna's recounting, I no longer doubted this.

Devlan Tygean made his move from a mere eight or nine feet away. He had clearly planned the attack ahead of time, which is why Adelyn could spot something in the young man's behavior that had her warning her neighbors. And, at least from Heshna's description, Devlan was handy enough with a sword that his thrust was quick and on target, propelled by an agile lunge. But Gueritus was faster, and more on target, and more agile, for he somehow (and really, this is so goddamned hard to do) got one of his two swords out of the scabbard in time to knock the attack askew. The Count's other sword emerged a heartbeat after, and this was the one that sent Devlan bleeding and yowling to the cobbles, his spade clattering from his fingers.

From there, chaos erupted. The melee was, by every measure, a bloodbath. This pitched street battle between the armies of Counts Gueritus and Tygean was a thing unwitnessed since the inaugural days of Beranardos Sherdane's Labyrinth, when the new High Lord launched an all-out war to crush those opposed to his contract system. In my teens, I had often tried to imagine the storied episode, and creativity was required again tonight, for Heshna's tale was filtered through a colorless drone. But I think I got it. Having already experienced the feral madness of the Raving Blade's soldiery on the night of the Shadowbiter duel, and then having been overpowered by the grim determination of Tygean's renegades, I could at least partially picture a street war between them.

Gray Bender is the canal that runs through Gessum's Cross, and in under a minute, bodies were falling into this murderous trench like storm trash, as the melee spilled in all directions. Coljin Helmgrinder and the other Shadow Bidder recruits were waiting at the ready, prepared to assist whichever side appeared to be winning, though, according to Heshna, the huge Contract Blade didn't take too long to make a decision. He chose prudently, I guess. Tygean's men were outnumbered. The Raving Blade himself was instantly delivering bloody murder to the enemies directly in front of him, plus his two most combat-oriented vassals, Viscount Szorticus and Baron Hurgis—the former a Kaszian weapons master, the latter a wooly brute who wielded twin battle axes with an almost lewd furor—were in the fracas within seconds, and the damage they inflicted was terrible.

Col and his team likely would have brought the situation to a stalemate had they opted for Tygean's side, but a stalemate was not a desirable thing in the mind of Coljin Helmgrinder. So, picking the man who had promised him a title, Col led his team into the fray, and they began to turn the tide. My Brood sister reports that the Shadow Bidders appeared unenthusiastic about the work, moving slowly from one side of Gessum's Cross to the other, hacking into the tumult of stabbing, hollering men. However, they got the job done, and in this way, all hope of Tygean's army was lost.

Heshna wasn't sure what happened to Count Tygean, Viscount Grieves, and Devlan, but it seemed likely that they were killed or captured. In any case, directly after the battle, Ulan Guertius went ahead and crowned himself High Lord, or so reliable sources in the Labyrinth were saying.

"Enough about them, Seer!" Terza interjected frantically. "Tell me about Adelyn."

This was one of Terza's many interruptions, which I have spared you. I was guilty of it too, probing at the anemic recounting when I found some description insufficient (all of them, pretty much), and my Brood sister's storytelling definitely suffered as a result.

"Adelyn fought," Heshna answered.

"She fought?"

"With that slim spade she uses, and a stil—"

"I don't care what weapons she used, Seer! Just tell me what happened to her."

"I don't know."

"What do you mean you don't know!"

"I lost track of her…after a while."

Terza was incredulous. She was also intimidating, and more than a little drunk—all recognizable from the days of our relationship, but not, perhaps, recognizable to Heshna the Seer, who seemed to wither before the onslaught.

"And why didn't you come and warn us? Why did it take you so goddamned long to reach the ambush site? We might have been able to help, instead of getting mauled in a bloody canal."

"I couldn't get out of there," Heshna reported quietly. "I had a good vantage for the meeting, but…I didn't expect all of that. I got pinned down."

In recent times I had witnessed quite a few interactions between Terza and Heshna, and I had been consistently impressed by Terza's kindness, the way, with no apparent difficulty, she skipped right over my Brood sister's social ungainliness. At this moment, something else was revealed, a thing that was strangely unpleasant for me to witness: the sight of Terza Falconbrow, the undisputed queen of all female Shadow Bidders (and many of the male ones too), raining her disgust upon the morose awkwardness of this misfit loner.

"I wanted to come…" Heshna tried again.

"Really? How bad did you want it?"

"It was hard for me—"

"It was hard?" Terza spat. "How hard could it have been, to slither through one of your holes? That's your job, right? If you're not going to pick up a spade with the rest of us—"

"Terza," I interrupted, and I placed a pacifying hand on her leg. "I'm not often in the habit of defending my Brood sister, but even I have to insist that whatever you're implying here doesn't fit. If Heshna says she couldn't get away, we should believe her."

I recalled the way Heshna had come to my aid in the tight alleys on the night of my reconnaissance mission and knew that simple cowardice didn't define her. My sense was that she had been a little too ambitious with the surveillance perch she had chosen for the meeting, and then found herself trapped once the fighting broke out.

"But you've looked for Addy since?" Terza pressed.

Heshna had. She had looked for Adelyn and the others in the day since the deadly melee, and the results of her explorations weren't promising. Adelyn could not be found anywhere, including all of their agreed upon meeting sites, and even other places that were less logical but still possible. Gratefully, her body was not among the dozens that littered Gessum's Cross following the combat. The desperate hope was that she was hiding somewhere and was too frightened to resurface. None of us really believed this, but we didn't yet wish to face the likelihood that she had been captured.

As for the others, there had been one confirmed casualty—Yurgen the Juggler, who, despite being the most agile member of the team, or possibly because of it, employed his dexterity in service of an extended combat with the attacking soldiers. This was something Heshna had actually witnessed from a secret vantage after she warned us. Dorcus Reed was stabbed through the shoulder early in the encounter and effectively lost the ability to fight, and her younger sister turned all of her attention towards extraction. Since the boat was overrun quickly by soldiers, the escape involved diving into the canal and swimming clear of the torchlight, something for which Getta Reed was well suited. She must have cut the straps on Dorcus's armor, since Heshna did briefly see the two sisters floating off into darkness.

Yurgen, by contrast, went on fighting. I'm not sure if he had drunk more during our stakeout than I was aware of, but he seemed strangely committed to covering Dorcus and Getta's retreat. At a certain point, Lethro came to his aid—Lethro, who definitely should have swum off with the Reed sisters—climbing into the skiff, so that the two of them could make a stand together. They killed four or five, according to Heshna. They fought well, but in the end, they were overwhelmed, which resulted in Yurgen's confirmed death and Lethro's capture.

"What about Blackstar?" I asked. "Did he ever arrive?"

This question had been grinding away in the back of my mind, but it had been superseded by other details. Now it needed to be asked, and in its answer, rendered haltingly and rather miserably by Cad, some of the more disturbing material came to light.

Despite Radrin Blackstar's assurances to the contrary, I had never been able to shake the sense that somebody who should have nothing to do with our mission would still choose to insert themself. My mind had been plagued by scenarios ranging from full-blown betrayal to a more targeted retribution, probably delivered to me personally, and ingeniously humiliating in some manner. I was referring, of course, to Shade of Night, and there was no need to wonder any longer, for this is what she verifiably did.

Shade apparently figured out the identity of Radrin Blackstar's Locksmith (Heshna swears on her life that she was not the source), and having a reasonable sense of when my operation would take place, she waylaid the Locksmith when he returned home after delivering keys at the ambush site. This was all learned later when Heshna arrived at Benni's dwelling in Dockside to find the old burglar bound, gagged, and bleeding. Shade at least had the decency to leave the door to his apartment unlocked, so that somebody would happen upon him eventually.

But Benni was damaged. He was damaged in that terrible way that only Shade of Night can damage, and while she did not sever the remainder of his fingers, as she promised she would, or his private parts, which she also promised, and confined herself to merely slicing off one of Benni's pinky toes (revenge for him letting Blackstar into my apartment the night she was attacked), the protracted intensity of her interrogation induced a level of trauma exceeding what the poor fellow had experienced at the hands of the magistrate. By the time Shade was done with him, Benni had violated his most sacred Labyrinth code by giving up Radrin Blackstar's whereabouts, and the nature of the plan. Thereafter, my vicious paramour made her way to our ambush site where she undertook her next harrowing interrogation.

Poor Cad. He only knew Shade as Jisselle, the property manager, with possibly some other identity, but nothing on the scale of the truth. This, combined with the fact that my protégé was wildly smitten with her (as he was with every woman over the age of thirty) put him at a terrible disadvantage. Of course, Cad was no match for Shade even on his best day, which this definitely wasn't.

"She was dressed all nice, Zeer, and pretty…and she seemed in need, and I didn't know who or what she really was, because you never told me."

Cad's aching discomfort as he recounted his portion of the tale was greatly exacerbated by the presence of Terza Falconbrow, upon whom he always tried to make a gallant impression, and who, in turn, might have taken this opportunity to comfort her young admirer. But she had no interest in that. The icy draft of Terza's gaze spread disapproval in all directions—towards those who had been pinned down, seduced, or insufficiently injurious to Underlord soldiers, which described all of us.

"What did you do, you little fool, have a smooch with her?"

"Cool it, Terza," I said. "Shade can be difficult to resist."

"So says the horny toad who can resist no woman."

"It wasn't like that," Cad murmured. "I was all confused, and she caught me off guard."

Of course she did. Dressed fetchingly, and appearing somewhat desperate, Shade approached Cad at his designated waiting point with a grateful sob of deliverance, as if the gods themselves had presented her with a friendly face in the least friendly of locales. The Dockside property manager, "Jisselle," did not bother to explain what she was doing wandering after midnight in the streets of the Lower City, or what incident had made her look so desperate. She simply threw her arms around Cad's neck, kissing and thanking him. During this hug, Cad felt a light pinprick on the side of his throat, which he thought might be a piece of her jewelry catching on his skin, but which turned out to be one of Shade's clever little implements, administering a knockout drug directly into an artery.

Cad did not go unconscious straightaway. There were no toxins quite capable of doing that; however, as Shade clutched him, he began to grow woozy, and that was all the distraction she needed to slide around to the side and put him in a choke hold. Cad is much stronger than Shade, and not a bad combatant when all is said and done; however, my wicked lover never allows circumstances to wind up as a strength versus strength affair, and she clearly knew that her only job was to neutralize his efforts at a counterattack long enough for the combination of the drug and her choke hold to do their work. Which is what happened, for Cad eventually slumped to the street, and when he awakened, his true nightmare began.

I would like to tell Cad, someday, when Terza isn't watching, that he shouldn't take this incident so hard. Shade of Night had done worse things to me, and she had bested me on three separate occasions without any aid from knockout toxins. Hopefully, I might put a little dent in Cad's dreadful feelings of shame. That task wasn't going to be easy, for Shade had really done a number on him.

When Cad regained consciousness, he had been dragged into a little alcove, and he was lying face down with his hands bound in front of him and his pants around his ankles. Classic Shade of Night. His tormentor was on top of his legs, clutching his private parts from behind, with a blade pressed there in such a way that the slightest twitch would slice the entire package from his body.

"My name is Shade of Night," she whispered to him upon waking, delivering a chilling alias that was well known to denizens of Sullward, and many other cities throughout the Empire. "In my apartment in Tergon, I have an entire display case filled with men's genitalia. I will gladly add yours to the collection if you don't do exactly what I say."

After that, Shade presented the situation as follows: Cad, whom she acknowledged as handsome and strapping, and ever-so-young, could either spend the remainder of his life as a ruined creature, incapable of enjoying or pleasing women, unable to have children, struggling to piss or to even think of himself as a man, or else he could avoid all of that, and Shade herself would come to him at a later date and reward those delightful male parts with pleasures that he didn't even know existed. All Cad needed to do to ensure the desirable outcome and avoid the horrific one was to let Shade quietly into the building where Radrin was hiding, and then assist her by calling out to the Finisher from the rear vestibule, requesting he come to take a look at something important Cad had found in the street outside.

"You don't owe this Imperial creep anything," Shade whispered to Cad as she forced him slowly, clumsily to his feet, gripping him painfully from behind. "He may impress a sweet boy like you, but he is a cold and wicked thing, who has plagued my life for many years. I left Tergon, in part, to avoid him, and now he has come here to haunt me again, and violate my personal chambers, and steal things from me. I must rid the world of him, and protect Vazeer at the same time, since our beloved Lashy should not associate himself with such coldness."

"But," Cad countered, or so he insisted, "if I do this, and you kill Blackstar, it will hurt Vazeer, and Terza, and the others... because they are counting on him to come at the right moment to finish the job."

Sitting at our little campfire, listening to this story, the group of us was morbidly spellbound, even Heshna, who had heard much of it already.

"How did Shade reply to that?" I asked, still grappling with the term "beloved Lashy," for which I had no cogent emotional receptacle.

"She told me not to worry," Cad answered, "that she had a plan to take care of everything."

"What the hell could that mean?" demanded Terza.

"It meant..." Cad resumed. "It meant that once she killed Blackstar, who she kept calling 'the Imperial creep'—once she killed him, she would fill in for him and finish the job herself. Benni told her the plan, and Jis—Shade of Night—said she could easily play the Finisher's role. Even though this attack wasn't really her style, it would be an interesting challenge for her, those were her words. To complete a contract in a street, in the middle of a battle. She was looking at it like a kind of career advancement."

"And you believed this?" Terza asked.

Cad wriggled inside his big security blanket.

"She just seemed..." he said, and his voice trailed off.

"She seemed like what, Cad?"

"She seemed like she might be goddamned crazy enough to mean it, Terza!" he barked, and then he pivoted to look at me and Heshna too, with a sort of miserable wildness. "When we reached the building, she was babbling all kinds of crap, about fixing the broken thing inside her, and that the path to repair must run through the two most wicked men—the Creep and the Roach—and her 'penance' was to rid the world of both of them, on the same night. I'm just saying, it didn't sound like somebody trying to ruse me. It sounded like a person who wanted to do this thing."

"She did," said Heshna. "I'm sure of it."

My Brood sister had been listening fixedly to this recounting, and it seemed likely that she was now hearing details that had not been included in the original telling.

"She didn't say any of this to me," Heshna quickly clarified. "But I know her, and this sounds like something she might come up with. But I don't think it would have worked, even if everything went according to plan. I witnessed Count Gueritus's reflexes at Gessum's Cross, and I don't think Shade could have pulled it off. I doubt if anybody could have done it…except, maybe, your Finisher, Brood brother. He was probably the only one."

We sat for a few moments, in gloomy silence, and then I finally asked the inevitable question.

"What happened inside the building?"

With this, Cad revealed the final, frightening details. It was a hard sequence for all of us, or at least three of us, since Heshna and I had our various attachments to the two combatants, and Cad had the terrible shame of having facilitated this thing. This is what we learned, filtered through a disconsolate recounting.

Cad followed orders, and with his hands still bound in front of him, and Shade exerting her terrifying pressure, he was able to open the door to the building. Benni had left only one lock operable on the rear door and cad used the temporary key to work it. Once inside, Cad whispered through the darkness, identifying himself. Radrin was waiting at the other end of the building, near the front door, prepared to emerge at the proper moment and perform his Finishing role.

"I said the thing she wanted me to say," Cad explained, "that there was something Radrin had to see with his own eyes, just outside the back. But I swear to you, I was already planning to screw it up for her because I knew she was gonna have to take her hands off of me at some point to get ready to fight. I was all set to yell out and resist. But she must've known that, 'cause she put me down before I could do it."

Indeed, Shade tugged Cad down into a kneeling position, and from there, she slipped the blade away and used the pommel to strike Cad on a pressure point on the back of his skull, knocking him unconscious. Shade was so damned good at this, nailing these sensitive spots in the human body to achieve all sorts of grisly objectives. If Radrin Blackstar stood alone in his ability to step through rents in the very fabric of space itself, so that he could emerge with his blade slicing through a man's throat, then Shade of Night was the reigning deity of finding, and exploiting, anatomical weaknesses one never even knew existed.

When Cad eventually came to, everything was over. Even the canal battle had finished, for he heard the sounds of a few men in the street outside, bantering with each other as they dispersed. He was so dizzy he could hardly drag himself upright, and it took him an inordinately long time to free his hands or even to pull up his pants. In addition to the pain in the back of his head, Cad felt intense soreness in his neck, and it occurred to him that after Shade struck him, she probably administered another, stronger dose of the knockout toxin to make sure he stayed down.

"When I finally looked around, the things I found inside that building were scary. It was like a slaughterhouse, and I threw up a little just looking at it, 'cause I was nauseous already."

What Cad found was blood. Blood everywhere, dripped and spattered, puddled and smeared. In one spot he saw a small bloody handprint on the wall—a woman's handprint—and then many boot marks of both male and female size, skittering and sliding through the space, as if engaged in a macabre ballet. The vacant apartment was only sparsely furnished, but in the largest living space, where the bulk of the combat had apparently taken place, the dining table and several chairs had been knocked over, and the wall mirror was shattered on the floor.

There was no way to know whose blood was whose; however, everything about this description suggested a protracted conflict. Having personally watched the two Finishers fight in my apartment—in that case, with Shade naked and unprepared for battle—I could only imagine the result when the two of them faced off fully armed and combat-ready.

"They were both gone," Cad said. "I found Blackstar's cloak, with a lot of blood on it, and one of Jisselle's earrings…and a fingernail, both with blood on them…but I didn't see either of their bodies. The back door was open, with a mess on the saddle. Like I say, the place was empty, and I have no idea what happened to either of them."

"She would have poisoned the blade," said Heshna when Cad was done with his tale. "So, if she cut him, he would succumb eventually."

"His blade was poisoned too," I replied.

I left it at that, for it seemed immaterial to explain where Radrin's poison had come from, nor was it worth noting that Shade had been divested of hers. A clever professional of her caliber would have had more stashed away somewhere. I sat several moments in heavy, firelit silence, feeling extremely lost.

This was an excruciating blow. Its inevitability did nothing to lessen the impact, and based on the way the others stared at me, I wasn't hiding it well. Even Terza, who could have cared less about either of the Finishers, and was consumed with her own private fears, kept her impatience at bay just a little longer as I digested this.

To whatever degree Shade of Night's return to savagery had muted my affections, those feelings had been at least partially restored by the knowledge that this eccentric, unstable entity had passionately cared about me. Unable to express herself like a normal human being (or even to remotely act like one), she conveyed her devotion in the form of the dangerous risks she was willing to take on my behalf. I was appalled by her latest escapade; however, I still understood, on some deep intrinsic level, that she thought she was doing me a service.

But that loss, personal though it was, was overshadowed by the other, for as decidedly impersonal as my relations were with Radrin Blackstar, his presence in my life had become a thing of extraordinary consequence. The principle of *alignment* was opening profound doorways, both inside and out, all of them hinting at a better future. Those doorways now felt shut. I noted a strange, hollowed-out sensation in my limbs, and I had the weird, disquieting sense that some critical piece of my internal machinery had just been removed.

"Okay, well…there's nothing we can do about any of that," said Terza, whose exasperation had finally reached its limits. "Only one thing should concern us now. We've got to find Addy, before she ends up in a goddamned rav…"

Terza couldn't complete the sentence. Having held it together through the telling, the full reality of the situation began to descend upon her, and tears glittered in her eyes.

"You all owe me!" she suddenly cried.

Terza stood, buckling slightly from the stiffness in her leg, but this did not mitigate the scalding disapproval she cast over us all.

"Every one of you let me down," she choked. "You let her down too, all of you. And now…."

Her voice trailed off for a moment, and she swallowed a few times, regaining her composure, just enough to release the final edict.

"As Yisva Herself is my witness, you will all be sorrier than hell, if you don't start planning, right now, to bring my Addy back to me."

26

A DANGEROUS PLAN

"This utility area is where they would be holding her, and the others," I said, poking my stick into a meticulous drawing I had made in the dirt. "It's the only logical choice for prisoners."

We squatted together around my muddy masterpiece, as the mists rolled slowly up the Grells, shrouding our campsite. The four of us crouched in a gossamer cave of the fire's pulsing light.

"There isn't a basement?" Terza asked.

"There is, but it took huge damage in the first Great Storm, and it would be flooded now, and probably filled with wreckage. I can't see Gueritus wasting time having his troops clear it out."

My drawing was a semi-detailed floor plan of Kaennamin Academy, and once again I pointed at the service area on the ground floor, cut off from the grander, public spaces.

"This utility zone actually makes for a decent dungeon, with a few different rooms that could act as cells, with some tweaks from a Locksmith. Dubin the Dicer probably possesses those skills...."

But I let the sentence trail off, since it wasn't going anywhere good, and Terza's reddened face had fallen into the most horrified of looks. Viscount Dubin Haiyes, aka "Dubin the Dicer," was one of Gueritus's two direct vassals, and also the man most often assigned to torturing prisoners.

"They won't start the ravings right away, Terza," I said, trying to distract from that dreadful name by using another worse one. "Ravings," a term that Gueritus himself had coined years ago, really needed to join "Dicer" on the list of banned vernacular.

"How do you know that, Vazeer?" Terza whispered, the anger now smothered to a gust of panic.

I didn't really know it, or anything, but I was trying to cast this scenario in the best possible light.

"Think about it," I said. "If they captured Adelyn, and that's a big 'if'…"

"They did, Vazeer, I know they did."

"You don't know it, Terza…but, okay, hold on a second. Supposing they did…they would have captured others at the same time—Tygean's men. Maybe Tygean himself, and his son. We already know they have Lethro. The point is, that would be a lot of people, people far more relevant to Gueritus than Adelyn. They wouldn't be in any rush to get to her—"

"Yes, they would," Terza said in a fierce wheeze. "They would be trying to find out information about us."

"They don't even know Adelyn is connected to us. She was working directly for Tygean, or that's how it looked. Why would they need to ask her things about Tygean? She would be low in the order of priorities."

Of course, this didn't apply to poor Lethro, who had been captured at the ambush site, thus making him a very good candidate for interrogation. Also, one of Tygean's people clearly gave away our position, probably by means of an impromptu street raving, so that same person might very well have disclosed Adelyn's role in the affair. But Terza's terror seemed at least partially placated by these reassurances, so I saw no reason to poke holes in my own theory.

"How will we get inside that building, Brood brother?" Heshna asked. "I have circled the place many times over the years, and there appear to be only two clear entrances, and both will be guarded. It doesn't look like an easy building to climb."

These were good questions. I had given this some thought and concluded that we had absolutely no chance of fighting our way past the guards, even if we had our entire crew reassembled. Therefore, a different approach was required.

"I'll need Benni Bones for this thing."

I pivoted to Heshna and Cad, the two of them sitting on the same log—sitting, it seemed, in the same exact leaden posture. The respective moods of these two, signifying hurts of an internal variety, were just about the last thing I felt like dealing with at that moment, especially when the group's bona fide champion was at the end of her own emotional tether and limping like a peg-legged mendicant. This was hardly an inspiring crew for an attack on the Raving Blade's compound.

"How would a Locksmith help?" Heshna asked. "It's the soldiers that will be a problem, not the doors."

"There's another way in."

"I've never seen it."

"It's not in a place you would think to look, and definitely not a fun route, but I think it could work for our needs."

"A waste line, into the canal?" Cad asked, making his first contribution to this discussion, though posing it with exactly the revolted apprehension befitting a sewage-related question.

"No."

I squatted down at the edge of the drawing, running my stick along the side that adjoined the canal.

"Sarien Kaennamin, and the rest of her family, were dead set against polluting the waterways, including the Grells, so they used large cesspools built into the bedrock. I'm sure the Underlords don't like admitting it, but many of their subterranean compounds were originally intended for turds, not treasure."

"Then what's our way in?" Terza asked.

I now poked my stick into the center of the main entry hall of the building.

"Sarien didn't use the canal water for waste, but in some cases, she did employ it. In Kaennamin Academy, she chose to place a dramatic reflecting pool in the front hall, and in order to supply fresh water for this, she ran it from the canal."

"The pool is dry," said Heshna. "I've entered the building more than once, and there was no water there."

I now brought my stick back to the area I was proposing for the dungeon.

"I've been inside too, everywhere. And I'm certain there is a clogged section of pipe, here."

I jabbed my stick in the thick wall separating the main hall from the service area.

"Sarien was smart enough to anticipate occasional backlogs of detritus," I continued, "so she created a vertical shaft that descends down to the water pipe. It's set in a back corner, near a drain, with a flat hatch on it. Not the sort of detail you would notice, unless you were an engineer. This allowed service staff to climb down there and clear accumulated debris from the grills."

"Grills?"

"Two, at least according to the drawings. I don't own the original set, but the copy I have is from that era, and I'm sure it's reliable. It clearly shows a three-foot diameter pipe, with a grill at the mouth of the water pipe, four or five feet below the surface of the canal, depending on the tide. That one has wide spacing between the bars, and water is always flowing past, so I doubt it's the source of the clog. The second one, which is deeper inside the pipe, just past the hatch, has a finer grating, to keep assorted canal garbage from flowing into Sarien's pretty pool. The pipe also shrinks in size there, so I'm sure that's where the blockage is."

"So…" Terza said, her face leaning in close now, and the firelight giving frantic jitters to her falcon, "…you want to fix your Kaennamin queen's reflecting pool?"

"Just the opposite. I want to leave the clog right where it is. The sight of the dry pool has probably removed any sense that there is an outlet to the canal. If my theory is right, and if we can simply penetrate the first grill, then we will be able to make it to the vertical shaft that leads into the utility space."

"Where Addy's probably being held…?"

"Exactly."

And now I looked around at each of them in turn and got, by and large, the reactions I expected. The one with the greatest vested interest appeared somewhat heartened by this report, and she let out a few robust puffs of breath. "Falconbrow" was back, and she was ready to execute.

"What the hell do we need the old Locksmith for?" Terza asked. "I'll tear that stupid grill off myself. Let's do this thing now, before it's too late."

"I don't think we could convince Benni to come anyway," said Heshna. "He was not in a good state when we saw him last."

Never one to express anything resembling positive solutions, Heshna's responses tonight were all trending towards "no," "don't bother," and "impossible."

"I don't give a crap what state he was in," I said. "He'll come or he'll have me to answer to. You tell him that."

"He fears the two Finishers more than you, Brood brother. Shade has maimed him already, and if Blackstar lives, Benni believes he will hunt him down for his betrayal."

"You remind him that Vazeer the Lash *does* live. If Benni Bones doesn't want to end up on one of my lists, he'll come here tonight, with his entire tool kit…everything remotely useful for a break-in. We're not only going through that outer grill, but also the hatch in the utility room, which won't be easy to open from below, and both jobs must be performed quickly and quietly. Just in case the threat of me isn't quite enough, Cad will guarantee Benni gets the message. Right, Cad?"

The final member of our group nodded, though he looked even less enthused with the task than Heshna, and I was really starting to lose my patience with this. Having myself survived Shade of Night's stabbings, chokings, and castration threats, I simply couldn't cut the kid much slack for his injured pride. On some level, I had to commend Shade for accomplishing what I never fully could: the final removal of Cad's desire to be a Shadow Bidder. Poor timing on that one, since, in no uncertain terms, a Shadow Bidder was what I now needed him to be.

"Up, up, you two. The sooner you get him the better."

I got them standing, then I began to shove them back in the general direction of their skiff. I did this in part to move them along, but also to get them quickly out of earshot of Terza, where additional missives could be conveyed.

"Okay," I whispered once we had rustled away just far enough to escape Terza's eyes and ears. "No more moaning from either of you. I need you both to treat this mission like it's the most important one you've ever run."

"A suicide mission," said Heshna. "I'm not prepared to fight with soldiers."

"And I think ya forget, Zeer," said Cad, swatting my hand away at last. "I ain't ever run a mission before."

Oh, Black Hells. More "no's" from her, and now his "*ya's*" and "*ain't's*" were back.

"You listen to me!" I snarled. "Adelyn needs us, and Lethro too, so we're not going to foul this up. Heshna, you're going to find Benni, wherever he hides, and Cad, you're going to make sure he comes, with all of his tools. And then, when you get back here—which you're going to do quickly—you're both going to come prepared to fight. Heshna, you're one of Holod Deadskiff's Brood, so spare me this peaceable horseshit. And you, you whiney bastard!" I said, grabbing the front of Cad's big cloak-blanket. "Shade didn't cut anything off of you, but somehow you lost your balls anyway. This is Terza and Adelyn we're talking about, your two most ridiculous crushes, and they need you. *Really* need you; is this the moment you decide to lose your nerve?"

"It ain't my nerve that I lost, Zeer," he muttered.

"Then what?"

Here, he sorted himself, searching for the right words.

"Terza's right," he finally said. "I failed. I failed all of you. That was my first real test, and I blew it. Probably got Blackstar killed, could've got all of you killed, and was no help to anybody but Shade of Night. I don't think you should rely on me again because I might blow it again…and get those two killed, which I couldn't live with."

Okay, this one struck an authentic note. On a very personal level, I knew the exact crucible he was passing through, since I had passed through it myself. Many times.

"I want you to hear me on this," I said, releasing his cloak but staying close. "When you and Heshna go rowing down the Grells in a few minutes, she can tell you all about the many tests that I've failed…stretching back to when I was a kid, but certainly as a Shadow Bidder. You've heard a lot of versions of the Gaff story, but Heshna can fill you in on the incident from her perspective, the perspective of anybody who was there that night, other than me, and it involves three people dying unnecessarily, and then a whole host of other horrible consequences, all because I failed to do the right thing.

"And now my Brood sister has information about the mistakes I made on the Narrow Bid. She can tell you about that too—how I decided things on that job that resulted, some of them directly, others indirectly, but the result was…the torture and death of my other Brood sister, my dear Flerr…" And I choked, slammed under the sudden, emotional weight of it, which I quickly tried to suppress.

"What you need to know," I said, recovering, but with a distinct crustiness in my throat, "is that I've screwed up to one degree or another on virtually every important job I've ever run. The difference, though, between me and you, is that I don't let it stop me. I push on. I always push on, and this way I correct at least some of my mistakes, find redemption in a part of the job, and this allows me to go on."

Now I gripped his forearm and spoke with sincere force, straight into the epicenter of his anguish.

"It's a tough battle, against your regrets, but you must win it. Because the alternative is to descend into a place where drink and Cojis and sometimes death are the only ways out."

And I left it at that, watching and waiting to see if the message sank home, which maybe it did. There was a perceptible tightening of the skin on his indented cheeks, a little flaring somewhere in those vibrant hazel eyes, which were catching tiny shards of dappled fire through the bushes. Their shape connoted resolve.

Perhaps he was thinking of his own mother, who had concluded, somewhere along the way, that her regrets were sufficient that alcohol and narcotics were her only means of continuance in this world. My final comment possibly hit that nerve, since Cad almost immediately began to look like himself again, albeit a bruised and bedraggled version.

But he wasn't the only one. Much to my amazement, the skulking Seer, bane of my early, and sometimes subsequent, existence, looked positively affected by what I had just said. "Sensitivity" simply wasn't a thing you ever saw on her face, but as the gods were my witness, I would swear that Heshna appeared moved. We were gaining only the faintest glow from the obstructed fire, along with a wan sliver of foggy moonlight, but there seemed to be a glossy sheen in her eyes. That shrunken mouth was somehow larger, as if she were trying to express something but didn't quite know how.

"We all make mistakes, Brood brother," she finally said, and then the two of us just stood there for a few seconds, hearing the quiet burble of the nearby Grells, being present to each other in an unfamiliar way.

"Okay, Zeer, you're right," said Cad. "I'm gonna shake out of this and go get Benni. And when I come back, I'll be ready to fight…to do whatever we gotta do to get Adelyn and Lethro back. You can count on me."

"I know that. And you too, sister. Just get the Locksmith for me, and I swear to you, on what's left of my honor, this is one job I won't screw up."

Then they were off, shuffling quietly through the brush towards the place where their skiff was hidden.

When I returned to the fire, Terza was bracing herself against a tree and conducting a series of strength tests of her wounded leg.

"I'm going to need to cauterize that thing before we go," I said. "The Kaennamins may have been opposed to dumping sewage in the canals, but the Underlords have no such qualms. We're going for a very dirty swim."

Terza took her hand off the tree and put it on my shoulder.

"Did you give them one of your speeches?" she asked.

"A good one, I think."

She now put both hands on my shoulders.

"So let me give you a little speech of my own, okay?"

"Okay."

"I need things from you on this job, Vazeer, serious things. Promise me you'll give them."

"I'll give you anything you want, Terza, though I'd sure like to know what you're talking about."

"What I'm talking about is the version of you I want to see as we do this. I've appreciated attentive Vazeer, with his sweet foot rubs and nursing—"

"You did? That's not what you said earlier."

"Well…I lied. I did appreciate it, more than you could know."

"I'd like to know."

"Later. I'll tell you after Addy's safe, after you've become the other Vazeer, the one I need from you now. Not the sweet man, or the heroic paddler, but Vazeer the killer. I want the one from the Gaff, and the one who fought Col—Col, who I wouldn't fight no matter how drunk I got—but you somehow did and almost won. I want that sick creature they're talking about from your Narrow Bid."

"Gods, you too? How does everybody know this?"

"The stories are starting to get out, Vazeer, and I must tell you, for once, this side of you is giving me hope. You did all of those things just to protect some mystery woman, who I know was your Midland Masque. I need you to go after Addy in the same way."

"Of course. I promise."

"Good, because I promise it too. You and I, if we're together on this, we have a chance."

"Falconbrow and the Lash," I said, with a grim smile. "There's nobody in Hell's Labyrinth…maybe in the goddamned Empire, who can stand against those two."

"Nobody," she replied.

And then, suddenly, Terza's fingers leapt from my shoulders and dug themselves into my hair, as she drove her mouth over mine with a reckless, smothering savagery. I was sent staggering backwards, and we almost lurched as a unit straight into the fire, though I don't think I would have noticed if that happened, or cared. Wetness slithered from our lips; our hot, gasping breath reeked of mead, but I wouldn't have changed a thing. My hands came up to her head in turn, and for several very long seconds, we kissed violently in this way. Then Terza pulled her lips away, while a thread of spidery saliva bridged our two mouths for a second, before it snapped and stuck to the side of her face like a glittering scar.

"Thank you," she garbled, hoarsely. Then she turned and limped back to her tree, where she promptly put her hands on the bark and continued her exercises.

It was many hours before the rest of our team returned. In that time, I once again cleaned and dressed Terza's wounds, none of which were looking bad, and then I set about the cauterizing process on the thigh. Throughout, Terza was her staunch self, though she found it necessary to bite a twig as I applied my heated blade to her skin, and her body trembled fiercely for a few seconds from the sheer agony of it.

As she lay in recovery, I set about prepping food for the two of us. We ate, then afterwards while Terza was once again resting, I heard Heshna's voice hail me lightly from the woods. This, I immediately interpreted as an improvement in our relationship, since scaring the crap out of me was apparently no longer the tickling pleasure it once was.

"I'm coming through," she said. "With the boy and the Locksmith."

I knew it couldn't have been the easiest thing for them to get Benni here, couldn't have been anything less than a painstaking Dockside hunt on Heshna's part, and for Cad, a pugnacious scrimmage to get the emotionally battered old burglar into a skiff. I was not only impressed as the three figures materialized one after another from the night, but even touched, for my two emissaries clearly took my rousing send-off to heart.

My Brood sister emerged from the bushes first, and as the campfire lit her, I was amazed to see what appeared to be a strangely pleasant look on her face. I don't think I'd ever seen this expression, one that seemed, dare I say it, appealing, with a feisty little lift to her sallow cheeks, an affable warmth down at the mouth. Could my speech have achieved so much?

Perhaps it had, for when Cad came through next, he not only looked like his old self—both in attire and demeanor—but he was actually beaming, which was quite a bit more than I was doing, and perchance inappropriate, though certainly a welcome sight.

And then finally came the Locksmith, shrouded heavily in a thick cloak with the cowl drawn. As this figure approached, he did not radiate the buoyant warmth of his two escorts, which made sense, because Benni had not been graced with my motivational speaking. In fact, his form looked rather diminished in that clothing, as if he was stooped and hobbling on that newly modified foot of his, though, come to think of it, he was neither stooped nor hobbling. The figure approached me in an aggressive, upright manner, with no gimpiness to speak of, which meant that Benni must have spontaneously shrunk in size.

Then, suddenly that cowl flew back, and I was left staring at a face that wasn't even remotely the right face; however, I was so baffled for a second that I couldn't make sense of what was wrong with it. There was an eye patch, for starters, and a nasty scar across the lips, neither of which were wounds I remembered Benni Bones having, nor were they details reported from his latest mishaps. Also, "he" was actually a "she," which I suppose I should have mentioned first, but I didn't necessarily note it first.

Yes, I was gazing at a small, freckly, female face—a scowling face, decidedly—with the one good eye boring at me like an accusatory brown bradawl, all of it surrounded by brittle auburn hair that poked hither and thither with the static from the removed hood. Then my perspective changed, for I was actually looking *up* at this short figure, which was explicable only because I had dropped to my knees and was in some danger of collapsing to the dirt entirely. Also, a choking, wheezing cry began to emerge from my throat, which was quite grating, but it couldn't be helped, for that collection of freckly, scowly, female features, circumscribed by bristly auburn, finally began to assemble themselves properly in my mind.

Somehow, against the laws of life and death themselves, I was graced with a vision of my heart's earliest connection in this world. Standing before me, damaged but very much alive, was my beloved Brood sister, Flerra Tellian.

27

SISTER

Have you ever simply lost it? Have you fallen so completely apart that even your very own sermon (given but hours before, and focused exclusively on the issue of grit and emotional forbearance) becomes effectively worthless? I try not to do this. On that night, for a second or two, I tried not to do it, but those were useless seconds, for a moment later I absolutely went to pieces.

Out came the tears and sobs, accompanied by clutching motions at my heart and throat as I knelt there in the dirt, trying not to faint. I was assaulted by disbelief, crushing guilt, questions about my sanity, or at least my eyesight; but there was also joy, oh yes, that too, in staggering loads, gushing over my consciousness like a muddy landslide, and this was not much undercut by the shame of seeing Flerra's disfigured face, or the reality that her one good eye was doing the angry, disapproving work of four, or the fact that she now walked forward the last few steps necessary to bring her boney fist within range of my face, then deployed said fist, cracking it into my left cheek and sending me toppling backwards onto my ass.

"Keep crying, you blubbering baby!" she shouted from those scarred lips. "The only reason I'm here is because I came to rescue

Lethro—Lethro, who you abandoned, just like you abandoned me. Otherwise, I'd let you go on thinking I was dead."

My retching precluded anything resembling a dignified response. While I would eventually need to understand how it was that she was *not* dead, I was way too compromised at the moment to find out.

Terza, who was less compromised, rose from her makeshift bed and came forward a few steps.

"It's good to see you, Flerra," she said. "And I'm glad you didn't let us go on thinking you were dead."

"I wanted to," Flerra snapped, stepping closer to me, and I prepared myself for some additional punishment—spitting or kicking or perhaps another punch—but she confined herself to words. "I wanted to make them both think it, him and Holod, so they could carry those wounds forever, just like I have to carry these."

She stabbed at her own disfigured face, with its eye patch, new lip scar, and, somewhere behind her hair, the stub of an ear. Her pale cheeks were flushed and showed hints of the ubiquitous freckles that had been so prominent in her youth. Despite the recent modifications, this was still very much Flerra's face, livid and animated.

At last, I got a couple of phlegmy words out.

"But how…did you—"

"How!" she yelled, halting the rest of my fraught sentence. "*How?* That's the first thing you want to know? Not, 'Oh Flerra, I'm so sorry. I care so much about you…but not enough to save you, to choose you over some dishy, Midland tart I just met. Who, by the way, froze up and almost got us all killed."

"I'm…."

Me again, trying to offer the requested apology; however, venturing in this direction brought me straight into territory that was not yet safe for passage. Full-blown weeping would follow, and my team couldn't afford this—Terza, who needed her killer, Cad, who needed his unfaltering mentor, Heshna, who needed to trust me when I told her to swim down a six-hundred-year-old Kaennamin rat hole, then do battle with the Raving Blade's soldiers. Yes, these three (perhaps Flerra too) needed something stronger from me at the moment. So, I cut off further attempts and wiped my sleeve over my puffy eyes.

"But you ask how?" Flerra went on, her wiry frame pacing around aggressively. "How am I not dead? Because, you stupid swamp monkey, they were supposed to take us *alive*! Didn't that occur to you? When you were rolling around on the floor of that parlor, and they were crawling all over your head, you don't think they could have killed you then? They wanted to interrogate us, not kill us…or not kill us right away, so they could figure out who was behind it."

That did occur to me, of course. It occurred to me even then, during the mission, and I made ample use of the soldier's restraint; however, I had heard Flerra's screaming, been present to Nester's vindictive hatred—Nester, the Master Sentinel, whom I later named "the Butcher," then, in turn, *butchered*, in the hallway where High Lord Sherdane died—and it did not seem to me that the man was going to stop until he had left a mutilated corpse on the rug. Add to this the fact that an hour or so later the Swell Driver arrived, submerging the entire compound beneath the frigid weight of the Derjian Sea. Plus, if Flerra had somehow survived these ghastly tribulations, she certainly would have come home to us by now. So, yes, it occurred to me, but all the other factors overrode my hope.

"That hateful shit lost control of himself," Flerra went on, a little quieter now, her one good eye now gazing off to the side. "I almost took out his eye, and I worked his men…killed one for sure, another too, I think. So, he didn't hold back, like he should have. When he finally did this…" Now she pointed again towards her eye patch. "…I passed out. No more fun for him. I woke up in a prison cell, and there was water everywhere and not a guard in sight."

"How'd you get out?" Terza asked from close behind me.

"Seriously?" Flerra shot back. "How many times have we worked together, Terza? You know there isn't a goddamned lock that's ever been made that I can't get through. And some rusted old hunk of crap, one that probably hadn't been used in years. I just spat on the thing and it opened."

"But the flood…" I ventured, now finally climbing up from the ground. "I hardly made it, and I'm—"

"You're a freak, brother, I know, made of river sludge, but I'm still one of Holod's little fish, remember? So I can swim too."

This was true. Holod Deadskiff used to impress this point upon all of his Brood: "If you work bids in this city, you're going to end up in the water." While he didn't push the apprentice Locksmiths, Eyes, Masques, and Blades quite like he worked the Grell Runners, Holod made sure we were all strong swimmers, able to hold our breath long enough to cut off armor or crawl out from beneath the keel of a ship. This was part of why I knew Heshna was entirely capable of joining our attack on Kaennamin Academy. She would probably be better at the first part—making it through that submerged water pipe—than either Cad or Terza.

"Plus, I didn't have to swim long," Flerra went on. "I found a vent shaft, not far from that holding cell, and it took me up to the top floor of the building above. Just one grate to get through, which wasn't hard. What *was* hard was doing all of this with my bloody eye missing, and also my ear, not to mention…"

She swiveled and stepped close to me again.

"…the pain from knowing that my own brother had abandoned me!"

Much to my surprise, to all of our surprise, I think, Terza came forward from behind to support me, putting a hand on my shoulder. I found this incredibly comforting. Flerra saw it differently.

"Oh gods, I heard about this," she muttered, that one fierce eye staring directly at Terza's empathetic hand. "You two at it again. After tossing me off for your Midland Masque, brother, you tossed that woman off too…so that you could get back into this lover's brawl?"

I couldn't tell how Terza's face reacted to this, but I did feel her hand slide off of my shoulder, for which I was sorry.

"You have no idea, Terza, how much whining I had to put up with back in the day," Flerra continued. "*Help me, sister, I think my girlfriend broke my nose again last night. How long can I keep doing this? I've gotta get out of this mess.* Every goddamned day, it seemed, I had to hear it."

And suddenly, Cad, who had been waiting quietly at the peripheries, let out a snorting sound, which got us all to look. My formerly stricken protégé was definitely his old self again, with complex, private damages no longer on display, making this some sort of speed record for recovery from emasculation. The healthy color was back in his cheeks, despite bruising on one side, as he stared at me with new appraisal.

Here I was thinking I needed to be Cad's model of emotional strength, when, in fact, just the opposite was required. He had arrived at the campsite grinning like a half-wit, and it now occurred to me that this was not because he knew how happy I'd be to see my Brood sister alive, but rather because Flerra had spent a good portion of that boat ride detailing the exact manner in which she was going to sock my ass into the dirt. Likely, she gave at least a partial recounting of my dysfunctional relationship with Terza Falconbrow, one that really couldn't have made me look too impressive, and all of this must have made Cad feel just a little better about himself.

"See, Cad knows the truth when he hears it," said Flerra, delighting Cad further by using his name. Delighting herself too, I think, for that one fierce brown eye was now rather spirited.

"I'm sorry, Flerra…" I babbled through the crap in my throat, employing the brief moment of levity to finally get the words out. "I tried…I tried—"

"Stop it, you overgrown infant," Flerra groused. "You're embarrassing all of us. And I swear, you're almost as bad as Holod. You should have seen him."

Flerra angled herself to better face everybody. She put her arms out in front of her and made an awkward waddle, at the same time taking gulping, histrionic breaths.

"Oh, my dear girl…oh merciful gods, will you ever forgive me…what can I give you? How about my fee for the bid? And would you like my kettle pot? Or…or, what about this old, smelly cod on my wall, will that make you feel better?"

The strangest of sounds erupted from a corner of our little theater. It wasn't the nasal explosion that Cad let off but more of a keening squawk, something that, if you missed the point of origin, might have connoted pain. Miracle of miracles, my other Brood sister released the first spontaneous laugh that I had ever heard from her. And it was one hell of an inaugural. Heshna's shoulders were shuddering, and that little gray mouth was split wide, revealing jaunty teeth.

Flerra was a true wit, did I ever mention that? In addition to the adoration she received at the Broodhouse for bringing home stolen treats, she quickly became the house favorite by virtue of her acerbic rants. These diatribes were invariably constructed on a wicked foundation of sarcasm, but they were perfect for a group of jaded young castoffs, relegated to a slum.

"'But…my dear little girl, you still look so angry with me,'" Flerra continued, clearly sensing the success of her routine. "'What if I leave you the Broodhouse in my will? And, while I'm at it, do you want some of the kids? Here, take this scraggly half-Tundrian bastard. You can have him right away, as down payment.'"

And with that, we all started laughing. Even Terza was in on it, and she didn't know Ichod (Flerra's obvious reference), plus she was half-Tundrian herself, but there she was chortling right along with the rest of us. I laughed hardest, I think, with all of that embarrassing choking abruptly channeled into jovial heaves that sent ripples of warmth coursing through my entire body. The feeling dispelled much of the pain, anxiety, and regret, which was, I truly believe, exactly what Flerra intended.

"Alright, enough of this," Flerra finally said, in a stern voice that was undercut by the giddy bloom in her cheeks, and also the fact that she was the main perpetrator. "Heshna tells me we've got some work to do tonight."

Here, I leapt in, seeing as this topic avoided sentimental obstacles, and also employed my skill set gainfully.

"Yes, it won't be easy, as I'm sure Heshna probably told you," I said, talking too fast and with an overabundance of manic energy. "Sarien ran a water line into the adjoining canal—The Sarentine, which is what that canal was called back in the Old Calendar. While she knew enough to allow access to that pipe, she was perhaps a little too optimistic about the ongoing cleanliness of those waterways, employing corrosion-resistant steel grates to stop only the largest—"

"Vazeer!" Flerra railed, and there was a fair measure of disbelief knitted into those speckled features. "You really think I want one of your stupid history lessons right now? Just show me where the outlet is located. There's nothing between here and the Black Hells that can stop me from getting us inside that building."

We crept in single file along the narrow canal lip, apishly hunched, hats and cowls low, trying not to make any jerky motions or expose flashes of skin. The Seer had already cleared this route and was waiting up ahead. The canal formerly known as *The Sarentine*, and now simply referred to as the *Queen's Canal*, did not here, or anywhere along its path, become a runner's ravine, which is why we had left our skiffs several blocks away. As it ran alongside Kaennamin Academy, there was a narrow pedestrian walkway across from the building.

Queen Sarien would have hated this encroachment. As the principal architect of the Lower City's greatest building, she wanted her iconic creation to be viewed from all sides, with ample space surrounding. However, builders during the Angiers Dynasty that followed had an almost maniacal obsession with filling space, and their oppressive urban planning ensured that views at the street level were all but nonexistent.

But gods bless the Angiers, for, in addition to being responsible for most of my beloved Virtuoso, they certainly gave great cover to all of us hoodlums in the current era. The same labyrinthine qualities that the Underlords so valued made our approach that night easier, though by no means risk-free.

"It's here," I whispered, and we came to a halt, the group of us hunkering on the dank canal lip, as the smokey waters of The Sarentine flowed past.

"I don't see anything," Flerra hissed from right behind me. "The water looks just the same."

"You wouldn't notice any disturbance, since the opening is too far below the surface. But look up there, about midway up the façade where the windows start. That single one with the arch is at the end of a hallway, and that hallway lines up closely with the water pipe. Sarien ran that passage to an internal balcony that looks down on the pool in the grand—"

I felt a vicious poke in my rear end that made my pelvis jolt forward and my head snap back. Flerra growled into my ear.

"Brother, this pick will literally go up your ass if you breathe another goddamned word about architecture."

A little farther behind I heard a low chuckle, and when I turned, I saw Terza's broad outline raised over my Brood sister's crouch.

"Remember this, Vazeer?" came Terza's low, amused voice. "When your sister and I were the two women in your life."

"It's coming back to me."

"I'm not *in* his life anymore, Terza," Flerra sniped over her shoulder. "I'm just here to rescue Lethro, then be on my way."

"And Adelyn, Flerra," Terza said. "We're here for her too."

"Of course," Flerra replied. "Lethro and Adelyn. After that, Vazeer and all his stupid dreams can go to hell."

I stood from my squat, my unarmored butt still feeling the nasty prick. Craning to see down the length of the pedestrian path, I tried to make out Heshna's shape where she waited somewhere near Academy Way, the next large street. As the name suggested, this avenue ran directly in front of the grand university, and Heshna, who was watching the activities of guards at the front door, had promised she would give the all-clear signal once it was time to make our move.

Then, suddenly, Heshna was right in front of me, or at least a lot closer than she should have been, speeding the last fifteen feet down the walkway.

"Something odd," she said by way of greeting.

Heshna had her head covered, like the rest of us, and I could just see the pinched end of her nose emerging from the hollow of her cowl. I couldn't tell if my Brood sister was agitated, excited, or completely unmoved by whatever she was about to tell me.

"A guest has arrived at the building, an important personage, to meet with the Raving Blade."

Now Flerra and Terza crowded in close, and Cad, who had been assigned to watching our flank, came forward a few steps as well.

"Who is he, Seer?" Terza asked. "Could you tell?"

"*She*," answered Heshna. "The personage is a 'she,' and she came with what looked like three retainers. I didn't get a look at her face, because she was wearing a veil. However, the style of her cloak, and the boots, and the way she walked…made it seem like she was a titled lady of some sort."

"A boat arrived from the Midlands two days ago," Cad interjected, in a voice that was a bit startling from behind. "Droden can always tell these things, and he said he thought the ship was from Tergon."

I swiveled towards him angrily.

"You're just telling me this now?"

"Why would I think anything of it? Ships come here from Tergon all the time."

"Not lately, they haven't. Did Droden have any idea who was on it?"

"No. But whoever it was, they didn't want to be seen. The dock boys told Droden a few passengers got off at night."

"Damn," I muttered, "your head really must've been up your ass."

"Why, Vazeer?" Terza prodded. "You know who it is?"

"I do," said Flerra. "There's only one sick little aristocrat I can think of who likes screwing with Underlords. I was wondering if she would get here eventually."

Around me, the others appeared confused, and I realized that I had largely skipped over this piece of the Narrow Bid story. The revelation about the long-term affair between High Lord Beranardos Sherdane and the Countess Shaeyin Odel was something I had left out of most renditions, as I had originally hoped to safeguard the Countess's reputation. Having subsequently received several unflattering portrayals, I felt less inclined to protect her.

Thus, in brief, unembellished fashion, I laid the whole thing out for them, and Flerra chimed in too, for she had been present when these truths had been revealed to us in the High Lord's compound. Together, we explained that it was some sort of jealous lover's spat that had ostensibly drawn Countess Odel to Sullward on the evening of our Narrow Bid, though, as far as I knew, she never arrived. I personally neglected to reveal what I had experienced later that night—the full, heartbreaking intensity of High Lord Sherdane's feelings for the lady, demonstrated by an emotional collapse of epic proportions.

"So, what the hell do you think she's doing now…meeting with this pig?" Terza asked.

"Looking for answers, probably," Flerra said.

Then they all turned to me. They did this (I would sincerely like to believe) because I was still the leader, the one capable of figuring things out. And what do you know, something did occur to me. It was a half-formed idea, composed of items syphoned from that same little brain cave where I stored all of my cleverest crap. Certain details had been filtering into my consciousness over the last couple of weeks, and even as this material entered, I had been vaguely aware that I didn't yet know how to use it, but eventually would. Tonight was possibly that time.

"I have a feeling that these two are trying to conduct some sort of deal."

Terza, who was closest, asked:

"What deal?"

"I don't know, exactly, but whatever it is, this agreement could explain why the Raving Blade doesn't fear the retribution of Tergon, why he thinks he can operate openly now, and has all sorts of grand ideas about his future as a ruler of this city."

"Blackmail?" Flerra asked. "Like we first thought on the Narrow Bid?"

"It could be something that simple…" I said and let the thought trail off there, for I didn't know how to communicate the alternative.

But I thought it. I considered another angle, without knowing exactly what it was. As Flerra had said, this was an aristocrat who liked "screwing" with Underlords, and while Beranardos Sherdane had been as different from Ulan Gueritus as a regal lion from a scorpion, there was always the possibility that the future Empress was seeking to derive benefit from a relationship with the *title*, High Lord of Hell's Labyrinth, as opposed to the man himself. Radrin Blackstar had hinted that Countess Odel would be facing an assortment of highly complex problems when she assumed the throne. Turning to a ruthless, ingenious individual outside the confines of the Midland power structure, one with enormous financial resources at his disposal and a lifetime's training in being discreet, did not seem beyond the realm of possibilities for an ascending leader of dubious character.

"So, what the hell do we do now?" Terza asked. "Is this a good thing, or a bad thing…for us?"

Yes, that was the question. I needed more information to answer it.

"Heshna, I want you to find out if this looks like a brief introduction or a real meeting. Is the Countess settling in for a few hours, possibly meeting with the Raving Blade and his vassals? See if you can figure that out."

Heshna merely nodded, then sped back the way she had come, a vanishing smudge against the dark.

"Why, Vazeer? Why do you care what sort of visit this is?" Terza was once again looking to me for answers, but Flerra interjected.

"Because he wants to know where security will be heaviest in the building, and for how long. That's the first thing you try to figure out when you're doing a break-in."

Basically, yes. I was concerned about issues of stealth on this operation, for there were some aspects of what we were about to do that were particularly difficult. For instance, I knew the interior of Kaennamin Academy extremely well, mostly from reviewing the drawings, but also from several furtive visits over the years, and while the ground floor utility area that I imagined as Gueritus's new dungeon was separated from the other spaces by solid walls, a sizable troop presence in adjoining rooms was a real threat. Men stationed there were likely to hear an attack if we were especially noisy, which, given the composition of this group, we probably would be.

I was somewhat confident in the group's ability to swim through the water pipe, and I was certainly confident in Flerra's skill at penetrating obstructions; what I was less sure of was how quickly and quietly our team could dispatch jailers. We didn't have in our midst Radrin Blackstar, who could drift into the space like mephitic smoke and eliminate men with neither sound nor tangible disruption. There was Terza Falconbrow (unquestionably the best of us), who was a warrior, not an assassin, and who could be given to yelling and cursing in her fighting. Additionally, there was me—whom Radrin Blackstar had chided for being "entirely incapable of killing quietly"—plus Cad, who, while drilled frequently in street fighting, didn't have a great deal of field experience, rounded out by Flerra and Heshna, both capable combatants, but only in limited engagements, when the primary goal was extracting themselves from bids gone bad.

So, indeed, it mattered a great deal to me where the troop presence might be most intense. If the meeting was conducted on a middle or upper floor of this six-story building (probably the third floor, since that's where the bulk of the classrooms were), and it carried on for some time, then we would be in much better shape. Plus—and I had not wanted to mention this on account of the poor imagery involved—bloodcurdling shrieks from the torture chamber would probably be kept to a minimum throughout the proceedings.

And so, we awaited Heshna's return. When she finally arrived, she came from behind, indicating that she had done another full perimeter of the building.

"I think it *is* the Countess," Heshna said. "I overheard one of the street guards talking to his companion, and he referred to her as the 'titled Midland whore.' She's meeting with her host on the top floor. I saw lamps brighten on the northeast corner of the sixth floor, and the timing seemed right. A male shape with long hair passed in front of the window, then I saw him close the curtain. I'm confident it was the Raving Blade."

I mentally scanned the floor plans, and I recalled immediately which room that was, and the implications. This was the Master Provosts' grand suite. It was an overawing space, one that I had glimpsed only once with the naked eye, but which I had studied on paper at great length. Considered something of a folly by historians, it was Queen Sarien's deference to the exalted role that architecture would play in Sullward's ascent, and the homage due to the individual who would inspire a whole new generation of master builders. It had full views of the river, a privy chamber the size of many Dockside apartments, a sunken couch area, and an enormous central fireplace. Unfortunately, every provost who inhabited Kaennamin Academy after Sarien died opted to sleep on the second floor, to spare themselves the climb.

If it was the Raving Blade personally closing curtains in that palatial suite, then he probably didn't have guards with him, or vassals. Which really did beg the question, what in the name of the gods were the two of them doing up there?

"Also," Heshna continued, almost as an afterthought, "the Countess sent her retainers away."

"What?"

"They all exited a few minutes ago, and it looked as if they were heading out of the Lower City."

Now I was truly taken aback, and at the same time somewhat revolted. This meeting really did seem to have improper undertones. I thought back to that wrenching moment at the culmination of the Narrow Bid, when High Lord Beranardos Sherdane, fearing that his own pride had led to a tragic mistake, offered his full bereavement up to the ears of long dead gods. Down in that tunnel, which turned out to be his tomb, he beseeched them to protect the one thing in this world he loved most of all. That "one thing" was currently lounging about with his betrayer up on the sixth floor.

"Vazeer," Flerra whispered harshly, drawing me back. "What are we supposed to make of this?"

Flerra had slipped off her hood, and in the faint amber light that misted from the windows, I could now clearly see the tautly strung black eye patch, the diagonal, off-color scar across her lips. With shrewish features that were never going to be beautiful, my Brood sister had now skewed in a decidedly ferocious direction, reminding me of some of the more intimidating corsairs I had met in my day. And yet, I could still see the little freckle-faced girl hiding in there somewhere, the one I had always cared about so deeply, and who had (at one time, at least) cared about me the same way.

"The news is mixed," I said, then I explained what the chamber on the sixth floor was, and how we needed to assume that the Raving Blade and the Countess were engaged in some sort of confidential discussion. While this would keep the Raving Blade himself occupied, along with perhaps a few guards outside the door, we could not count on a large portion of the garrison being relocated to an upper floor.

"Screw them," Terza muttered, crowding me and Flerra with her breathy vexation. "I'll take out the whole army myself if I have to. Let's just do this damned thing already."

28

CHAMBER OF HORRORS

It is an unsettling experience to swim underwater in the dark. It is even more unsettling when the water is filthy and cold, and you need to locate and work on things down below—things upon which lives depend, including your own. This is exactly what transpired, and it is fair to say that Vazeer the Lash and Flerra Tellian were the two Shadow Bidders in all of Hell's Labyrinth best suited to the task. In the annals of burglary masterpieces, this dirty gem by my sister and me needs an honorable mention.

To begin, I slipped into those sludgy waters with a rope tied loosely to my belt, took one of my huge, lung-filling, Deadskiff-honed gulps of air, then disappeared below the inky surface to start my hunt. I found the pipe grill almost exactly where I expected it. It was still intact—a testament to the Kaennamins' unique metallurgy processes—and I was able to tie my rope off easily. This allowed Flerra to make her way to the spot, and with files, chisels and additional implements at the ready, she set to work. Meanwhile, Cad and Terza waited fretfully on the lip of that canal, as Heshna roved in silent surveillance.

It took Flerra less than a quarter of an hour to get that grate off, and she was, as always, quiet and astonishingly efficient about it. She located the flakiest spots in the mortar, opened little crevices that allowed her file to get through to rusted bolts, then pried against the weakest spots in the steel, causing them to snap. In the meantime, I supported her in this task, holding the excess tools, pulling her up for air when her maniacal determination was keeping her down too long, and finally, I wrenched the grate off with her.

Next came the part I had been dreading the most, even if it wasn't the greatest threat: I needed to make it through that pipe and locate the vertical shaft that ran up to the utility area. I am, as noted, the ideal candidate for this job, having conducted many underwater drills along these lines, always at night, feeling my way through a silty world of sweeping currents and jagged debris. This was my ultimate means of escape when bids went belly up, but I can't say I enjoyed it.

On that submerged, pitch-black pipe crawl, I experienced some genuine shudders of panic. Two or three episodes of heart-slamming, oxygen-squashing terror erupted as I became snared on poking things that had made it into the pipe through the relatively wide spaces in the outer grill. All the while, I kept running my hand along the curved stone ceiling, trying to find the shaft. I found it—eventually—which was an extraordinary relief.

The climb up the shaft was easy, for there was a steel ladder imbedded in the wall of the chute, and it brought me six or seven feet above the water line to the underside of the hatch. As expected, there was no simple way to open the hatch from below. The metal was mostly undamaged, though some minor rusting had caused small gaps to form in the intersection between the horizontal lid and the shaft. Through these, I saw the faintest twitch of firelight, and in the otherwise pitch-black confines of the vertical, grouted passage, this small glow allowed for limited visibility. I tied my rope to the top rung, pulled it a few times to make sure it was secure, then I descended once again and set about the painstaking work of clearing the pipe for my team. This would ensure that their only job was to pull themselves along the rope the forty or so feet necessary to get to the shaft. They too would face the specter of panic, and I wanted to remove as many causes for it as possible. Next, it was time to get Flerra.

"The hatch has two stuck points," she whispered, once she and I had climbed together, dripping, up the ladder. Flerra had dispensed with her bulky cloak and was in the streamlined leather and cloth outfit she wore to all of her bids. Her arsenal of specialty implements were strapped to her everywhere.

"I can see one of the hasps through the crack, so I can work it with a slimpick. But the other's a problem, because there's no crack. It's over here, above this bolt."

Flerra gently tapped the underside of the hatch, where there was an excess of steel from the weld.

"Are you going to chisel it?"

"Too loud. I'll cut into the seam, until I can get a flat bar in and snap it off. Once it's gone, I'll be able to pop the bolt out the top, using some oil. I've got to tie the rope to my belt so I can use two hands."

"Forget the rope, I'll hold you."

I reached down and grabbed the rear of her belt. She stiffened, and I sensed that she was about to spit back something to the effect of "*I don't trust you enough to hold me,*" but pragmatism ruled, and she drew a slim cutting file and started working on the weld.

"I should get Heshna before you go much further," I said. "She'll be able to tell if there's somebody in the room above."

"There's nobody near the hatch," Flerra muttered. "You think I need to drag Eyes along on every job I do? Unless you're starting to miss your replacement sister. You sure cleaned that up quick."

"It's not totally clean…and you're one to talk."

"Heshna was never my enemy."

"No?"

"That was your fight, then you got me all riled up. I was just a little kid who trusted my older brother, which shows you how dumb I was."

I actually had to take a few musty breaths just to calm myself. Heshna, who was hardly the persuasive type, had somehow managed to infect Flerra's head with this nonsense in the few short hours of her resurrection. The Flerra I knew wouldn't fall for it, unless…

…unless, of course, it wasn't entirely nonsense. Which begged the question, how clearly did I grasp anything about my past?

"You're cinching the belt too tight, you clutchy monkey! Support me, don't choke the life out of me."

I loosened up a little, trying to use more palm and less fingers.

"You know who always supported me?" she mused after another minute of quiet cutting.

"Let me guess. Lethro?"

"Good guess."

"Well, Lethro never worked a Narrow Bid with you, Flerra. Nothing you two ever faced came close to what happened to us."

"So? That doesn't change anything. I know for sure that Lethro wouldn't have left that parlor, left me to die. He would have gone down fighting, trying to save me."

I had no rejoinder to this, for Flerra was probably right. Lethro, who had just proved himself very much the hero by joining Yurgen in a suicidal fight to cover the Reed sisters' escape, probably would have remained in that parlor during the Narrow Bid. He also would have died, or been captured, along with the Masque in the party. In this way, the entire team would have been doomed, for with no lure to pull the soldiers out into the marsh, and with their Underlord host seeing with his own eyes that the visitors were impostors, the whole thing would have ended right there. A quick, brutal interrogation would have yielded all the relevant information, and then the three prisoners would have been executed.

But it was useless to say this, for I obviously hadn't thought any of these things through that night. I hadn't really been thinking at all, which I now tried to explain.

"I wasn't entirely myself, Flerra. Or even partially myself."

My Brood sister stopped cutting and spent a moment wiggling the weld with her fingers. Then she turned to me in the dim light.

"Was it that thing again? Like what happened on the Gaff?"

"Essentially."

A few quiet breaths and some staring. While I had never explained to her the full scope of the void I experienced during the infamous Cross-Bid, Flerra understood that I didn't really know what happened that night. Not to mention, she had seen this phenomenon herself, in various mini blackouts throughout our upbringing. One episode, in particular, stood out, when I stumbled zombie-like back to the orphanage with a clump of hair in one fist and a bloody rock in the other, and only repeated slaps across the face from the house matron brought me out of my pre-pubescent battle trance. I had no idea what happened, though I did later surmise that the incident involved juvenile bullies from the Wags, for the little mongrels gave me a wide berth after that.

"Well," Flerra finally said in our dank flue, "if you ask me, you *were* yourself. The real you."

"I hope not."

She now drew a slim bar from her thigh and raised it to the weld.

"Whoever it was," she said, starting to force the bar under the weld, "that person knew enough to find the prettiest woman in the room and leave with her."

I heard a sharp click, producing a quick metallic echo against the walls of that shaft. Unmistakably, it was the sound of the weld breaking off, and somehow Flerra's hand fired out and caught it. Really, in all of Hell's Labyrinth, only Flerra Tellian could have managed this—hindered by near total dark, with only one good eye, and her body angled precariously, she nabbed the weld from the resonant blackness, so that it wouldn't fall with an oversized splash into the water below. Chances were, nobody would have heard it anyway, but Flerra was the most thorough burglar you might ever hope to work with.

She stuffed the weld away, then set about oiling and then poking the cut bolt, and after a minute or two of this, she expressed satisfaction.

"It's moving a little, so I can definitely pop it, and I've tested the other hasp. It will go quick and quiet, once we're ready. Go get the others."

I continued to support her until she had slid all her implements away, then she took hold of the ladder again. I started to make my way down, but she snatched the cloth on my shoulder in a snarly grip.

"Vazeer," she murmured.

"Yes, Flerra?"

She paused, clearly assembling something important in her head.

"Terza's in our group," she finally said, "and hopefully, soon, Adelyn. I'm definitely going to be the ugliest woman on this bid. Even Heshna would win a pageant against me now. So don't go ditching me again…so you can grab those others."

This comment seared into me, sending a terrible tremor right up from my bowels into my throat. At that moment I wanted (possibly more than anything, ever) to be somebody other than I had been, to erase all of my repulsive missteps, that I might never let Flerra down again. I placed my free hand over hers, and it was unsteady as our flesh touched.

"That's not going to happen, Flerra," I breathed. "I swear it."

She kept her hand under mine for a moment, then slid it away.

"Go then, get the team."

With that, I scampered down the ladder and back into the cold, muddy water.

It took quite a while to get our entire crew into that small six-foot section of shaft, and it wasn't a pleasant operation. As expected, Heshna was best at it, and she clearly drew upon all of those unpleasant hours in her youth, when Holod turned us into a school of delinquent tadpoles. But Cad and Terza never received such training. They could swim, certainly, and Cad could swim quite well, having been one of Droden's dock boys, but they both found the sightless, airless pipe crawl an event of claustrophobic terror, which it was. This did not bode well for extracting traumatized torture victims via that panicky route.

Eventually, we managed to get our little assault squad crammed into place, even though Terza was essentially stepping on Cad's head as the two of them gasped and hyperventilated for several minutes after the swim. On the plus side, being confined within that hellish chute did make the prospects of storming into a big, spacious dungeon filled with armed torturers just a little more appealing.

"Pop it," I whispered.

Flerra busted out the formerly bolted hasp. She used a small, felt-covered mallet and an oak driving pin, accomplishing the task with such delicacy that there was only the lightest scrape over our heads as one half of the hasp came loose. Then she turned to the other with her slimpick, and she unfastened it in under ten seconds. After that, she and I gently hoisted the lid and slid it off to the side.

I crawled alone out of the shaft and into a dim room that was receiving torchlight through an open doorway. Scattered on the floor were several stone blocks, half-rotted barrels, and rusted iron cannisters, which I remembered from my last visit—building supplies shoved back here in the decade following the first Great Storm. Half-hearted campaigns had been launched then to repair the damage; however, King Denevaego, grief-stricken with the loss of his two sons, simply couldn't follow through with any of it.

Seeing that the room was empty, I signaled the others, and they slipped out of the hole one by one. While the Seer was technically our scout, the person at the vanguard needed to be able to kill without thinking, which was a specialty of mine. I was ready, willing, and able to perform that function, and a hell of a lot quieter than Terza; so I led, with Heshna just behind, then Terza, Flerra, and finally Cad bringing up the rear. In this way, our dripping snake shuffled its way out of the shaft, through the initial utility space and into the next.

In the second room we encountered our first grim confirmation. This long, torch-lit space felt more like a corridor than a room, and here we spotted the tools of the Raving Blade's favorite pastime. Pincers, scalpels, awls, and branding irons were lying on thin wooden tables lining the walls, and, far more horrifyingly, blood had leaked and spread from these implements, leaving rust-colored caterpillars on the floor. Behind me, I heard Terza release a tiny screech, and I turned with a hand up, to make sure she didn't launch herself into the next room. She was breathing hard, and moisture had started to well in her gray eyes, as she grasped how these implements had been used, and upon whom.

Heshna tugged at my sleeve and pointed to her ear. Sure enough, I began to detect the mutterous undertone of dialogue, so I slid forward until I could hear the sounds more clearly. I picked out two distinct voices, one low, gruff and male, and the other....Yisva be praised, female! Now, I could not slow my approach.

I don't know if the others could hear the voices too, or if perhaps Heshna gestured, but suddenly we were shambling forward as a fervent mass. It did, just then, occur to me that we might be in for some terrible surprise. That female voice did not sound victimized. She sounded, I would say, flirtatious, suggesting that it might not be Adelyn at all, but rather some member of the Gueritus housekeeping staff making coquettish small talk with the torturers as she came to mop up blood.

Closer I crept, and as I did, I tried to cull out pieces of dialogue. Suddenly, I was pulling up short, for a new voice had asserted itself. A third person seemed to have just arrived, shrieking with rage.

"What the hell is going on in here?" came this new voice, which was male, though rather high-pitched. "Have you lost your bloody mind, Jaex?"

Our assault team froze.

The first two voices seemed similarly halted, their flirtation disrupted. At last, the man in the pair replied.

"What's the rush, Dubin? There's nothing to learn, and I'm having some fun…for once."

"You unspeakable half-wit!" Dubin screamed. "This isn't a Harmony Festival. You were supposed to rave her to pieces by now! The others lost eyes, feet…cocks, but this one…just a brand!"

"Calm down, Dicer. I was getting there—"

"You call me Lord Count now—"

"And you call me Lieutenant Commander."

"You've been played, Lieutenant Jackass. She's a Masque, didn't you realize that? Give me that goddamned scalpel, I'm taking this whore's tongue, before she convinces you to cut off your own cock!"

And I was running. I Launched from the fore, flinging myself towards that opening with such bloody determination I probably could have crashed straight through a locked door. Down the length of that room I sped, bursting within seconds into Dubin the Dicer's chamber of horrors. No matter what it took, no matter what the cost—including my life—I was going to stop that scalpel.

The torchlit utility chamber beyond was a pulsing, vaulted grotto, one that smelled to me instantly of ash and sweat. Here, the stakes were revealed. Sometimes, the biggest surprise is that there isn't one. Fate can, on the rarest of occasions, reward one's planning with continuity, and so it was that night, for this new, terrible place was being deployed just as I had imagined, and those we sought to rescue were, in fact, stowed here. Our opponents, mercifully, were but three men, our element of surprise complete, and there was still time to spare one of the victims a fate that would leave her heartbreakingly silent for what remained of her days. However, there was a choice.

I could see the choice, before I could see many other things, for it was directly before me. Against the far wall, standing in a tattered white undergarment and chained by her wrists, was our damsel. Lovely Adelyn was bloodied, but only slightly. On her round, dusky forehead, between the tendrils of damp, curled hair, was that terrible mark: the two coiled blades, puckered and oozing from the branded heat. To one side of her, broad and heavily armored, was the new Lieutenant Commander of the Raving Blade's army, a man I recognized at once. This was the big, blond-haired soldier with the ugly scar on his neck, who had been present in The Crossbiter when I met with Gueritus. That night, he and another man had dragged one of the vassals from the room and assisted Dubin the Dicer with the subsequent raving. Thereafter, this big, blond killer had presided over the duel I fought with Coljin Helmgrinder in the courtyard outside.

"Jaex," as I now knew him, was the sort of warrior one needed every conceivable resource to beat. I should not, by all dictates of logic, surrender even the slightest advantage to him (advantages that I now had, for he was not yet looking in my direction, nor had he drawn a blade). This was the moment to run him down and do him dirty before he had time to ready himself.

But, like I said, there was this choice. On the other side of our damsel was another man, a shorter, rounder man, pink and pudgy of flesh, with thin light brown hair mussed into dancing bedlam, and this other man was one of the sickest, most depraved souls who had ever walked the soil of Derjia. Probably not a martial threat, Dubin Haiyes—aka Dubin the Dicer—formerly a Viscount but now promoted to Count, was holding the scalpel he had taken from the Lieutenant Commander, and this scalpel was frighteningly close to our damsel's mouth.

So, I made my decision. Jaex might pull free a blade, Jaex might use his little reprieve to butcher me, but he wasn't likely to hurt Adelyn. She had already worked her wiles on him, and with combatants charging, the Lieutenant Commander's function as the compound's lead warrior would take immediate priority over his role as a part-time raver.

But not so for Dubin the Dicer. This sadistic man might opt to use his remaining seconds in this world to inflict one last act of mutilation, his only real hope of causing us pain, and I simply could not take that chance. So, I went for him. I put my faith, once again, in the indomitable Falconbrow, trusting that she could limp her way behind me fast enough to cover my back. I also had to trust that Cad and my two Brood sisters could take down the third jailer, a soldier I saw loitering off to the left in the vicinity of the other prisoners. Yes, I had to trust all of that, for Dubin's scalpel had to be stopped.

And wouldn't you know it, my concerns were well founded, for the poisonous heart of Dubin the Dicer saw fit, in that doomed moment, to deface, not to defend, to gouge, not to guard. His awful instrument (with a blade smaller than my finger but with eyeball-puncturing, jugular-severing fleetness that could bring tragedy in the space of a breath) turned not towards me, but towards Adelyn.

The problem for Dubin the Dicer was that I was not moving just then like a normal human being. I moved, so help me, like Yisva's searing weapon, blasting towards the vicious pig and his vicious instrument with this one last mission in life, a final purpose in my questionably worthwhile time among the living, and that was to stop his blade. Not even to kill him, but to halt that goddamned thing before it released one more drop of blood in this world. And in this mission, I am profoundly gratified to say, I was successful.

Adelyn helped me. She threw herself away from Dubin, to the full rattling length of her chains, and this gave me just enough time, just the tiniest extension, to make it to that flabby wrist of his, which I grabbed and slammed back against the mortared wall. The scalpel fell from his fingers, and my other fist, gripping my spade, came around to crack him so hard on the side of the head with the pommel that there was a hollow pop. I didn't have the distance to drive the blade in, but the collision with his skull was so concussive that his head flew back, and he brained himself on the granite wall. He dropped unconscious to the floor.

But Jaex wasn't unconscious. The hefty, blond thug instantly became everything an Underlord would want from his staff, whipping a spade and stiletto free faster than most men could have drawn a jack. He saw Terza coming and went into a fighting crouch, which meant that our advantage was gone, and we were now going to have to face off with this well-armed, well-trained, fully prepared combatant. Except, we still had an advantage.

Sweet, helpless Adelyn was not so helpless, we now discovered. For the last decade I had only known her as a Masque. Before that, when Adelyn joined my bids as a Blade, I had never seen her in action, and honestly, I wouldn't have imagined this *action* to have been particularly impressive. Tonight, I learned that I had underestimated her, just as the Lieutenant Commander had.

Gripping her chains and levering her lower body upright, Adelyn promptly scissored her bare legs around the Lieutenant Commander's neck and head. That female place he had hoped to ravish was now up against the back of his skull, and those thighs and calves were pinioning him into his death posture. Our clever damsel not only began an immediate choking process with the crook of one leg, but she made sure to cover the Lieutenant Commander's eyes with the back of the other. This allowed Terza and me to lunge in low and essentially pick our targets.

We were very efficient about it. Terza went for his ribs, specifically the seam between his front and back plate, and I for groin, thrusting up into the gap just to the side of the codpiece. I have been told that every warrior hopes to meet his end in battle, or, barring that, nestled snugly between a woman's legs, and irony of ironies, big, scar-necked Jaex, Lieutenant Commander of the High Lord of Hell's Labyrinth, had the rare privilege of dying both ways. We jammed this menacing piece of shit straight through with steel, and he never even mounted a counterattack. There he expired, cleanly spitted and dangling from a pretty noose.

Glancing beyond our mele, I saw quickly that Cad had made a spectacularly good choice, something for which I had prepped him repeatedly.

"When you go one on one with a trained swordsman, take the bastard straight to the cobbles. Wrestle and pound; don't fence."

That's exactly what Cad did, using his considerable strength and grappling capabilities to dive at the third man's midsection. Down the two of them went to the hard stone floor, and within seconds, my Brood sisters had swooped in like a pair of trained falcons. They slid around to each side of the fallen man's head and drove their slim blades straight into his neck.

There was one last threat, one final place from which disaster might emerge, and Dark Gods bless her, my one-time nemesis, Heshna the Seer, having just killed a man, possessed the presence of mind to spring up and run for the room's door. This stout, iron-bound portal was down a hallway and, at present, closed, but we needed to know if it would remain that way. Heshna was there in an instant, pressing her ear against it, with her fingers brushing the wood as if fondling forth secrets.

After a few seconds she glanced over, giving me a thumbs-up. Then, with the other hand, she quietly turned the deadbolt, effectively barring entry against all who did not carry keys.

And in this way, we won. We won quickly and quietly, very much according to plan, with no casualties taken and several delivered. In those seconds as I stared at my Brood sister, having just received her hopeful signal, I do think I experienced something on the order of elation. Many things seemed possible then, for we had done it. *I* had done it, utilizing my knowledge of history and architecture, politics and psychology—the whole arsenal of irritating extravagances, which, right about now, were looking a lot less extravagant—and compiled them into a plan that actually worked. Not to mention, I had been personally heroic, for once. I had saved a real-life damsel, who did not turn out to be some other thing that thoroughly mortified me. Dare I hope that this wonderful, chained maiden might desire me at last, shed her resistance after all these years? And if not her, might her best friend take me back, seeing as I had done everything she asked?

I don't think I consciously thought any of this, but I subconsciously felt all of it, and this delightful illusion remained for the three or four breaths I spent staring at my new best friend, Heshna the Seer, and her ever-so-hopeful thumbs-up. Would that I could have gazed that way just a little longer.

29

DISILLUSIONMENT

When I turned back to the others, I was met with an astonishing sight. Adelyn had released the collapsing bulk of Jaex's corpse from her legs, and Terza had dropped her bloody blades, allowing the two of them to throw themselves wholeheartedly into a fettered embrace. But this "embrace" was not the grateful clasp of two relieved friends, with pats and squeezes and hearty laughs. Instead, I found myself staring at a gasping, passionate kiss, complete with ecstatic cries and the tinkling of chains as two bodies strained to break natural laws and meld. Shackled still, but with her form slumped into the most magnificent state of release, Adelyn surrendered to Terza's desperate mouth and fervent clutches, and the sight left me stunned.

In this life, I have often questioned my capacity for love, but that doesn't mean I can't recognize it when I see it—can't, from the emotive fountainhead at my core, sense when humankind's most precious inner treasure is present. That furious, sobbing kiss, with catching fingers through soiled hair, was an unmistakable thing. Terza had never kissed me like that. Even earlier this evening, when she threw her hands around my head and her saliva-drenched lips closed over mine, she was expressing something different—gratitude, mostly. Optimism, too, for she had been in the grip of the poignant notion that she might soon be reunited with this woman, the one hanging in an Underlord's chains, but entirely hers. This clearly wasn't some exploratory tryst between friends. Adelyn was the person in this world to whom Terza Falconbrow had given her whole heart, and who, in return, had given the same. It was a beautiful sight, but for me, painfully disillusioning.

I snapped out of it quickly. The needs of the moment could not be ignored, for Adelyn was still in chains, and there were others to consider. I looked around and spotted what appeared to be a set of manacle keys hanging on a peg on the far wall. Retrieving them, I returned to the lovers and promptly set Adelyn free. She looked over at me with a sweet, tear-streaked smile, but her mad embrace did not come off of Terza, as it probably never would.

"Vazeer!"

The angry growl had emerged from the far end of the vaulted chamber. I hurried there and en route passed Cad, who was standing in awestruck confusion, gaping at Terza and Adelyn. If my protege was suffering his own form of disillusionment, it seemed to be born less of pain than wonder. Which was entirely appropriate, for neither woman had ever been a real prospect for him.

"Go barricade the door with something heavy," I muttered as I brushed past to the place where Flerra crouched.

When I arrived at my Brood sister's side, I was met by another shock, this one coupled with new pain. Flerra was clutching Lethro in her arms. The veteran Blade had been released from his shackles, but the happy ending here was less complete, for, in addition to the oozing brand on his forehead, crusted trails of blood ran from the poor man's eye sockets. Flerra was blocking some of my view; however, I was still able to do a quick survey, and it did not appear that the Ravers had taken more from Lethro than that. Still, this was bad, and I felt terribly sorry for him.

"Don't you worry, Lethy," my Brood sister said, stroking his hair. "Flerra's going to take care of you."

"Alive, girl," Lethro croaked. "I just can't believe you're alive."

I squatted down and gripped Lethro's arm.

"I wish I'd gotten here sooner, Lethro."

Lethro took a moment to orient himself to my presence, then replied hoarsely.

"It's okay, Vazeer. I'm amazed you got here at all."

"You can thank Flerra for that; without her, the plan wouldn't have worked. Also, I want you to know that your sacrifice wasn't in vain. Heshna saw the Reed sisters escape, which they only accomplished because of what you and Yurgen did. I'll make sure everybody knows."

"I'm glad," he said. "And there are no words for how happy I am to have my Flerra back."

"I'm back, Lethy," Flerra cooed as she stroked him. "You and I won't be apart again."

I stayed silent, allowing them to share this moment, to share a thing that was obviously deeper than I had realized. Perhaps it was deeper than they had realized, for I sensed that there was more going on here than friendship.

"Vazeer," Flerra said, without looking at me. "Did you kill the Dicer?"

I glanced over to the place where Count Dubin Haiyes was sprawled. He was just now starting to move, kicking his legs as he came back to consciousness.

"No," I replied.

"Drag him here."

I must have looked at her strangely, for my Brood sister's one eye glowered with a degree of menace that said this was not a good moment to question her. So, I jogged off to the place where Dubin was now attempting to roll over, and I stomped his head back to the floor. Then I grabbed him by the collar and dragged him across the flagstones, past the deceased Jaex and Terza and Adelyn, who were currently addressing the oozing forehead brand with a piece of cloth.

When I neared the place where Flerra held Lethro, I saw that four additional figures were chained to the walls beyond them. They looked like Underlord soldiers, and I could only assume they were Count Tygean's men, captured in the battle at Gessum's Cross. These unfortunate souls were in even worse shape than Lethro, all with missing limbs and two who appeared to be dead already. I wanted to go to them with the shackle keys and see what could be done, but Flerra had another agenda.

"Wake the Dicer, Vazeer," she said when I had towed my groaning load to her. "Then hold him down."

"Flerra, this doesn't—"

"Vazeer!" she hissed with a viciousness that alarmed me. "If you want any chance, any chance at all…in this lifetime of me forgiving you, you'll do this thing."

"It isn't necessary, Flerra," Lethro croaked.

"Yes, it's necessary. For me, it's necessary. Now wake the god-damned Dicer, then hold him down."

And so I did. Dubin hadn't really gone unconscious again with my stomp, so a few swats on his fleshy cheeks were sufficient to rouse him. Then, as instructed, I pressed his arms to the floor, and Flerra reached to her thigh harness and pulled forth a pair of plyers and a Derjian slip blade, which she brought straight to Dubin's mouth.

"Gotta keep the pig quiet, first," she muttered.

After that, she set to work.

What followed was a ghastly thing. It was ghastly on so many levels, which I'll refrain from describing, since recalling this incident literally makes me sick to my stomach. Flerra was, horrifyingly enough, rather good at this work. From a practical standpoint this made sense, seeing as there was nobody in the entire Labyrinth who was better at inserting her implements into tight spaces, and also busting through small obstructions (like teeth, for instance) to reach her goal. So, in this respect, I get why Dubin the Dicer's tongue, and then the rest of him, came apart so quickly. What I can't quite fathom is how my Brood sister could do all of this with such cold-hearted calm. I knew she had killed before. Over the years it had happened, but, per her reporting, she had derived no pleasure from those incidents, as well she shouldn't. Tonight, this was not the case.

Dubin the Dicer, inflictor of untold torments and sorrows, did not die well. He whimpered and squawked, thrashed and heaved, inducing Flerra to crawl up on top to better control his bucking midsection. She then instructed Lethro to hold down the legs. Our newly blind Blade seemed about as repulsed by this project as I was; however, he swatted around until he got a hold of those kicking hose and immobilized them. And in this way, we allowed our dear Flerra to execute her raving.

It's hard to say what a person needs in this life to repair themself. I'm certainly in no position to judge. Perhaps this is what Flerra needed, to make right the loss of her eye and ear, the full loss of Lethro's sight, the crushing disappointment of having her Brood brother abandon her, and earlier abandonments—a father who fled before she was born, and a mother who succumbed to sickness when Flerra was so young she retained only the most ethereal and melancholy of memories. Could this one heinous act of dismemberment possibly repair all of that?

Either way, what's done is done. Count Dubin Haiyes, aka Dubin the Dicer, and arguably one of the worst creatures who ever drew breath in this world, was most assuredly done, in every sense of the word. For this, at least, I was not sorry.

As Dubin was reduced to the last shuddering, splattering convulsions, I finally stood from my now obsolete restraining role and went to attend to Tygean's men. I glanced back once at the others and noted that Terza had carefully wrapped Adelyn's forehead with a linen bandage, covered her shoulders with Jaex's cloak, and was now helping her to take sips of water from her canteen. Beyond them, I saw that two heavy blocks from the first storage space had been deposited at the base of the room's door, and since Cad was nowhere to be seen, I could only assume he was in the process of retrieving more. Heshna was still listening at her guard post.

In this reprieve, I addressed the chained soldiers. The first of them I did not recognize, though he wore the blue Tygean ribbon on what remained of his bloody tunic. There was no reason to free this man, as he was dead already, which was fortunate, for the sad wretch had been divested of almost a third of his body. The next individual was entirely recognizable to me, since it was none other than Viscount Owen Grieves. While I'll not deny the man had given me significant trouble in my two meetings with him—separated by a decade—he had also gifted me with my street alias, and I felt a painful clench in my throat at the sight of him. Grieves was actually alive, though just barely, and I quickly saw to it that he wasn't, for his suffering was ungodly. My guess was that the bulk of the Tygean soldiery had been given a choice to swear fealty to the new regime and thereby avoid this horror. These men had either been too proud to submit or were too senior in the organization to be granted clemency.

When I reached the next figure, I again experienced recognition, for it was Devlan, Count Tygean's son. My sense was that he had suffered the worst torments of all, based on his horrible condition. Here, too, I won't elaborate, other than to say that some of the things that Shade had threatened to do to Cad had been done to this young man, and that wasn't the half of it. I couldn't tell if Devlan was quite dead, but the loss of blood had rendered him motionless, and I quickly saw to it that his consciousness never returned to his mutilated body.

Finally, I arrived at the last prisoner. Of all of them, I felt the greatest sadness here, for slumped on the floor, with his wrists shackled in a painful pinion above his head, was Count Halsin Tygean. He was still alive and had likely been kept this way so that he could listen to the torments of his son. However, he was not in a condition from which a man ever hopes to recover. Like Lethro, his eyes had been gouged out, and they streamed viscously below the coiling evil of that forehead brand. But, unlike Lethro, a great deal more had been done to him than that, starting with the loss of his nose, something I had once heard Gueritus promise he would accomplish.

I knelt down and quickly freed his wrists with the shackle keys, and his hands flopped limply to his lap. He released a low groan and opened his lips, revealing, thankfully, that he still had a tongue.

"Vazeer? Is that you?" he whispered.

"Yes, Lord Count. It's me."

His blond hair was greasy and dirty, his handsome cheeks stubbled, crusted with blood, and creased by sorrow. He took a shallow, strenuous breath.

"The fault is mine," he wheezed, in a congested voice, weirdly altered by the loss of his nose. "My son, Devlan, meant well, I think. But he has always been too impetuous. I did not do right by him as a father."

To this I said nothing, and I squatted there in withering silence.

"Is he gone?" Tygean finally asked. "My son?"

"Yes."

"And Grieves and Borden?"

"Gone."

"And your friends? The Blade, and Adelyn…lovely Adelyn, so good at her craft. I hope they did not suffer too terribly."

"They both survived, Lord Count. They will recover."

"Oh," he sighed quietly. "That's very good to hear."

Another grave spell of quiet followed. I heard Flerra murmuring with Lethro, and I glanced over to see that Terza and Adelyn were now joining them. Surprise was sure to follow, since Adelyn, like Lethro, had not known until now that my Brood sister still lived. I turned back to Tygean.

"Lord Count," I said, after a moment's pause. "Do you want me to help you from this place?"

Tygean sat with this for a moment, then brittlely shook his head.

"No, just end my suffering."

This was as I expected, though I couldn't bring myself to agree to it out loud.

"Vazeer," said Tygean.

"Yes, Lord Count."

"Once you leave here, you must flee. You *all* must flee…and disguise yourselves, for Gueritus will not let this rest. He has been preoccupied, and his army is currently small, but these things are about to change, and he will see to it that every one of you is hunted across the Empire. He will use every means at his disposal to make sure you wind up like me. I have been acquainted with this terrible man for many years now, and I can promise you there will be no expiration on his vengeance. Especially now that he is High Lord."

I heard the warm sounds of reunion, and I glanced over to see the others affectionately clinched in a shared hug. My eye was drawn to Terza, and I took special note of her smile—her full smile, something I hadn't witnessed in over a decade. Perhaps I'd never really seen it, for it appeared almost sun-drenched in this gloomy grotto. Terza Falconbrow did not seem "almost beautiful" any longer. She was magnificent—a gallant, radiant being, not other than I had known her to be, just somehow more. And Adelyn, who was likewise luminous, seemed every bit Terza's equal, bandaged and bedraggled though she was.

"I'll take good care of him," I could hear Flerra saying, her sharp voice audible, even though her back was to me. "We've got one good eye between us, which should be more than enough for this ugly shithole."

To this Lethro must have made some droll reply, as the four of them laughed, and they did so robustly, almost hysterically, a sound which had the telltale signs of unfathomable relief. Terza then looked over to me, and a little flick of her chin indicated that it was time to get going. I turned back to the Count and reached forward to grip his forearm.

"I appreciate the warning, Lord Count," I said. "But it won't be necessary."

Tygean took a few slow, labored breaths, then he replied.

"I think we can drop the formalities at this point, Vazeer; call me Halsin. And why…why won't it be necessary?"

"Because…Halsin, I won't be leaving. And my friends won't be fleeing the city and living as fugitives. You can depart this world knowing that the terrible man who did this to you, who did those things to your son, is about to meet a very unpleasant end. Just as Dubin the Dicer did."

Tygean absorbed this, then I saw the vaguest hint of a smile quake at the corner of his crusted mouth.

"I thought I heard a rat squeaking earlier, but it didn't quite sound like him."

"That's because his tongue had already been pulled out, to keep him quiet for the rest of it."

"Smart planning there," Tygean replied. "But whatever you are planning now, Vazeer…it's not a good idea. You cannot reach Gueritus. He is somewhere upstairs, far upstairs. Your team will never make it with so many men in the building."

"There's a way. Leave that to me."

"It's a suicide mission."

"That's the only type I take these days."

This actually got him to chuckle. Through his agony and grief, his blindness and the imminence of his demise, Count Halsin Tygean, one-time repository of my many grand hopes and ill-considered dreams, brought himself to wheeze out a shuddering laugh.

"I hope you still have your Finisher with you," he finally said. "Gueritus is a devil with those swords. I always knew it was so, but having just watched him fight at Gessum's Cross…I don't think there is anybody who can beat him blade for blade. He's almost inhuman."

"Perhaps he's *almost* inhuman, but I'm entirely inhuman, and I'm quite practiced at revenge. This may be my one useful talent in this world."

Tygean shook his scraggly head and returned my grip.

"No, Vazeer," he breathed, "you have more talents than that. Sherdane always remarked on it, and he was right. You must see to it that you come down from that tower, once you complete your business. There is important restoration work to be done, as we discussed."

It was right around then, I think, that I began to feel something strange happening to me. To a certain extent, the experience was counterintuitive, for I recognized that this was a moment when I might have felt stirred, and committed, and possibly even hopeful, but I didn't. I felt sick. There arose, somewhere deep within me, a low creaking, like the straining of wood being crushed beneath a terrible weight. I didn't know which obscure, mental cellar was emitting this, but I did sense that whatever was in there was not a good thing.

"I cannot promise that I will return," I said. "Somebody else will have to do the restoration."

Once again Tygean shook his head, though it appeared to cause him increasing pain to do so.

"It has to be you, Vazeer…*Vazeer the Lash*. Did you know that I was the one who came up with that name? When Grieves told you about it, all those years ago, did he explain why I chose that word?"

"Because of my insane habit of *lashing* on to my cargo, of refusing to let go, no matter what the cost."

"Yes…" he garbled through a swell of maimed congestion, "but it's more than cargo. You refuse to quit, Vazeer the Lash. You won't give up a job, even when perhaps you should. I want you to lash on to this project of ours in the same way, make it your cargo. Complete your bloody work tonight, but after that, go and find your Nascinthé of Levell and bring her back here. She will be your inspiration."

This caught me off guard, and I found myself shaking my head, which was pointless.

"I doubt I would be *her* inspiration," I replied. "And she deserves a better place than this."

"Which is why you must rebuild it, so that you can bring the Spellbinder back. Promise me you will do it, Vazeer, that you will live long enough to see this undertaking through, and that you will create a place for her. Make it so that the Spellbinder wants to perform here. Let my wife and daughters finally see her, even if I never will."

After that, he descended into a fit of coughing. The sound was a low, whistling bark, which eventually released a stream of blood from both corners of his mouth. His injuries were starting to kill him from within, as was the sheer agony of his fate.

"Vazeer," came Flerra's strident hiss. "It's time to go."

I raised a hand in her direction but didn't look over.

Count Tygean squeezed my arm with surprising force.

"Make me that promise, Vazeer," came the clog of his fading voice.

"I promise," I muttered, but I didn't really know what I was promising, for all I could see in my mind's eye was the brutal thing that came next. I wanted the Count to leave this world thinking brighter days lay ahead—for his family, for the city, for me—but I sensed it wasn't so. Something much, much worse was coming, making this feel like one of those moments, ominous and unpredictable in my life, when I might get pulled inescapably into the void. However, that's not what occurred, and I remained painfully awake as I bid the Count farewell.

"It's time for you to go and be with your son, Halsin. May the two of you find peace together in a better place."

And with that, I reached over and cleanly slit his jugular, causing his form to sag as the red curtain fell. So ended a hopeful and improbable friendship before it had ever truly begun.

I stood and approached the others. They were clustered before me, framed with ribbed vaulting, overhung by massive stone. There was a vague slickness on the ceiling blocks, and as the moisture picked up little convulsions from the torches, the room seemed to throb like the embers of a dying fire. The air still smelled of smoke and human suffering.

"Are they all dead, Vazeer?" Adelyn probed once I had reconvened. Only Heshna was absent, for she was still listening at the chamber's door.

I made the tiniest inflection of my head.

"Flerra, do you still use that same healer?" I asked.

She pointed to her eye patch.

"That's who fixed me up after the Narrow Bid."

"You're going to need to take Lethro straight to him after you leave here. Also, bring Terza and Adelyn, since the muck in the canals has the potential to infect even a branding, let alone the more serious injuries."

"I'm not an idiot," Flerra said, and for a moment she seemed ready to school me, but she paused. The cinching of her eye indicated that she realized something was up. On the front of my Brood sister's shirt, I noted the new dark stains, and also a few sprinkly marks on her neck. Dubin Haiyes's death freckles seemed to have combined seamlessly with her own.

"Why are you saying these things, Vazeer?" Terza asked. "We can discuss all of that once we're back in the skiff."

Her healthy blush was still present; however, it was cooling quickly. Where Flerra looked merely suspicious, Terza now looked concerned.

"I'm saying it because I'm a sensible man, and I like to plan ahead."

Whether or not they perceived the irony in this, nobody scoffed.

"As such," I continued, "everything is going to proceed from here very sensibly and efficiently…just as it has so far."

"He's not coming with us," said Adelyn suddenly.

Adelyn's round, soiled features gently furrowed, and I sensed that her uncanny appraisal skills were largely unhindered, despite her exhaustion.

"What the hell are you up to?" Flerra snapped, now with some alarm.

"Cad," I said. "I need you to do something for me."

Cad had just joined our gathering, and while he appeared much restored from his pre-mission despondency, he still seemed under the daze of the Terza and Adelyn revelation. He only tore his gaze from those two once I addressed him directly.

"I'm going to need you to move those blocks away from the door," I said. "Then stack them back up once I leave. You row the team straight to the healer. Flerra will show you where."

"Enough of this, Vazeer," said Terza, one of her hands coming off of Adelyn to grab my bicep. "We're leaving right now, all of us. We got what we came for, and there's no reason to stay."

"No, Terza," I said as I slipped out of her grip. "I only got part of what I came for; the other part's upstairs. Flerra, give me your plaster saw and a pry bar; also a couple candles from your sealed tube."

"Vazeer!" Terza's radiant mood collapsed, and there was a notable quiver in her voice. "Stop acting like a crazy person."

"No chance of that. Flerra, give me those tools quickly."

Flerra began to pull the implements out, handing them over with a somber scowl.

"You have a choice," my Brood sister said, "which I didn't have. So, I'm not abandoning you…by not coming with you."

"I understand. Just get Lethro to your healer, and the others too."

"But *I* don't understand," said Terza. "Why would you go up there…to kill him?"

"Why else?"

"But do you really need revenge?" she demanded, reaching forward once again to grab me. "Revenge on behalf of your phony Count, who Addy tells me never gave you a diven, and whose son screwed this whole thing up? You don't owe him anything."

"It's crazy, I know," I said, looking towards the doorway that led back to the water hatch. "But I've always been crazy, so there's nothing to be done about it at this point. Now, it's time for you all to get out of here. Cad, help me move those blocks, then put them back once I leave."

"He's lying."

These two words, and the conviction with which they were spoken, halted everything.

Adelyn stepped forward, gently took my chin in her hand, and pivoted me back to her.

"Why are you lying to us, Vazeer?"

And there it was before me, her once-upon-a-time indeterminately alluring face, now more than alluring and not at all indeterminant. Adelyn was tired and drained and barely holding herself together, but she still had enough power left in that persuasive core of hers to open my own core, releasing the many hazards it contained.

"Tell us," she said with greater force, pulling my chin.

Between Adelyn's face tugging, and Terza's bicep squeezing, and Flerra's suspicious scowl, I found myself beyond cornered. Knowing just how short our time was, the truth was the only way to move things forward.

"Because," I said, pulling free. "None of you will ever have a restful moment again if I don't do this. Terza, you want to make another painting, or spend a happy, carefree afternoon with Adelyn? That's never going to happen if the psychopath on the sixth floor lives. We have only survived this long because the man has not fully established himself as High Lord. Now that his opposition is defeated, and he's making the gods know what deal with the future Empress, he will unleash untold resources to nab us. Tygean said it before he died, told us to flee. But I have another way, which will allow you all to go on living your lives."

"Then I'm coming with you, Zeer," said Cad, pushing his way between Terza and Adelyn. "If you need a plaster saw and a pry bar, that sounds like a job for me. And my hopes for marriage just went to shit, so I really don't care how bad it is up there."

"You dumb boy," Terza said, grabbing his shoulder and pulling him back. "Dumb and so sweet. But I need you for something else. You've got to take Addy out of here and row her to the healer. I'll go with Vazeer."

"And Lethro," Flerra said. "Take Lethro, Cad. My stupid brother needs those tools for some kind of break-in, and whatever the hell he's planning, I'm the one for that."

"Nooo!"

It came out as a growl. It came out as a prelude to something far more threatening, for the dark thing had been rising steadily in me since my conversation with Count Tygean, since I was forced to empty his blood, and my dreams, in a crimson bath.

"None of you are coming with me. You're all going out that pipe, and you will stay on alert in case I fail in my efforts and you're forced to flee."

"No." "I'm coming." "Vazeer."

Makes no difference who said what, for I instantly scorched the lot of them.

"Shut the hell up, all of you! And listen. Flerra, you think, after what happened to you—after what I allowed to happen—I'll allow it again? Lethro needs you, not just to swim through that pipe but to live his life. You've promised to take care of him, and you damned well better. And Terza, you want to put Adelyn through the same thing you just suffered, you want to leave her alone in this world? I have never seen anything so beautiful, so perfect, in my entire life, as the two of you. I don't know which of you I'd rather be, that I might get to be with the other one. There's simply no way in hell I'm letting this thing get torn apart. And Cad, forget it. I failed an innocent young man once, a horrific event that everybody else in this room can tell you about, and it's not happening again, not on my watch. You are a master builder in the making, not some doomed Shadow Bidder."

Again, the protests, a little weaker this time, whereas my scorching was even stronger.

"This is a one-way trip, you morons!" I snarled. "You've all had your fun, slapping Vazeer around, chiding and sniping at him, but that man is gone. The one who remains is not to be screwed with; it's the creature you asked for, Terza, the inhuman thing who can't be stopped. I'm going up to the top of this building, and I'm destroying everything in my path. The rest of you are just a hinderance."

They readied themselves for additional volleys, but their feeble efforts were overridden by an unexpected ally.

"He's right. Let him go."

Heshna the Seer had left her listening post and slipped soundlessly into our gathering. She stood directly before me, though she wouldn't quite meet my eye.

"It's that thing," she murmured. "It's best if we leave him alone now."

"What're you talking about?" Terza asked, swiveling to Heshna, bewildered and visibly distraught. "…like…how he behaved on the Gaff?"

Heshna nodded. "But it's worse this time. I can feel it, the cold thing, buried deep inside him…but now, not so deep. It's always bothered me, since I was a girl."

The group turned to me with varying tinges of apprehension and mystification, and all I could see in those faces—nervous, concerned, sympathetic—was weakness. Human weakness, into which the Lash could drive his ominous will.

"Get the hell out of here, all of you! I'm not going to say it again."

And they started to listen. The group began to amble over towards the door we had entered, with only two exceptions: Cad, who remained behind to move the stone blocks, and Terza, brave Terza, who seemed unable to let me go.

"Vazeer, this just isn't right—"

And I lunged, grabbing the top of her leather armor and driving her back, my other hand swinging to strike her in the face. Terza's combat instincts took over, and a hasty block mitigated most of the blow, but I still managed to cuff her in the side of the head. I also heard a tearing sound where my fingers had grabbed the tunic below her armor.

"I will beat you bloody, Falconbrow, if you're not gone in seconds."

Terza looked both frightened and appalled, and she wrenched my fingers off of her collar as if they were the dirtiest, goriest digits that had ever sullied Hell's Labyrinth, which, I felt certain, they were about to be.

"Leave him, dear," said Adelyn, pulling Terza's shoulder from behind. "There's no talking to him now."

And there wasn't, which Terza apparently understood. Adelyn was never wrong about these things, and I had never been this way, the sort of monstrous brute my ex-lover wouldn't have suffered for one moment in her life.

Cad accompanied me to the door where the blocks were piled. As we dragged the obstructions aside, I spoke my final words to him.

"You listen to me. I'm giving you the keys to the safe. All of the items in my home are to be divided equally between the people in this room, along with half the money. The rest of the money should be given to Droden, Merejin, Selene, Ichod, and the Reed sisters. Also, find out if Yurgen had any family, and if he did, give them his share. You tell everybody what he did, his sacrifice. You got it?"

Cad nodded.

"Get Flerra to help you," I continued, "if you have problems with the math."

"I'll manage."

I looked up to find that Heshna was right in front of me, suddenly and soundlessly, which would have been startling if I was still capable of being startled, which I no longer was.

"Brother, can you get to the top floor?"

"Yes."

"I'm certain the Countess is the only one in that chamber with Gueritus. If you can get to the sixth floor…get inside that room, you will have them alone."

"How could you know that?"

For several seconds we simply stared at each other in a weighty stasis, joined by something even deeper than our history.

"The same way I know many things."

I stepped closer, possibly frightening her, but she managed to hold my gaze.

"Is this why you hate me?" I asked. "Because you know things, things that are worth hating?"

"I don't hate you, not any longer. But I do hate that thing… the other part of you. Try to leave it on the sixth floor, if you can."

This I considered, inhaling the ashy, dungeon reek, staring down the arched length of this once hallowed, now cursed place.

"One way or another," I finally answered. "It's not coming back down."

Then I opened the door, stepped out, and left my fellows, and the very idea of fellowship, far behind.

30

DARK THING

I am, in the end, a creature of violence. Violence birthed me, violence built my career, violence infected me right up through that night when I slithered through Sarien Kaennamin's bygone tower of lost imaginings and sought to murder a demon pretending to be a man. I threaded and wove, and all the while the hatred rose like fumes inside my mind, heaving up images of maimed Count Tygean, eyeless Lethro, poor half-mad Brand from the abandoned orphanage, trying to signal meaning in a meaningless place. There was nothing left inside of me that felt worth saving. I had become entirely a vehicle of vengeance.

The world just beyond the torture chamber was a dim complexity of vaulted service passages, originally for Academy staff, but now, apparently, only for those given to ravings. There were no soldiers moving about here. I did hear the sounds of men talking, and possibly dicing, down a particularly well-lit hallway, but it wasn't along my route, so I avoided it.

It didn't take me long to reach my goal. This would mark the true start of my journey, a once-bustling chamber that had not seen proper use in over two centuries. It was the Kaennamin Academy laundry room, and there was a secret buried in the wall here, a secret known only to me, because I read books and others do not. The Raving Blade once told me that he also liked to read, but I doubt that he had culled through the entire history of the school and ferreted out this one unique detail.

According to records, and confirmed by a small, faded square on the original floor plans, Queen Sarien, in deference to the exalted stature of the Master Provost, designed a personal laundry chute that ran from the sixth floor's palatial suite all the way down to the ground floor laundry room. This flourish was enjoyed greatly by the First Provost, and to some degree the Second; however, the Third Provost responded differently. A dour, distrustful man, he came to fear the shaft, from which he claimed cold drafts, queer noises, and occasional rats emerged. Therefore, tactfully waiting until the city's beloved old Queen passed away, he promptly had both openings sealed up, which, according to a small, barely legible note, he accomplished with wooden studs and plaster. This would allow the new sections of wall to match the existing, without precluding a re-opening at some later date by a less paranoid provost.

Ironically, a few years after fortifying his quarters, the Third Provost decided he no longer felt like making the climb each day, so he promptly moved to the second floor. Thereafter, his successors all followed suit, and the buried shaft was forgotten.

But I had not forgotten it. I had, at one time in my youth, fantasized about inhabiting that suite, of restoring it to its former glory, which would include, among far more relevant repairs, reopening that chute. Tonight, I would perform at least that one small restoration. I'd tap and knock until I found the first sealed-up opening, cut my way in, then shimmy up to the sixth floor, where I would stealthfully cut my way out. In so doing, I had a decent chance of catching the Raving Blade by surprise.

When I entered the laundry chamber, I found it to be a

forlorn place, a neglected relic of a bygone world. The ancient, bronze pump was still standing in the center of the main basin, erect but heavily oxidized, lording over its dry pool like a decrepit heron. The adjoining tubs with their clever sluices and drains had chipped and cracked and were now covered in mildew. Gueritus's soldiers hadn't even bothered to light a torch here, so I snatched one from a nearby hallway wall bracket to assist with my search.

I found my opening easily enough. Following the first Great Storm, the wall tiles in this room had been partially restored; however, no such efforts had been made in the ensuing centuries, and certainly not since the recent cataclysm. With many of the ceramic squares dashed underfoot in dusty potsherds and gaps aplenty in the plaster, it didn't take much in the way of educated jabbing to find the weak spot on the shaft wall.

The cut I made was narrow, requiring the prying of only six wall tiles and the sawing of a relatively small section of plaster; I didn't even need to remove a framing member, as the spacing was just sufficient to squeeze through. I lit one of Flerra's candles with the torch, returned the brand to the hallway, then entered my forgotten conduit, prepared for my climb. The chute was roughly a two-and-a-half-foot square, ideal for a pressure shimmy, and with the candle in my teeth, and my back and all four limbs pressing against the stone walls, my journey began.

As I started the ascent, smelling stale air, seeing the grouted chimney box spearing away into blackness, the weird creaking tone inside my head intensified. Formerly shrouded behind a wall of mind, buried just as I was, it began to emerge from its turbid crypt. I knew at once that this was the thing that Heshna had sensed. In fact, it was the very phenomenon that others had experienced in so many ways, and which had always stayed just hidden enough that I might go on pretending to be a normal person. But I was not a normal person, and this thing wasn't staying hidden any longer, working itself free, at last, of the void.

Murmurously, the entity emerged, stripped of any illustrative elements. I saw no whirling arms, hooked ends, or spiraling center. This absence was, quite possibly, because the "symbol" was linked to Radrin Blackstar in some way, and the Finisher was gone. Nor was there lyrical sequence, like the one I had experienced in Merejin's study—that primal poetry, disgorged in the meter of wanting. What I experienced, instead, was understanding.

Squeezing and shimmying my way up the old, buried shaft, insights came to me as if a secret provost was whispering directly into my ear canal. I never actually heard words, but the creaking and buzzing began to cogitate inside my brain, and it all coalesced into one clear truth. The abstruse thing moving about inside me wasn't supernatural. It wasn't an occult phenomenon, or a divine entity. It was a rupture. The Summoner from Darkness was a subtle fabric tear, a split in reality's camouflaging skin.

I couldn't quite see this torn section, but I continued to hear it, initially as a sound like wind pressuring an old barn wall, then as a deeper, crueler moaning, as if that same wind began to penetrate a partially open window. There was also a sensation, an irritable tickle against the underside of my flesh. As to what lay through the breach, that was unseeable, but this is not to say that I was entirely unaware of what was down there, at least in principle.

Just on the other side of the rupture dwelled the source. Through those whistling, frayed edges lay life's substratum, the power that had summoned all things into being. It continued to summon even now, for I sensed it boiling just beyond the break like lava, felt it heaving like a nighttime ocean. This was the raw material from which all creation was derived, and, astonishingly, I had access to it, or at least a portion of it, directing a sliver of that summoning force through my psyche.

I even knew why. The fracture had been caused by obsession—maniacal, one-pointed obsession—stretching out over many years. Water dripping on a rock can, in time, penetrate it, if the same spot is hit again and again and again. So it must have been in my case, when a single, improbable fixation repeated itself within me, dominating my consciousness since childhood, filling me with one purpose in life: *resurrect a dead thing, breathe life into a fallen world*. Over and over again came those interminable drips, eventually cutting the rock.

Was this enough to create the opening? Could such thoughts, in their own right, channel a path to the core? And might this explain other, saner skills, like those I witnessed around me: Adelyn, who could halt men who were in the act of killing each other, Flerra, who could open locks with a puff of her breath, Heshna the Seer, who could see whatever the hell it was she saw, and ferret secrets straight out of the walls? Just possibly, inadvertent brushes with the substratum were the source of all mysterious talents; and also, just possibly, I was different from those others given the intensity of my pursuit, having taken things, as always, too far.

Up, up, up I crawled, through the dark artery, and yet, paradoxically, it felt like I was descending. As that square of smokey ceiling retreated before my candlelight lance, it seemed I was plumbing depths, not heights, and now a new, darker truth made itself known. There was a terrible danger inherent in what I had done. There was a terrible danger inherent in me. Just like those students from Merejin's past, I had become a contaminated piece of society's puzzle, an unstable component that was more likely to destroy than to create. I need look no further than my own conscience to see this—I no longer cared about other people, no longer cared about the misfortune I might cause. Alone, and disconnected from even the tiniest sense of amity, my spirit had skewed wildly in a direction from which the most destructive elements might be summoned.

Merejin had warned me. That which lay through the rent, the amalgamative power whispering in the space beyond, could not, should not, be contained inside a single human heart. I did not imagine that the generative force was an evil thing, but it was unambiguously a selfish thing, selfish in that way that all creatures are, at least at first. Like the tiny organism in the tide pool, clawing and killing, eating the others, it wanted, above all else, to survive. It needed to dominate; to win. Only with a sense of sharing could the deadly selfishness be overcome, and I, most assuredly, was in no position to accomplish that.

What I *would* accomplish—the very thing I had done before—was to pull some new, murderous entity out of the dark.

I noticed the change in the shaft wall with my own eyes. I did not need Summoner for this, as I could see the precise place where the stonework became studwork with lathed plaster filling the gaps. However, the whistling winds seemed much enrolled in my endeavors, and they nosed to the fore of my slaughter mission like overeager hounds. My fingers veritably hummed in anticipation of the coming violence.

As had been the case downstairs, there appeared to be just enough room between framing members to squeeze through, and I went about the plaster cutting meticulously. There weren't likely to be wall tiles here, for even though the mouth of the chute lay within the confines of the bath chamber, it was located on a section of wall adjoining the wardrobe and was nowhere close to the pump, tub, or rinsing basin. Still, I did a light exploratory poke just to make sure and was rewarded with a clean penetration to a place of brazier light.

I picked up the distant murmurs of conversation immediately. Suspended at the top of the shaft, pressing the walls with my back and legs, I listened for a bit, until I was sure that the sounds weren't coming from the bath chamber. I heard no splashing or pumping, no rustling or pouring, which meant that my target and his companion were in the living chamber—probably the sunken conversation pit near the fireplace. I continued sawing, working along the studs and creating a clean extractable rectangle.

I was through quickly. The material was old and ready to give way, plus Flerra's saw was particularly sharp. Also, perhaps, I was imbued with inspired energy, so ready were my hands to deliver on their promise. I crawled out of the new opening, scrabbling quietly across the tiled floor like one of the Third Provost's phantom rats.

I knew the layout of the suite extremely well, as I am almost a savant when it comes to this, retaining details with just one viewing of a floor plan. Therefore, when I opened the bathroom door a crack, I did so without fear of being seen, knowing that it faced the side wall of an alcove. However, there was the small matter of rusted hinges to contend with. Though clearly oiled by Gueritus's staff, and in one spot reinforced by an additional iron band, the door still made a low groan as I worked it open a body's breath. I stared through the slender reveal at a section of plaster wall, newly painted in light mauve.

For a few seconds, I remained motionless, trying to determine if the conversation had ceased. Not only had it continued, but now that I was unhindered by a closed door, and stark still as death, I keyed into its animated dimensions. And what a strangely animated thing it was, for the man's voice, grating in the most unmistakable of ways, was unquestionably that of High Lord Ulan Gueritus, and the other was, indeed, a woman…a very, very arrogant woman.

"Oh, Ulan, you silly man," she pearled off in an haughty Midland accent, "teaching you will be something of a chore. How small are your ambitions, here in this churlish place."

I was, for a moment, taken aback. The impropriety of it shocked me, and I was quite sure that I had never heard a more condescending tone in my life. The voice itself possessed a bit more trill than Nascinthé's impersonation from the Narrow Bid, and it was definitely more snide.

"Yes, yes, Countess, but I don't see what benefit there is to me in any of this," came the scratch of Ulan Gueritus, who did not sound offended by his chastisement. This was, I recalled, one of his strange virtues, the fact that he took no overt offense to the most overtly offensive material, though this did not entirely reassure me that Countess Odel hadn't just been mentally slotted in for a raving.

"The benefits are copious, and the problems you head off even more so," she replied.

"What, what, then? For it is not a stretch, not a stretch at all, when I say that fifty percent of our income comes from Midland merchandise. Refusal to deal in your Tergonian baubles would cut us off at the knees."

"Refusing my deal will cut you far worse," she snapped. "Consider this: what if the Emperor decided one day that it was far easier for him to make war on you than to chase Kaszivar's wretched ships across the sea? What if Nesabedrus were to decide that? It's worth considering, for I am in a unique position to tell you that such thoughts have crossed his mind."

Standing there, captivated and somewhat appalled, I awaited a response to what could only be construed as a threat. Indeed, the Raving Blade saw it that way too.

"Do you consider it wise to provoke me like this, Lady?" he rasped. "I would think you wiser than that, much wiser."

"And I would think you wiser than to rebuff me," she shot back. "Eager friendship is what you should be offering, for I am a very good woman to befriend. And I'm explaining exactly how to do it. Promise me this change, make it known you will turn back all items from the Midlands, and I will return to the Capital with a win, which is something I need right now. Such a favor, coming at this critical juncture, would not soon be forgotten, even when, inevitably, I ascend to greater things."

"Right, right, but wouldn't it soon be forgotten, Countess Odel?" Gueritus asked, and there was something baiting in the hoarse inflection of his tone. "You seem to have forgotten my predecessor quickly—so very quickly—and it is now my understanding that he eagerly offered you his friendship. His eager, eager friendship."

I knew it was time to get on with my business. I should, by now, be sliding into position, but I found these maneuvers difficult in the presence of such riveting discourse. Once before, I had been faced with a similar situation. On the night of the Narrow Bid, as I waited with fatal expectancy to kill our target, I became hypnotized by the laments of High Lord Beranardos Sherdane. Given that Sherdane's tragic breakdown had been spawned entirely by love for this very woman, the one who was right now making indecorous deals with his killer, it seemed of no small consequence how she might respond.

She did respond, and I soon wished she hadn't.

"Dear me," she snooted, "how predictable of you to bring that up. It's certainly none of your business, though I will say this: Beranardos's friendship turned a little *too* eager in the end. Such things were diverting for a puerile girl, but when the girl grew into a woman, with bigger issues to consider, that's when all the romantic garble became less entertaining. I don't anticipate that happening with you. You, my dear Ulan, are a pragmatist, like me."

Quickly, (and I would also say utterly) I found that I hated this woman. Her insouciant words pained me in odd ways, which was no small thing, for I was not entirely myself. However, perhaps the little segment of confidential banter had opened a door back to my humanity. Ear was now being given to an unmet figure who had played such a significant role in my life. Countess Shaeyin Odel, whose letter had launched a Narrow Bid, whose affections had reduced a mighty High Lord to sniveling collapse, who had been friends with my own Nascinthé of Levell, back when she was Nirabella Spellbinder and the Capital worshiped at her feet—this very one was finally being revealed.

But, as both Shade and Radrin had attested, Countess Odel was not a grand figure. She was something small and self-seeking and every bit as conniving as the Finishers had implied, and I found myself sickened. "Sickness," as such, broke the spell, and I readied myself for the work at hand. While it would be easiest to lie in wait in Gueritus's privy chamber, ambushing him when he came to relieve himself, time was not on my side. The rescue operation in the torture chamber would eventually be discovered, at which point a frantic messenger would come knocking, and all hope of completing the job would be lost.

Thus, I squeezed my way out of the bath chamber and began

to survey things from the safety of the antechamber. As noted, the provost's suite was an unreasonably large space, one that had elicited some eye rolling back in Sarien's day. Nonetheless, it definitely had its charms, and as I slid close to the threshold of the broader living area, I took in some of its finer details: the huge wraparound window seat, which, in daylight hours, surveyed much of the Lower City, as well as three sinuous bends in the river Grells; the hefty plaster crown molding (no longer gold-leafed but still magnificent), and an elegant dome rising gently above, which made the ceiling tall but not towering.

I squatted low, then poked my face around the doorframe, scanning over the dining area, the door to the private kitchen, and finally the edge of the conversation pit, the suite's most eccentric feature. Sarien had made some odd choices here. Recessed a full five feet below the surrounding floor (too deep, in my opinion, and now dangerous, since the gold-plaited railing had long since been scavenged) with a single set of steps giving access, the semi-circular breadth of this space was sufficient to host a gathering of two dozen, which rarely happened. The real explanation was the fact that both Sarien and the First Provost were given to compulsive pacing, and they apparently wore out the original rug as they bandied design concepts back and forth in front of the fire.

Some of these flourishes had the potential to be helpful to my cause, others harmful, and as I crawled from the alcove, I tried to determine which would be more relevant. I soon learned that Gueritus was seated, with his head below the rim of the conversation pit—helpful—however, he was facing in my general direction, with his pale hands gesturing over the lip—definitely harmful. This meant that I would need to slither on my stomach to get any closer.

"Well now," Shaeyin Odel said. "I certainly hope you have the capacity to move off of this subject, since it's starting to bore me terribly."

I had tried to close my ears to the banter, which involved several innuendo-laced barbs from Guertius, and a few (I must confess) adroit counters by Shaeyin Odel. She was proving to be a rather dexterous opponent in the face of the Raving Blade's intimidation tactics.

"Perhaps you delight in salacious material of this sort," she went on, "because of your strange, cloistered lifestyle. You ought to get out more, Ulan."

Oh, that was a good one. I do believe the lady may have hit a vulnerable spot, given that Ulan Gueritus had informed me during our meeting at The Crossbiter that he was thoroughly done with Beranardos Sherdane's policy of *Ruthless Caution* and planned to "step out into the light," as he put it.

"Yes, yes, well…about that," Gueritus rasped. "You have now moved me in a direction, a very interesting direction, which I was going to get to soon enough."

There was little chance of slinking up on my target from behind, since making it all the way to the far side of the conversation pit would involve an extended, leather-creaking, scabbard-scuffing stomach crawl that would become far too noticeable as I drew near. After that, I'd have to leap down into that pit, which I probably couldn't do fast enough to prevent him from releasing a cry. Nor would I be able to stop Countess Odel from screaming, and the moment either of those things happened, I was as good as dead.

The Raving Blade would have left the front door of the suite unlocked, and the guards outside would be quick to respond to a disturbance. Therefore, my best bet would be getting to the door of the suite where I could carefully slide home the bolt. That locking mechanism, and the door itself, were among the paranoid fortifications made by the Third Provost, and I felt quite confident that if I could simply secure the door, I'd have more than enough time to get the job done.

I began to shimmy on my stomach across the marble floor, moving ever so carefully in the direction of the front vestibule. I was tucked against the far wall, perhaps as much as fifty feet from my enemy, so he had very little chance of hearing me, and, as long as he remained seated in the pit, I was invisible.

"…this, this, you see, is the point, Countess Odel," the Raving Blade was saying, though I had missed the first part of the sentence. I reached a faded Kaszian rug, which prickled my armor and added new friction to my movements.

"I had always wondered, wondered a great deal," Gueritus continued, "where Beran got his precious intelligence—such secret, secret intelligence—which only the Emperor and his closest staff would know. I understand now, of course, and this makes me admire him more, a great deal more."

"Okay…?" she replied, with an exasperated lilt. "Where are you going with this?"

"Well, well, Countess," Gueritus continued, "I simply want you to understand, understand completely, that it wasn't the man's indiscretions that I resented, for I knew nothing of that… not until recently. What I *resented* was that he learned all the wrong lessons from the intelligence, that he wanted, in fact, to remain 'cloistered' in that very manner that you so scorn."

"Dear me, Ulan, you are really dragging this out. Might you explain how this pertains to our business?"

"I'm simply explaining, Countess Odel, explaining as best I

can, that I know things, courtesy of you, and your eager, eager friendship with Sherdane. For instance, I'm well aware of the Empire's clandestine war with the Inland Kingdoms, and the terrible drain on Tergonian resources that this has become. I have even been told that the Sullward Imperial Garrison will be vacated, all but vacated, within a year, and the Emperor will merely leave behind a bunch of clerks to examine our cargos, under the pretense that our City Watch will enforce your laws. All of this, as you can imagine, does very little to chasten me, and it leaves me in no great hurry to turn back Midland merchandise. No great hurry at all."

This got me to pause. I was on the verge of sliding out of the main living space, but I was slowed by the sheer weight of the revelation and the numerous threads it tied. This explained why Gueritus felt such confidence in his flagrancy, why he thought he could run his fencing operation without Shadow Bidders. It also made it clear that Countess Odel, despite showing some surprising nimbleness up to this point, had likely just been boxed into a corner. A dangerous corner, since she had lost her leverage.

I resumed my exodus, soon making it out of the room. The provost suite was designed in such a way that the entry vestibule and the main living area were technically the same space, with the wide stone fireplace column dividing the two zones. This allowed for an imposing entry vestibule on one side and the half circle of the conversation pit on the other, with room to pass around either wing of the fireplace wall. I had just made it beyond the left wing and was now entirely shielded from view.

I got to my feet and approached the entrance. The suite's door was an exceptionally thick, oak slab, which had adequately withstood the ravages of time. So too had the bolt, which, as expected, had not been thrown. However, there was a problem. The heavy steel of the locking mechanism, while intact, had some corrosion at the bands, guaranteeing that I would make a loud screeching noise as I slammed it home.

"Oh, dear me," I heard Countess Odel croon out from the conversation pit. While her voice was muted by the intervening fireplace column, its extreme hauteur got through. "You do have that look, Ulan Gueritus, that insufferable look of a man who thinks he's won. How I enjoy seeing that look at court, knowing that one day soon I will grind it down to minced lamb."

Once again, I was pulled from my endeavors by the shocking tenor of this conversation. What the hell was she thinking? At this point, I truly had to wonder if Countess Odel had some sort of unexpressed death wish. Using that tone with anyone in this city was risky, but this was High Lord Ulan Gueritus, the Raving Blade of Hell's Labyrinth.

"Woman," Gueritus snarled. "You have just, you have most certainly overstepped—"

"Ohhhh, have I?" she scathed back, cutting him off. "Am I due now for one of your ravings? Or, just shy of that, to be tossed out the door on my head? I would not consider either course, if I were you. Do you think I would come here without informing others of my intentions? Do you think, for one moment, that I would undertake this enterprise without informing Nesabedrus? That's right, he knows exactly what I am up to and supports it. Which is why he and I have devised the perfect way to bankrupt your system, should you prove a stubborn fool."

Gueritus garbled something, which I couldn't quite make out, but soon it turned into his familiar, "What, what—" which she again cut off.

"What? What?" She laughed. "Is this your normal manner

of speech, or have I finally gotten you to stutter? *Yes, yes*, I have *plan, plan* in place, starting with the lifting of the statute of limitations on stolen merchandise, which will, with a pen stroke, cut the value of your Ripening Halls in half. All of that painstaking time you spent squatting over your baubles like a mother hen… wasted. You'll be just another common thief, trying to hawk pilfered items to lowlifes."

If I was having trouble concentrating before, I now moved into slack-jawed territory. This discussion really belonged on some sort of short list of inconceivable conversations. Before me lay my conundrum—the rusted bolt, and the noise it would produce—but, for the life of me, I couldn't get my mind out of the conversation pit.

"You, you wouldn't dare," Gueritus hissed. "The Southern Traders and the auction houses—"

"Won't like it," Countess Odel finished for him. "No, they certainly won't, not at first, but they will accept it, eventually, because we have a generous bundle of benefits worked out for them, ranging from a substantial reduction in taxes, to preferential berthing at all Imperial ports, to, the prize of the lot, first call on the plunder that we will be hauling home from that clandestine Inland war that you thought was your great bargaining chip. Turns out it's *my* bargaining chip, in more ways than you can know. As Empress I'm going to win that war, and win it decisively, initiating the largest campaign of Tergonian expansion since the Imperial Armada took the West."

Gods, the boldness of this gambit. While I duly agreed that there was very little to *like* about Shaeyin Odel, I was quite sure that Tergon's Grand Dispatcher, Radrin Blackstar, had thoroughly underestimated her.

"But please, my dear Ulan," the Countess said, in a softer,

more congenial voice, "you can sit back down, and take that horrid look off your face, the one that says you're about to clobber me. There is truly no need for it. I haven't the slightest interest in doing any of the things I just described; I simply needed you to understand that I have thought this all through. What I'd very much like is for you and I to come to an agreement, one that suits us both. We will then clink glasses, share some laughs, and before you know it, you will be offering me, and I in return, some eager, eager friendship."

Gueritus made a few mutterous noises, which did, in fact, sound de-escalatory. After that, I heard the rustling of fabric, suggesting that he had once again taken his seat.

I turned my attention back to the door. I tried, again, to resolve the dilemma. I could pound the corroded bolt into position, thereby losing the element of surprise, or I could leave the door unlocked and try to quickly kill my target—a target who was, by all accounts, not an easy kill.

"*Lock the door.*"

The voice was clear. The tone was lucid, deep, and authoritative, to such a degree that I actually glanced around, which was preposterous, because I knew the source. It had come from within.

"*Lock the door,*" it said again.

It was my voice, I think. But it had never sounded like this—crystalline, poised, fountaining up like a melodious wellspring. Rising from the core.

"*Lock the door,*" it said a third time. "*Your partner has been summoned.*"

Now, a shiver arose, warm and supple. It wriggled straight up my torso into my neck and finally pulsed around my lips.

"Please, my dear High Lord," I heard Countess Odel saying from the far side of the wall, "there is no cause for chagrin. I simply have a gift for this, which I take great pains to hide at court, but not from the man who matters most. There is a reason that Nesabedrus wants me to crown myself Asadeissia II."

"*Summoned,*" the inner voice intoned with the low, vibrating resonance of a gong. "*Your partner has been summoned out of the dark.*"

My fingers stroked over the cool burnish of the bolt, absorbing the textured mass, a deadly calm overtaking me. Suddenly, it all made sense. Suddenly, I felt I could see the full arc of things, grasp the inexorable pull that had brought the proper pieces into position. Here, at the top of this forgone place, my shadow partner would arrive, as he always did, surviving poison and betrayal, bypassing guards and obstructions, that we might complete this mission together.

This was alignment. This is how it was when the raw power of a dream—as Asadeissia put it—"razored a pathway to the light."

"*Lock the door.*"

And I did.

31

SHADOW PARTNER

The noise was loud. The clank and metallic shriek disturbed the suite like the rusty release of an ancient crossbow, not the sort of sound one would confuse with the antics of the guards outside, or an object falling over in the entry hall. It was deliberate. The steel bolt made it most of the way home on the first pound, requiring just one more rap with my pommel to drive it snugly into the catch.

"What was *that*?" I heard Countess Odel ask.

Gueritus did not answer, though I did hear the abrasional scrape of a blade, likely two, being pulled from their scabbards. I began to move towards the main living space.

"What is it?" she said again in a lower voice. "Who's here?"

"Please, stay in your seat, Lady," he said, and I heard the jingling rub of his clothing, and perhaps armor, as he approached the small flight of stairs that led up out of the pit. But I did not let him climb those stairs. I came quickly around the wing of the masonry wall, and just as he was about to put his foot on the first step, I arrived at the top of the flight, towering over him.

We locked gazes. It was strange to see this man again, with so many plans having been created and destroyed, so many horrors put on display, since our last encounter in The Crossbiter Tavern.

All of that created an even bloodier glaze through which to view him. High Lord Ulan Gueritus was dressed well, with a finely woven purple blouse, belted with a darker purple sash, and he wore black hose with tall leather boots. Makeup seemed to have been applied, improving his pallid complexion, and this only added to the sense that this conference with Countess Odel did, indeed, matter to him, that he might even be trying to woo her, of all things. I also saw that his formerly stringy hair had been washed, neatly combed, and drawn back into a fine, aristocratic ponytail. Pairing all of this with the fact that he had come forward with his two jeweled long swords leveled, ostensibly playing the role of the lady's protector, made the spectacle almost impossibly ironic.

A series of hammering bangs came to us from the suite door.

"My lord, is everything alright? Was it you that threw the bolt?"

The guard's voice was quite muffled, for the door was almost four inches thick.

Gueritus and I simply stared at each other. He stayed motionless at the base of the five shallow steps, gazing up, the obsidian shine of his eyes picking up hints of the brazier light.

"Well, well, isn't this a devilish twist," he muttered.

"Who, in the Emperor's name, is that?" Countess Odel asked from behind the Raving Blade. She had not remained seated, as instructed, and had instead come forward a few steps in a sort of rapt uncertainty. I gave her only a quick look, as I could not risk taking my focus off of my enemy and his two leveled blades. Still, even with a cursory scan, I could see that Shaeyin Odel was a tall, shapely figure, garbed in an elegant gold silk dress, with frilled white at the collar and sleeves. Her hair was long and blonde, with the color skewing closer to honey than the pale yellow that

Nascinthé had achieved in her disguise. Additionally, the shape of the Countess's face was rounder than Nascinthé's, with fuller, more sensual lips and stronger brows. Her eyes, though a little shaded from my current angle, were a striking blue color, and I could ascertain, without much additional gawping, that she was an extremely attractive woman.

"Yes, yes, my lady," Gueritus intoned hoarsely. "I'm afraid I have some unfinished business to attend to here. Please stay back out of harm's way as I deal with this matter."

"But who is he?"

Another round of heavy slams concussed the door, with the same guard's muffled appeals just reaching me where I stood.

"It's of no consequence who he is, no consequence at all," Gueritus answered, "for he won't be with us much longer. Indeed, not much longer at all."

I took my first slow step down the stairs. I held a spade in each hand, and while these weapons were half the length of the opposing swords, my opponent still shifted backwards, which felt oddly familiar. How analogous this moment was to that prophetic dream I had experienced aboard the Elena's Guile. Then, as now, I stood on high, with the raspy, twin-bladed Gueritus wavering below me in the face of my resolve. And yet, there were differences.

In the dream it was the murky Gueritus who exuded malice, whose spirit was of such tarnished substance that it projected outward into the surrounding cityscape. In this place, the roles were reversed. It was me who came as the bloody shadow man, violating the sanctity of an architectural treasure with an aura of darkness. High Lord Ulan Gueritus was, strangely, the gentleman, valiantly shielding a lady from harm. The twists of fate here seemed absurd.

I took two more steps down into the pit, and Gueritus continued to retreat, though I suspect he did this more out of a desire to bring me down to his level than fear.

"Well, well, Vazeer the Lash," said Gueritus. "It seems the Dark Gods have been kinder to me than I might have hoped."

Beyond Gueritus's form, I saw Shaeyin Odel twitch at the uttering of my name. I dared not focus on her too closely, but I would swear there was a small tic of shock in that elegant frame. Perhaps Bernanardos Sherdane had mentioned me to her, or maybe she was familiar with recent events in my city. In any event, the Countess was now glaring at me with a sort of ferocious scrutiny.

"There is no kindness coming to you, Ulan Gueritus," I replied as I reached the floor of the pit. "Not from the Dark Gods, not from me. Your time in this world is running short."

Standing on the same level, I noted that the Raving Blade and I were of roughly the same height, though the elevated heels of his boots likely accounted for some of this.

"No, no, Shadow Bidder, I think not," he said, revealing his boney fence of perfect teeth. "I have big plans, very big plans in the making, and some of them involve you and your friends; Dubin and I have discussed this at length."

"Dubin the Dicer is now a pile of bloody body parts," I replied. "As is your Lieutenant Commander, Jaex. The prisoners have been freed, and I have made it up to this chamber unimpeded. All in all, I'd say that your plans are off to a poor start."

Ulan Gueritus was a difficult man to rattle, something I had learned in The Crossbiter. But I do think this litany disturbed him, for the pearly grin morphed in a direction I distinctly recalled from our last meeting, when his merriment was spoiled by disgust. It was time to push things a bit and see where I could take them.

"Also, as you probably heard," I continued, "the door to your suite is securely bolted. So, no help is coming to you. No surrogates are here to buffer you, which means you must face me…"

And I attacked.

This, as I have amply noted, is my thing. I get the jump on those of greater skill, or size, or numbers by deploying such deceptions, and most of the time it works. I had achieved some impressive trickery-generated results against Coljin Helmgrinder in our infamous Lower City duel, and when it comes to the brigands, sailors, and assorted miscreants I've had to deal with over the years, there are far too many misdirectional assaults to quantify. I expected to achieve something similar tonight.

However, it did not play out that way. Not at all. In fact, so completely did I fail to catch the Raving Blade off guard that he instantly used my ploy against me, utilizing the most fiendishly skillful swordsmanship I had ever seen. My attack involved flicking my right spade at his loosely held left blade—his lead—by which I sought to clear a path for myself that way and simultaneously thrust my other weapon from an off angle at his throat. I am right-handed, which the Raving Blade knew, so using the left for the killing blow, combined with the oblique skew of the assault, combined with my mid-sentence launch (emerging from such an irritating line of discourse) should have been at least partially successful. But it was me who wound up bloodied, with an almost fatal injury, which is not a good way to start a duel.

Inhuman reflexes, or some sort of Masque-like ability to read his opponent, had Gueritus nonchalantly dropping his lead blade as I flicked for it, causing me to miss the steel entirely and plunge a little too far forward. I did manage to stab with my off-hand weapon, but not from quite the proper angle, and Gueritus was ready for it anyway, deflecting with his right and simultaneously jabbing with the other sword. It was that poke from the lead blade, the one that I had tried and failed to flick aside, that almost put an end to me.

He caught me in the upper ribs, just below my breast, and only the fact that this was a reinforced spot in the armor, he was jabbing as opposed to thrusting, and it was the right, not the left side, kept me from collapsing in a heap. But the situation was bad. While I couldn't tell exactly how deep the puncture was, I knew for sure that Ulan Gueritus had just tilted this fight wildly in his favor. He might very well defeat me in a matter of seconds if something didn't change immediately.

I sprang back and to the right, my two blades raised, ready for him to press the assault, but he didn't. Instead, he simply smiled in that malevolent way of his, watching me wince and bleed as a pleased sound emerged from his throat.

"See, see, Shadow Bidder, it is as I explained. There is no need for surrogates when it comes to my swordplay. And most certainly there will be no need for surrogates with my other form of play—such fun play—when I slowly take every last piece of you apart."

I bent over slightly, pressing my right spade hand against the wound, trying to determine how bad it was. There was limited pain on contact, from which I gleaned that I had probably gotten off lucky, though a heavy dousing of Nettledown was going to be required to fix this. Of course, the Raving Blade couldn't know exactly how serious the wound was, so I decided to exaggerate it, taking a few shallow breaths, coupled with a sickly little cough. I thought this might draw him in, but he seemed content to stand where he was and watch my pantomimes of pain.

"Your Ladyship," he rasped, glancing back. "Would you be so kind, so very kind, as to slip around to the entrance of the suite and unbolt the door? I would like my guards to secure this man before he entirely bleeds—"

And I attacked again. This move was less slanting, with a driving thrust straight at the torso, deploying both spades simultaneously. I came fast and stayed low, showing more athleticism than he should have reasonably expected from a coughing, gasping victim of a chest wound. But, somehow, the Raving Blade wasn't fooled. Maybe he had witnessed too many of my tricks during the Shadowbiter duel; or, perhaps I had derived disproportionate help from the crowd in that fight; or, finally, there was a distinct possibility that the Raving Blade truly was the most dangerous swordsman in all of Hell's Labyrinth, not excluding Coljin Helmgrinder, and without the ability to come at him from behind, the fight was lost.

My spades were suddenly deflected off to the left, and while Gueritus needed to twirl both of his weapons to accomplish this, and also to aggressively pivot his body in the process, he still managed to get the edge of his left blade down to my thigh where he delivered a wicked cut. Slashes are better than punctures, but this one was deep, causing my leg to buckle and forcing me down to one knee.

As before, the Raving Blade did not push his advantage and instead took a step back.

"Well, well, Shadow Bidder, it seems that none of your tricks work on me, have never worked, when you think about it. Countess Odel, may I again trouble you, trouble you just a little, to go and unbolt the door? I am growing tired of this man and his tactics."

"Yes." Her answer was quiet. It reflected, perhaps, anxiety, or perhaps something else.

I gave her a quick glance, and while she was partially obscured from view, standing just a few feet behind Gueritus, I detected some sort of engrossed deliberation in her posture. I didn't know what it meant, or how any of this was playing out in her mind. However, what I did know was that if she made it to that door and slid back the bolt, I was as good as dead. Actually, worse than dead, as Gueritus had promised. Shaeyin Odel, even more than the Raving Blade, needed to be stopped, at least until I figured out how to beat this man.

Or, until my "*shadow partner*" arrived.

"Bring the bastard already," I muttered under my breath.

"What, what, Shadow Bidder?" Gueritus asked. "What sort of curse are you mumbling? Or prayer?"

Behind the Raving Blade I saw Countess Odel starting to move. She stepped hesitantly, and her initial trajectory seemed like it would send her around her host's right side, towards the little flight of stairs I had used earlier. I wasn't blocking that path any longer, though the stairs weren't far off, and already I began to strategize how I might lunge and knock her legs out from under her as she made the ascent. After that, admittedly, I didn't have much of a plan.

But perhaps my shadow partner did. The promised ally from darkness would be most helpful right about now, and in truth, his arrival was something I could envision. As I glanced up at High Lord Ulan Gueritus, saw that macabre gauntness of his face, improved slightly with makeup but ultimately grotesque, I could all but see Radrin Blackstar's knife cutting cleanly across his throat. How often had I witnessed that? How wonderfully it would complete the arc and bring this dreadful drama to a close.

But that's not what happened. Conspicuously, it didn't, for Countess Odel continued around her host, the Raving Blade remained unharmed, and in the meantime, the wraithlike, collared phantom known as Blackstar did not elevate out of shadow and rescue me. However, something *did* happen. Something very strange.

As Shaeyin Odel came around the side of High Lord Ulan Gueritus, edging towards the staircase, I noticed that she was carrying an object in her hand. Her arms were at her sides so the item was half obstructed by the billowing folds of her gold dress, but I was quite sure she gripped the wine bottle that she had been sharing with her host. It was an odd sight really, for I couldn't imagine that this highbrow lady planned to guzzle straight from the bottle as she unbolted the door. No, that's not what she planned at all.

The Countess was just passing Gueritus when suddenly she spun in a swirling billow of gilded silk, and, jacking the bottle clumsily overhead, she rained it down with a sort of convulsive savagery on the Raving Blade's face. Her swing was graceless and even bungling, but her surprise attack was imbued with such jolting violence that the bottle exploded against the side of Gueritus's head in a paroxysm of green glass and gouting scarlet. Only a last-second pivot kept the blow from landing directly in his eyes, but he was still thrown sideways, with his right forearm sweeping over his face to clear away the stinging wine and broken glass.

This was clearly my moment. I should have leapt up from my injured squat and launched myself at my enemy, but I'll confess I was so utterly shocked, so mind-bogglingly mystified by this turn of events, that for a second or two I was almost as incapacitated as Ulan Gueritus.

"You killed the one thing I loved!" shrieked Countess Odel, the broken bottleneck clutched in her bleeding fist. "My one love, and you murdered him!"

And just like that, she was flinging herself at Gueritus again, upon him, hopping up to land in a sideways clinch like a rabid weasel. Her movements were so manic, awkward, and incensed that Gueritus's capacity for recalibration seemed temporarily suspended. I, too, couldn't quite make the turn, for, above and beyond the non-sequitur insanity of it, there was something so brutally real, so sickly passionate about this act, it almost seemed to snap the flow of time. A singular thing had just been summoned up out of the dark.

"You took it from me!" screamed Shaeyin Odel, her face contorting furiously. "You took my heart, you sickening freak!"

And then, from her oblique piggyback, she began to stab the shattered remnants of the bottleneck straight into the Raving Blade's skull.

Immobilized by the sight, the Countess's heartbreak seemed to plunge straight into my core. Beyond questions of how she could have disguised these feelings, what the hell her plan was, who told her about the Narrow Bid (and, quite possibly, my personal role in it) was this stunning moment of unhinged emotionalism. All matters of personal safety, Imperial ambition, reason itself fractured like the bloody, gouging splinters in her fist. Shaeyin Odel had, at last, revealed herself to be the matching consort to Beranardos Sherdane, the mighty High Lord from whose inconsolable lips emerged wailing prayers to forgotten gods.

Then the moment was past, and the Raving Blade reacted. Dropping one of his swords, he reached up and grabbed the Countess by her hair, and with a quick hinged duck of his upper body, he was able to flip her onto the floor. The second she hit the ground, the Raving Blade's boot shot out at her face. A panicked twitch of her head prevented direct contact; however, his heel scraped abrasively across her cheek, sending her lolling back in a honey-colored tousle. Gueritus could have killed her then. He could have butchered her with his remaining blade, but he checked his swing, recognizing, no doubt, that this was not a person that he could afford to kill. His plans, his aspirations, and, indeed, his own life would be forfeited if he struck down Countess Shaeyin Odel. So, he kicked her again, in the torso this time, and she rolled several feet across the carpet in a spin of wine-speckled gold silk.

But my partner in shadow had done her job. She had created the opening, for as that first kick scraped her cheek, I shook out of the daze, and as the second thudded home, I blasted forward. Gueritus was fast. He had uncanny reflexes and was a true fighter, who had been tested in real battles, not just fencing matches, but he was severely hindered. Wine, glass, and a profuse supply of his own blood were still splattered in his eyes, plus the initial blow to his head must have dizzied him; plus (not to be dismissed), his mind was registering its complicated reactions to kicking a woman across the floor, a gratifying activity for him under normal circumstances, but one that was substantially complicated by the fact that this was the future leader of the Empire. All of this must have unbalanced him, which is exactly the sort of thing I like to exploit.

Propelling myself off of my good leg, I made a high fake with one of my spades, drawing his remaining blade up, then dove low at his thighs. Releasing my weapons, I got my hands around the backs of his legs and power drove him straight across the pit until we rammed into one of the couches. The furniture had been pulled away from the walls, probably to make the seating more intimate, and we knocked the tasteful piece onto its back as the two of us flipped over it to the tight space beyond.

The Raving Blade instantly dropped his remaining sword, which was an essential act if he had any hope of countering me, and his left hand went groping for a dagger at his belt. He moved quicker and with greater purpose in this situation than I was used to from a toppled swordsman, especially one bleeding from cuts to the head.

I had already pulled a jack from my right thigh as we tumbled, and in an effort to stop Gueritus's left hand, I stabbed the inside of his forearm, where there was a knot of tendons. He wore a cuirass underneath his clothing, but it was something light (probably so it wouldn't interfere with the comely cut of his blouse), giving my jack a good chance of getting through. I couldn't quite tell if it did, but either way, Gueritus's hand jerked back, the dagger still hanging halfway out of the sheath. He snarled, and punched at my head with his other hand, but this too I had anticipated, and I tucked my chin, presenting him the top of my forehead, which is a damned boney thing to hit. In fact, more than one set of knuckles that I knew of had broken on that very spot, and while I can't say if this was the result in Gueritus's case, I do know he gave up after two grunting attempts.

In the meantime, I had drawn a stiletto with my other hand, which would allow for a killing blow; however, my position wasn't perfect. I was a little bit too low on Gueritus's body, and while I had no problem stabbing him in a whole host of unsavory places en route to the heart or throat, I was cognizant of the fact that his right hand was now fumbling around for another weapon. Additionally, he was clever enough to start wriggling madly, which meant he understood the basic principles of close-quarters combat. This was indeed one of the first things Holod had taught me—to stay in constant motion, to never allow your enemy to get into a balanced position, to hit a stationary target, to know where your weapons would be coming from next. As such, the Raving Blade alarmed me a second later when I heard the quick, soft grating of that left-hand dagger being drawn.

I had miscalculated. That leather cuirass was clearly thicker than I had imagined, or possibly had steel strips woven in at key spots, as the gouge to his forearm should have made that hand inoperable for the remainder of this fight. As I glanced up from my chin tuck, I saw the dagger levering back to take a stab at my head. There were only two options here: jab at his waist and hope that the pain was sufficient to cause him to blow his attack, or else break away from the clinch, retreating from range. The former appealed to me more, but the Raving Blade had already shown some extraordinary toughness, and I didn't have enough faith in a nonlethal stab to distract him. So, I rolled violently off to the side as his blade drove at my head, missing by a hair's breadth.

This was turning into a problem. I still had the advantage, more or less, with two small blades in my fists, but my injuries were starting to hamper me, and Ulan Gueritus was proving to be an inconveniently versatile combatant. He rolled away from me so that he could attempt to get back to a standing position. There, his superior fencing skills might come back into play, even if he only wielded daggers.

"Damn, damn you, Shadow Bidder," he snarled, as he started to rise, "as the Dark Gods are my witness—"

But he never finished that sentence, nor did he ascend out of a kneeling position. If the Dark Gods witnessed anything, it definitely wasn't the thing the Raving Blade was talking about.

She came at him from behind. Her hunched form was a bedraggled mess of stained silk, chaotic tresses, and wine-splattered flesh, and the only weapon she had within reach was one of the cushions from the couch, but she swung this down on her nemesis's rising head with such shrieking belligerence that the green pillow exploded in a pandemonium of torn velvet and fluttering feathers. And this, ironically, turned out to be the balance-tipping blow. Ridiculous as her implement was, it was one hinderance too many for him, for the combination of the whacking rear assault, the blinding storm of the goose down, plus (I had to imagine) the deep, injurious loathing of this regal woman that he had tried so hard to impress, all simply halted him for a heartbeat. And a heartbeat was all I needed, because this time he was the only one who froze. I was upon him instantly, driving my stiletto so hard into his upper arm that it pierced straight through the armor, making havoc of the complex web of muscles there. That troublesome dagger of his somersaulted from his hand, and once that happened, it was all over for him.

I did not complete the task alone. My partner was indeed with me to the end, emerging as she had from a place of darkness and loss, retribution and madness, and she promptly swept up that fallen dagger as I slid up onto the Raving Blade's thighs. While I began targeting lower spots where I knew my jack and stiletto would get through—his groin, his waist, his ribs—the Countess rose up on her knees, gripping the dagger in both of her hands, and began to plunge it down repeatedly at Gueritus's face, screaming all the while.

The Raving Blade's extraordinary toughness prolonged this nightmare for him. He refused to quit, writhing to avoid my fatal stabs, waving his one good hand in front of his face to try to stop Shaeyin Odel's blade. But there was no stopping us. I am, as I have explained, eminently reducible to a state of violence, and she, unskilled though she was, had now entered a genuine battle frenzy. Taking in the oblique sight of her, with her spattered silk dress, her disheveled golden hair, her mauled, shrieking face, Countess Odel had transformed into a thing of the most feral human need, stripped down to its core. The desire for her then, above and beyond all other desires, was to murder the hateful thing that had stolen love from her in this world.

It was quite possible that she would turn that dagger on me next, given the efficacy of her intelligence operation. On some level, I didn't care. The unfathomable bravery of this noblewoman, whose entire training with blades probably involved proper etiquette with a butter knife, was of such an astonishing order that dying at her hands would almost seem an honor. She had come here to face death alone in this pit of darkness, and while I couldn't begin to imagine what her original plan had been, she had somehow pulled it off anyway.

At the door to the suite, all sounds of yelling and pounding had ceased, which probably meant they were searching for a battering ram; however, those sounds—or the lack thereof—were entirely superseded by much closer ones. As our bloody act reached its crescendo, the whistling inner winds arose again, keening sharply through my mind, rustling outward into my limbs. This time, I no longer felt alone. My ally was aligned with me in every sense, cohort in vengeance, sole companion in what was likely my final act, participant in the pulsations of Summoner, which—I would swear—shook her body in time with mine. Heaves of force appeared to rock us both, shuddering her frame just as mine shuddered, routing the glossy path of her knife. Up and down went that dagger, correlated perfectly with my stabs. It was some kind of sequenced dance of murder, elemental and devastating, like twin forks of lightning, or two gyrating tornados dragging unsheltered lives into the sky.

High Lord Ulan Gueritus, the dreaded Raving Blade of Hell's Labyrinth, left this world in a painful and gruesome manner. His own durability was in part responsible, but that wasn't all of it. His dual executioners had become terrible things, barbaric and passionate beasts, for the two of us were entirely taken with the act. Some part of me knew I shouldn't feel this. Perhaps Shaeyin Odel knew it too, but neither of us cared enough to stop. And so, we just kept stabbing and gouging, screaming and slaughtering, until the atrocious creature known as Ulan Gueritus was nothing but an oozing pile of flesh and tattered cloth.

There was a grim silence in the aftermath. The slams against the suite door had not resumed, which didn't do much to reassure me. It was probably only a matter of a few minutes before that barrier came crashing down.

I stared across at Countess Odel, taking in her features clearly for the first time, and I must say the sight was terrible. Her silken, gold body, with the white laced collar, was shaking painfully as she strove to suck in air. And that body did not look right. Formerly statuesque, with beguiling curves and prominent breasts, her trunk was oddly misshapen, as if Gueritus's kick to her torso had unbalanced her entire upper half.

But even worse was her face, which appeared nothing short of mangled. Exquisite from a distance, her visage now bordered on grotesque in close quarters. In addition to the worming trails of Gueritus's blood running everywhere, and a handful of gory feathers gummed to the wild nest of her hair, her features had been damaged in weird ways. Her lips seemed warped and flattened, as if someone had pounded her repeatedly with a grain pestle, and that scrape from Gueritus's boot heel had done something bizarre to her right cheek. There, the flesh had been torn back like a fish skin, and indeed a piece of it was actually dangling free from the side of her jaw. I watched in mute horror as the fleshy swatch broke off and fell in a puttyish strip to the floor.

I stared into her eyes and noted that they were watering heavily, as quiet, choking sobs emerged from that distended chest. I also found that this was the first pleasant resting place for my gaze. Here, I was no longer aware of the deformities. I didn't see the maulings and warpings, the smashed bits and torn strips. All I saw was the color. The most improbable of shades—a translucent blue-green, so unalloyed and luminous one might think humanity's first hopes and dreams had taken birth in such a hue. And they were ever so unique, these eyes, brilliant and unmistakable, for who in this world could look upon them and not remember his very first viewing? Who would not recall, viscerally, that initial meeting in the Boathouse, when she turned her gaze to him, when something between them was exchanged and locked and (now known beyond all shadow of a doubt) joined forever.

With a ferocious, convulsive gasp, I suddenly understood the true identity of my partner in shadow.

"Well, my love," said Nascinthé of Levell, the damaged putty of her false lips quivering softly, "I guess I've finally grown used to men's blood splattering across my face."

32

SPELLBINDER

For a suspended moment, I simply stared at her. I gaped into the watering blue-green, encircled by grisly filth and a deformed disguise, and I knew in the deepest, core-level part of me that only one thing could have made this happen. Only one motivation could have drawn her here, compelled her to overcome fear, trauma, and a complete lack of training, and that motivation, unfathomable though it seemed, was me. *Me*, otherwise known as "my love"—the only title I ever wanted for the rest of my life.

And suddenly we were flinging ourselves at each other, knitting together in a soiled junction of misshapen lips and blood-spattered limbs. Wet with violence, Nascinthé's false face dropping away like leprous waste, we inhaled each other in the middle of the Raving Blade's polluted pit. All the while, I was aware of the astonishing change as it burned through me. It was as if a searing fire iron was being thrust through my inner spaces, pressing down on the torn section of spirit with a fiery hiss. Suddenly, the wound started to close. That mysterious rupture, plaguing me throughout my life, the place from which strange winds blew and uncaring causality exerted itself, was abruptly and achingly sealed.

But even this development was eclipsed by the other. It paled before the reality that, after decades of doubting my own personal capacities, wondering if there was some jammed mechanism in the fugacious gateway of my heart, I learned it wasn't so. I was in love. I was madly, violently in love with her, Nascinthé of Levell, whom the Capital knew as Nirabella, whose spectacular presence lingered on in many a wistful memory as the Spellbinder. This feeling did more than cauterize, for it was as if my mind and body had previously been some unlit edifice—a great Lower City building languishing in gloomy disrepair—and now, by clever engineering contrivance, every room on every floor was simultaneously alight. Dazzlingly illumined, with a brightness that made the subtle particles of my soul feel excruciatingly alive.

This might not seem like an opportune moment to describe being in love. With a corpse leaking away below, and the eerie silence beyond that fortress door, no doubt signifying the gathering of reinforcements, one might think it wise to consider more practical matters. But I don't care. Really, I don't give the slightest goddamn, because this was my moment, my life's greatest moment, arriving—befittingly—drenched in blood and overlying an act of revenge.

Besides, we might both be dead inside of ten minutes, so when else am I going to tell you about it? What better time than now to relay the single most important thing that had ever happened to me? It charred through my consciousness like a bursting star, illumining the forlorn spaces, the inoperative chambers, driving the darkness and madness right the hell out of me. Truly, I could no longer feel any of it: the insane dreams and obsessions, the vindictive campaigns and poisonous fixations—gone, gone, gone, the whole psychological mess, replaced by a piercing luminance that made everything clear.

I had no idea how Nascinthé had managed to pull this off, what in the world her plan had been, but there was one thing I did know with absolute certainty: she whose smashed putty lips were gulping at mine with jerking, covetous wheezes was instantaneously, and irreversibly, the single most important thing in my life. For the rest of my life.

Period.

Can a person know such a thing so suddenly? Given the circumstances, was this even graspable? I assure you, it was, because that's exactly what happened. I felt, in those revelatory seconds, as if everything that had transpired before had been some sort of blurred-over mirage. The misty substance of my past simply burned off in the face of this stunning emotional daybreak.

"My love, we must leave this place," said Nascinthé, pulling her sullied face from mine and introducing a hint of pragmatism into our rapture (in truth, only a short interval had passed on the outside, though it felt like a lifetime's worth of change within).

"Yes," I said, nodding emphatically. "We will use the same route I took to get in. They won't even know we left."

But it was not meant to be. Time, which had never truly been on our side, was done handing out favors, and it announced this with a loud, shattering crash in the vicinity of the suite door, accompanied by the scuffling of boots and a bad-tempered dissonance of male voices. Suddenly, they were swarming inside the vestibule, and though they had not yet spilled around the masonry wall into the living area, I implicitly understood it all.

That silence beyond the door had been the guards trying to give false hope to the intruders, while the proper device was gathered to bust down the door. Their presumption must have been that the "Countess" was in fact a Finisher, and that if she was dangerous enough to take out the Raving Blade, then the best bet was to catch her by surprise. While I doubted that the soldiers had yet discovered my little crevice in the derelict laundry chamber, they probably guessed that the Finisher had help, and all of this ensured that Nascinthé and I would be facing a sizable force. As I learned a moment later, my worst estimates undershot the problem.

We had only managed to gather our weapons and get upright before the full troop filed inside, separating around the wide chimney column to come at the pit from both flanks. They fanned out quickly to encircle the sunken area, looming above us in that same bristling, vulturine display that I had witnessed on the canal bridge. But this was much worse, for there were at least forty of them, and we were surrounded.

When I looked up at the top of the stairs, I noted that the Raving Blade's lead vassals had taken a position there. Count Gahvin Szorticus, "The Kaszian," stood at the fore of the invading entourage, and he was further flanked by Viscounts Hurgis and Piragen, all three of whom had been present during my meeting at The Crossbiter Tavern. I also wasn't surprised to see that the newest member of the family was standing just behind them. Baron Ujendus—otherwise known as Coljin Helmgrinder—towered over the lead vassals, and he had on his glistening features the intensity of a man who had come to settle business once and for all.

"Theese...theese cannot be," gibbered Gahvin Szorticus, the bronzed leather of his face rumpling as he stared at his lord's corpse. "How is theese could happen?"

Szorticus's raven hair was once again oiled into a phalanx of greasy little quills, and he was robed entirely in sashed black cloth, with an array of sword and dagger hilts poking forth, along with less recognizable weaponry. His expression seemed locked in some sort of wonder-affliction hybrid.

As for the rest of the throng, they had now crowded the edges of the pit, and as I gazed around at the forbidding Lower City faces set off against the beige ceiling dome, I observed that there was some variety here. Many of these soldiers were the Raving Blade's diehards—some familiar to me from The Crossbiter, and some merely standing in close proximity to those men. This group had that awful, pitiless look that years of observing and administering ravings will give you.

But there were new faces too. These were likely staffers from the other lines—Count Tygean's men, primarily, and soldiers from Sherdane's third vassal, Count Donblas. As a whole, this blend of new recruits didn't wear quite the same sadistic patina as members of the Gueritus family. Additionally, there were a half dozen ex-Shadow Bidders present—the men that Col had enlisted—and as I scanned over them, I realized that I had worked bids with most of them. Of particular note was Dolan Mael, one of the Contract Blades who had ambushed me during the infamous Gaff. Dolan had typically coarse North Derjian features, short-cut dark hair, and a brooding temperament that usually made him the least sociable person in any gathering.

"Theese is…we must understand…" Gahvin Szorticus was muttering, still locked in his incapacitating mental prison.

"We will understand it soon, Gahvin," said Viscount Piragen. This older, white-haired Underlord was dressed tastefully, in a cinched lavender waistcoat and a gold-trimmed scarf. Those icy blue eyes seemed to reflect a bit more cognizance than the others.

"Dubin will extract it from them," he said. "Piece by piece."

Well, maybe not cognizance. Piragen didn't even realize that his own lord, Dubin the Dicer, was moldering away in the dungeon, which told me this entire operation needed some work on its scouting protocols.

"Shadow Bidder," said wooly Viscount Hurgis, the nappy welter of his facial hair hackling as he slid forward to the top step of the staircase, "you've just guaranteed yourself the sickest death in the history of Hell's Labyrinth. You and this two-faced whore, who will be given to the soldiers for a month, before we set the scalpels to her. I'll be first in line for both duties."

With his two axes in hand, Hurgis proceeded down the first two steps, and the movements of his stocky, armored frame had the sort of surly nonchalance that suggested he had spent much of his life in combat.

"Wait, Hurgees," said Count Szorticus, and now he drew from his belt some sort of peculiar, chained weapon that looked like a dreadful marriage between a flail and set of shackles. Rattling and glinting, the weird chainy thing fed through his hands like a metallic cobra, its clinking noises intimating subdual, captivity and torment. "We must take theese two alive. I will do theese with you…with Edgrin and Jaex."

Once again, there had clearly been a failure of communication here, seeing as Lieutenant Jaex was drawing flies down in the dungeon. However, "Edgrin" was present, and as he started to make his way around the edge of the pit, I noted that this was the bald-headed soldier with the gap between his teeth who had taken charge of proceedings during my duel with Col. Edgrin had also been part of the duo that incapacitated and abducted an Underlord right in front of me at The Crossbiter, shunting him off to ungodly torture. This was clearly a specialty of his, which must have been viewed as a highly desirable skill in this organization. If memory served me, Edgrin was Gueritus's Master Sentinel, the officer in charge of compound security.

At my side, Nascinthé gripped her dagger with one hand and me with the other, and this display—not lost on anyone—made it clear that she did not believe another beguiling masquerade was possible. I held a stiletto and a fighting dirk, and while my spades would have been more useful, they seemed too far away to risk running for. And it was pointless anyway, since cutting our way out of this mess was hopeless.

Count Szorticus now joined Viscount Hurgis on the steps, whispering something to his fellow Underlord, pertaining, no doubt, to prisoner-seizing matters, while Master Sentinel Edgrin drew ever closer to the stairs. As all this occurred, I found that no inspired ideas were coming to me. When I checked with my tongue, which was pressed in a gluey sheath against the roof of my mouth, it had nothing clever to say. I did at least know to whom I might say the clever thing, were it to come, and I stared up at him now.

Coljin Helmgrinder, aka Baron Ujendus, and I locked gazes, our eyes forming a visual weld in the open space over the Gueritus family leadership. My former comrade still had that serious business expression on his glossy face. He was fully armored, like the others, and while I couldn't see his hands, his enormous, muscled shoulders had a certain gravitational compaction that suggested he was holding heavy weaponry. Our exchange lasted but a couple seconds, yet in that time, I watched an interesting thing occur.

Col started to smile. He smiled at me, but also at Nascinthé of Levell, whose identity he had clearly surmised, and the expression had about it an unmistakable look of respect, something you didn't often see on Coljin Helmgrinder's face. Honestly, you never saw it, and as the big, intimidating warrior grinned down at me and Nascinthé (two people he had tried, at various times, to kill), it did seem to me that something on the order of approval was present. In any case, the man certainly recognized his moment when he saw it.

I will probably never be friends with Coljin Helmgrinder. I may, very well, fight him to the death one day, as has been promised on multiple occasions by both parties, but I do concede that I made one key error in assessing his character. The fellow did not, as I had so obnoxiously stated, lack for creativity.

"Now!" Col bellowed, and suddenly, those hitherto unseen blades were up and whirling—his massive broadsword in his right fist and an exceptionally long spade in his left, possessed of slender, tapered blade more akin to a huge stiletto than a short sword. With these, he descended on Szorticus and Hurgis from behind, and while the two startled Underlords did manage to turn, and had their weapons at the ready, this was effectively a surprise attack. I'm sure a formal duel between Coljin Helmgrinder and the vaunted weapons master, Gahvin Szorticus, or the ornery bull, Viscount Hurgis, would have been a fascinating spectacle, worthy of betting and cheering and rousing entertainment. But Col wasn't a fool, and this was no time for honor. It was time to cut the head off the snake.

Hurgis was first in line for that ghastly, death-dealing broadsword, since he was on the right side. Having faced the horrible implement myself, I might have felt some sympathy for him, had the bastard not just promised to rape and murder the woman I loved. Therefore, no sadness at all as the pugnacious Viscount splattered in front of me like a watermelon slammed by a mallet. I don't even understand how so much gore was possible, given the presence of armor and clothing and general compression of the man's shape. The only real answer was the fact that he had been struck by the biggest, heaviest blade in Hell's Labyrinth, wielded by the biggest, heaviest warrior our city had ever known, and these two factors, coupled with the fact that Hurgis hadn't quite gotten his axes crossed into a proper block, produced the dramatic and rather disgusting effect.

Before the nappy bundle of blood and broken armor even hit the floor, Col was funneling his energy straight at Count Szorticus. I'll say this for the Kaszian weapons master, he did manage to deflect the initial flurry, his body torquing and weaving, while that weird chain thing spun and scraped off of Col's blades. One piece of the gangling weapon actually whipped up and around to clink off of the armor on Col's upper back, but this obviously wasn't the ideal implement to counter such an assault (as if there was one).

I've said it a hundred times already, but won't refrain from blabbing it again: when it came to combat, Col lived in a class by himself. Were it his size and strength alone at play, he might have been properly matched by the likes of Gahvin Szorticus, whose superlative training and agility established him a very dangerous adversary. But Col was also superbly trained, and astonishingly agile, capable of making his blades gambol and twirl in impossible ways. Really, I have no bloody idea how I stalemated him in the Shadowbiter duel. If we ever fight again, I'm certain he'll kill me in seconds.

Which is about how long it took him to do away with Szorticus. The Kaszian did not cascade forth in a geyser of blood like his vassal Hurgis, but I did get to watch the point of Col's stiletto spade poke in a syrupy glint straight out the man's back. I'm unclear what move Col put on his adversary to achieve this, as Szorticus was blocking my view, but I think a whirling sweep of that huge, man-halfing blade was sufficient distraction to cause the Count to lose track of the smaller, pointier implement, and then fail to anticipate the startling speed with which it might advance. Something like that. Regardless, so much for Gahvin Szorticus and his short, baffled reign as Gueritus's stand-in.

As Col made his move, all six of his newly recruited Shadow Bidders sprang into action. I saw Dolan Mael and another Blade named Tobus of Gealtwhal leap at the approaching Edgrin from either side, catching him entirely off guard. Here, too, the same business applied: the Master Sentinel would have been a tough opponent, not to be taken lightly, a thrill to watch in a duel…etc., etc. Forget it; they drove their blades straight into his ribs, back, and neck when he wasn't looking, which was what happened to two others in the crowd, each taken down by a pair of flanking Shadow Bidders. Those victims were unknown to me, but based on the highly coordinated nature of this ambush, I had to assume they were respected figures in the Gueritus family, the removal of whom left the sadistic army effectively leaderless. Except for Viscount Telris Piragen, who, perhaps, had been neglected…

…but no. Col got him. As the older Underlord drew a slender sword from his scabbard and took an uncertain step in Col's direction, he was splayed to the floor with one overhead chop.

"Soldiers of Tygean and Donblas," Col roared after felling the three top members of the Gueritus leadership. "This is your moment to avenge your lords. We can divvy the spoils afterwards."

Col understood the dynamics here. A shortage of qualified soldiery had forced the Raving Blade to absorb a host of resentful parties, and while these men might, in time, have become inured to the killing of their comrades, the dismemberment of their lords, the humiliating fealty that had been demanded of them, that time had not yet come.

"Tygean!" a man cried from the section of crowd directly in front of me. It was Baron Medgen, the young, attractive Underlord from Tygean's line who had been present during my meeting with Gueritus at The Crossbiter, and who had been forced to swear fealty shortly before my arrival. Memorable in that encounter was Gueritus promising Medgen Count Tygean's dismembered nose as a gift, and seeing as I had found the unfortunate Count so divested, I had to assume the souvenir had been received. Vengeful motivation clearly wasn't lacking, and since Medgen likely held the highest rank from his lord's defunct lineage, it was no surprise that the others responded to him.

"Tygean!" rang out the pugnacious reply.

"Donblas!"

"Donblas!"

Within seconds the room descended into a churning pandemonium of stabbing blades, toppling bodies, and barbarous screams. When my Brood sister, Heshna, described the ferocious street battle that transpired at Gessum's Cross, I actually felt a degree of macabre jealousy to have missed the spectacle. I can now put those regrets aside, since the virulent bloodbath that occurred on the encircling edges of the Master Provost's conversation pit had everything a grisly voyeur might hope for. And the view was striking, for how often does one get to observe a battle from below? Nascinthé and I, still joined by her grip, swept our gazes up and around to watch the heavy, scuffling bulk of those bodies—grappling, thrusting, pounding, plunging—and it was such a graphic event, such a monstrous human cyclone that for a few moments, the two of us were entirely frozen.

I saw two men run each other through at the same time, and then, grimacing and intwined, topple as a duad over the edge to the floor of the pit. Elsewhere, tandems and trios were putting their backs to each other, facing off against adversaries who threw themselves riotously forward. It became clear, within seconds, that it was the Gueritus troops who were on the defensive, and while I don't think they were technically outnumbered, morale was not on their side. Several tried to surrender, but they were instantly butchered, laying bare the fact that no one on the attacking side was looking to integrate these men into future plans.

The full-scale disintegration of High Lord Beranardos Sherdane's system was underway, and nobody here seemed to care, nor did they appear troubled by the imminent arrival of Lave Kaszivar and her plundering armada. Somewhere in the very back of my own mind, these issues murmured, but they were largely superseded by another agenda, which was getting the two of us the hell out of there.

An opening appeared when four men in close proximity were displaced in quick succession: one collapsed and bled his life out on the lip of the sunken area, his arm flopped listlessly below, another was knocked unconscious when he tumbled headfirst into the pit, and two others rolled to the side in a frenetic, heaving ground scuffle.

"This way," I hissed, and Nascinthé and I sped across the carpet to the encircling wall. I leapt onto the edge, then helped Nascinthé do the same. Clear of our arena, we made a low, scuttling sprint towards the bath chamber, threading through the banging, grunting juggernaut. No one bothered with us. They couldn't afford to waste a precious sword stroke on two meekly fleeing noncombatants, seeing as everybody else within reach was furiously trying to kill them.

We soon arrived at the bath chamber, and once inside, I closed and locked the door. The mechanism was a mere turn bolt and not the sort of thing that would stop a determined assault, but I didn't anticipate anyone using the privy just then. Escaping via the building's central staircase would have been easier. There was even a chance we could have gotten away with it, given the general chaos, but there was an equally good chance that building's main, vertical channel was filled with sprinting figures—those ascending to the battle, or possibly fleeing from it, or just as likely engaged in the conflict themselves, seeing as this poorly stitched army was ready to rip apart wherever it sprawled.

So, down my buried shaft of ancient laundry we went. I quickly tied off the wound in my thigh, and stuck a packed kerchief over what I now discovered to be a rather shallow jab below my chest. Then I inserted myself into the chute. I employed no candle, as I did not wish to singe my climbing companion.

"I'm not sure I can do this," Nascinthé gasped, as she slid her legs and the frilly width of her dress into the little rectangular opening above my head. I was a few feet below, pressed and suspended.

"You can do it. And I am here to catch you if you slip."

"Should I mention," she said, groaning as she eased the rest of her body into the shaft, "that I'm not trained for this sort of thing?"

"You weren't trained to slaughter Underlords either, and look how naturally it came to you."

"About that," Nascinthé replied, her pretty shoes scrabbling nervously at the grout lines above my head. "You should know that I am officially done with that line of w—"

And she slipped, the edges of her soles scratching down the stone, her breath keening from her in a terrified screech. I tucked my chin, allowing her crotch to land heavily on my shoulders, her dress a pleated, perfumed tent around my head. The slightest skittering abrasion occurred where my own feet gripped the walls, but otherwise, my four-point hold withstood the weight.

"Please let me know if you're planning to do that again," I said from below her fumy straddle.

"Don't joke," she wheezed, "this is very scary for me."

Scratch by scratch, slide by shuffling slide, we descended. Nascinthé fell a second time about midway down, her constricted wail again warning me, but this time the sole of her shoe landed on my arm, and we were able to stabilize her before she slid farther.

"I'm not like those girls you grew up with, Vazeer," she gasped when she had gotten her breathing under control. "I'm not made for scampering around in places like this."

"Which is why I love you."

"Is it…and do you?"

"Yes, with all my heart," I said. "And you'll never scamper again, I promise."

"What a relief. Both things."

We eased into what felt like the second half of our descent, pressing and groaning within the pitch-black confines of our conduit. Throughout, I was intensely aware of how different this experience was from my earlier ascent, how altered the descending man was from the one who had so balefully climbed. There were no inner winds, no torn sections of self, nor was there any sense that I could summon things, except perhaps a vast storehouse of devotion, as I attempted to get the woman I loved to safety.

I did, at least, retain a small portion of my capacity for insight, since something started to come to me. As I slid downwards, I kept repeating one of Nascinthé's phrases in my mind: *those girls you grew up with.* These words, combined with the "scampering" imagery, at last produced an idea.

"Did you, by chance, meet my Brood sister, Heshna?"

"I did."

"At Eastcove, where you docked?"

"Yes."

"Is that how you pulled this off…by promising my sister you'd get the target alone in a room, and her promising to direct me there?"

"Of course."

"Son of a bitch!" I growled. "And you two couldn't have let me in on the plan?"

"Would you have allowed me to go through with it?"

"Never."

"Your answer, then," Nascinthé said with a grunt as I heard a heavy, clothy ripping, indicating that her dress had briefly snagged between her and the wall before working itself free.

"Plus," she continued once she was moving again, "my safety was contingent on the High Lord thinking I was Shaeyin Odel. As long as he believed that, I was untouchable. Your concern for me would have blown my cover."

"But what if I hadn't come?"

"I knew you would."

"But what if something went wrong and I never made it?"

"Then I would have talked my way out, just as I talked my way in. I'm good at both things."

"So I'm gathering."

We were now almost at ground level, and below me I could see the faint luminance of the laundry room opening.

"What I'm *not* gathering," I said, when I finally put my feet down on the flagstone floor and reached up to take Nascinthé's waist to help ease her the last few feet, "is how you were able to spin all of that...those brilliant political maneuvers, and box Gueritus in."

"Shaeyin and I used to duel endlessly," she replied, "debating every imaginable issue, to the point where flipping the tables on each other became a matter of reflex. She was very good at it, but I was better."

"Better than anyone, I think."

"Yes, I think so too."

For a few moments we simply slumped against each other, allowing our sweating muscles to recover from the arduous descent. My leg was throbbing, but it was otherwise holding strong.

When we finally emerged from the opening into the old laundry chamber, all was quiet, eerily quiet, since guards should have been patrolling the ground floor. We encountered no one. Skulking carefully down musty, brazier illumined corridors, passing doorway after doorway, some open, most closed, none emitting evidence of humanity, it felt as if the ghosts of the forlorn Lower City had finally arisen and stolen away the souls of the living.

When we arrived at the grand atrium, we found it as deserted as all the other ground floor spaces, though somehow not as desolate. The Kaennamin Academy entry vestibule had an undefinable tranquility to it. We walked past Sarien's broad reflecting pool, which had been dry on prior visits, but which now, compliments of the Swell Driver, was puddled just enough to catch the room's torchlight. How elegant it was. How inspiring, this horizontal mirror, sending eyes back to great heights. Staring up at the surrounding balcony with its pillared stone railing and bas reliefs (a whole series depicting the building trades), I realized that I had never seen these carvings clearly, having only viewed them by incidental light. Nor had I been able to fully take in the elliptically vaulted ceiling, with its flower-petal ribs, or the patterned inlay in the marble floor, cleverly replicating the interconnected circles of a compass.

Torches alone didn't explain this. The hall felt clean, it felt untainted by pollutants of all sorts. I looked on this great place as if for the first time, no longer choked by obsession, no longer confusing my desire for external restoration with a far more essential repair that had been needed within. Up ahead I saw the massive, iron-bound doors, which hung beckoningly open. Here we detected our first sign of humanity, but not life, for there was a pair of corpses sprawled in the vicinity of the great doors. The leathery inertness of those shapes merely reinforced the sense that we were entirely alone.

"There were guards here when you came?" I asked Nascinthé in a low voice, which still fell prey to sonorous echoes.

"Many."

"I can't fathom…"

And I let it trail off. I let it trail because I could, when all was said and done, fathom it, fathom a great deal, since the incentives in this subterranean society were well known to me.

"They are free," I muttered. "All of them are free…us too, I think."

And I allowed the full reality of it to settle over my mind. The soldiers in this building were indeed free, released from the coercive threat of the Underlords, whose promises of retribution had kept so many reluctant parties employed. I didn't know the identity of those two corpses on the floor, but whoever they were, they had probably tried to bar the path to liberty, to poor effect.

From somewhere far upstairs came a noise, a distant steely knell. It might have been the clash of weaponry, or it might have been the breaching of treasure vault doors, but either way it seemed many floors away, and I heard no shambling descent of footsteps. I heard nothing anywhere, not in the atrium, nor on the front steps of the building, which I could see quite clearly through the gaping doors.

I took Nascinthé's hand, and we cautiously proceeded towards those yawning doors. As I neared the vaulted aperture, I again recalled the phantasmal hallucination I had experienced at the height of the Swell Driver, when, in the shadow of this very building, I had been visited by three figures in succession. The first was King Aurellis Kaennamin, the man who had envisioned the astonishing Lower City. This night, as I exited his granddaughter's commodious shrine, I felt I might be saying goodbye to him once and for all, just as Holod had always wanted, for the only thing of any concern to me now was the woman by my side. I simply refused to shunt even one piece of myself away from her in the name of that obsession.

I would also be saying goodbye to High Lord Beranardos Sherdane, the next phantasmal visitor from that dream. Sherdane had done so much for me in this life, but he had also created a crooked thing, an ultimately unsustainable thing, that was coughing up its last breath upstairs. Let it die. Let the whole intricate, illegal system die, even if it made our city vulnerable to the rapacious ambitions of others. And "our city" was perhaps no longer *my* city, for wherever Nascinthé wished to go, I would go with her.

Finally, I had to make my peace with that last figure, the one who had, in his enigmatic way, set all of these events in motion.

With that bloody cut across Sherdane's throat, Radrin Blackstar had started a sequence that eventually brought this world down, just as he intended. Just as, possibly, I intended, which I now needed to face.

I still didn't know who Radrin Blackstar was, not specifically. But I did sense that he and I were the same. The very thing that had happened to me, the chasmal rent at my core, had also happened to him, though in his case he had mastered it more fully. Perhaps somebody had trained him (a fugitive student from Merejin's class seemed feasible), since he had clearly restrained the wanting so completely that he came across, at times, as a vacuous thing, devoid of human emotion. While it would take time to confirm a theory of this magnitude, I felt certain it was so.

The question was, which of us had summoned the other? Whose vision was it that held sway here? Or was it possible that we had performed this conjuring collectively, that we might execute a brutal overlap in our respective dreams? Someday, I sincerely believed, I would be able to answer these questions. For now, my attention belonged with the partner, the far better partner, who had been summoned to take his place.

Nascinthé and I reached the threshold and stood beneath the hemispherical weight of ancient engineering, staring out into the cool sheen of night. A light drizzle had started to fall, and it delivered, faintly, the smell of rain, mixed with other, unseen waters. Somewhere, far beyond the newly repaired docks, slicing the wrinkled field of a nocturnal ocean, came the Red Armada. In my mind's eye, those flared, weather-beaten sails were a sight to rival Ventrilus's bygone masterpiece, and whether the inscrutable Lave Kaszivar was a mere marauder as Radrin claimed, or if she was (as Terza and Adelyn hoped) the second coming of Giradera of Azmoul, significant change would accompany her arrival.

"Is it really true then?" Nascinthé asked as she stared down those broad, sweeping steps. "Are we free to go…or to stay, if we choose?"

I turned and took in the full sight of her. Nascinthé had discarded her torso padding and rubbed off most of the putty, making that ethereal face, notwithstanding a swollen cheek, the one I knew and loved. Even in the huffing light of the entry torches, the astonishing aquamarine color was a radiant burn. Those elongated lips, stripped of theatrical excess, were trim and expressive again, delivering questions and staggering hope.

"Might you truly wish to stay?" I asked. "Here, in Sullward?"

"Why wouldn't I? Droden tells me you have all sorts of ridiculous ideas about the future of this city, which I'd like to hear, because I'm similarly ridiculous, and a very good politician. Actually, I'm a *great* politician, which the world has yet to learn."

When I heard those words, a ticklish thread of heat ascended straight up my throat. I palpably recalled the strange incident that occurred when I retrieved Nascinthé's contract payment from a hidden burrow along the side of the road. Holding her pretty jewelry box in hand, I had this bizarre sense that the sequential flow of time, and to some extent the trajectory of my life, would divide cleanly between the period when the box remained closed and the forever after, once it opened.

The feeling was fleeting, and all the more forgettable after *I, Asadeissia* was revealed, and then the discovery of a close friendship between Nascinthé and the future leader of the Tergonian Empire. But in this moment, I could not shake the sense that I had experienced a premonition. While I had no doubt that the Red Siren's impending arrival was a matter of great consequence, I did wonder if maybe we had focused a little too much upon her. Possibly, we had concerned ourselves with the wrong "second coming."

"Besides," Nascinthé said, the numinous glow of her making me almost lightheaded, "didn't you and I just go through the substantial trouble of getting rid of these people…or at least the worst of them? It would seem a shame not to take advantage of it."

Suddenly, the vast, emotive upswell became almost unbearable, and I forcefully took her in my arms.

"I don't deserve you, Nascinthé of Levell," I whispered, through a clog of phlegminess.

In pressed closeness, Nascinthé regarded me through the honey static of her hair, a deep, sober appraisal consuming that lovely face, then the corners of her lips bent wryly skyward.

"Probably not," she agreed, "and yet, you definitely have me. So, I must ask you, my love…are you going to send me away again?"

"Never. Never so long as I live. I'm yours entirely."

"Okay then," she sighed with a soft, fatigued happiness, crumpling herself ever more completely into my body. "In that case, would you kindly take me home."

THE END

ABOUT THE AUTHOR

Peter Eliott is a lyrically gifted author and winner of over a dozen literary awards. He combines his passion for poetic literature, grim humor, and suspenseful adventure in the critically acclaimed Shadow Bidder series. He currently lives with his wife in Amagansett, NY, where he devours literary fiction to grow his ever-expanding arsenal of creative ideas. Stay in the loop with Peter Eliott, and never miss his next release!

Website: petereliott.com
Instagram: petereliottofficial
Facebook: petereliottofficial